GW00359337

Julia James lives in England with its peaceful verdant countryside [and nearby] Cornwall. She also loves the [... steeped] in myth and history, with its sunbaked landscapes and olive groves, ancient ruins and azure seas. 'The perfect setting for romance!' she says. 'Rivalled only by the lush tropical heat of the Caribbean—palms swaying by a silver sand beach lapped by turquoise water… What more could lovers want?'

Clare Connelly was raised in small-town Australia among a family of avid readers. She spent much of her childhood up a tree, Mills & Boon book in hand. Clare is married to her own real-life hero, and they live in a bungalow near the sea with their two children. She is frequently found staring into space—a surefire sign that she's in the world of her characters. She has a penchant for French food and ice-cold champagne, and Mills & Boon novels continue to be her favourite ever books. Writing for Modern is a long-held dream. Clare can be contacted via clareconnelly.com or at her Facebook page.

Also by Julia James

Cinderella's Baby Confession
Destitute Until the Italian's Diamond
The Cost of Cinderella's Confession
Reclaimed by His Billion-Dollar Ring
Contracted as the Italian's Bride
The Heir She Kept from the Billionaire

Also by Clare Connelly

The Boss's Forbidden Assistant
Twelve Nights in the Prince's Bed

Brooding Billionaire Brothers miniseries

The Sicilian's Deal For 'I Do'
Contracted and Claimed by the Boss

The Diamond Club miniseries

His Runaway Royal

Discover more at millsandboon.co.uk.

THE BILLIONAIRE'S DEMAND

JULIA JAMES

CLARE CONNELLY

MILLS & BOON

First published in Great Britain 2024
by Mills & Boon, an imprint of HarperCollins*Publishers* Ltd,
1 London Bridge Street, London, SE1 9GF

www.harpercollins.co.uk

HarperCollins*Publishers*, Macken House, 39/40 Mayor Street Upper, Dublin 1, D01 C9W8, Ireland

The Billionaire's Demand © 2024 Harlequin Enterprises ULC.

Greek's Temporary Cinderella © 2024 Julia James

Pregnant Before the Proposal © 2024 Clare Connelly

ISBN: 978-0-263-32023-7

09/24

This book contains FSC™ certified paper
and other controlled sources to ensure responsible forest management.

For more information visit www.harpercollins.co.uk/green.

Printed and Bound in the UK using 100% Renewable Electricity
at CPI Group (UK) Ltd, Croydon, CR0 4YY

GREEK'S TEMPORARY CINDERELLA

JULIA JAMES

MILLS & BOON

For HB

CHAPTER ONE

LEANDROS KASTELLANOS NODDED at familiar faces, exchanging civil pleasantries as he made away across the crowded function room at this top Athens hotel, popular with those wanting to throw a lavish party, as was the case tonight. All around, Athens high society was mingling and enjoying itself, the men all in tuxes, as was he himself, and the women all in evening gowns, glittering with jewels.

He was here only because he'd returned unexpectedly early from a business trip to New York, and out of civility to his hosts, the parents of the newly engaged couple whose betrothal party this was.

His expression tightened. He wished the couple well—but not all engagements led to a happy-ever-after marriage...

He should know...

No! He pulled his thoughts back sharply. No point remembering his own disastrous engagement. It had been six long years ago—in the past. A past he had no interest in revisiting. He was no longer the fool he'd been at twenty-six, swept away on a tide of romance. Blinding himself to the true nature of the woman he had fallen so hard for.

Until he'd seen her true nature for himself—had his face slammed into it.

It wasn't me she loved—it was the Kastellanos money. And if that wasn't going to be coming her way—well, she was off. Dumping me faster than you could say—as his father had spelt out to her—disinherited.

The realisation had been brutal.

My faithless fiancée.

Bitterness filled him. So much for love.

Hadn't his father warned him? And been proved right?

Now, though, the Kastellanos millions were all his anyway. His father's untimely death three years ago had left him one of the richest men in Greece—and the most eligible. But marriage was not on his agenda; he stuck to the kind of passing liaisons in which he had indulged in his youth—before he had been beguiled by the oh-so-deceptive and deceiving *ingénue* beauty of the woman who had proved so faithless.

The function room opened on to a spacious roof terrace, set up for dancing later on. On impulse, he stepped out, wanting to clear his unwelcome thoughts, his toxic memories. The ever-present illuminated Parthenon was visible atop the distant Acropolis and the festoons of hanging lamps around the dance floor cast a soft glow.

The scent of flowers from all the lavishly filled planters at the perimeter of the terrace caught at him.

And one more thing caught at him.

On the far side of the terrace, half in shadow, against the dark foliage, was the pale, slender outline of a woman.

For a second—an instant—time ceased. Then it crashed and crushed him.

Eliana saw him. Saw him step through onto the deserted terrace.

Cold dismay seared through her.

Oh, dear God in heaven, no, no, *no*!

She'd been deeply reluctant to show up here at all—to show up anywhere in Athens!—but Chloe had been adamant.

'You can't hide for ever, Elli—please, please come!'

With deep misgivings she had agreed only when Chloe had sworn that even though her future in-laws, long-standing friends of the Kastellanos family, had invited him, he would not—could not—be there tonight! He was in New York, safely across an ocean.

That, and only that, had persuaded Eliana to show up, out of loyalty to her old school friend. Not that she'd kept in touch much with Chloe since her own marriage—even less since the shocking ending of that marriage.

Arriving tonight, seeing all those faces—many still familiar—she'd felt her nerves get the better of her, and she'd bolted out to the sanctuary of the deserted terrace.

No sanctuary at all—the very opposite.

She felt her lungs turn to stone. He was here—less than ten metres away from her. Imposing upon her consciousness as if he'd been ringed in fire.

The last man in the entire world she could bear to see.

On whom she had not set eyes for six long years—

Yet his final words to her, his denunciation of her—scathing, bitter, contemptuous and cruel—were as clear as if they'd been spoken yesterday.

For a second her vision blurred, then cleared, bringing him back into focus. He had frozen, just as she had—but now he was walking towards her. Striding. Purposeful. Powerful.

Almost, she flinched away. But then, with a strength she had not had to summon for so, so long she steeled herself. Inwardly, she gave a kind of silent, manic laugh—after what life had done to her, why should she flinch from this blow now?

He came right up to her and she could see the lamplight slant across his features. Features once so familiar. Features now etched like acid on stone. Light glinted in his eyes, but it was a light that was darkness—darkness visible.

He stopped a mere metre from her. Eyes holding hers. Dark and condemning.

His expression changed minutely, and it was taking all her strength just to stand there, immobile, her shoulders steeled, her whole body steeled.

'Well, well—Eliana.'

His voice was like a knife...a blade drawn down her cheek.

'After so long. And as beautiful as ever.'

That dark, killing glint came again into his eyes.

'Tell me, are you here to catch another husband? Another *rich* husband—the only kind you go for...?'

From somewhere—she didn't know where—she found the willpower to hold her ground, outface the contempt unhidden in his taunt.

'No,' she answered. Her voice was cool...as cool as a mountain lake.

'No?' The taunt was still in his voice. 'I'm sure there might be rich pickings to be had here tonight.'

She did not flush. She would not. 'You must excuse me,' she made herself say, her voice still cool. 'I have yet to offer my congratulations to Andreas for being so fortunate as to gain Chloe as his bride-to-be.'

She made to move past him, but he was staying at her side as she headed across the terrace. He was speaking again.

'And likewise I shall congratulate the happy bride-to-be on catching Andreas Manolis, with all his millions.'

Eliana threw a glance up at him. 'Chloe has her own millions,' she said.

'Then it should prove a happy marriage indeed—with no impediment on either side.'

The cynicism—the unspoken accusation over their own thwarted marriage—was open in his voice, but she would not flinch. She simply headed inside. She would find Chloe, then escape.

Escape, escape, escape—dear God, just get out of here!

Her friend saw her, gave a cry of pleasure.

'Elli, you came! I'm so, so pleased. Andreas—here is Eliana, one of my dearest friends for ever! And with her is—'

She stopped short. Suddenly silenced.

Leandros wanted to laugh, but if he did, he knew it would be a savage sound. A snarl. As it was, he leashed his response into a terse, tight-lipped throwaway.

'Don't read anything into it. It's chance, that's all.'

Malign chance—mocking him.

Had he known—had he had the slightest idea that Eliana would be here—he'd never have shown his face. But it was too late now.

He let Andreas's parents introduce him to their son's fiancée, and said whatever it was that the occasion required. As he uttered his pro forma good wishes, Eliana stepped a little aside, as if to increase the distance between them.

As if it were not infinite already.

She was talking to someone else—an older couple, whom he took to be the bride-to-be's parents. He turned away, letting more guests approach the engaged couple, heading for the bar. He needed a drink—a stiff one. Then he'd get out of here.

As for Eliana—

He blanked his mind—blanked her name. Blanked her very existence. Just as he had for six long years. As he would go on doing. Because anything else was unthinkable.

She's out of my life—and she's staying out.

But as he knocked back his shot of whisky at the bar he could still see her, imprinted on his retinas.

As beautiful as ever…hauntingly beautiful…

He slammed the empty glass down on the bar. He needed another shot.

* * *

Eliana stepped inside her room at the small two-star hotel which was all she could afford with a sense of shuddering relief. She stripped off her evening gown—a leftover from the days before her marriage. Her hands were shaking, heart hammering painfully. Weak suddenly, she sank down on the bed.

Oh, dear God, she had seen him again! Seen Leandros!

She had not set eyes on him since that hideous day when she'd slid his ring from her finger, told him she was not going to marry him, and walked away from him.

Gone to the man she was going to marry instead.

Shock broke over her at what had happened this evening, delayed and all the more devastating for it. She felt her tremors increase, the hammering of her heart become more painful yet.

To see Leandros again and to know…to know…

That he hates me with as much hatred as he ever did! That I am as loathsome to him now as then!

He held her in contempt, and she deserved it—that was the hardest thing to bear. To bear as she had had to bear it for six long years. Since she had walked out on him, rejecting him for another man. A man she hadn't loved—a man she had married only for his money.

Guilt bit at her for what she had done to Leandros—the man she had once loved, whose love for her she had destroyed with her faithlessness.

And she felt guilt of another kind too—survivor guilt. For the man she had married instead of Leandros was now dead—smashed to pieces in a fatal car crash eighteen months ago.

Well, she was getting her just deserts now. She'd married for money, but widowhood had taken that away from her, reduced her to the poverty she had married to avoid. A poverty she deserved, and to which she was now condemned, eking out what little she had. And even that small portion came with a claim on it she could not refuse...

As her thoughts went in that direction they gave her a crumb of comfort. If there was anything to salvage from the wreck she had made of her life, it was that.

As for seeing Leandros again, feeling his scorn, his contempt for her as stinging as it had been six years ago, she must just put it behind her. She did not live in Athens. She would not see him again. Tomorrow she would be heading back to Thessaloniki, the city she'd lived in since her marriage. Back to the life she now led—had to lead—leaving Athens far behind as she had done before, when she had ruined her own life.

And broken her own heart.

Leandros stood out on the terrace of his house in the wealthy Athens suburb of Psychiko, a whisky in his hand, his mood as dark as the night around him. He had left that benighted party as soon as he decently could, wanting only to put it behind him—to wipe the image of the one woman he wished to perdition from his mind.

But she would not go. She was still there, imprinted balefully on his retinas in all the beauty that had once so captivated him. And he saw her here, too—as if she were with him out on the terrace, gazing up at him with those wide-set eyes. And in them was all that he poured down into hers.

He'd kissed her here, on this very terrace, her lips like velvet beneath his, her heart beating like a wild bird as he held her in his arms.

She'd been like no other woman he'd ever found. Till then he'd enjoyed all the privileges of his family wealth and his own good looks, knowing that any female he smiled on would be only too keen to get his interest.

But Eliana was shy—hesitant. Even though her beauty was a loveliness that stopped me in my tracks.

For the first time in his life he'd fallen in love. Determined to win her—overcoming her shyness, the hesitancy born of the sheltered upbringing she'd had—he'd wanted to see in her beautiful blue-grey eyes fringed with smoky lashes all that he himself felt for her. And when he'd asked her to marry him he had seen just that. She had given a little cry and come into his arms, as if she had belonged there all her life—as if she would never leave him.

But leave me she did.

She had walked out on him—gone to another man. Married him instead.

And it was his father who had told him why—who had warned him from the start.

'Her father's financial affairs are seriously shaky. Rumours are flying all over town that he has debts he cannot pay. If he goes under, she'll want a rich husband instead.'

The words stabbed at his head now—and yet he had disbelieved them, right up until the moment when Eliana had slid his ring from his finger. Then, with a bitterness that had been like a knife in his throat, he'd realised his father's warning had been right.

Just as he was right to tell me he was going to test her, by telling her that if I married her he would disinherit me—that our marriage would come without the contents of the Kastellanos coffers for her to enjoy.

He'd told his father to go right ahead—knowing that Eliana would not care, that her love for him was all that mattered to her, not his wealth.

How wrong I was.

Bitterness seared through him again, as strong now as it had been that fateful evening when he'd watched her walk away from him...walk away for ever. Eviscerating him.

He wrenched himself away, heading back indoors. He wanted another whisky. And another one after that, if need be. Anything to block memories.

But they came all the same And just as toxic.

Eliana and me, on that sofa there. She curled up beside me like a kitten, her head on my shoulder and my arm around her. And I was kissing her, and her mouth was sweet like wine, and her body was soft against mine, and all I wanted in the world was to lift her up, carry her upstairs to my bed...

But that had been impossible.

Impossible not just because this had been his father's house then, but also because he'd known Eliana would not have yielded to his mounting desires. She'd wanted to wait till their wedding night.

That ugly twist to his mouth came again. Had that been part of her machinations as well? Withholding her body from him to make him all the more eager to marry her?

He set the empty whisky glass aside. What the hell was the point of standing here, remembering what had happened and what had never happened? Remembering a woman who had never been the woman he'd thought her. Who had made a fool of him...

And then walked away from him.

He had never set eyes on her again—until tonight.

He strode from the room, wrenching his black tie undone as he did so, making for the staircase. He would put tonight out of his head. Tomorrow he was flying to Frankfurt on business, and he was glad of it. Putting as much distance as possible between Greece and himself was the smart thing to do. The only thing.

CHAPTER TWO

ELIANA STEPPED OFF the train on to the platform. She felt dog-tired. She'd slept almost not at all, and the train from Athens to Thessaloniki seemed to have taken for ever. She'd dozed only fitfully in her seat during the five-hour journey, and she still had a bus ride to her destination.

She hefted her small pull-along suitcase, grateful it was on wheels, heading out of the station. As she passed the waiting taxis, her mouth thinned. A bus ride was all that she could afford. Just as her pokey studio flat in a run-down apartment block was all she could afford.

The meagre widow's allowance made to her by Damian's grudging father, Jonas, was supplemented a little by her work in a local supermarket, stacking shelves and minding the till. She would put in a shift this evening, tired as she was.

A wave of depression sank over her. Was this now all her life was going to be? Because how could it be otherwise?

Would to God I had never seen Leandros again...

Stirring up the past. Six years—six *years*—since she had last seen him. Surely she should have become immune to him in those six endless years? But all it had taken was that one single moment of seeing him again for her to know that Leandros Kastellanos, with every reason in the world to hold her in contempt for what she'd done to him, *still* had exactly the same power over her useless, pointless, pathetic senses as he ever had. As if those six long years had never existed.

It was a galling truth—a hopeless one.

I made my choice—I made my life—now I must live with the consequences.

And it was a life without Leandros—a life that could never have him in it again.

Never.

Leandros was back from Frankfurt. He'd returned via London and Brussels, but as he'd come back to Athens it had been as if the city closed over him again. Restlessness had possessed him, and he'd wanted to be off again on his business travels. But right now that wasn't possible. Since his father's death three years ago he'd taken over the running of the company, and it was more than a full-time job. Working lunches, like today's, were the norm.

Today's was in Piraeus, with a couple of directors of a shipping brokerage who were keen on Kastellanos investment funds. Leandros was in two minds about it, and wanted to discuss it with them in person.

The problem was he was finding it an effort to focus on business—ever since seeing Eliana again he'd been finding it so. Try to block them as he might, his thoughts kept gravitating back to her. They did so again now, as his chauffeured car made its way out of Athens south to Piraeus.

He'd heard about Damian Makris's death in a road accident some eighteen months ago now—the news had been all over the press and had circulated amongst his circle of acquaintances. Though it had been shocking—how could it not be, for a young man still in his twenties to die?—Leandros had not wanted to think about it. Not wanted to think that now Eliana was no longer Damian's wife but his widow.

Jonas Makris, Damian's father, had made it big in construction, and was based in the north of the country, with lucrative building projects all over the Balkans. That Eliana had taken herself off to Thessaloniki with the man she'd preferred to him had been a sour source of what might have passed for comfort to Leandros. Their paths had never crossed.

Till that damn party for Andreas Manolis and his fiancée...

But at least she hasn't shown up in Athens again—I can be glad of that.

The taunt he'd thrown at her—that she was now set on lining up a new husband, rich, of course, the only kind she went for—came back now, twisting his mouth. Well, she was welcome to go husband-hunting in Thessaloniki—or anywhere else that was not Athens.

Though maybe his taunt had been misplaced. Maybe she was perfectly happy being a wealthy widow, burning through whatever her hapless husband had left her.

He gave himself a mental shake. Hell, he was thinking about her again...

His car was arriving at the entrance to the prestigious yacht club where he was to meet his hosts for lunch. With an effort, he switched his mind into business gear, running through the issues that would need discussion and clarification if they were to reach agreement.

An hour later he had made his mind up. Though lunch had been lavish, and his hosts clearly very keen, he had not taken to them, and considered the deal they wanted carried too much risk for him. He veiled that decision from them—there was no point being blunt when it was not necessary. For now he let them think he would consider it, and they were happy enough with that as they moved on to coffee and liqueurs.

He was only half listening to what his hosts were saying—they were making general conversation about various aspects of the business and political life in Greece in which they all shared an interest—until one of them mentioned a name that suddenly drew his attention sharply.

'A lucky day, though, for Vassily Makris. He'll scoop the lot when old Jonas calls it quits.'

Leandros paused in the act of lifting his coffee cup.

'Vassily Makris?'

If there was an edge in his voice, he veiled it. His engagement to Eliana had been brief, and unannounced—few had known about it, and few knew of his own connection to the widow of Damian Makris.

Her friend Chloe did, though. At that party her reaction had shown that plain enough.

His host nodded. 'Yes—Jonas's nephew. Damian was Jonas's only son—his only child. There's no grandchild either, apparently. Only a widow—Aristides Georgiades's daughter. Jonas, understandably, was never happy that the marriage was childless. And the widow is the loser for that.'

'Yes,' Leandros's other host corroborated. 'Jonas has all but thrown her out on the street, from what I've heard. Of course if the Georgiades money had lasted she'd have been OK, but we all know what happened to that...'

Leandros frowned, before hearing himself ask a question he didn't want to ask, but asked all the same.

'Didn't Aristides Georgiades's property not pass to the daughter when he died? Some historic old place way out in Attica?'

'No,' came the answer. 'Jonas Makris's kept it—it went to him with the marriage. Had his daughter-in-law given him the grandson and heir—any heir at all!—he might have put it in the child's name, but as it is it will all go to the nephew, Vassily.'

Out of nowhere, in his head, Leandros heard Eliana's

voice—a voice from long ago—talking affectionately about her childhood home.

'My father loves it—he grew up there, and I did too. It's one of those few remaining neoclassical mansions, built after Greek independence in the nineteenth century by my great-great-grandfather, with beautiful grounds and gardens, and a glorious view!'

Leandros's thoughts came back to the present. So the old Georgiades family mansion was no longer that.

A random thought pricked.

That will have hurt her.

He shook it from him. Why should he care whether Eliana had lost her family mansion? Or that it seemed she hadn't done well financially out of being widowed.

The conversation moved on, and Leandros was relieved.

I don't want to think about her or know anything about her.

He was done with her. Had been done six years ago. And yet...

If she hasn't profited from widowhood, and there's no Georgiades money for her, then she'll definitely be on the lookout for a new meal ticket.

Another thought came.

And with her beauty, it won't take her long to find one...

Eliana was staring at her bank statement on the screen of her laptop. It made depressing viewing. Her income, such as it was, mostly went out again almost immediately, right at the beginning of the month, leaving her precious little to live on. As for credit cards... She had her own now, with a low limit—all that the bank allowed her in her new penurious circumstances. The credit cards she'd enjoyed as Damian's wife had been stopped the day after his funeral—his father had seen to that. Seen to a lot else, as well.

He hadn't bothered to confront her himself—had communicated only through his lawyer, who'd called at the villa she'd shared with Damian and informed her that she must vacate it, taking only her own personal possessions. And those did not, he'd spelt out, include any of the jewellery she'd worn as Damian's wife.

'They were not gifts to you, merely provided for you to wear,' the lawyer had informed her.

The same had applied to her wardrobe as well, and all she'd been permitted to take had been what she'd brought with her when she'd married Damian. She would be granted a small allowance, and she must make do with that. She knew even that was grudgingly made, and had been done for the sake of appearances only. She had wanted to refuse it, but she was in no position to do so.

She knew well why she was getting such harsh treatment. Jonas Makris had been unforgiving of her for failing to present him with a grandson. He'd been keen on her marriage to his son originally—a trophy wife who was beautiful, well-born, and old money—and the fact that the 'old money' was all but gone had appealed to him, too, for it had meant he could dictate the terms of her marriage to Damian. Terms she'd agreed to. Just as she had agreed to terms with Damian.

Her face shadowed. Jonas had been a harsh father. She might never have loved Damian, but she had come to pity him.

Their marriage had been useful to both of them, but—

No, don't go there. It's a mess, and that's all there is to it. And now you just have to cope with it.

And that included coping with a financial situation that was precarious in the extreme, and one from which there seemed to be no way out. She'd just have to budget yet more draconianly. Her eyes went to a rare extravagance that she had indulged in that day, reduced for clearance at the supermarket she worked at. She hadn't been able to resist splashing out on it, unwise though it had been to do so. A colourful plastic toy boat—just right for bathtime fun...

She sighed. She'd ask for another shift at the supermarket...get a little more money in, feel a little less precarious. Night shifts paid a fraction better, and as she had no social life whatsoever, what did it matter if she spent her evenings working as well as her days?

But it was wearing—she knew that...felt it. Wearing, tiring and depressing. With no end in sight—none. Just on and on. She was stuck now.

She gave another sigh. There was no point dwelling on it. Her life was what it was. She had made her choice six long years ago, and now she was living with the consequences. Stuck with them.

In her head she could hear again the taunt that Leandros had made, out on the terrace at that hotel where she had so disastrously set eyes on him again, wishing with all her being that she had not.

'Tell me, are you here to catch another husband? Another rich husband—the only kind you go for...'

His words mocked her—and condemned her.

She had no defence against them.

None.

Nor against the torment of seeing him again. The man she had once loved, and whose love she had so faithlessly betrayed.

Leandros was at his laptop and he was searching the Internet. He knew he shouldn't, but he couldn't stop himself. A demon was driving him as he typed her name into the search box.

Eliana's name.

Photos leapt on to the screen. Photos from the glossy magazines and tabloids that loved to highlight those living the high life. And Eliana had done just that.

Leandros's gaze bored into the screen. Image after image…

Eliana in a ball gown at some charity gala in Thessaloniki…at a private party on a yacht…at a fancy restaurant…at the opening of one of her father-in-law's prestigious properties… The images went on and on. Eliana with the man she had preferred to himself, Damian Makris. Nothing much to look at—but then his appeal had not been his looks, but his family money.

Leandros frowned involuntarily. He'd barely known the man, but to be dead at twenty-nine was a cruel fate for anyone. His gaze rested now on a sombre image: Eliana without her husband at her side, in a black dress, her father-in-law beside her, leaving her husband's funeral.

Thoughts flickered in his mind as he recalled what those two brokerage directors had said about how Jonas Makris had all but cast his daughter-in-law out of the family. And again that taunt he himself had thrown at her at that party in Athens. That she must be on the lookout now for a replacement for Damian Makris. A wealthy one, of course.

But not necessarily to marry.

Just someone to provide her with the luxury lifestyle that apparently she was now deprived of.

Someone…anyone…

Anyone who might find her beauty appealing…beguiling… Tempting…

Thoughts were circling now, coming closer like birds of prey—thoughts he must not have, must not allow. To do so would be madness—what else could it be? For six long years he'd blanked Eliana's existence, refused to think about her, relieved that she was away up in Thessaloniki so he wouldn't run into her. Wouldn't see her with the man she had preferred to himself.

But that man was gone now.

So she's available again—and missing her luxury lifestyle...

The birds of prey that were those thoughts he must not have circled closer, talons outstretched, taking hold of him...

His eyes went to her photo on the screen. He was unable to tear his fixed gaze away.

And everything that he had blanked for six long years came rushing back like a tidal wave. Drowning his sanity.

He felt his fingers move again on the keyboard, calling up another tab. Slowly, deliberately, he clicked through the screens, reaching the one he wanted.

Booking his flight to Thessaloniki.

Eliana had just got off shift and was dog-tired. She'd worked a twelve-hour day—seven in the morning till seven at night—not even stopping for lunch. She gave a sigh as she let herself in to her shabby, depressing studio apartment. Was this really going to be her life from now on? This miserable hand-to-mouth existence?

But what could she do to improve it? She had no marketable skills other than basic ones. She'd skipped on higher education in order to be with her father, and then, for those few, blissful months now lost for ever, tainted by the memory of how they'd ended, she'd thought that her future would be the everlasting bliss of being married to Leandros, making a family with him.

After that she'd been an ornamental, dressed-up doll of a wife for Damien, shown off to his father, to his father's friends and business associates, dressed up to the nines, bejewelled, smiling, making polite small talk as Jonas

Makris's docile daughter-in-law. A daughter-in-law who had become an increasing disappointment to him in her failure to present him with the grandson and heir he demanded.

As for Damian...

Her mind slid sideways. Back into the grief she still felt at his death, at the waste of it all. The sheer sadness.

He'd left such a mess behind...

And she was caught up in it.

She gave a tired sigh. Her life now was what it was, and nothing would change it. Nothing *could* change it.

She went into the cramped kitchenette, with its cheap fittings and broken cupboard, stained sink and chipped tiling. She needed coffee—only instant, which was all she could afford these days. She'd brought back a sandwich from the supermarket, marked down at the end of the day, and that would have to do for supper with a tin of soup. Meagre fare, but cheap—and that was all that mattered.

She had just taken a first sip of her weak coffee when something unusual happened. Her doorbell rang. She replaced her mug on the worn laminate work surface, frowning. The rent wasn't due, and no one else ever called except the landlord's agent. The bell rang again—not at the door itself, but at the front door to the apartment block. Still frowning, she crossed to the door to press the buzzer to let it open.

She knew she ought to check who it was first, but the intercom had never worked, and she lacked the energy to trudge down to the main door. It was probably for a different apartment anyway.

She took another mouthful of coffee and then, moments later, there was a knock on her own door. The safety catch was on so, setting down her coffee again, she opened it cautiously—and froze in total shock.

CHAPTER THREE

LEANDROS WAS STILL in shock himself. Eliana lived *here*? In this run-down apartment block in the back end of the city? Had she really been reduced to *this*?

Disbelief had hit him when the airport taxi had dropped him off in this street, and he'd stared around, questioning whether he had possibly got the wrong address. But no, he had not. And that was definitely Eliana standing there, her face ashen, in the narrow gap of the safety chained doorway.

He watched her fumble with the safety chain, as though her hands wouldn't work properly, and as the door opened more widely he stepped forward. She stepped away, as if automatically, and then he was inside, casting a still half-disbelieving look around him at the tiny studio, with its shabby furniture, worn floor, cramped kitchenette and totally depressing air of chronic poverty.

Eliana had not just gone down in the world—she had reached the bottom.

Her face was still ashen, her eyes distended.

'What—? What—? I don't understand… Why—?'

The disconnected words fell from her lips, uncomprehending, as filled with shock as her expression. Leandros's gaze snapped back from surveying her unlovely living quarters to her face. Not just ashen, but with lines of tiredness etched into it. She did not look good…

But that was to his advantage. Just as seeing the daughter of Aristides Georgiades, whose forebears had hobnobbed with the long-gone kings of Greece, now the widow of the son of one of Greece's richest men, reduced to living in a dump like this was to his advantage.

She will do anything to get out of here.

'You really live here?' he heard himself ask.

Something changed in her face. 'As you can see,' she answered tightly.

She crossed her arms across her chest, chin going up. She took a breath, kept talking, her voice less faint now.

'Leandros, what is this? What are you doing here?'

There was blank incomprehension in her tone, but a demand as well.

His own expression altered in response. 'I thought you might like to come out to dinner with me,' he said.

She stared. 'Are you mad?'

He ignored the voice that was telling him that, yes, he was in fact mad to be doing what he was doing. 'I have something I want to speak to you about,' he said instead.

Her face closed. 'So, speak.'

'Not here,' he said dismissively. 'I'll tell you over dinner. It could be...' his voice became silky '...to your advantage.' His gaze flicked around the dump she lived in—had been reduced to living in. 'I could get you out of here,' he said.

Something moved in her eyes—a longing so intense it overrode everything else in her tired face. For a moment he felt pity for her—then he pushed it aside. It wasn't the emotion he intended to feel. As for love—she had killed that six years ago. Now all he wanted from her was something else. Something that had nothing to do with love.

He saw her handbag—a cheap one—on the table, and handed it to her, along with the apartment keys beside it.

'Let's go,' he said.

She seemed totally dazed, and he took advantage of it, guiding her out of the apartment, ushering her downstairs, and into the waiting taxi, which promptly drove off. She sank into her seat, still looking blitzed. But then, he was blitzed too.

All the way up to Thessaloniki a voice inside him had told him that what he was doing was madness. But he was doing it all the same...

He stole a glance at her, sitting silent and immobile, staring ahead blankly. He felt something move within him that was confirming of his mad impulse to come to Thessaloniki like this. For all the tiredness in her eyes, the cheapness of her clothes, her face with not a scrap of make-up, her hair caught back in a straggling knot, her beauty was undimmed.

He let his gaze rest lingeringly on her. She might be beaten down by her new poverty, but she was unbowed.

An air of unreality hit him—was he really sitting here in a taxi with Eliana? Or would he blink and wake up? Find it was only a dream after all?

His expression hardened. He was done with dreams about Eliana. She'd destroyed them six years again—ripped them from him and trampled them into the mire. Now what he wanted from her was a lot more basic.

The taxi made its way out on to the seafront of the city, where there were any number of restaurants—Thessaloniki was the foodie capital of Greece. But tonight was not for gourmet dining—Eliana was hardly dressed for it—and the mid-range fish restaurant the taxi driver had recommended would do fine.

It was quiet at this early hour of the evening, and he chose a table far from the few other diners. Eliana was focussing on her menu, and Leandros knew she was doing so to avoid looking at him.

'Made your decision?' he asked.

She gave a start, naming one of the fish dishes, then look-

ing away again. Leandros beckoned the waiter over, relayed
their order, then ordered water, beer for himself, and a carafe of house red. The waiter headed off, returning a few
moments later with the drinks order, and a basket of bread
with some pats of butter.

Leandros reached for his beer, taking a long draught—
he suddenly felt he needed it. Then he poured water and
wine for them both.

'Eliana—'

He said her name, and as if on auto-response her eyes went
to him. And immediately veiled. Her hand jerked forward to
take a piece of bread, which she then crumbled into pieces
as if she were doing something to distract herself. She still
looked strained…tense as a board. Yet for all that there was
a haunting beauty about her. Haunting—and so, so familiar.

Emotions churned in him, but he fought them back. He
didn't want those emotions. They were from the past, and
he wasn't interested in the past any longer. He was immune
to it and inured to it. It was just the present he was interested in—and the immediate future.

'I expect you're wondering why I'm here,' he opened,
helping himself to some bread and buttering it. 'As I said,
I have something to put to you.'

He glanced at her semi-covertly. Her expression did not
change.

So he spoke again. Not prevaricating, or circling around,
or delaying in any way. Cutting right to the chase—to the
reason he was here.

'I want you to come back to me,' he said.

Eliana heard his words, but they did not register. It was impossible that they should do so. Her expression, veiled as
it already was, froze. So did her fingers, pointlessly crum-
bling her piece of bread.

'I am quite serious,' he said.

His eyes were on her like weights. A weight she could not bear.

'You can't possibly be,' she heard herself say, her voice faint, hardly audible.

A new expression crossed his face. He was cynical. She could see it in the slight twist to his mouth, the acid look in his eyes. Eyes so dark…so drowning…

'And yet I am,' he returned.

He reached for his wine glass, took a hefty slug, then resumed his regard of her.

'Don't get any ideas, however,' he said. His voice held the same acidity as his eyes. 'I want something a lot more limited this time.' He paused 'You'll do well out of it, all the same.' His eyes narrowed, sweeping over her. 'You really have hit rock bottom, haven't you? I'd heard old man Jonas hadn't gone easy on you—but surely Damian left you something?'

If her face could have gone even more blank, it did. Then, with a tightness that was in her voice as well as her throat, she spoke.

'Evidently not.'

He frowned. 'Why not? Unless…' That acid look was in his eye again…that cynical twist to his mouth. 'Unless he had reason not to?'

She didn't answer. It was none of his business, her marriage to Damian, and the years she had spent as his wife. Nor was what had happened after his untimely death. Nothing about her was any of his business any more…or his concern. Not that he felt any for her—that was obvious.

But why should he, after what I did to him?

And why, most of all, had he turned up here like this—said to her what he had…?

Waves of unreality were hitting her…slug after slug. How could she be here, sitting opposite Leandros, out of nowhere—

absolutely nowhere? For all the desperate blankness in her eyes, they were still fastened on him. Her senses reeling.

Leandros—here—physically so close—

His face...the once so familiar features. His sable hair, his dark and gold-flecked eyes, the line of his jaw, his sculpted mouth, the breadth of his shoulders, the lean strength of his body... All here... All real...

She felt faint with it—with the scent of his aftershave, still the same as she remembered...

Jerkily, she reached for her wine. She needed it.

His face had tightened.

'Looks like you got your just desserts,' he said now, as she stayed silent. 'You married him for money, and now you haven't got it.'

She still said nothing. There was nothing she could or would tell him.

Their food was arriving and she was grateful. Hungrily, she got stuck into her fish, and Leandros did too.

'So, my offer to you...' he opened, as he started eating. 'I want you to come to Paris with me.'

His voice was brisk, without expression. But Eliana stopped eating, eyes fastening on him. Emotion knifed through her before she could stop it.

Paris—the destination that had been going to be their honeymoon...

Leandros was still speaking in that brisk, expression-less tone of voice.

'I have to go there on business next week. I want you to come with me.'

His eyes lifted from his food, looked straight at her. There was a glint in them that was like acid on her skin.

'We'd planned to honeymoon there, remember?'

Her hold on her fork tightened. His eyes were resting

on her. Unreadable. But the feel of acid on her skin ate through her.

'We won't be recapturing the past, Eliana,' he went on. 'We'll be…updating it to our current circumstances.'

He ate some more of his fish, washing it down with some wine. He looked across at her again.

'And in these present circumstances I think my offer to you is entirely…appropriate. I am willing to take you on. It will suit us both. I'll provide you with a new wardrobe, and when we part I'll be generous. You will have enough to get you out of the dump you live in, get you back to Athens all fixed up to go husband-hunting again. Just what you want. As for me… Well, I'll get what I want too, Eliana.'

She set down her fork. Looked straight at him.

'Which is what, Leandros?'

Her voice was flat.

A dark, saturnine glint showed in the depths of his night-dark eyes.

'What I was denied, Eliana,' he said softly. 'What you denied me.'

He set his cutlery down too. Reached a hand forward. Folded it over hers still resting over her fork. It felt warm, but like a weight that would crush her to pieces.

Faintness drummed through her.

'You in my bed.'

He had said it. Spelt it out. Laid it out. Bluntly, coarsely, brutally. No hearts and flowers—they had rotted years ago—nothing but the blunt, visceral truth.

He lifted his hand away. The hand that had not touched her for six long years.

'You denied me during our courtship—prating on about wedding nights and so forth. Were you already hedging your bets, even then? Just in case a better offer came along and you wanted to go as a virgin to his bed? I assume you did with Damian? Did he appreciate it, I wonder? Appreciate all your fantastic beauty? Well, whatever... I most definitely *will*. I set no prize on virginity—that would be hypocritical, wouldn't it? Even when I wanted to marry you it was your choice, not mine, to wait until our wedding night—whatever your reason for it. Now, we'll be...let us say "equal" in that respect. Both experienced. We'll make, I am confident, good lovers.'

He went back to eating. The fish was good, tasty and filling. And his mood was improving, his confidence in his own decision increasing. He confirmed it to himself. For six years he'd done his best to ignore the continuing existence of the woman who had once meant all the world to him—now he was going to reverse that policy.

But on his own terms this time. Not hers.

'I'm due in Paris tomorrow. I propose I fly up here again then, and we'll fly to Paris from here. Don't bother packing—we'll hit the fashion houses first thing. Give me your current phone number and I'll text you the time you'll need to be at the airport.'

He was being brisk and businesslike, and he was glad of it. He looked across at her, waiting for her reply. She'd picked up her cutlery again, and was absorbed, it seemed, in eating her own fish.

'Eliana?' he prompted.

She didn't look up, and he waited a moment longer.

'Do you require something on account? Is that it?' he said. 'If so, I expect I can run to that.' He reached into his jacket pocket and took out his wallet. 'If you have expenses here to settle, will this cover it?'

He extracted a few hundred-euro notes and put them by her place.

She stopped eating. Pushed them away from her. Looked across at him.

'Thank you, but no,' she said politely. 'And thank you,' she went on, in the same polite voice, 'but no, in fact, to your kind invitation to go to Paris with you and keep you company in bed.'

He paused again. Then: 'Why not?' He kept his tone casual.

'The past is gone, Leandros. I don't want to try and ex-hume it. What would be the point?'

'The point, Eliana,' he spelt out deliberately, 'is what I have already said. I will bankroll you, get you back on your feet. You'll be able to start again—look for another rich man to marry you. You can't do that,' he said, and his voice was drier than ever, 'from some dump in a backstreet in Thessaloniki.'

He drained his glass of wine and went on eating, as did she. For all its non-gourmet status, the food was good, and he ate with a will now. He didn't say anything more—he'd let Eliana think over what he'd offered her.

When they'd both finished eating, he settled the bill, then got to his feet.

Leandros was guiding her outside, into the warm air. The seafront stretched along the wide bay. City-dwellers were making their evening *volta*, strolling along—a familiar scene at this hour of the day along every seafront in Greece.

'Let's walk a bit,' he said to her.

Passively, she fell into step beside him. She was still in a daze, unable to believe what was happening. That Lean-dros had reappeared like this—and what he'd said to her.

Unbelievable.

Unbelievable that he should have said it—or thought she might agree.

Suddenly, he spoke.

'We used to do this every evening—do you remember?

In Chania, walking along the curve of the harbour that time when we went to Crete?'

Eliana felt her heart catch. How could she not remember her hand being held fast in his, as if he would never let her go?

But it was me who let him go—went to another man.

Pain—so familiar, so impossible to relinquish—stabbed at her for what she'd done.

'That was a good holiday...'

Leandros was speaking again. There was reminiscence in his voice, but then it changed to hold wry humour.

'You insisted on separate bedrooms.'

Suddenly, he stopped, stepping in front of Eliana. His hands closed over her shoulders. Stilling her. Freezing her. He looked down at her, his face stark in the street light.

'Had...had we not had separate bedrooms all the time back then...'

He drew a breath. She heard it—heard the intensity in his voice when he spoke again.

'You would not would have left me.'

There was something in his voice—something that was like a stab of pain. Then it was gone, replaced by hardness.

He dropped his hands away.

'No—stupid to think that. With or without sex, you'd still have walked out on me, wouldn't you, Eliana? Because I wasn't going to be able to give you what you wanted. Not me...not even sex with me.'

The twist in his voice now was ugly, and she flinched.

'Just money. That was all you wanted from a man. Any man. Did that hapless fool Damian know that? Know that if his father had done what mine did, and threatened to disinherit him, you'd have dumped him as ruthlessly as you dumped me?'

He quickened his pace and she was forced to do likewise.

Emotions were smashing around inside her, but there was nothing she could do about it.

Oh, dear God, why had Leandros turned up like this? Wasn't her life now grim enough as it was, without him twisting the knife that had been in her heart since what she had done to him?

'You don't answer?' Leandros said now, cynicism in his voice. 'Well, what does it matter? Damian knew the risk of marrying a woman who'd just dumped the man she'd been keen to marry until his money vanished.'

And something else entered his voice now—something that made it seem to Eliana that he was trying to convince himself.

'I know the risk I'm taking.' Now his voice had hardened, conviction made. 'Which is why I'm keeping my offer strictly limited. I'll lift you back out of the gutter you've fallen into, but on *my* terms, Eliana—my terms only. Be very clear on that. This is the finish of something old—not the start of something new.'

She didn't answer—there was no point. Instead, she stopped walking.

'I'm tired,' she announced. 'I don't want to walk any further.'

She hadn't wanted to walk at all, but she'd been too dazed, too passive, to do anything else.

'All right. I'll see you back to your apartment.'

He summoned a taxi and she sank into it, closing her eyes. She could not bear to see Leandros. Yet his presence dominated her. She knew he was only a few centimetres away from her…that she would only have to reach out her hand to take his…to feel his fingers mesh with hers as they once had.

Anguish filled her suddenly, flooding her with the sheer misery of it all.

I loved him, and I left him.

And what they'd had so briefly in their lives—what she'd willingly, wantonly destroyed—could never, never come back...

He didn't speak to her again, and she was glad, keeping her eyes shut, terrified that tears might come. Tears he would think deliberate, artificial...manipulative.

At the shabby apartment block the taxi drew up at the kerb, and she stumbled out.

'Eliana—'

Now he spoke. Demanding she halt. She did, unwillingly turning back as he leant towards her from his seat.

'You haven't given me your mobile number.'

She stared at him blankly. Of course she hadn't. A look of irritation flashed across his strong features, and then he was reaching inside his jacket pocket, taking out a card case, removing a card and holding it purposefully out to her.

'Take it,' he said. 'And text me your number. Then I'll give you the flight details.'

He was still holding the business card out to her.

Nervelessly, knowing she shouldn't, but doing it all the same, she took it. Then she turned silently away.

She could barely stay upright. The shock of the whole evening was catching up with her, and she had to get inside—get away, get out of his presence.

She heard him pull the car door closed, speak to the driver, give the name of the city's best hotel. Heard the taxi move off. Then numbly, dumbly, his card burning her fingers as if it were a hot coal, she went inside the apartment block, trudged up the stairs as if a weight were on her back. She was barely able to function.

She got herself inside her studio, collapsed down on the bed.

And just lay there. For a long, long while.

Anguish consuming her.

CHAPTER FOUR

LEANDROS LAY SLEEPLESS on his bed at the hotel. On the other side of the city was Eliana…

He was still shocked by the brutal reality of just how low she had sunk. The cramped, run-down studio flat, the whole shabby apartment block in the back end of town—was that really what she had come down to?

Well, he could get her out of there. Lift her back up to something more like the life she had once lived.

He frowned. Why had she not bitten his hand off when he'd made her his offer? Did she have anything better in mind? His expression hardened. Well, if she did, she wouldn't be getting it from him. He'd been totally upfront with her—she wasn't going to get the chance to have any illusions about what he was offering.

And there was nothing sordid about what he was offering. He wanted an affair with her, a temporary liaison that would give them something each of them wanted. She got a ticket out of that dump of an apartment, and he—well, he got what had been getting under his skin ever since that damn night in Athens all those weeks ago.

He stared, hands behind his head, up at the ceiling of his hotel room, but what he was seeing was not that. It was the image of Eliana, sitting opposite him at the taverna, without a scrap of make-up, in those chain store clothes, her hair pulled starkly off her face—and yet with the same unforgettable beauty that she had always possessed.

His mind slipped further back…back to that holiday he'd reminded her of, their week in Crete. Happiness had consumed him. He'd stepped into another world, with Eliana at his side. The week had been magical—and intensely frustrating too. For her kisses had been an incitement for so much more—and yet she had always drawn back. His only consolation—and it brought a twist to his mouth even now—was the fact that she had found it as hard to draw back from him as he had from her. She'd wanted him—and he'd done his damnedest to show her just how much he wanted her! Done his damnedest to show her just how much she wanted him in return even as, breathless and bemused, she'd pulled away from his embrace in the shadows of that quiet cobbled street in the old part of Chania, where their hotel—a converted merchant's mansion—had lain a few metres beyond.

'Let me come to your room tonight…' His voice had been husky as he'd moved to reach for her again.

She'd held him at bay. 'We agreed. Oh, Leandros, don't make it harder for me than it already is. I want so much to wait for our wedding day…our wedding night…'

There'd been a catch in her voice, her eyes glowing partly with pleading, partly with the desire that he knew had quickened in her as he'd kissed her as seductively as he'd known how.

And he'd honoured her plea—knowing how important it was for her.

His expression changed again, became etched in bitterness. Now, with the acid lens of hindsight, he knew just why it had been so important for her.

So she could go a virgin to Damian's bed.

Had she kept her virginity deliberately from the off? In

case something happened to prevent her from marrying him? Would she have given herself only when his ring was on her finger, her access to the Kastellanos wealth secured?

Well, now there would be no ring—and all that she would get from him materially, as he had informed her over dinner, would be the couture wardrobe he would provide, and whatever piece of jewellery he chose to bestow upon her when he had sent her on her way, which she would be able to sell to fund her in Athens.

When I've had enough of her.

And then he could get his life back and be free of her—finally. Finally free.

She will never haunt me again, neither in dreams, nor in waking. I'll be done with her and her power will be gone.

A nerve ticked in his cheek, and he felt his hands clench behind his head as he went on staring sightlessly at the blank and empty ceiling overhead.

'Oh, for heaven's sake, watch where you're going!'

The angry outburst from a shopper was lost on Eliana as she made a muttering apology. Her mind was not on restocking shelves. It was like a tangled skein of wool—knotted and impossible, riven with emotions, a tormented mess. It had been like that all week. Ever since the bombshell Leandros had lobbed at her—as if turning up at her apartment hadn't been bombshell enough.

Through the tangled mess in her head one phrase kept going round and round and round. She kept hearing his voice saying it.

'I want you to come back to me.'

It was incising itself into her ceaselessly, remorseless, by day and by night. Not letting her go. Tormenting her. She'd tried to overlay it, to smother it, to deafen it with the words she'd said to him, dragged out of her numbly as she'd sat opposite him in the restaurant.

'Thank you, but no.'

She wanted to hang on to them—needed to hang on to them...was desperate to hang on to them. But with each passing day they were getting fainter and fainter.

Oh, dear God, why had Leandros come back into her life? Why couldn't he have stayed out of it? Just gone on ignoring her existence as he had for six long, bleak years.

I don't need this, and I don't want it—I don't, I don't, I don't!

She had enough to cope with—oh, so much more than enough.

She stretched up, replenishing the packets of pasta and rice. The tangled mess of her thoughts and emotions was writhing now, like a nest of snakes, and Leandros's voice was in her head, over and over and over again.

'I want you to come back to me.'

She closed her eyes in anguish. She must not listen to those words—must not heed their power...their tainted temptation to claim again in any way, on any terms, what she once had had.

Leandros desiring her...

As she still desired him...had always done...would always do...

The knowledge was impossible to deny.

In her mind's vivid eye she saw him again as he had been at that fateful party to celebrate Chloe's engagement—and then as he had been only a handful of days ago, striding back into her life. Saw that he still possessed exactly what he had always possessed—the ability to kindle in her that flame of desire.

But I forfeited my right to desire him.

Her eyes shadowed. She had no right to him...to anything of him. Not any more...

Yet memory played again in her head of how they'd walked along the seafront, how she had denied him, all the while trembling in his arms at his kisses.

Guilt smote her again—always, always guilt. Guilt at having betrayed his love for her and denied him his desire for her. The desire he had told her he now wanted to slake...

The tangled, tormenting knot of thoughts and feelings in her head writhed again. How could she be free of her endless guilt? Free of Leandros—finally free? Free of what she had once felt for him? Free of the desire that now could only be tainted by what she'd done to him?

Slowly, fatefully, the words shaped themselves in her head.

If I went to him now, as he asks of me—if I did I could finally move on...put behind me what I did, what I destroyed.

Her guilt would go—the guilt she had felt ever since she had returned his ring, accepted Damian's in its place.

I could be free of it—free of that guilt. Because I would be offering him now what I never offered him then, what is all that he wants of me. And that would free him, too, wouldn't it? He can be purged of me. He can hate me still, but I can make amends—and in doing so free myself.

If she simply went to Paris with Leandros...

All through her shift the thought stayed with her.

All the while she walked back to her studio that evening.

Stayed with her as she sat down on her narrow bed with its lumpy mattress, reached inside her handbag. Took out the business card in the zip pocket. Stared down at it.

She got out her cheap phone and numbly, without thinking about it, without letting herself think about it, she started to tap in the number from the stiff white card.

Sent a text to Leandros.

Scarcely believing that she was doing so.

And yet she was.

Leandros sat in one of the several business lounges at Thessaloniki airport, where he'd just arrived off the shuttle from Athens, drumming his fingers on his briefcase. His flight to Paris was about to be called—and there was no sign of Eliana.

Yet she had agreed to be here. He hadn't spoken to her—she wouldn't take his calls—but she had texted, and it had been by text that he'd told her when to arrive.

So, where was she?

Was she going to show up or not?

He could feel tension whipping across his shoulders. His expression was set, his gaze fixed on the entrance to the lounge. He was oblivious to the fact that he was being eyed up both by the hostess in charge of refreshments and by a female passenger across the lounge, trying to catch his eye. Oblivious to everything except his impatience to see Eliana walk through that damn door...

The flight announcement started, and his tension cranked up even more. OK, so they would want to board the business class passengers first, but there was no immediate urgency. All the same...

She was burning in his head.

And there was only one way to extinguish that flame, that fire.

His gaze darkened. He hated it that it should be so... Despising himself for his weakness... Resenting her for her power to make him so weak.

I should not want her. I should not want to have her with me, to take her to Paris, to claim what she denied me— denied me before she betrayed me, my faithless fiancée...

But it did not matter that he could hear his own thoughts jeering at him—it made no difference. Nothing had made any difference—not since seeing her again in Athens, and then, last week, succumbing to the temptation, to the fire in his head that she had kindled, to confront her here in Thessaloniki. To put to her his contemptuous offer, knowing she would accept it—because how else was she going to get herself out of the gutter she'd fallen into by failing to give Jonas Makris the grandson he'd craved?

So… His darkening thoughts circled back to the present. Where the hell was she?

One of the airline staff was approaching him, a smile on her face and a clipboard in her hand, inviting him to board.

'I'm waiting for someone,' he said curtly, and she nodded smilingly and moved on to another passenger—but not without a lingering glance back at him, to which he was as oblivious as he was any other female's attention.

There was only one female he wanted to pay him attention—to turn up.

And she was there—there in the entrance to the lounge.

He felt emotions stab through him—a mix of them. Anger that she'd run so late, relief that she'd arrived at all, and something even more potent…more stabbing. Something that made his gaze focus on her like a laser beam, taking in the entirety of her in an instant, imprinting it on his retinas.

She was looking fraught—that was the only word for it. Strain in her face, in her eyes, as she hesitantly showed her boarding pass to the attendant at the door, gripping her bag—a shoulder bag that seemed, he thought, to be doubling as a carry-on, bulky and bulging.

He'd told her not to pack, that he'd be supplying her wardrobe, but presumably there were first-night necessities she would need before he took her shopping in the Faubourg Saint-Honoré tomorrow.

He pushed the thought of 'first-night' from him...got to his feet, strode across to her.

'You've cut it fine,' he said. His voice was still curt, and it came out like an admonishment.

She flushed. 'The bus took longer than I thought it would,' she said.

He frowned. 'I told you to take a taxi—that I'd reimburse you the fare.'

She didn't answer, only paid attention to the airline staffer who was hovering, keen for them to board.

Leandros nodded, taking Eliana's elbow. He felt her freeze, and for some reason it annoyed him. But she went with him all the same, disengaging as they left the lounge to make their way towards their gate.

Leandros glanced at her as they walked. She was looking neat, but that was about the only compliment he could pay her. He frowned inwardly. It was...strange... That was the only word he could come up with. To see her dressed so cheaply. Almost as strange—and that was definitely not the only word—as seeing her reduced to living in that squalid rental apartment.

He quickened his pace slightly, unconsciously. Well, that poverty-stricken, squalid existence she'd been forced into was about to change. From now on her luck was looking up—courtesy of himself. Courtesy of the fire burning in his head that only she could extinguish.

When he had got what he wanted from her—then, and only then—he could be free of that burning fire, so disastrously rekindled. He wished to God it wasn't so—wished to God he'd never set eyes on her again. Wished to God that she'd never been widowed, simply so that their paths would never have crossed again and she would have remained out of his reach for ever by her marriage, instead of only six long years.

But now...

Now she was boarding a plane with him, and they were heading to Paris. To have the 'honeymoon' she had denied him. And after that, and only after that, he would, if there was any justice in this world, finally be free of her.

Finally.

'Champagne, madam?'

The steward was proffering a tray with two glasses of gently foaming flutes on it, together with little bowls of salted almonds.

Eliana shook her head, but Leandros simply reached out and took the two flutes with a swift 'thank you', placing them on the table set between their spacious seats. The steward placed the nuts down as well, and then disappeared.

Leandros picked up a flute and held the other one out to Eliana. Passively, she took it, trying to calm her jangled nerves. Trying not to be so burningly aware of sitting there beside him in the capacious first-class seat. But he was dominating her senses—as he always had.

He always did—always! From the first moment I saw him there was never another man for me. Never...

Not Damian—poor, hapless Damian. Trying to please his overbearing father with a bride Jonas Makris considered suitable for his son—irrespective of what his son might want...

Poor Damian—and yet we both got what each of us wanted from our marriage.

A marriage that had ended with his car smashed to pieces on that treacherous road a year and a half ago, leaving the consequences that it had...

'To Paris—and to our time together there.'

Leandros's low voice interrupted thoughts she didn't want to have…memories she wanted even less. He clinked his glass against hers, a smile pulling at his sculpted mouth. Yet it was a smile that was disquieting. Like the silky note in his voice.

'To our days,' he said. 'And to our nights…'

For a moment his eyes held hers, and then she broke contact, knowing colour had stained across her cheekbones. Knowing why. Because when he looked at her like that…

More memories she must not have came to her. Of how he had once looked at her like that all the time, making no secret of his desire for her—a desire that she, in those heady, intoxicating days of her love for him, had made no secret of returning.

She took a hasty sip of her champagne, letting the soft mousse fill her mouth, divert her senses from the burning consciousness of Leandros so close beside her.

His power over her senses was as undeniable as ever—and yet now, in the toxic aftermath of what she had done to him all those years ago, he had never been more distant…

Sadness filled her. Yes, she had decided…chosen…resolved to come to him now, like this, for the reasons she had justified to herself and for the sake of the freedom that they must somehow find from each other. It had been her choice—and yet now the reality of it weighed her down. Mocked her.

Had this been our honeymoon six long years ago…flying to Paris, newly wedded, setting off on our life's adventure together…oh, how blissful it would have been.

Instead…

She suppressed a sigh. There was no point in looking back. She had destroyed a past that never was—now she had to cope with the present.

She took another mouthful of champagne. It would likely

make her light-headed, but it would provide an insulating layer over her ragged emotions.

Leandros had got some kind of business journal out of his briefcase and was immersed in it. She was glad of it— it gave her time for her breathing to steady, her colour to subside. She helped herself to the salted almonds, feeling a pang of hunger. She'd been far too stressed to eat today, trying to summon the nerve to actually get to the airport at all. She hoped that some kind of meal would be served on the flight. Presumably there would be dinner that evening. And then afterwards, later on—

Her thoughts cut out—absolutely cut out. She could not think ahead to the coming night—dared not. The resolve she'd felt as she'd sent that fateful text to Leandros last week seemed impossible to believe in now.

She felt the aircraft push back, the engine note change. They were taxiing towards the runway. Airborne, she leant back in her seat, closed her eyes. Perhaps Leandros would think her asleep. It would be easier if he did. Though 'easier' was a relative term…

'Are you all right?'

Leandros's voice made her open her eyes, turn her head towards him. He was frowning.

'Thank you, I'm fine,' she said. Her voice was clipped.

'I've never flown with you before,' he said slowly. 'When we went to Crete we went by sea.'

Memory was instant and painful. Standing on the deck of the ferry, leaning on the rail, the wind in her hair, Leandros's arm around her, her head nestled against his shoulder, not a care in the world. And so incredibly happy.

She dropped her eyes, reached for her champagne again. No point remembering that happiness. It was gone. She had destroyed it and it could never return. *Never.*

'So, are you a nervous flyer?'

She couldn't say there was concern in his voice, but the fact that he was asking at all showed something—though what it was she had no idea.

She shook her head. 'No, though I haven't flown much. When my mother was alive we went to England sometimes, to visit the relatives who hadn't objected to her marrying my father, and for her to catch up with friends from her youth. But after she died that all stopped, really. I just stayed with my father, because—'

She stopped. Her mother's death when she was eighteen had devastated her father, and she had centred her life around him, forgoing college, keeping him company in their beautiful but isolated house out in the countryside. It had been a quiet existence.

And then one of her school friends had invited her to her twenty-first birthday party at her family villa in Glyfada, on the Athens Riviera, and she hadn't been able to resist going, even though her father had fretted. And it had been there, out on the terrace, bathed in lights and music, guests dancing and partying, overlooking the waters of the Saronic Gulf, that she had first seen Leandros.

She had fallen for him on the spot, ineluctably drawn towards the tall, self-assured, oh-so-good-looking man in his mid-twenties, unable to tear her eyes away. He'd been talking—flirting—with a sophisticated female wearing a lot of make-up and a revealing dress, who had clearly been all over him. Then he'd glanced across the crowded terrace—and their eyes had met.

For a timeless moment the world had stopped, the music had been silenced, the noise and chatter too—and then, as if in slow motion, she'd seen him turn back to the other girl, smile pleasantly but dismissively, and make his way across the terrace. Straight to her.

He'd smiled down at her.

And she'd been lost.

That was all it had taken—for both of them.

'Because…?' Leandros's prompt brought her back to the present—the present in which that enchanted past could never exist again.

She gave a tiny shrug, not wanting to think about any aspect of the past.

'It was convenient,' she answered.

She saw the flight attendant moving down the gangway, proffering more champagne, handing out menu cards, and held her flute out for a top-up. It was probably rash, but she felt she needed it. Then she studied the menu, choosing the chicken option. Leandros glanced briefly at his, selecting beef. Then went back to his business journal and Eliana could relax a fraction—but only a fraction. A fraction of a fraction…

The meal when it came was welcome, and she tucked in. For her, decent food, let alone gourmet food, belonged to a different life. Now Leandros was offering that life back to her—

But only if—

Her thoughts cut out. Impossible to think them.

As he began his own meal, Leandros addressed her again.

'So, tell me—which fashion houses in Paris are your favourites now?'

'I don't have any,' she answered. 'Whatever you want.'

'Eliana, it's what *you* want.'

She looked at him, puzzled. 'This is only for you, Leandros,' she replied. 'I'm here because you want me to be here.'

Even as she spoke, she felt her thoughts betray her. Was she truly here, like this, only for his sake? To make what amends she could to him? To do what was still in her power to do—to give him all that he still wanted from her? But not her love—never that…not any longer.

And I will get closure too, won't I? That is all—there is nothing more than that…

Yet once again her betraying thoughts plucked at her…

To be with Leandros again, so tormentingly conscious of his physical presence at her side, with all of Paris awaiting them…it was not just closure she was after…

Emotion twisted inside her—knotting and tangling.

But Leandros's next words cut through the tangling. Made things simple again—brutally so. His voice was edged, like a knife, to cut through that tangled knot of impossible emotions.

'Really?' he said. 'I thought you were here because you wanted to get out of that hellhole you've been reduced to living in. To climb back out of the gutter—get your old life back again.'

Her eyes pulled away. The hardness in his was the same as it had been when he had seen her at Chloe's engagement party, that disastrous encounter in Athens. And the same as she had seen six years ago when she'd walked away from him, his denunciation of her ringing in her ears even as got herself out through the door with the last of her shaken strength, her stomach churning at what she was doing. Handing him back his ring…telling him she was going to marry Damian Makris.

She didn't answer him now. There was no point. Instead, she asked some innocuous question about what time they would arrive in Paris.

He told her, adding, 'I'll be dining out tonight—a business dinner. You can have room service. Tomorrow morning I have an appointment, but then we'll head to the Faubourg Saint-Honoré and get your wardrobe sorted. After that…

Well, whatever suits us.' He paused, then continued. 'What might you like to do?'

His tone was courteous enough, and she matched hers to it. It seemed the easiest thing to do. Requiring the least effort, the least involvement.

'Whatever you like,' she said.

He made a noise in his throat. 'Don't go complaisant on me, Eliana. You never used to be—and I always liked you for speaking your mind. Other girlfriends...' there was a cynical twist to his mouth now '...they always agreed with everything I wanted—tediously so. You never did, and that was part of your appeal to me—your honesty. Be honest now. So, do you want to do the cultural stuff, or the histori-cal stuff, or just stick to spending my money?'

Only with that did an edge creep into his voice. She heard it, but did not respond. 'I'd like to see anything of Paris,' she said civilly. 'Even the touristy things. It will all be new to me.'

'We can see beyond Paris too, if you like, and if the weather holds.'

His voice was civil now, too, and she was grateful. Maybe if they could just continue to talk in this way, without him cutting at her all the time—*as though I don't know what I did to him, how badly I treated him!*—being with him would be more bearable. Less unbearable...

'What about Versailles?' he went on. 'We had that high on our list, as I recall—'

He broke off abruptly, reaching for his wine and taking a hefty draught.

Eliana paid attention to her food. Somehow she'd drunk her champagne, and now she was starting to sip her chilled white wine. Another layer of insulation over her nerve-endings.

'Then there's the Trianons, too, near Versailles—we

could do them…the Grand and the Petit Trianons,' Leandros was saying, back in the same conversational tone.

'Yes,' said Eliana politely, 'we could do that.'

We could do a lot of things, but all you're really taking me to Paris for is sex.

She felt her throat close, anguish clenching it tight, and felt her eyes blinking suddenly.

This might have been our honeymoon together! Starting our lives together. Living our dream together.

But she had made that dream impossible. All that was left to her—and to Leandros, claiming from her the one thing he still wanted of her—was this poisoned present.

Nothing else.

She reached for her wine again. To conceal the tears that threatened…

CHAPTER FIVE

THE PARIS TRAFFIC was bad as they crawled around the Périphérique to make their slow way into the centre. They were staying, so Leandros had told her, on the Left Bank, near Les Invalides.

'You can add Napoleon's tomb to your sightseeing list,' he remarked. 'Our hotel is one of the former grand residences of the city. Once owned by one of Napoleon's marshals, so I understand.'

He was being civil, making conversation, and though Eliana was glad he was not making any more cutting remarks to her, his politeness was detached, impersonal.

I could be anyone—anyone at all.

But how could it be otherwise? she thought painfully. Since she had tugged his ring from her finger, her voice stilted, telling him of her change of plan, everything they had once had between them had been obliterated, as if an axe had fallen. All intimacy severed for ever.

The car was gaining the centre of Paris, familiar from a hundred films, and she craned her head to catch a glimpse of the sights. Leandros pointed them out to her and she realised he must, of course, be far more familiar with the city than she was. She had not travelled abroad much with Damian—his father had liked to keep him close by and under his watch.

An unexpected start of excitement pricked at her now as

the iconic Eiffel Tower came into view nearby. She was here, in Paris, and however...*difficult*...the reason, it was something to be here—and a change, she had to acknowledge honestly, from the dreary, dismal, endlessly grinding impoverishment to which she had been confined since Damian's death.

A sudden yearning smote her.

If only... If only I were here with Leandros as we should have been!

She crushed it down. There was no 'if only' possible. Face set, she kept on gazing out of the window, not looking at Leandros, the man she had betrayed and abandoned. Who would never, *could* never, forgive her...

The hotel was, as Leandros had said, a former grand townhouse, and as they arrived Eliana looked about her with pleasure at the way past and present were intermingled in the luxurious interior.

'We're in the Résidence,' Leandros said to her as he checked them in. 'The main top floor.'

He guided her into the lift, inset beside a grand staircase sweeping upwards, and Eliana felt her nerves start up. The reality of what she was doing was hitting her...the reason for her presence here. At their floor, they emerged on to a wide landing set with a pair of gilded double doors, which Leandros opened with a flourish.

She stepped inside into a beautiful drawing room—there was no other word for it—eighteenth-century in style, with a carpet in rich hues of blue and gold and furniture which, although modern, looked as elegant as the rest of the room, and was styled for comfort as well as elegance. Paintings adorned the walls—again, a skilful mix of modern and classic—and there was a large mirror above the marble fireplace. Long blue silk curtains graced the French windows which, she realised, led onto a little Juliet balcony, overlooking a narrow formal front garden and the quiet street below.

Several doors opened off the drawing room. Leandros crossed to open one of them.

'Your bedroom,' he said.

Eliana's eyes flickered to him, and then to the doorway, and she walked through into the room beyond. It was a double bedroom, with a silk-covered bed, more silk drapes at the windows, and the glimpse of an en suite bathroom through another door.

'Mine's next door,' Leandros said.

Was his voice dry? She didn't know—knew only that her breathing had quickened, as if in agitation, and that nerves were plucking at her again.

'I'll leave you to freshen up,' he was saying now—and he walked back out, closing the door behind him as he did so. 'I need to change for this evening.'

Slowly, Eliana let her shoulder bag down onto the beautiful counterpane and looked about her, still feeling her heart thumping. Dear God, she was here, in Paris, in a hotel suite, and there was only one purpose for her presence here.

Faintness drummed through her, and emotions she could not name—would not name at all. She took a deep, steadying breath instead. The best way to cope with this—the *only* way—was not to think, not to feel, just to keep going, one moment at a time.

'Freshen up', Leandros had said. So she did just that, repairing to the en suite bathroom.

It was a long time, it seemed, since she'd got up that morning, and as the bathroom facilities in her studio were both primitive and limited, the contrast with the palatial bathroom here was total. Almost without realising it, she felt her spirits lift as she stripped off, turned on the shower, stepped inside. The vanity unit came with an overflowing basket of expensive toiletries, and within minutes she was revelling in the feel of washing her hair under a strong, hot stream of water, lathering her body with richly scented bodywash.

Oh, but it felt *good* to have such a shower again—not since she'd lived with Damian had there been such luxury for her.

Luxury she'd once taken for granted.

Luxury that had come with her marriage.

She felt a kind of sudden hollowing in her stomach. And now it was going to be hers again—courtesy of the man she had rejected marrying.

She cut the shower—cut the thoughts starting to invade her mind. They were too disturbing and for too many reasons. Disturbing reasons. Because they were conflicting reasons…reasons she was fighting against admitting.

Being here like this—in Paris, with Leandros—was not simply for the reasons she had been telling herself. Because she owed it to him…because she wanted final closure, so she could move on with her life, move on without Leandros…

She reached for a towel to wind around her wet hair, another to wrap around her naked body. She was conscious of avoiding looking at her reflection. Yet she saw it all the same. Slender…so slender…her nakedness covered only with a towel, her arms and shoulders bare, her legs bare, her breasts pressing against the confines of the towel. She felt an awareness of her own physical body…felt as burningly conscious of herself as she had been of Leandros on the flight over…of the body that soon Leandros would—

Urgently, she tore her thoughts away again. Too disturbing…too conflicting. Just like her emotions. Ragged and raw. Tangled and tormenting.

Impossible to make sense of.

Leandros stood by the Juliet balcony, hands thrust into the trouser pockets of his tuxedo. His mood was strange, his thoughts disjointed, contradicting each other. Had this been a major mistake, letting Eliana back into his life? An act of insanity he would regret all his life? Was he just raking up dead ashes that should be dug into the earth and never exhumed?

Even as the thought came, its negation came even more swiftly. It was his love for Eliana that was dead and gone—nothing else. Seeing her again had rekindled—instantly, totally—everything else he'd ever felt about her. And it was that 'everything else' that he was reviving now—reclaiming now.

That and nothing else.

He felt his heart harden the way he had taught it to—the way she had caused it to. No, there was nothing left of love between them. His face hardened along with his heart. Not that she had ever felt any love for him. It had been self-interest, that was all. The moment his father had threatened to disinherit him she'd cut and run...

But now he'd brought her back into his life. Deliberately and consciously.

On my terms only. For a limited period—and a limited purpose.

To get her out of his system once and for all. It was all he asked for.

The door from her bedroom opened and she emerged. His eyes went to her immediately. She'd changed, and was now wearing something a little more suitable for her surroundings. A below-the-knee dress with a slight floral print, high-waisted and with a blouson bodice. Her hair—newly washed, he could see—was drawn back into a still-damp ponytail.

'That dress isn't chain store,' he heard himself saying.

She gave a little shake of her head, as if his remark had taken her aback.

'No, it's one my father bought me. Like he bought the

gown I wore to Chloe's party. They're old now, but good quality.'

He frowned. 'You must have had a decent wardrobe from Damian?' he said.

'I was not allowed to take it when I had to leave the house we lived in,' she said quietly.

Leandros's mouth twisted. Jonas Makris had certainly done the works on her all right.

But I don't want to see her in clothes she wore for the man she rejected me for.

'Well, you'll leave Paris with a new wardrobe,' he said. He crossed to the drinks cabinet. 'I've some time before I need to leave. Would you like a cocktail?'

Into his head came the answer she would once have given instantly. A Kir Royale—champagne infused with *cassis*. It had always been her favourite.

'G and T,' she said now.

He glanced at her, reaching for the bottle of gin out of the plentiful array in the cabinet, together with tonic water and ice cubes.

'Very English,' he said dryly. He frowned. 'You used to like sweet cocktails.'

'Well, now I prefer something more astringent.'

There was an edge in her voice, and he could hear it. He mixed her drink, and then a martini for himself, coming across to hand her glass to her where she stood in the middle of the room.

He looked at her a moment. 'You look tired,' he said abruptly. 'Worn down.'

She took the glass, met his eyes. 'I'm a widow, Leandros. And I've no money. I've had to take a job with long hours and little pay. So, yes, I'm tired.'

He frowned. 'I know your father died a while back, but surely he left you something?'

She took a sip of her cocktail. 'He had nothing to leave,' she said. 'When I married Damian, Jonas paid my father's debts, but put a charge on his estate. When my father died the charge was executed. There was no money to repay it, so… Well, Jonas foreclosed.'

Leandros was still frowning. 'What about your mother's family? I know you'd said they weren't keen on her marriage.'

'No—they wanted her to marry the man she'd been expected to marry until she came out to Greece on holiday and met my father.'

There was a sour taste in Leandros's mouth suddenly.

Like mother like daughter…

'So she jilted her English boyfriend to marry your father?'

Eliana did not answer him, only took another mouthful of her drink.

'Have you no English family to turn to?' he pursued.

This time she did answer. 'There are only a couple of cousins now, and an aunt who was always jealous of my mother—she wouldn't help. And anyway—'

She stopped short. He did not press her to continue. His veiled gaze rested on her. Her youthful dress, her tied-back hair and lack of make-up made her look younger than her age. More like the age she'd been when he'd romanced her, entranced by her natural, radiant beauty.

His expression hardened. She might have looked like an ingenue, wide-eyed and innocent, gazing at him so ardently, adoringly, whispering sweet nothings to him, but *nothing* was all that he had ever meant to her. She'd walked away from him without the slightest hesitation once his father had made it clear he'd cut his own son out of his inheritance, cut him off without the proverbial euro if they married.

She is venal, and worldly, and material wealth is all she cares about.

He spelt the words out in his head deliberately, harshly. He must remember them—not forget them.

Or I will never be free of her.

The sound of the house phone was welcome against such dark thoughts. He crossed to the sideboard to pick it up. He listened, hung up, and turned back to Eliana.

'That's my car. I must go.' He paused. 'I have no idea how long this dinner will go on, so don't wait up. As I said, order whatever you want from room service. This suite comes with its own butler, so discuss it with him.'

She simply nodded, saying nothing. His eyes rested on her for one last moment. She looked...frail. That was the word.

He shook it from him. He hadn't brought her here to pity her, but to get closure—finally to achieve that.

He strode towards the door and was gone.

Eliana lay in bed. After Leandros had left for his dinner she'd stood a moment, wondering what she should do, feeling strange. Had she really just had a cocktail with Leandros, all dressed up in his dinner jacket, as effortlessly devastating as he always was in a tuxedo? But then, of course, he was devastating at any time—any time at all...

She felt emotions flicker—conflicting, confusing. But how could they be anything else at seeing Leandros again—having him physically in front of her, with the sheer overwhelming impact on her that he'd always had—but for that to be dominated by all that now separated them.

She went across to the sofa, sat herself down on it, sipping her G and T, wanting the alcohol to numb her nerve-endings.

There was a complicated-looking remote control on the

low table in front of her and she picked it up, clicking it. The mirror above the fireplace sprang into life—a wall-hung TV. She channel-surfed idly, not engaging, and then let it settle to an English language news station. Perhaps the miseries of the world would take her mind off the moment. So, too, might ordering dinner for herself—drinking on an empty stomach was not wise.

She picked up another handset, placed on the side table by the sofa, and got through to Reception, gave an order for dinner. She'd asked for something she could eat while watching TV, and was duly obliged, with the politely attentive butler setting out her repast on the coffee table, then taking his leave.

She ate, then took her empty plates through to the kitchen that came as part of the Résidence, and busied herself washing them up. Then she made herself a herbal tea and went back to the sofa. She found a nature programme, and then a history one—they whiled away the time.

She ought to relax. Here she was in a luxury hotel, with nothing to do but indulge herself. Yet she was strung out like a piece of wire.

After a while she gave up on the TV and retired to her bedroom. There was a well-stocked bookcase in the drawing room, many books in English, and she'd selected an old favourite—*Persuasion*.

But as she sat up in bed, wearing the Victorian-style nightdress that she had worn long ago as a teenager, the soft mattress a world away from the lumpy bed in her studio apartment, propped up on luxuriant pillows, she thought maybe *Persuasion* had not been a good choice. Jane Austen's heroine had ruined her own life over the lack of money. Turning down the man who'd loved her.

She got a second chance, though.

Bleakness sat in her eyes. Second chances did not always come.

They can't for me. Leandros only wants closure—nothing else.

And so did she. Surely that was all she wanted? All that it was sane for her to want?

Wearily, she dropped the book, shut her eyes. She had committed herself to this—to being here in Paris with Leandros—but the more she faced the actual implications of what was going to happen now that she was here, the more tangled she became, emotions meshing and twisting, troubling and tormenting.

She gave a start—that was the door of the Résidence opening. She heard Leandros moving around...heard, she thought, the clink of a glass, then the sound of his bedroom door opening. Then silence.

For a long, endless moment she just went on lying there. Her heart was beating fast in her chest, she could feel it. Emotions, tangled and tormenting, twisted inside her. Wanting and not wanting. Not wanting and wanting...

Wanting...

Leandros was here—so close, a mere room away. Leandros who, for six long years, had been impossibly out of reach, impossibly distant. Leandros from whom, six years ago, she had walked away. And now... Oh, now he was back in her life—for whatever dark reason, whatever bitter purpose... He was here now, and so was she...

So close—so very, very close...

Leandros.

His name cried out in her head.

Without any consciousness of what she was doing, letting some impulse direct her—some impulse she could not repress, could not deny—and with her heart still beating audibly within her, the breath stopping in her throat, she

felt herself slide out of bed. Set her feet on the floor. Cross
the room. Open the door…step through it.

On leaden feet, impelled by the guilt that had consumed
her for six bitter years, and impelled by so much more…by
those tangled, twisting, tormented emotions…she headed
towards the door of Leandros's own bedroom.

It opened with a click, and she stepped inside.

Leandros was reading. The bedside lamp was sufficient to
illuminate the text of the international business journal he
was attempting to look at. *Attempting* was the only word
that was appropriate. He couldn't focus on the contents. His
thoughts were all over the place.

Correction—they are in one place only…

The bedroom next to his.

She was there. Eliana. Real, live and no fantasy. No
dream. No long-lost yearning.

So go to her.

The words were in his head, in his will—but he was re-
sisting them. Yes, he'd brought her here to Paris for precisely the purpose that was now urging him on, but with
his head—if not, alas, his body—he knew that now was not
the right time. Tonight it had been a formal dinner, tomorrow he had his client appointment—he wanted all business
affairs out of the way before he turned his focus on Eliana.

And there was another reason too. He wanted to give
her time. Oh, she deserved no consideration, but he would
allow it her all the same. He would treat her well—whether
she deserved it or not.

He forced his gaze back on to the article he was attempting to read. He wished he felt sleepy, at least, not as if this
edgy restlessness was possessing him.

And then, as his eyes glazed over yet again, not seeing
the text, he heard his bedroom door open.

Immediately, his gaze flashed upwards, pulse leaping.
It was Eliana. Standing in the doorway.
And Leandros's blood leapt again.

Eliana forced herself forward. Her feet felt like blocks of
lead, and her heart was thudding in her chest at the thought
of what she was doing. But she made herself pad forward.

Leandros's gaze had lifted from his magazine and gone
straight to her—eyes fixed on her like lasers. She felt her
cheeks flush, then whiten, as her own gaze took in, instantly, the fact that he was sitting in bed, bedclothes casually drawn over his lower half, his torso bare. Smooth,
muscled, lightly tanned, lithe and powerful...

She swallowed.

She had to say something. Of course she did. But her
throat was as narrow as a crushed straw.

She swallowed again, halted halfway across the room.

Leandros let his magazine drop, his lasering eyes never
leaving her. Saying nothing.

So she spoke instead—she had to. With an effort, she
managed to get the words out, past the deafening thudding
of her heart, the blood drumming in her ears. She felt hot
and cold all at the same time, weak and faint, forcing herself to stay upright.

'Leandros...' She said his name, faint and hesitant. 'I...
I...'

It was all she could manage. Something changed in his
face. His expression was edged...became guarded and
loaded at the same time.

'Yes?' The edge was in his voice too.

She took another halting step forward, half lifted a hand,
then let it drop again.

'Leandros.' She got his name out again, less hesitant
now, but with a husk in it that even she could hear. She

swallowed once more, took another step forward, lifted her hand again.

Was she imploring him? And if so, for what?

'Eliana.'

He echoed her style of address, his voice flat now. The edge was still in his face, and in his voice.

'What is it that you want?'

It was a polite inquiry—or could have been. But she knew it wasn't. She felt herself flush again and made herself speak. He obviously wasn't going to help her out.

She took a larger breath, lifted her chin—looked straight at him. 'You brought me here to Paris for one reason only, so—' she took yet another breath '—here I am.'

She let her hand drop, knowing she was just standing there, wearing her ankle-length nightgown, a few metres from the end of his bed. And he was sitting there, propped up by his pillows, his bare torso exposed, looking at her.

Like a pasha waiting for his chosen female from the harem to approach him...

Dark stories from the grim centuries of the Ottoman conquest and occupation of Greece were in her head. Was that what she was? One of those hapless females procured to serve...to service...their imperial masters?

Her face tightened. No, she was not.

I'm here by my own choice—because I choose to be here.

And whatever the tangled and tormenting reasons for doing what she had done—coming here to Paris with Leandros, coming into his bedroom now—they were *her* reasons.

She pressed her lips together a moment, then spoke again. Firmer now, more resolute, though the blood was still thudding in her ears.

'You said you wanted the honeymoon I denied you. So now I...' she took a breath, knowing it was ragged, knowing her heart was still beating audibly in her chest '... I give it to you.'

It was all she could say. She wanted to say so much—but that was impossible. All she could do was take another step forward, and then another, as if drawn towards him. At the foot of the bed she stopped. She was so close...so very close. She felt her heart rate quicken...emotion quicken. But which emotion? She didn't know—there were too many inside her...

Something was wrong. His expression had changed and she could see the planes of his cheekbones, taut beneath the skin. A sudden shaft of dismay struck her.

'Ah, I see—the sacrificial maiden.'

His words dropped into the silence between them, into the yawning gulf between them.

He shifted position suddenly, flexing his sinewed shoulders. The metallic glint in his eye was steel. And there was steel in his voice as he spoke.

'Well, as it happens, Eliana, I don't require a sacrificial maiden—not that you qualify as a maiden any longer. I don't want a sacrifice at all—and least of all...' the steel was a blade now '...do I want one who thinks she can assuage her wrongdoing by making such a virtuous sacrifice...'

She cried out with protest in her voice at what he was saying. 'No! It isn't like that—'

He didn't let her say more. His voice was twisted, sarcasm knifing in it. 'Do not think,' he said, and each word was a twist of his knife, 'that you can make me feel bad about bringing you here—that you can present yourself as some kind of victim, required to lay down her beautiful body for my vengeful lust!'

His words were stripping her, but he was going on, leaning forward suddenly.

'You don't get to play that convenient role. Because, my

sweet, faithless Eliana, when you do join me in my bed, believe me—oh, *believe* me!—you will be as eager for me as you so fondly think I am for you. Honeymoons—even mockeries of honeymoons, like this one—are mutual. Don't comfort yourself by thinking otherwise!'

The steel in his eyes glinted in the lamplight as he leant back against his pillows, deliberately picked up his magazine. He cast one more look at her, not steely this time, but scathing.

'Get back to bed—your own bed. We've a full day ahead tomorrow.'

She was dismissed. It was as blunt, as brutal as that. Colour flared in her cheeks. Humiliation and more than that—worse than that.

With what self-control she could summon, she turned, walked back to the door. Blood was surging in her, flaring in her heated cheeks. In her room, she flung herself back into bed, felt emotions surging along with the blood in her distended veins.

Was he right? Was that why she had gone to him as she had? Just to assuage her own guilt at what she had done to him six years ago? Making a sacrifice of herself? Atoning for the wrong she'd done him?

Is that the only reason I went to him? Truly the only reason?

Easier to think so. Or was she deceiving herself? Suppressing a truth she dared not face…emotions she dared not arouse…?

As she huddled into the bedclothes, turned out her bedside light, she could still see in her mind's eye Leandros in his bed, torso bared, looking at her. And she felt her emotions writhe and twist like snakes with poisoned fangs.

CHAPTER SIX

'OK, TAKE YOUR PICK—plenty to choose from.'

Leandros was speaking, sitting next to her, as he had on the drive from the airport yesterday, in the chauffeured car now cruising through the Faubourg Saint-Honoré, with luxury fashion houses all around.

'I… I don't mind,' Eliana answered. She glanced briefly at him. 'You're paying—you choose.'

She was feeling even more awkward in his company this morning after last night. She had slept fitfully, her emotions more tangled than ever, waking only when the house phone by her bed rang and she groggily answered it to hear Leandros's brisk voice telling her he was off to his client appointment, and would be back after lunch to take her shopping. The butler would serve her breakfast whenever she was ready.

She'd been relieved not to see him, and determined, if nothing else, to enjoy the luxury of her surroundings after so many grim months of poverty and deprivation. She'd decided she would deal with being with Leandros again when she had to—and till then she'd make the most of a filling and leisurely breakfast in bed, then a lengthy, pampering bath.

Then, dressed in the same outdated frock she'd worn the previous evening, since her choice was very limited, she'd gone downstairs to explore the hotel, making her way out into the rear garden. The day was pleasantly warm, sunshine shafting across the small but elegantly laid-out space, and she'd found a quiet bench and read some more of *Persuasion*.

Captain Wentworth was despising Anne Elliot with ill-concealed disdain. Anne was enduring it painfully.

Eliana felt for her.

At least Anne Elliot hadn't had to endure Wentworth's scathing tongue. As Eliana did Leandros's now.

'Eliana.' Leandros's voice was bladed. 'I told you last night—drop the martyr pose. You're here with me of your own choice and now you can choose the clothes you'll be wearing here.'

She named a fashion house—one she could see they were nearing, and which she did personally like—and the car pulled up at it. She was left to make her own choices as the *vendeuses* ushered her to the fitting rooms, to emerge some time later with her choices made.

Leandros was sitting in the plush waiting area, reading a magazine about upmarket cars from a selection thoughtfully provided by the fashion house for attendant males.

He looked up as she emerged. Eliana felt his eyes go to her. Rest on her. Saw his expression change.

There was approval in his eyes—and more. A light she had not seen before, yet could remember, oh, so well. She felt colour flare...walked forward hurriedly. To see Leandros look at her like that, letting her know, quite openly, that he liked what he was seeing, that she was pleasing to his eyes...

'Finally,' he said, nodding slowly.

He got to his feet, his gaze still taking in the change in her appearance.

She wore a belted two-piece in cinnamon-coloured fine

wool jersey, gracefully skimming her slender figure. It was both chic and comfortable to wear. She'd accessorised it with a plain but soft leather handbag, moderately heeled matching shoes, and a printed silk scarf that went with the short, lightweight jacket with bracelet sleeves. She'd added some fashion jewellery—topaz beads and a chunky bracelet.

One of the *vendeuses* had discreetly inquired whether she would like to avail herself of the fashion house's own-brand make-up selection, and she had done so. She hadn't used it lavishly, just applied some tawny eyeshadow and mascara, and a tinted lip gloss to give a soft sheen to her lips, finishing off with a spray of the fashion house's latest perfume. She'd redressed her hair too, changing it from the plain ponytail to a stylish French pleat fastened with *faux* tortoiseshell combs.

As she'd put the final touches to her face and hair, she'd told herself that it was because her outfit deserved it. That it was part of her attempt to make amends to Leandros...

But it was more than that, she knew. Knew it when she saw his eyes resting on her with approval in them—and more than approval.

He used to look at me like that all the time. Is that what I'm yearning for? To recapture that?

She put the thought aside—it was too painful, too difficult.

Too tangled.

Instead, she simply said, 'I've bought quite a lot—you said I should.'

He made no demur, merely settled the hefty bill to cover a good half a dozen carrier bags bearing the fashion house's name with the flick of a platinum credit card.

'Now for evening dresses—but not here,' he said.

They got back into the dutifully waiting car, and the carrier bags were stashed neatly in the capacious boot by the chauffeur. Leandros named a fashion house that Eliana knew made a speciality of ultra-alluring designs. She'd never shopped there. It had been too sophisticated for when she'd been young, and not conservative enough to please her father-in-law. As for Damian—well, he'd just wanted her to wear whatever his father had wanted her to wear. That had been his sole concern—not contesting his father's dictates or defying his will. Except, of course—

She pulled her mind away. Gave herself over to what was happening now. This time it was Leandros making the choices, not her. Well, if that was what he wanted, that was his call. This whole expedition was his call, after all. She would not be keeping any of these clothes when her time with him was over. However venal he thought her, she would not prove it to him in that, at least. Even if she could not defend herself for her past actions and they would stain her for ever…

She was grateful to him for diverting her thoughts, her painful memories, by saying, 'Time for some sightseeing— shall we see what's happening to Notre Dame?'

'Why not?' she said.

She kept her voice studiedly neutral. But it was an effort. Somehow, when she'd just been wearing her poverty-stricken, cheap-of-necessity clothes, making no effort to look good, it had been easier—easier to ignore, or downplay at least, the impact Leandros had on her. But now, chic and elegant, with her flattering hairstyle and a touch of make-up to enhance her appearance, she was more conscious than ever of the man sitting beside her in the confines of the chauffeur-driven car.

More like old times. When I only wanted to look good for him, to revel in his finding me beautiful. I thrilled to see him looking at me…wanting only to gaze at him in return… feeling myself melting inside…

Deliberately, she made herself look out of the window, away from the temptation that was Leandros, and away from the memories she should not allow herself, for those times had gone for ever. Instead, she watched as the car crossed over to the Île de la Cité, closing in on the great cathedral.

'It's still in repair after the catastrophic fire a few years ago,' Leandros was saying. 'But we can look at the outside. Would you care for that?'

'Why not?' said Eliana again.

They got out, walking on to the great concourse by the west front. It was milling with tourists, and there were plenty of noticeboards showing the extent of the original damage and what was being done to restore it. She saw Leandros gazing up at the solid, four-square towers, at the Romanesque arch between them with its ornate carvings.

'I first came here with my father,' he said. 'We went up on to the roof, saw the gargoyles. Great for a twelve-year-old.'

There was a fond, reminiscent note to his voice. He had been close to his father, Eliana knew. Although their fathers had been very different, it was something she and Leandros had had in common, and they'd talked about it sometimes. Unlike her, sadly, Leandros had no memories of his mother—she had died when he was a baby.

He glanced at her now. 'I know your father didn't like travelling, and his health was not great, but why didn't you take off as a teenager, Eliana? Do Europe with your friends?'

She wondered why he was bothering to ask, but she answered all the same.

'My father would have worried about me,' she said. 'And I didn't want to leave him.'

'You were very sheltered,' he said slowly. 'Cossetted.'

His eyes were resting on her, and what she saw in them hurt.

'I didn't think you were spoilt, simply...naive. Entitled,

I suppose, but not really realising it. I didn't think it mattered. As my wife, you'd have everything you could want, so what would it matter if you'd grown up taking that for granted, expecting to go on being looked after, cossetted, for the rest of your life?' His voice changed, hardened. 'How wrong I was.'

Eliana was silent. What could she say? Nothing in her defence—nothing at all. Instead, she started to walk away a little, as if studying some other aspect of the cathedral. But she was taking little of it in.

He thought me entitled, but after the desolation of losing my mother, my father feared me leaving home, leaving him. It made him shower me with gifts and protect me, which I let him do because I knew it gave him comfort to do so... made him feel...safe. Just as I knew that he was glad that, since I was so keen on marrying, at least it was to someone who would be based in Athens, not too far away.

It was painful to remember...painful to think that. And pointless too. Her father was dead, and she had never married Leandros...

Leandros came up to her.

'The crypt is open, if you wanted to visit? Otherwise I was going to suggest Sainte-Chapelle—it's a short walk from here, and we can go inside, unlike here.'

Eliana resisted the impulse to say *Why not?* again, lest it draw an edged comment from Leandros. So instead she said politely, 'That sounds good.'

Did it sound good? Did anything they were doing sound good?

But then, how could it? How could anything about the tangled, knotted, twisted mess of emotions she was caught in, ever be 'good'? It was a tangled mess—and Leandros was at the heart of it. Confusing and conflicting, jostling past and present. How overwhelming it was for her to be with Leandros again, however painful the reasons.

The reasons she was admitting.

The reasons she was not…

Her eyes went to him now, as they started to walk away from Notre Dame. How tall he was…how familiar. Once so dear to her so that her breath would catch with it, at seeing his strong profile. She felt a sudden impulse to reach for his hand, to take it and walk along beside him, hand in hand, as they had once always done…

She felt her hands clench at her sides in painful self-denial.

'Just along here,' Leandros announced, and she looked to where he was indicating, at Sainte-Chapelle, instead of where her eyes wanted to linger—on him at her side.

Leandros got entrance tickets and they went inside. Immediately, Eliana gasped in awe. Sunshine was pouring through the narrow windows that soared the height of the walls, one after another along the length of the nave, leading the eye towards the glory of the vast rose window above the altar. She gazed, amazed at the sheer incredible beauty of it.

'It's like being inside a jewel box!' she exclaimed wonderingly, gazing around her.

'The rose window depicts the Apocalypse,' Leandros was saying. 'The Four Horsemen are there somewhere, and all the other signs of the end of the world.'

She gave a little shudder. 'I won't look too closely,' she said.

She turned her attention to the painted pillars, as brilliantly coloured as the stained glass, and then to the vaulted ceilings running alongside the main aisle, painted in French blue with the French royal fleur de Lys.

'The chapel was commissioned by Louis IX, the saintly

King of the early Middle Ages,' Leandros remarked beside her.

'He was the one whose first wife was Eleanor of Aquitaine, wasn't he? Before she went off to marry Henry Plantagenet, King of England.'

'No, she married an earlier Louis, then Henry Plantagenet of England. Two glittering marriages—a queen twice over. Of course, as an heiress in her own right she didn't need to marry to enjoy a lavish lifestyle.'

Eliana made no answer—there was none to make. If it was yet another dig at her, then it was one he was, after all, entitled to make. She wandered away a little, moving to examine one of the many painted statuettes adorning this jewel box of a chapel, knowing that the sting of his words was both hurtful and to be expected. And there was nothing she could do about either. Yet they hung in her head for all that, heavy and hard.

Leandros let her be and she continued her exploration, wanting diversion. As she returned from her circuit he said, pleasantly, 'Seen enough?'

She nodded, and they made their way out again.

He glanced at his watch. 'We should be getting back. You'll need time to get yourself ready—we're going to the opera. Puccini's *Manon Lescaut*. It should suit you.'

That was definitely a dig—it was an opera about a poor girl who rejected her equally poor lover in favour of a wealthy suitor. She wanted to protest, riposte, find some way of answering back. But how could she? Like Manon, she had chosen wealth over love.

Not that that had stopped her first love from wanting her to want him still.

As she got into the car that Leandros had summoned to their side his words from the night before were in her head—how he did not want her to make a sacrifice of herself. Taunting her that she would be eager for him.

He wants me to want him.

Her eyes shadowed as she pulled her seat belt across. The man she wanted was the man she had once known, so long ago. The man she had once loved—and rejected. This man now—this Leandros—was not that man. And she was not the woman he had once loved either.

So what is there left? Nothing that I want.

That was the truth of it, she thought bleakly. Leandros here, now, only wanted a sexual affair with her—she had forfeited anything more. But for herself…?

Her eyes went to him now, in profile, as they crossed over the river to the Left Bank. Emotions flowed within her as turbid as the waters of the Seine—and as unknowable.

She gave up on her thoughts, which were as hopeless as her emotions to try and untangle, as the car made its way through the Paris traffic. Leandros was studying his phone messages, absorbed and silent.

Back at their hotel, in their suite, he spoke.

'The Paris opera is very grand, so look your best. Wear one of the new evening gowns. I've taken a box—a *loge*—and there will be people there this evening whom I know.'

She nodded acquiescently, before disappearing into the sanctuary of her bedroom. It would take time to get herself ready.

Memory played tormentingly of how once she had rejoiced in making herself as lovely as she could for an evening with Leandros, taking endless trouble with her hair, her make-up, wanting to look wonderful for him, wanting…longing…to see his eyes light up when he saw her. Light up with love.

And now…

Now it will only be with desire.

Pain twisted inside her and, knowing how useless it was, she went to select from the three evening gowns Leandros had bought her. All were fabulous—and revealing. Designed specifically to show off her beauty—and her body.

She picked the pale blue one, because its décolletage, though low cut, was draped, and she could pin it higher than it would otherwise fall. For all that, when she finally slipped it over her head, letting the silk glide down her body, the bias cut clung to her hips, the length of her thighs. Her shoulders were all but completely exposed by the thin straps.

She wished she had a shawl, or a stole of some kind, but there was only a luxuriously soft fake fur evening jacket, which would have to be discarded once they were seated.

She gave herself one last look in the floor-length mirror on the wall, her expression troubled. Even after pinning her bodice higher, she still felt it was too low. She also knew that with her ice-blue slinky evening gown, her full *maquillage*, and her hair in a sophisticated upswept style, it was almost as if she were a different person. A new person. Not the drab, work-worn pauper living the poverty-stricken life forced upon her, not the jewel-laden trophy wife of Jonas Makris's son, and nor—she felt a painful pang go through her—the youthful self she had once been, romantically gowned, her hair loose and flowing, wide-eyed and adoring for the man she loved.

Now she was the woman Leandros wanted her to be— alluring, tempting, a *femme fatale*...

The only way he wants me to be now.

Her expression changed.

And what do I want to be now?

The question hung there, unknowable and unanswerable, all part of the tangled mess of her emotions, confusing and conflicting.

A sharp tap on the bedroom door made her turn away from her disturbing reflection, her disturbing thoughts. She slid her bare arms into the short fake fur jacket, picked up the satin evening clutch bag in matching ice-blue, and walked to the door on heels much higher than she was used to. Outside waited the man who had once loved her—then hated her.

Now he only desired her.

A poisonous, toxic mix.

She opened the bedroom door and walked out.

CHAPTER SEVEN

LEANDROS STILLED. SHE'D cut it fine, timewise, but *Thee mou*, it had been worth it! His gaze went to her like a magnet. Six years ago her beauty had been that of a young girl, just on the brink of womanhood. Now...

She has become the woman—no longer the girl.

No longer the sweet, innocent ingenue he had known.

His heart hardened. But she had never been that, had she? Not when she'd been threatened by a reality she did not wish to accept.

She wanted me only when she thought me wealthy.

Well, now his wealth would lift her out of the poverty into which she had sunk at least for the duration of his desire for her. Then she would have to make her own way in the world again. He would be done with her.

'The car is waiting,' he said.

His voice was curt, his thoughts dark. Her beauty, her allure, mocked him.

Mocked him even as his eyes went to her as they took their places in the limo and it set off through the Paris traffic for the opera house on the Right Bank. He made no attempt at conversation—his mood had darkened and he saw no reason to disguise it.

There was something about the way she was just sitting there, resplendent in the soft white faux fur jacket nestled around her shoulders, the upswept hair exposing the line of her neck, the cut of her cheekbones, her always beautiful eyes deepened and darkened by make-up and thick, blackened lashes. Her face was semi-averted from him and she was looking out of the window, studiedly taking no notice of him. All he could see of her gown was the sweep of silk from waist to ankles, her legs slanting away from him.

She was remote from him, withdrawn from him—as if he did not exist for her.

Something flared in the depths of his eyes and he rested his gaze darkly upon her averted profile. He would *make* himself exist for her—she *would* take notice of him. He would make it impossible for her not to.

I want to be rid of this desire for her—dear God, I just want to be rid of it! I want it not to be able to torment me ever again.

It was his only wish.

The car had pulled up outside the opera house, the Palais Garnier, and the driver was opening her door for her. Eliana stepped out carefully, her gaze going to the grand edifice— a legacy of the opulence of the Second Empire of Napoleon III in the mid-nineteenth century. Then Leandros was beside her, taller than ever, it seemed to her, in his evening dress, guiding her in.

The glories of the interior were breathtaking, and she gazed around the lobby, already crowded with women in evening gowns, men in black tie tuxedos. The sheer opulence was almost beyond belief. Her eyes went to the massively imposing staircase that divided in two to sweep to the upper floor with a flamboyance that only the extravagances of the Second Empire could justify. Everywhere there were columns and carvings and statuary, gilded and glowing in the lamplight. She all but blinked at the dazzle.

She felt a touch at her elbow and started.

'This way,' Leandros said at her side.

And then she was being guided up that magnificent staircase, gazing around her as she went. She gathered the skirt of her evening gown with one hand, her heels ringing on the marble stairs. Others were doing likewise, making the ascent to the next level up. There was a chattering of mostly French but other languages too all around her, and the scent of expensive perfume in the air.

They were shown into their *loge* and she stood gazing out over the auditorium, filling up now, and at the other boxes all around as well. She felt hands on her shoulders, and started again.

'Let me take your jacket,' Leandros said.

She was reluctant to part with it, but he was already sliding it from her shoulders—and besides, she was already too warm. Yet with it gone she felt horribly exposed, knowing just how much of her flesh he was seeing—her shoulders, her arms, and the expanse of her décolletage that she had been unable to cover, even with the aid of the safety pins raising the drape of her bodice.

She sat herself down on one of the gilt and velvet chairs, leaning forward slightly to continue her perusal of the spectacular interior of the opera house—and to avoid having to pay any attention to Leandros. Her nerves were on edge, and she was supremely and uncomfortably conscious of her appearance, and of his presence behind her.

She heard him saying something in French to someone who seemed to have come into the back of the box, and she wondered if they were to share it. But then the exchange ceased, and instead she heard the sound of effervescent liquid being poured. A moment later Leandros was standing beside her, proffering a glass of lightly foaming champagne. She took it without thinking, and he raised his own glass

to her. The light from the wall lamp threw his features into
chiaroscuro, accentuating the planes of his face—hardening
them, it seemed to her—and she felt herself tense.

'To my very own Manon,' he said.

His voice was as edged as a knife-blade inserted between her ribs.

'My faithless fiancée...'

She paled—she could not help it. The blade in her flesh
twisted, and she almost cried out in pain. Yet she had no
defence against it.

She had only the glass of champagne he had bestowed
upon her.

She took a mouthful, ignoring the delicate mousse, simply swallowing it down, needing to feel its impact. Yet for
all that she could still feel her eyes sting, and she lowered
her gaze, letting her mascara-laden eyelashes veil it from
him. What good would it do to let him see her pain at his
scathing taunt? He would only think she deserved to feel it.

And I know I have no defence to make.

She took another mouthful, welcoming its effervescence
in her mouth, in her suddenly constricted throat, as she
swallowed it down. She felt its kick and was glad. Grateful.

Leandros was taking the seat beside her—too close, far
too close—angling his long legs away from her, then handing her a programme, which presumably had been delivered
along with the bottle of champagne.

She was grateful for the programme, which gave her
something to do other than knock back her champagne.
She balanced the glass carefully on the unoccupied chair on
her other side and bent her head to peruse the programme.
It was in French, and she had to focus on trying to understand its explanation of the contents of each act. But she
knew the sorry tale well enough—even though *Manon* had

never been a favourite Puccini for her. How could it be with such a heroine?

Though 'heroine' was scarcely the word for her. She was vain and conceited and unrepentant, as well as faithless and venal.

Does Leandros truly think me as despicable as she was?

She reached for her champagne again to block the anguished question. As she did, she realised that the house lights were starting to dim, and the audience had taken their seats. The orchestra was done with tuning up, and a hush was descending over the auditorium. The emergence of the conductor—a famous name, she knew—heralded the start of the performance.

Setting aside her programme, she held the champagne glass instead, finding some comfort in sipping from it as the music sprang into life and the curtain rose on the first act, where the hapless lover, des Grieux, would meet the woman who would destroy his life.

Despite the innocuous opening scene, with its cheerful crowd and carefree students, how could she possibly enjoy so sad and sordid a story? Only when the tenor singing des Grieux—another famous name—launched into the celebrated aria, one of the best known of the opera, did she feel unwilling emotion welling up in her as the familiar cadences caught at her, caught her up in des Grieux's headlong plunge into total, overwhelming love at first sight, swept away by so fatal an indulgence.

Yet it wasn't des Grieux that she was thinking of.

I'm thinking of myself—falling for Leandros the very first time I set eyes on him.

The memory was in her head...instant—indelible.

'Donna non vidi mai...'

Never did I see such a woman... sang the tenor, and the joy and wonder and passionate yearning in his voice soared above the orchestra, out over the audience, reaching up towards her.

Echoing within her.

For, just like des Grieux, never before had she seen someone who made it impossible to turn her head away. At that party in Glyfada, where they'd met, she'd fallen so totally in love in that very moment.

She felt her head turn now, powerless to stop it. Felt her gaze go to Leandros's profile, carved as if from stone. Felt, as Puccini's music soared around her in passionate voice and swelling orchestra, filling her head, her heart, something call from her out of nowhere, it seemed to her. And she was unprepared, unwarned…with emotion rising up in her—an emotion she had thought long extinguished, smothered and lifeless, for six long, bitter, painful, endless years.

But it had not been banished, not extinguished. It was still there, hidden deep inside her—and it was summoned now, against all reason, by the passion of the music. It powered up inside her, all the emotion that had once filled her and which she had thought could be no more, thought impossible. And she could not stop it—could not force it back, force it down, force it back into the oblivion where it needed to be—where it *must* be. For how else could she go on living?

For a moment she was blind as it swept over her, possessing her entirely. Repossessing her.

And then suddenly, unstoppably, it was sweeping from her, sweeping away all the tangled, tormenting, confusing and conflicting emotions that had plagued her since the moment she had set eyes on Leandros again, made the fateful decision to come here to Paris with him. And they had plagued her every hour since. Now they were simply gone—as if they had never been. Swept away to leave uncovered, unhidden, one emotion—only one—that had been there all along. That always would be…

She tore her gaze away, forced it back to the stage below as the aria ended. And yet she was shaken to the core, to the very core of her being, as she realised, saw and knew the truth that had been there all along, concealed in the heart of that tangled confusion of emotions.

Six years might have passed—she might have walked away from Leandros and she might have been wed and widowed since, might have buried the man she had married, with tears for his sad, sad fate—but nothing could now conceal from her what she knew, what blazed within her.

What she still felt—would always feel, could never *not* feel for Leandros, whatever happened, whatever life did to her…

I am here with him now, here with him again after so, so long. And though all he wants of me is what he has declared, that cannot, will not, and does not change what I now know—the truth I now know. About myself.

Unconsciously, she started to sip at her refilled glass again, letting her eyes rest on the stage below, watching the events unfolding that would eventually lead the lovers to their doom. Unconsciously, she let the music take over, flowing over her even as what was happening to her inside was flowing through her.

She knew they were the same—that they shared the same name, the same truth.

That however flawed, however doomed, however one-sided, love always survives somehow—impossible though it must seem.

And now she knew, with a certainty that filled her, that it was still true.

Leandros gave his polite social smile.

'Permit me to introduce Madame Makris. A fellow Hellene, like myself.'

It was the interval, and they were mingling in the spectacular Grand Foyer. Eliana was at his side, drawing admiring glances all around. But how should that not be? Her beauty was radiant—breathtaking. Turning every head. Turning his...

He was glad of the obligation to make small talk with the couple to whom he was now introducing Eliana. The man was a business associate, the woman his wife—ultra-chic as only a Parisienne could be. Did the couple wonder why he was with a woman he had introduced as married? He gave a mental shrug. The French took such things in stride.

The couple smiled at Eliana, and Eliana murmured something in halting French, then stayed silent. Conversation focussed on the performance, and Eliana was asked what she thought of it. She made a polite comment about the soprano and the tenor, and then made an equally polite comment in careful French about the magnificence of their surroundings.

It felt strange to be in company with her. The last time had been six years ago—another lifetime. He pulled his memory away. There was no reason for it...no purpose. The woman at his side now was not the woman he had once thought her.

She never had been.

She had stripped his illusions from him—and the process had been painful. Perhaps it was retaliation, therefore, that made him say to her, as they headed back to their *loge* at the end of the interval, 'The ice-blue of the gown suits you.' His eyes rested on her now, half lidded. He gave a smile. One without humour. 'As icy as your heart?'

She made no answer, but a look passed across her eyes that he did not recognise. Then, with a shock, he did. It was a look he had not expected to see from her.

Sadness.

'You have reason to think so,' she said quietly.

'At least you have the grace to admit that.' His voice was terse.

She looked at him. There was still that same expression in her eyes.

'I admit everything, Leandros,' she said, in that same quiet voice. 'Everything I did to you.'

They reached their *loge* and took their seats again. Her words echoed in his head. And the sadness that had been in her voice. Then his mouth tightened. She might admit what she had done to him—but she had not said she regretted it.

And if she did regret it? Would it make a difference? Would I think less ill of her?

Restlessly, he crossed his legs as the curtain rose. He could catch the faint scent of Eliana's perfume, hear the slight rustle of her gown as she slanted her legs away from his. The sense of her presence at his side in the dim light of the auditorium pressed against him. He focussed, instead, deliberately, on Puccini's passionate music and the events unfolding on the stage, darkening to their desolate conclusion.

The faithless woman was dragging the hapless lover to his death, and hers. He should feel no pity for her—none. And yet as, in the final scene, Manon's besotted lover staggered to seek water in the desert in which they were marooned, and Manon lifted her lovely head to cry out, despairing and agonised, against her fate—*'sola, perduta, abbandonata'*—lost, abandoned, alone—he could not help but feel her anguish.

He felt his eyes go to the woman at his side, sitting as motionless as he.

Abandoned and alone. Her husband dead, cast out by his ruthless father, all but destitute, scraping a living, bereft of all hope of anything better...

He felt emotion stab. It could not be pity. How could it be? She deserved none, had earned none. Not from him.

His expression hardened even as the final anguished notes from the dying lovers on stage brought down the curtain on the final act. There would be no second act for Eliana—not if she had hopes of one from him. He had brought her here only to rid himself of her—to exorcise her former power over him and to free himself.

That, and only that, was his purpose.

A purpose he must abide by. Or risk far too much…

'What might tempt you?'

Leandros's query made Eliana look up from the menu. After the performance they had removed, as it was popular to do, to the opera's restaurant. Unlike the ornate Second Empire style of the rest of the building, the restaurant had been created as a startling contrast, with modernist style and lines—and a celebrity chef to entice those in the expensive seats to equally expensive post-performance dining.

'I'm not quite sure,' she answered now.

The gourmet menu was full of tempting possibilities, and she would be happy with any of them. Happy just to sit here and have Leandros across the table from her. She seemed, she thought, to be inhabiting a new world—it looked just like the one she had been in before, and yet it had changed. Profoundly, permanently. For there could be no going back now, she knew. She had faced the truth about herself. All that confusion and conflict within herself had gone.

Would it make her happy? No, that was impossible. Leandros's justified bitterness was indelible—she knew that too, accepted it. Just as she accepted the truth of what Puccini's heart-rending music had revealed to her. The truth about herself.

She let her gaze rest on Leandros, feeling again that upwelling of emotion that had come over her, accepting that truth—welcoming it. She was happy just to be here with him, discussing their dining options in the busy restaurant, with chatter and conversation all around them, other diners enjoying the gourmet offerings just as she and Leandros were about to do.

'I'm having the lamb,' Leandros was saying now. 'I recommend it.'

'Then, yes, the lamb,' she agreed, setting aside the menu and agreeing, too, to his recommendation of a salmon and seafood first course.

He was back to being civil to her—no more cutting remarks likening her to Manon. She was glad of it, but she knew now that the pain it caused her did not matter any longer. His bitterness against her was as justified as ever— how could it not be?—but she knew she could not change that. Accepted that she could not. It was only she who had changed, not him, with her new self-knowledge, her new self-awareness. She was no longer confused, or denying, or conflicted. Only clear and certain.

As they dined, they made conversation, as they had that afternoon. Careful, yes, and civil, about neutral matters— the sights of Paris, what was of interest, history and art. Yet all the time she was aware of his eyes lingering on her as he reached for his wine, as he set aside his plate. He did not make it obvious, but it was there all the time.

She welcomed it.

Welcomed, too, her own answering response, knowing how much she wanted to let her gaze rest on him, glory in him…rejoice in what she knew he wanted of her…

Even though it could never match all that she wanted of him…

A sliver of a needle slid under her skin, but she accepted the pain. Leandros would not—could not—think differently about her. He desired her—and despised her. He had brought her here to Paris for the reason he had told her. That would not change. Only she had changed.

I told myself I owed it to him, that I could assuage my guilt at what I did to him by acceding to what he wants of me. That that was all I wanted. But I deceived myself—that was not all.

But now there was no more self-deception, no more denial. Not any more. Now, as his gaze lingered on her, she knew—with every passing moment, with every lingering glance exchanged between them, with her newfound clarity and certainty and acceptance, with all that was flowing within her, lifting her, changing her, quickening her—what tonight would bring.

For Leandros—and herself.

CHAPTER EIGHT

LEANDROS TOOK A slow mouthful of the cognac he'd poured for himself and taken into his bedroom. On their return to their suite, Eliana had made a point of murmuring good-night to him and disappearing into her own room. Lean-dros had watched her go, wondering whether to stay her. His mood was strange—but then so was hers.

She seemed…different. He wasn't sure how, only that she was. Since the curtain had fallen at the opera she had been different. Over dinner—different. In the car on the way back to the hotel—different. But he didn't know how, or why.

What he did know, as he took another mouthful of the fiery liquid, was that all evening it had become increasingly impossible to take his eyes from her. Even now he could feel heat beating up in his body, filling him with a restlessness that he knew could be assuaged in only one way.

Should he respond to it? Go to her room? Fulfil the rea-son he had brought her here to Paris with him? Why should he not? She'd agreed to it, gone along with it, so why should he feel this reluctance now?

He swirled the cognac slowly in its glass. His body was telling him—increasingly so—that now was the hour. Her beauty, so breathtakingly displayed in that ice-blue evening gown, had been inflaming him all evening. Yet his own scathing words to her the previous night, spoken right here in this room, saying that he wanted no sacrificial martyr in his bed, that he wanted her as eager for him as he was for her, were sounding in his mind.

But there was no sign of that. Not tonight. His mouth twisted a moment. Maybe he should stop jibing at her, cutting at her to relieve his own bitterness, indulging in his accusations of her. He'd made an effort over dinner, keeping conversation civil, even though sometimes it had been an effort. His mouth twisted again. Not for that reason, but because his eyes had kept going to her, distracting his attention.

He had known his blood was quickening... And it was doing so again now. Tormentingly so.

He knocked back the rest of his cognac, knowing he was doing a disservice to its XXO status.

Maybe he should consider a shower—that might take his mind off where it wanted to go.

He set the empty cognac glass down on the antique mahogany chest of drawers with a click, reaching up to rid himself of his bow tie, loosen his collar.

Restlessness was possessing him again.

And he knew why.

Carefully, Eliana cleansed her face of make-up, taking trouble to do so, making full use of the generously supplied toiletries in her en suite bathroom, then she washed her face with scented soap, patting it dry gently with a soft towel.

She gazed at her reflection, eyes wide and clear.

I told myself I came to Paris because I owed it to Leandros—because I saw it as a way of finally getting closure for myself.

But she knew that now for the self-deception it had always been. She knew the truth now—had seen it, felt it, faced it as Puccini's heartbreaking music had soared all around her, revealing to her the truth she had been hiding from, denying.

Her hands lifted to her head, removing the pins one by one from her hair, so that it started to fall in luxuriant tresses to her shoulders. She shook it out, cascading down her back in soft, silken folds that framed her face, then reached to the bodice of her gown from which she now removed the two safety pins. Immediately, the drapery dipped across her breasts, exposing her cleavage, the soft swell of her breasts.

She gazed once more at her reflection.

Glorying now in her own beauty.

Beauty that had one purpose only.

She felt a quickening of her pulse, felt a quiver go through her...a shimmering awareness of her own body. With shallow breathing, she turned away, walking out of the en suite bathroom, back into her bedroom. She felt the silken folds of the beautiful gown she was wearing brush her thighs as she crossed to the door, opened it and stepped beyond.

A replay of what she had done last night.

But now, this night...

Oh, it was so different.

As different as dark from light.

As denial from acceptance.

Lie from truth.

Softly, slowly, she opened the door to Leandros's bedroom and stepped inside.

Leandros turned. He was unknotting his tie, his dinner jacket already discarded, draped around the back of a chair, cuff-links slipped off and placed on the tallboy.

His hands dropped away. He stilled completely.

She was walking towards him. Not as she had before,

halting and hesitant. Now she was simply approaching him—in all her breathtaking, matchless beauty. Her gown was slinking around her slender, shapely body, the décolletage low over the sweet swell of her cupped breasts...

He felt something spear within him, and knew it for what it was.

And her hair—

His breath caught. It tumbled in golden glory over her bare shoulders, her bare back, luxuriant and wanton. She had wiped the make-up from her face, but she needed none to enhance her beauty.

His breath caught again, emotions storming within him, unleashed and potent.

She came up to him—unhesitant, unforced, unresistant. She said not a word, and nor did he, as she lifted her hands, wound them around his neck, drew his mouth down to hers...

And he was lost.

His mouth tasted of wine and aromatic coffee, and her fingers at the nape of his neck speared into the sable of his hair. She felt her breasts peak, engorge. Felt desire—oh, sweet, sweet and glorious desire—stream within her. This—*this* was why she was here...why she had come to Paris...why Leandros had had to come to her, ask her to go with him. Six years...six long, anguished years...bereft and punishing... Anguished years she had deserved, yet which now vanished as if they had never been.

His mouth was crushing hers now, and his hands had caught her waist, pulling her against him. Her pliant body yielded to his, hip to hip, thigh to thigh. She felt his body surge, and where once, long ago, in her innocence, it might have shocked her with its sure sign of masculine arousal, now she gloried in it.

He was hers, and she was his. And for this night, this time, this long-deferred union, she would take, and give, and possess and yield what she had never done before.

That all he could feel for her was raw desire she did not care about—could not care about. If that was all she could give him that had any value to him it would be hers to give—and claim. And she would glory and rejoice in the giving and the claiming, now and for ever.

Desire was creaming through her and she gave herself to it, consumingly and passionately, with so much pent-up longing, with so much time to make up for—lost time, damaged time. But she had this time now, and this night. And it was hers to give to him, and to take for herself. Now. Oh, now...

She was pressing her hips against him, feeling his need for her, glorying in it, and in turn pressing her engorged breasts against the hard wall of his chest. The frottage against her cresting nipples was making desire course through her even more powerfully, more urgently.

Without taking his mouth from hers, their tongues still entwining, ravenous for each other, he scooped her up into his arms, swept her across to the waiting bed, coming down with her as he laid her upon it. Then he was shucking off his clothes, ridding himself of them and then setting himself to free her of hers. She lay back, lifting her arms above her head against the pillows, her body displayed for him as he knelt over her, easing the narrow straps from her shoulders, turning her over, sliding down the zip and lifting the pale silk from her body.

She heard, low in his throat, his guttural response to what he had revealed for his own pleasure, his own desire—and she saw it was his desire to have that pleasure. His eyes were dark, glittering with naked desire. His mouth was demanding on hers, his hands shaping her breasts, drawing from her intensities of pleasure she had never known, never dreamt could exist.

Then his mouth descended to the straining peaks, laving and caressing, teasing and delighting with little whorls of pleasure that drew from her throat low, helpless moans of bliss. His hands were moving down her body, smoothing her flanks, slipping beneath her, lifting her hips towards him, his mouth never leaving her silken flesh.

She gave a gasp of wonder, of shock, swiftly followed by intense, unbelievable pleasure. Her hands closed around his shoulders, holding him where he was as his lips glided to where she most exquisitely sensitive. She felt her legs widen, her thighs slacken, as if her body had a will and an appetite of its own. And she could not resist it, must go with it, must give herself to it—could do nothing but be helpless, to crave the pleasure, the exquisite, unbelievable pleasure he was arousing in her.

Desire quickened, became urgent, like a wildfire taking hold of a tinder-dry forest. Her whole body was aflame, her breath shallow, her neck arching, her spine curving, to offer herself…

She felt the pleasure mount, intensify—it was unbearable, it was exquisite, it was all the world, it was her whole being. Little cries broke from her, pleading and imploring. Her fingers indented into his strong, sinewed shoulders and a tide was building in her…a tide she could not stop, would not stop, creaming through her, mounting and mounting, intensifying yet more, until she thought she must surely die of it unless…unless…

And then suddenly, brutally, he was lifting his mouth away from her. She gave a cry of loss, of anguish. But he was moving over her, his powerful thighs parting hers yet more widely, his forearms lifting him now. He was readying himself, poised, and she realised that all that had come before had merely been preparation—to quicken her, arouse her, take her to the point he himself was now at.

She felt his urgency and knew it to be her own as well. His hunger for her was her hunger for him. Wanting…craving…needing more and yet more… And now her hands were fastened around his flexing spine, seeking only to draw him down to her, to let him fill her, make her one with him…

She was blind, lost in a hunger that was a tornado of flame and urgency. Reaching for him, pulling him down to her, she wanted this, only this…his possession…now… Oh, now…now…*now*…

His hands were cupping her flanks, lifting her to him. Her spine was arching like a bow, offering her yearning, pleading body to him, and then he was there, poised at the moment of their ultimate fusion. For one last moment of unbearable hunger he kept her waiting, and as her bliss-blinded gaze clung to his, his eyes burned with a desire that was darkness visible.

She heard him speak—a low, impassioned rasp.

'Now I make you mine…*mine*—'

He drove into her. Full and thrusting and complete.

She screamed. Pain spearing through her like a knife.

Leandros froze. His blurred vision cleared and he was staring down at Eliana's contorted face, realising, dimly, that her hands were pushing desperately against his chest, pushing him away…pushing him out of her.

In some kind of disbelieving slow motion he withdrew from her, knowing his heart was pounding, his breathing was ragged, his consciousness in freefall.

As he came free of her she buckled over, jack-knifing onto her side, curling into a foetal position—protective and rejecting. He put his weight on his knees, staring down at her. In the low light from the bedside lamps he saw her hair was totally swamping her face.

'Eliana—*Christos!*—what is it? What's wrong?'

Consternation was in his voice, bewilderment, incomprehension... The contrast from a moment ago, when he had been blind with desire, craving only one consummation, with what was now pounding through his blood was total.

His answer was only that she hunched her body even more, hugging her drawn-up knees, and from her throat broke a noise that could only be a sob.

With a shaking hand, he smoothed away those tresses from her face. It was still contorted.

He said her name again, his voice shaking now, as did his hand as it lifted away from her. Instinctively, he let his hand close over her shoulder, but she only wrenched herself away the more, and another noise tore from her.

'Dear God—I didn't mean to hurt you!' His own voice was broken, with shock—more than shock—racking through it.

What had happened? What the hell had happened? She had been aflame for him—and he for her.

It had been an instant conflagration as his eyes had gone to her, walking into his room when he had thought her in bed next door. He had felt a shaft of searing gratification at the sight of her, at the clear purpose in her as she came towards him, her body shaped sensuously, gloriously, by her clinging gown, her hips swaying, breasts all but bared by the revealing drape of her low décolletage, and her hair loosened and, oh, so wanton, cascading over her shoulders...

She had come up to him...kissed him. Her lips lush and velvet, claiming his, her hands winding around his neck to draw him to her. And that instant had released from him all that had been waiting for release.

His response had been instant, unstoppable—and all-consuming. Urgent and overpowering—overwhelming. He had been unable to resist—and why should he have? She had not come to him as she had the night before, as some kind of unwilling sacrifice, the difference had been absolute.

Lush and sensuous, desirous and desiring…

It's what I wanted—all that I wanted.

And he had taken what she'd offered, what she had so clearly wanted as well. Every touch, every kiss, every yielding, every low, sensual moan in her throat, every caress and every arching of her body had been an invitation to him to take more, and yet more…

To take all he craved and hungered for.

Until—

His mind reeled, incomprehension possessing it totally. Not knowing what to do, he moved away. He must do something—but what? And how? And then, as he drew away from her, his eyes went to the bedsheet, where they had been lying.

And he froze all over again.

The pain was ebbing, and abject gratitude that it was doing so shuddered through Eliana. Slowly, slowly, she was surfacing from it, and feeling not just the pain, that sudden agony like a knife-thrust, convulsing her, but all the other sensations that had been flooding her overheated, over-stimulated flesh.

Cold was creeping over her now, and she felt her body shiver.

Then the quilt was being drawn over her, and her shoulder was being taken, and slowly, but insistently, Leandros was turning her towards him. Her knees were still drawn up, but she felt them slacken, felt the hectic pounding of her heart rate slow a fraction. Pain—a searing ache—still pierced her.

Leandros was beside her, a sheet pulled half across his

waist. He was raised up on one elbow, on his side, and his other hand was carefully, gently, drawing her tumbled hair clear of her face.

He looked down at her.

'I think you need to explain,' he said.

Disbelief was still his dominant consciousness. Yet the evidence was pounding at him. Her scream, her cry of pain when he had entered her—and then... *Thee mou*, that smear of blood...

It isn't possible—it just isn't possible.

She was looking at him. Her features were no longer contorted, yet there was a pallor to her face that told she was still shaken. Her eyes were huge, distended, barely meeting his. But he wanted answers. Needed answers.

'Eliana, you were married for six years—six years! How was I to think—?' He broke off.

Words formed in his head, unspoken but vehement. What the hell kind of marriage had it been for those six long years? Clearly not the kind he had assumed it to be. Had raged that it would be...

And more of his assumptions had self-destructed as well. She'd given Damian no children—no grandson for his father. By choice? To avoid pregnancy? Or had there been chance of pregnancy...? No chance because either she or Damian had been incapable? Or—?

They'd never consummated their marriage.

But *why*?

He looked down at her. And as he did the explanation came to him. The one and only obvious and ineluctable explanation.

'Damian was gay,' he said.

His voice was flat.

But his emotions were not.

Somewhere very deep inside him, emotion was welling—turbid but powerful, seeking entrance to his consciousness, seeking the light. But this was not the time for it.

She hadn't answered him, but her gaze had shifted, and he knew without a doubt that that was the reason for what had happened just now. The reason that, after six years of marriage, she was still a virgin...

Or had been.

Until a few brutal moments ago...

Compunction knifed through him. Had he known—had he had the slightest suspicion—he would never—

'Eliana, I am *sorry*.' His voice was vehement. 'But I never dreamt— How could I? If you had only said... Dear God, I would have been...'

'I didn't know it would hurt,' she said.

Her voice was low and her eyes slipped past his again.

'Not like that.' She swallowed, and now her eyes did meet his. 'And I am sorry too... I... I've shocked you. Shocked myself.'

He saw her start to tremble, saw beneath her lashes tears start to bead. He drew her against him, holding her, as carefully as if she were the rarest porcelain. His breathing was ragged still, but his heart-rate was slowing now, his body subsiding. Passion spent before it even was. But that did not matter...did not exist. All that mattered—all that existed—was his careful holding of her, appalled by his unintentional hurting of her. She was bundled up beneath the protective quilt, his arm around her.

After a while, he spoke. 'Would...would a warm bath help, do you think?' he heard himself ask. 'I can draw it for you. It might be...soothing.'

She swallowed, nodding faintly. 'Thank you,' she said, her voice still low.

He slid from the bed, seizing the bathrobe from the door

and wrapping himself in it, heading into the en suite bathroom and turning on the bath taps to full. Not too hot, just warm and...soothing, as he had said. Would bath salts help? Surely they might. And the scent of them, too, would be soothing. What else? What else could he do? Carry her into the bathroom, that was what.

He went back into the bedroom. She was still lying there, bundled up beneath the quilt, still in a foetal position.

'Your bath's all run,' he said.

He didn't ask, only drew back the quilt, scooping her up in one smooth movement. She felt as light as a feather and, naked as she was, he felt her to be terrifyingly vulnerable. He kept his eyes from her, out of consideration, lowering her to her feet beside the fragrantly full bathtub. He turned away, not wanting her to have him seeing her vulnerable nakedness.

'I'll... I'll leave you to it,' he said uncertainly, not knowing what else to do. A thought struck him. 'There's a shower cap, if you don't want your hair to get wet...'

He closed the bathroom door, left her in peace and privacy. His thoughts were still all over the place, his emotions even more so. Disbelief was still uppermost, and things were rearranging themselves inside his head—things he had thought for six long years that now needed to be re-examined. Understood...

What kind of marriage did she have?

Obviously, not the kind that he had thought she had. Not the one that everyone else had thought she had. There had never been a whisper of Damian Makris's sexual orientation that he had known of. But then... His expression darkened. With a domineering father like Damian's, being gay was something no son would freely admit.

Did she know beforehand?

That was the question that burned now. The question he had to know the answer to—*had* to.

Because if she'd known...

Then she didn't leave me for another man—not in that way. Not in the way that lacerated me, carved knives into my flesh...my heart...

His face hardened. The woman he had once loved might have walked into a celibate marriage, but that didn't exonerate her for her decision. She had still married Damian for his money.

Rejecting me because she thought I would be poor and she couldn't face poverty.

It was that that had shown her true nature. Her true character. That was all he must remember about her.

And yet...

Even with the Makris wealth to give her a luxury lifestyle she can hardly have been happy in that marriage. Having a father-in-law holding her at fault for his lack of grandchildren when all along it was his son who had borne the responsibility for it.

Had Damian let her take the blame? Shoulder his father's ire and disappointment?

So that after Damian's death old Jonas had thrown her out of the family, cut her off with nothing?

He frowned again. And if she hadn't been cut off like that...

Would she be here with me now?

The question forced its way into his head—demanding an answer. An answer he did not want to give. To face.

An answer he did not have.

Last night she tried to come to me like some sacrificial victim, making me feel bad about what I was demanding of her. Yet tonight...

He gazed blindly at the closed door of the en suite bathroom.

Tonight she was a different woman...

He felt emotion buckle through him, confusion and conflict. He turned away, busying himself straightening the bedclothes, tidying the pillows. His eyes went again to the slight telltale stain on the sheet. He should strip the bed.

Instead, he only pulled the quilt over it, smoothing it flat. They would sleep on that. And under the one in her bedroom, which he'd fetch now.

He halted. Would she want to spend the rest of the night with him? His expression changed again with his changing thoughts. He wanted her with him. It was why he had brought her to Paris. Not for her to sleep alone, away from him. Not any longer.

Not now.

He strode out, walked into her bedroom, lifted the quilt up and then, as well, scooping up her nightdress. It was only a cheap garment, with a popular chain store label in it, but if she'd feel more comfortable wearing it tonight— well, that was understandable.

He glanced around. What else might she need?

He saw a tube of face cream on the bedside table, and picked that up too. Plus there was whatever was in the vanity in his own bathroom.

He returned to his own bedroom, laid her quilt over his, draped her nightgown over the pillow on her side, placed the face cream on her bedside table.

Another thought struck him. Hot milk—that might be comforting too, after her bath.

He went out again, heading into the kitchen. He made fresh coffee for himself, heated milk for her, sweetening it with honey, adding some delicate almond biscuits to the tray, carrying it all back with him.

He could hear the bathwater emptying, and he knocked gently on the en suite door, having picked up her nightdress.

'If you open up, I'll pass you your nightgown,' he said.

She did so—just a crack—and he handed it to her, hearing her thank him in a low voice. When she emerged, his eyes went to her. She looked pale still, but better somehow. Her hair hung down her back, a little damp from the bath, curling around her face. She looked younger.

Like I remember her.

'How are you feeling?' he asked.

'Better—thank you. The bath was a good idea.'

She looked around, clearly uncertain what to do.

'I thought you might like some hot milk and honey,' he said. He made his voice encouraging.

'That was kind—thank you.'

He folded back the quilt on her side, gesturing that she should get in. She did, and he propped up the pillows for her, before stepping away again. Then he went round to his side of the bed. He realised, with a start, that he was still naked beneath his bathrobe. He snatched his sleep shorts from underneath the pillow, swiftly pulled them on, adding a tee as well, out of the chest of drawers. Sufficiently decent, he discarded the bathrobe, climbed into bed beside her.

'One hot milk coming up,' he said, and reached for the mug from the tray on the bedside table. 'And almond biscuits.'

'Thank you,' she said, and took the mug and a biscuit. She cupped the former and nibbled the latter.

Leandros reached for his coffee. He'd made it milky, with some of the hot milk he'd heated for her. He helped himself to a couple of the biscuits.

'Be careful of crumbs,' he warned her. 'They're hell to sleep on.' He kept his voice light.

She gave a slight smile, sipping at her milk, easing her shoulders back into the pillows. She turned to him.

'Thank you,' she said. Her voice was still low. 'For the milk, the bath—and for…being understanding about…'

He felt his hand reach out, touch hers. Lightly. Gently. Saying nothing. Simply wanting…

But he didn't know what he wanted. Things had changed. But how, and to what extent, he still didn't know.

One thing he did know.

That to sit here quietly, side by side with her like this, in the midnight hours, in the soft light around them, not speaking but sharing this moment, companionably finishing their warming drinks, sharing the almond biscuits, was good.

And for now, that was enough.

CHAPTER NINE

ELIANA WAS DREAMING. It was the sweetest dream she had ever had. She was warm and safe and tucked under a strong, protective arm, her body nestled back against another body, fitting into the curve of it as if it were the only place in all the world for her to be. She felt herself smile in her dream... a contented, happy smile...knowing with a certainty that was permeating through her, sure and blessed, that this was the only place she ever wanted to be.

Had ever wanted to be...

A happy, contented sigh breathed from her and she snuggled back more still against the warm, protective body cradling her, the strong arm holding her close, holding her safe...

Safe from all the sorrows and difficulties of her life... from all the grief and the sacrifice, all the loss and heartache.

From all the guilt.

She went on dreaming. This was the sweetest dream she had ever had...

Light was filtering through the heavy drapes across the windows, slowly rousing Leandros to consciousness. But he did not want to wake. He was fine as he was...where he was. Just fine. His arm was over Eliana, and somehow his own body was cradling hers, separated from him only by the cotton of her nightgown. It felt good. So very, very good.

He hovered a while between sleeping and waking, but slowly the latter gained ground, as daylight played on his closed eyelids. He opened them, seeing first the glorious swathe of pale golden hair across the pillow, exposing the tender curve of Eliana's neck. He could not resist it. He moved slightly to drop a kiss on her nape, as lightly as a feather.

Would it rouse her? He didn't know—knew only that her limbs were starting to stretch languorously, her low breathing changing subtly. He stilled. Full consciousness came to him, and the memory of all that the night had brought.

He eased away from her, sliding out of his side of the bed, sitting for a moment, taking in all that had happened. His mind was unsure, uncertain.

He twisted his head, looked back at where Eliana had slipped back into sleep again, lying still. He could not see her face—he had been holding her from behind—only that glorious swathe of hair across the pillow and the tender nape he had just kissed.

For one moment longer he felt that uncertainty, confusion, hold on to his head. Then, with a decision he had not known he had already made, he let it fall away. Oh, it might still be there somewhere, ready to rise again, to pluck at him, disquiet him, but right now...

He got to his feet, walked across to the windows, drew back the drapes. Sunshine flooded in, mild and autumnal, filling the room. He glanced out of the window. The roofs of Paris stretched beyond...the whole city stretched beyond. Inviting and entrancing. He gave a smile. The day looked good.

He padded quietly from the room. Out in the drawing room he phoned through to the butler, ordering breakfast to be served. While he waited he went back into his bedroom, not disturbing Eliana, but whisking away the remains of their midnight milk and coffee, busying himself with the washing up, finishing just as breakfast arrived.

The aroma of fresh coffee filled the air, and of freshly baked croissants, rolls and pastries, along with the crisp tang of freshly squeezed orange juice. He thanked the butler, then dismissed him, wheeling the trolley carefully into his bedroom.

He paused by the bed. 'Breakfast, *madame*, is served,' he announced.

His voice was warm, and his mood, he knew, with a sudden lightening that came as a gift of the morning, of the day ahead, was the best he had known for a long time.

And it stayed good.

And he knew it would stay good all through the leisurely breakfast in bed he would have with Eliana beside him.

She stirred as he made his announcement, and groped herself up into a sitting position, pushing back her long, tangled hair and looking at him. Her expression was uncertain, and he knew that memory was piercing her too, that she didn't know how she should be now, this morning after the night before.

He made it easy for her. Smiled down at her.

'Let's just have breakfast, shall we?' he said.

And in those words were words unspoken—words that did not need to be spoken yet. He did not even know what they would be—what they *should* be. So as he didn't know what those words should be, he set them aside, sticking to words he knew he could say...wanted to say.

'It's a glorious morning,' he said. He paused. 'Let's just take things as they come.'

He'd said enough. He could see in her expression that she was glad of his words, for the sudden confusion and tension that had been there a moment earlier had ebbed away. In its place was a new expression, and one that caught at him.

Shyness.

As if finding herself in my bed is something she had not expected.

But then a rueful thought darted in him pointedly. There was a lot about Eliana that *he* had not expected.

He put it from him—he'd resolved not to go down that complex and confusing path. Not this morning...not this day.

He pulled the breakfast trolley against his side of the bed as he slid back in under the quilt, propping himself comfortably on his piled-up pillows.

'OJ to start with?' he asked, turning back to Eliana.

'Oh, yes—thank you,' she said.

She sounded a touch awkward, but he glossed it over. He didn't want her feeling awkward, or shy, or feeling anything other than that it was good to be sitting with him, side by side, on this glorious morning, with all of Paris awaiting them for the day.

He poured her a glass and handed it to her. Her fingers, he noticed, were careful not to touch his. He did not mind. It was not rejection, he knew, only self-conscious shyness.

A thought came to him, flickering in his mind.

That was the way she'd have been after our first night together, on our honeymoon...

Another thought, a realisation, came hard on its heels.

But this was our first night together...

It hung in his head for a moment—but there were too many other currents, too much confusion, too much shock circling around that truth and he would not deal with it. Not now. Not when he'd resolved, as he had just said to her, to take the day as it came. And right now it was coming with breakfast in bed, to be consumed enjoyably and leisurely.

Companionably.

That was what he felt, sitting back again with his own glass of orange juice. He let her be…let her get used to being here, like this, with him.

OJ consumed, he asked her what she might like to eat, then handed her a personal tray with croissants, butter pats and apricot jam, and a cup of coffee with hot milk. She placed it on her bedside table.

He got stuck in to his own breakfast—a more robust, seeded roll, with butter and a dollop of blackcurrant jam. He was hungry, and it went down quickly, and he reached for another.

At his side, Eliana was neatly getting through her croissant.

'You can't beat the French for breakfast in bed,' he said, helping himself to yet another roll. 'Though for a really substantial experience I'd always vote for a—what's that expression?—a full English. Bacon and eggs, smoked kippers, devilled kidneys—the works!' he said humorously.

He glanced at Eliana. She was more at ease now, he could tell, as if she was getting used to sitting here beside him. He wanted her to be at ease.

We're starting afresh.

The words were in his head and he knew them to be true. Knew it with that same lightening of his spirit that had come as he had got out of bed, welcomed the new day, the new start.

What had gone before in their lives was still there—how could it not be? But last night had changed things. Though just how he still did not quite know for sure…

But he wasn't going to work that out now.

For now, he was going to do just what he'd said—take the day as it came.

For now, that was all he wanted.

* * *

Eliana sat back on the padded seat on the deck of the river cruiser. They were heading down the Seine to Giverny, to see Monet's famous gardens. The sun was warm on her, the breeze off the river as the cruiser gently made its way downstream pleasant on her face.

Outwardly, she and Leandros were spending the day much as they had the previous afternoon—sightseeing. And yet it felt fundamentally different. It *was* fundamentally different, she knew.

And it was not just because of what she had realised so undeniably the evening before, feeling Puccini's heartrending music pierce her own blind heart, piercing so much repression and denial, declaring to her the truth about herself and about why she had agreed to come here with Leandros.

Yes, that had changed her completely—she knew it and accepted it.

But it isn't just me who is changed.

Last night—as she had yielded willingly, wantonly, discovering in herself a passion and a sensuality to which she had given herself completely, knowing the truth about herself and accepting it, acknowledging it, instead of denying it and suppressing it—the revelation of her virginity had shocked Leandros to the core.

She bit her lip now, still troubled at how it had happened.

I didn't think he'd find out—I didn't realise just how... obvious...it would be!

Her marriage to Damian and the constrictions under which she had made it had no relevance to the truth she had faced up to as she'd sat in that *loge* at the opera and watched the two ill-fated lovers on the stage below, tormented and tormenting, destroying their own lives by the decisions they made. And yet, for all that, love had survived—even if the lovers themselves had not.

So it is with me.

She had given up on what she had once felt for Leandros six long years ago—buried it deep under the guilt she felt for what she had done. Yet it had survived despite what she'd done, despite the fateful decision she'd made all those years ago to abandon him, reject him.

Her eyes went to him now. He was standing a little way from her, but not far, leaning on the railing, looking out over the river at the passing scenery as Paris gave way to the countryside of Normandy. He looked relaxed, at ease, and she was glad—and grateful.

With feminine instinct and a little pang, she knew that his discovery that her marriage to Damian had been celibate had come as welcome news. That it had lessened, in some way, his sense of rejection by her when she had married Damian and not him.

Does he think it part of the retribution I deserved? To be denied a normal marriage with the husband I had chosen over him?

No—there had been no sense of that in him. And that knowledge, that certainty that came from somewhere she knew not where, warmed her.

Her expression softened as her gaze fixed on him, the breeze ruffling his sable hair, the sleeves of his jumper pushed up to show his strong, tanned forearms as he leant against the railing. And the way he was being with her now warmed her too.

He'd been different from the moment she'd woken. Woken from that dream—the sweetest dream in all the world. A dream that had, as she'd woken, suddenly been no dream. Leandros truly had held her close, protected her, all night long...

Emotion welled in her, but there was sadness too. Sadness for all that might have been in her life. It pierced her now, the knowledge that however last evening and last night had changed things between them, it could never make right all that had gone wrong.

But for now, in this moment, this day, during this time with him, given to her as a blessing that she had never thought could be hers, what she had was enough.

'You can see why Monet loved his gardens so much,' Leandros said. 'Immortalising them in so many paintings.'

After the tour of Monet's house and gardens, he had repaired with Eliana for a late lunch in a nearby restaurant with a vine-covered terrace, busy with other visitors. The day was still warm enough to sit out, though he was glad of his lightweight sweater. Eliana wore a short-sleeved top with a matching bolero-style cardigan around her shoulders, paired with a flared skirt—all part of the wardrobe he'd supplied her with the previous day.

His gaze lingered—and yet it was not the gaze of the previous day, veiled and assessing, holding at bay the part of his mind that was deploring the rashness of his decision to have anything to do with Eliana ever again, presenting her with an outward civility that masked the turbid, bitter emotions that warred with the driving desire for all that he sought only to sate and quench. To be free of for ever by indulging it. To taste and take the beauty that tormented him…

No, now it was less her beauty that held him—more her expression. He wanted to read it—be reassured by it.

'It was a good place to live out his life,' she answered now, her tone ruminative. 'There is always peace to be found in a garden.'

There was a softness in her eyes, as if she were thinking of more than Monet's garden.

'The garden at your father's villa was beautiful, as I remember,' he heard himself saying.

'Yes, it was always a comfort to him—as was the villa itself. He loved them dearly. I was always glad—'

She broke off, busying herself with breaking open her bread roll as they waited for their food to arrive.

'Glad?' he prompted.

She lifted her eyes and looked across at him. 'Glad he was able to end his days there.'

'Were you able to be with him?'

'Yes—Jonas granted me that, and I was grateful. After his stroke, my father...lingered...for two months. I stayed there for the duration.'

Leandros's eyes rested on her. There was a sadness in her face now, and he felt it pull at him.

'I... I heard that the villa will now pass to Damian's cousin.' He felt uncomfortable saying it, but he did not mean it cruelly. Just the reverse.

Her marriage had not been easy. For whatever venal reason she'd made it, she had paid a high price for the rich living that was so important to her that she could not do without it.

She could not face poverty—even with me to share it with. She wanted what she was born to, and the threat of losing it made her reject me.

'Yes. Vassily will get it now—unless Jonas sells it, or pulls it down and replaces it with something modern, then sells that at a greater profit still. It's his business, after all, and how he made his money. Construction.'

'Or destruction,' Leandros riposted tightly. 'I only visited once, but it deserves keeping—whoever owns it.'

Leandros frowned again. Her father-in-law had driven a hard bargain when Eliana had married his son.

But it gave her what she wanted—she lived the high life with Damian.

Even if a celibate one...

A childless one.

He looked at her. 'Did you never think to give Jonas the grandchild he was set on? Even if Damian was gay, there was always the choice of conceiving through IVF and so on.'

She shook her head. 'Damian didn't want that,' she said.

She spoke calmly enough, but her expression was evasive. Leandros studied it.

'And you didn't want a child either?' he asked. 'A child would have ensured that you would still be part of Jonas's family now—he would not have cast you off as he has. Reduced you to the poverty I found you in.'

She didn't answer. The waitress came up with their dishes, placing them down in front of them, then heading off again. The moment passed, and Leandros let it. What point was there in probing Eliana's marriage? He would not disturb the day. There had been revelations enough last night—confusion and complexities. Today he wanted only ease and peace and Eliana at his side.

To pass the day as they were doing.

Companionably.

That word came again, just as it had come to him over breakfast, and then as they'd headed down river to take their leisurely, easy, peaceful cruise to Giverny, to explore the magical gardens of Monet's water lilies away from the cares and troubles of life, whether past or present.

He got stuck into his steak frites—simple, traditional French food—and washed it down with table wine, robust and drinkable. Eliana was eating fish, nothing delicate or sauced, but a grilled fillet of white fish, served with *pommes parmentier* and green beans.

He turned the conversation back to Monet, and to what they had seen.

'Though the water garden is extraordinary, and of course

the famous Japanese-style bridge, and all the even more famous waterlilies, I don't like that it's separated from the house and the immediate garden of the house. Going through that linking tunnel was a disappointment.'

'Yes, I agree. It would be much better to have a house whose gardens encircled it—but then Monet had to buy what became the water garden from a neighbour, so I suppose that limited him.'

Leandros looked across at her. 'What kind of house and garden would you ideally like?'

The moment he spoke he regretted it. She would answer and say it was her father's villa, and that was lost to her.

Unless her next husband bought it back for her.

Next husband?

He had taunted her with being on the lookout for another rich husband to ensure she never had to face the poverty she'd always been determined not to experience—had bribed her, if it came to that, into agreeing to coming to Paris with him by saying he'd kit her out with a wardrobe suitable for ensnaring another rich husband—or even merely a rich lover.

And I'd move on once I had done with her.

He felt his jaw clench. Had he really thought that? Said that? Taunted her with it?

And I taunted her last evening, calling her Manon for betraying and rejecting a poor lover for a rich protector.

No—he would not go down that path again. Not now—not today.

Things had changed between them. Just how he did not know, and he did not want to. Not right now. Not today.

Nor the next day either. Or the one after that.

For now...

Just take the day as it comes.

And he knew—as he had known that morning, and knew

now as he sat here with her, companionably, over lunch at this simple restaurant, eating a simple meal, having wandered in the gardens at Monet's house, with the afternoon and the rest of the day before them—that it was enough.

Eliana set her knife and fork down on the plate, feeling replete, reaching for her glass of wine. Dappled sunshine shone through the vines shading the terraced seating area and played on her face. Her mood was strange—yet peaceful. Despite Leandros asking her those questions.

Had she wanted to answer them?

All but one.

And that she had avoided. Must avoid. He would not be interested anyway, so what did it matter?

That he was asking questions at all was…was what? Curious? Surprising? Unexpected? Perhaps predictable. The revelation last night of how her marriage to Damian had not been what he'd assumed invited questions.

Not that her answers to any of them mattered—any more than why she and Damian had never tried to have a child.

None of it matters, because no answer I give can ever justify what I did to Leandros.

That was all there was to it—all the truth that it was necessary for her to face.

And the truth she had discovered last evening.

Her eyes went to him now, softening as they did so, and emotion flowed within her, strong and irrefutable. That was all that mattered to her now as she sat here with him, in this time she had.

It would not last. How could it? He had brought her here to free himself of her, purge himself of her, to take from her all that was left of what he'd once wanted.

And I will give it to him—freely and willingly. Even if it is all he wants of me, it is his...

Last night—and the debacle that had ended it—had merely been a…a delay…that was all. Now, tonight, she would be different—fulfilled.

All that he wants—and all that I want to give.

She felt that precious emotion flow again within her, warming her and comforting her. She would pay a price for it—as she had six years ago—but for now, *this* now, it would be her joy and her gift to him. And now she knew, with that certainty that had filled her since the discovery of the truth about why she had come to Paris with Leandros, that it was a gift to herself too.

'Shall we eat in tonight?'

Leandros's enquiry was tentative as they made their way back into their hotel. She might prefer to go out—see and be seen. If so, he would oblige. He was being…considerate. That was the word that came to him. Going easy on her, as he had all day, because—

Well, because. That was all. Still taking the day as it came.

And it's been good today.

The river cruise, the gentle ambling around Monet's gardens, a leisurely lunch, some more ambling around the village of Giverny itself, then back to the river to glide serenely back upstream to Paris, looking out over the riverbanks that another painter, Seurat, had made equally as famous as Monet's waterlilies, with his river-bathing youths and his bourgeois promenaders along La Grande Jatte, immortalised in his trademark *pointilliste* style.

They had discussed it amiably, agreeing to differ—Eliana preferring the beauty of Monet, he the technical brilliance of Seurat.

We used to agree to differ all the time…

Even with her sheltered upbringing—or was it because of

it, perhaps?—Eliana had been happy to disagree with him. It had been a novelty for him—the females he'd favoured had tended to agree with him. Too eagerly.

I called Eliana naive, overprotected by her doting father. But was I, in turn, spoilt by my looks and my wealth? Did I take it for granted that I could always have what I wanted? Feel entitled to it?

It was a disquieting thought. If it were true, then had it only exacerbated the blow of Eliana's rejection of him? And besides...

I knew my father was only testing her, warning her he would disinherit me if I married her. I knew he only wanted her to prove her love for me—get her to marry me even with the threat of disinheritance and then relent. He would never have gone through with it. Would even have bailed out her father.

But Eliana had not known that. Had only known that if she went through with marrying him there would be no money—no money to keep her in the lifestyle she was used to, which she could not face losing when her father ran out of money.

So she had chosen Damian instead—and lived to see her father die, and all that he possessed pass to her father-in-law. Lived to face the very poverty she had married to avoid.

Come full circle.

Karma? Was that the word for it?

What we flee from we must eventually face?

The door to the elevator was slicing open, cutting off his thoughts. He was glad. He wanted to go back to his mandate for the day—to take things as they came.

And that included Eliana's preference for dinner.

She glanced at him as they entered the Résidence.

'That would be good...eating in,' she said.

'I think so too,' he affirmed. 'How about some coffee now?'

'I'd prefer tea,' she answered. 'But let me make it—and your coffee. Silly to summon the butler.'

She headed for the kitchen and Leandros followed her, discovering that a platter of fresh *patisserie* had been left for them. It looked good, and lunch had been a while ago now. He lifted a cherry, succulent and inviting, from the top of one of the mouth-watering selections, and realised that Eliana, kettle in hand, was looking at him, her expression strange.

'You used to pick the nuts off the baklava,' she said. 'Even though they were tiny and covered in syrup.'

'So I did,' he recalled. He'd forgotten. 'Then you'd dampen your serviette with water from your glass and hand it to me to wipe my sticky fingers...'

So long ago...so slight a gesture...so slight a memory. And yet—

He put it from him. It was the present he was dealing with. And one issue in particular.

'I was thinking,' he said, 'whether you'd like another bath.'

She looked at him blankly.

He busied himself with the coffee machine, selecting his choice.

'After last night,' he said. 'In case—well, in case...'

He looked up, straight at her. He must say what he wanted to say. Needed to say.

'Last night...it changes things. So I want you to know—' He broke off. Then made himself go on. 'I expect nothing now, Eliana. Not any more.'

Where that had come from he didn't know. Knew only that he had needed to say it. That, in the end, was that what this day had been about—separating what had been before from what now was.

He was looking at her still. He could not read her face, nor her stillness. He went on speaking.

'So we'll just go on taking things as they come, OK? We can be as…as we are now. We can go on with our visit to Paris. Or…' he took a breath '… I can take you back to Thessaloniki, if that is what you prefer. It's…it's your call.' A thought struck him. 'Everything I bought you yesterday—all the clothes—obviously you will take them with you. That goes without saying. Anyway,' he carried on, wanting her to understand, 'for this evening, at least, let's just do what we agreed—eat in, take it easy…whatever.'

He paused again. She was still looking at him, her expression still unreadable. He needed a way out of there, so he took it, lifting up the platter of *patisserie*.

'I'll take these through,' he said, and got out.

Not knowing if he felt relief or its very opposite.

Or both.

Or why.

Eliana deposited her tea and Leandros's coffee on the low table by the sofa. Leandros was at one end, and he switched on the TV to an English language news channel. Her mind was still processing what Leandros had just said to her. She busied herself pouring milk into her tea, and Leandros did likewise for his coffee, then pushed the platter of *patisserie* towards her.

She selected one of the enticing-looking confections, depositing it on one of the two small plates she'd brought through for that purpose, handing the other plate to Leandros so he could make his selection. A small gesture…an intimate one.

A domestic one.

As if—

No—there was no 'as if' about it. She hadn't married him, she had never been his wife, and she never would be. Whatever was happening now had no domesticity to it at all.

Does he really want me to go back to Thessaloniki? Does he regret bringing me here?

She didn't know and couldn't tell. Knew only, with a clutch of emotion that she kept tight within her, what it was that *she* wanted.

In this sea of past bitterness and present doubt, of that she was sure.

I don't want to leave him—whatever he might want of me here, and however briefly. While he wants anything of me at all, I don't want to leave him.

Because this time, she knew, was all she would have—all she could ever have—of the man she had once loved and knew she still did.

CHAPTER TEN

LEANDROS STOOD BY the open windows giving out on to their Juliet balcony. The early-evening twilight was gathering. Gently, he eased the cork of the champagne bottle and it gave with a soft pop. As it did so, he heard the door of Eliana's bedroom open, and she emerged.

After tea and coffee she'd gone off to take another soothing bath, and he'd been glad, repairing to take a shower himself, and change into more relaxed clothes—a lightweight fine cashmere sweater over an open-necked shirt with turned-back cuffs. He'd touched base with his office while he had the opportunity. He'd left matters in good order, and they still were. He was glad of it. He didn't want distractions. Not now. Right now he had only one focus.

And she was standing right there.

She was hesitant, he could see, and he wanted that dispelled.

He made his smile warm, his voice warmer. 'Ah, there you are—how are you feeling?' There was genuine concern in his voice.

She didn't answer him directly. 'I soaked for ages—it was a real indulgence,' she said lightly. 'My apartment only has a shower, and the water is very seldom hot anyway.'

'Then have a bath every day!' he said, keeping his tone

as light as hers. He picked up an empty flute. 'Champagne? Or something different? Another G and T?'

Even as he asked her, his eyes were drinking her in. She'd put on one of her new dresses, softly draped in sage-green, halfway between dressy and casual—just right for dining in. She'd drawn her hair back into a low, loose chignon at the nape of her neck. He fancied she'd put on a little mascara, and maybe some lip sheen—just a very light touch of make-up to enhance her features. Whatever she'd done, with the dress and the hair and her own beauty she looked effortlessly lovely...

Something moved inside him as he looked at her—part of this strange new feeling he had about her that he knew was changing everything, even if he still did not understand how...

She stepped forward. 'Thank you—champagne would be very nice.'

She was still a little hesitant, and Leandros found himself wanting her to relax more. He wanted that sense of simply taking the day as it came to continue—without the complications, the confusion, the complexities that lay between them.

He filled her flute, and then his own, holding hers out to her.

She took it, murmuring her thanks.

'Santé,' he said in the same light tone. And as he did, he recalled the toast he'd so acerbically given the previous evening at the opera—'My very own Manon.'

It had been designed to taunt.

To mock.

To wound.

Regret, or something like it, smote him. Reappraisal— maybe that was the right word? There was a reappraisal he should apply—one that she deserved.

Maybe I was being unfair—oh, not in saying that she only wanted to marry for money, but knowing that, having done so, she paid a price for it. A heavy price. To be unjustly accused by her domineering father-in-law of failing to give him the grandson he demanded when that was entirely because her marriage was celibate because her husband was gay! And then her father-in-law punished her by reducing her to poverty in her widowhood.

His thoughts were sober.

Maybe she did not deserve any more retribution from me for what she did.

Maybe retribution—if that was even the right word now—had already been exacted from her...

Maybe she had already paid her price for her faithlessness.

And maybe, therefore—the words from that morning came again into his head—*we should start over.*

They'd made a start—today had been a good day, a much easier, more peaceable day, without their previous guarded, superficial civility. He had the grace to acknowledge that the bitterness he harboured was as deep within him as it had ever been, while she'd kept to an air of passive detachment. But today had not been like that. It had been—

Companionable.

There was that word again—the one that kept coming to him.

Almost like we used to be.

The thought flickered in his head like a light that might or might not dispel the shadows.

'*Santé,*' she echoed, dipping her head to take a taste of the gently beading champagne.

'I've taken the liberty of ordering dinner for us,' he said. 'I hope you don't mind.'

He told her the choices he'd made, saying there was still time to change them, but she shook her head.

'It all sounds delicious,' she said. 'Thank you. And thank you, too, for taking me to Giverny today.'

He glanced at her. 'You don't have to thank me,' he said. 'It's all part of…'

He stopped. Part of what? Part of what he was offering her because of what he was getting in return? Like the clothes he'd bought her? This stay in a luxury hotel?

Put like that, he didn't like the implication. Which didn't make sense. It hadn't troubled him when he'd put it to her in Thessaloniki over dinner. Outlining what he was offering her—what she would get out of it in return.

'Yes,' he heard her say quietly, acceptingly, 'I know. But thank you all the same—for dinner tonight, and last night, and taking me to the opera, and to Giverny today, and Notre Dame and Sainte-Chapelle yesterday.'

He shook his head in negation. 'I didn't mean it like that.' He paused. 'I don't want it to be like that.'

He had wanted it—but not any more. Now he knew he no longer simply wanted her gratitude for bringing her to Paris—and the reason he had brought her here.

For sex—that's what you brought her here for. You spelt it out plainly enough.

Yet somehow, right now, it was an uncomfortable thought. He felt his mind sheer away. And not just because there was suddenly a sordid edge to it…to what he'd offered her.

Because even if she's only accepted to get out of that wretched dump she has to live in and get her hands on a decent wardrobe again, so she can kickstart her way back into a luxe lifestyle, that doesn't justify my offer. Because what does it say about me that I made such an offer? Doesn't it just reduce me to her level?

His mouth twisted. Well, right now there wasn't much likelihood of his making good on the reason he'd brought her to Paris. Not after last night. And it wasn't just a question of enough soothing baths...

He'd hurt her physically. He hadn't meant to—hadn't even known he could, in that way—but that didn't change the fact that he had done so.

'I think,' he said haltingly, knowing this was something he wanted to make clear to her, and finding the resolve to do it, 'that from now...well, separate bedrooms.'

As he said it, there was instant conflict in his head. He'd said the right thing, the decent thing. But the moment he'd done so scorching memory had come—vivid...leaping into punishing hyper-consciousness...

She'd torn herself away from him, in his bed, almost at the very consummation of the inferno that had been consuming him—consuming her too. For she had lit that inferno by coming to him as she had, and he had gone up in flames, and so had she, with mutual desire burning them with the white heat of passion unleashed.

But from the moment of her shocking revelation to this moment now he'd assiduously, doggedly, refused to let into his head what had come before. Yet now it seared white-hot.

Gliding up to me, hair loose and wanton, body sensuous and irresistible to me, winding her arms around me, reaching for my mouth with hers...

He had been lost instantly, totally. That had been no self-sacrificing abasement, no offering herself to him as some kind of atonement. That had been Eliana just as he'd said he'd wanted her to be—eager, aroused, passionate. And he had been likewise. Instantly. Consumingly...

He slammed down hard on the memory. It was the situation now he was dealing with. A situation that made any repetition of what had happened last night completely out of the question.

'So you can be comfortable,' he said now.

She was looking at him questioningly, uncertainly. 'Leandros, why…why are you being so nice to me?'

He frowned. 'I'd be a brute not to be, in the circumstances. It appals me that I hurt you—'

She shook her head. 'I don't just mean separate bedrooms. I mean…well, all day today. And…and last night too. Making hot milk for me…all that… And you're being nice to me now too.'

He took a mouthful of champagne. Her question had been direct—his answer was not.

'Why shouldn't I be?' he countered.

Her frown remained. 'Because you hate me,' she said.

He stilled. '*Hate* you?' His voice was hollow.

'I don't blame you for that—I have no right to do so.' She spoke as if she had not heard him. 'But…' She took a breath and he realised she was not as calm as she was appearing. 'But even though you discovered that my marriage was not…not what the world thought it was…not in that way…that doesn't change anything between us, does it?'

He didn't answer, only lifted his champagne flute to his mouth, taking another slow mouthful, as if to give himself time, then lowering it again.

His expression changed, and he looked directly at her.

'Eliana, even if…even if you went into your marriage with Damian open-eyed about his sexual orientation—and I hope that you did…that you knew what you were letting yourself in for—do you…do you ever regret it? Regret marrying him instead of me?'

He had said it—asked the question that he had never allowed himself to ask before. For what purpose would there have been in her answer? Not while she was married to Damian certainly.

But if she had come to regret it she could have had the marriage annulled for non-consummation...or just gone for a divorce—

'No.'

Her one-word answer was quietly spoken, but there was in it something that made Leandros know she had spoken only the truth.

'No, I don't regret marrying Damian. It was my choice to do so—and it would be my choice again.'

Leandros felt a heaviness inside him at her answer. He pursued it to its conclusion—the conclusion he already knew...had known for six long years. Now stated again.

'Because if you'd married me you'd have faced poverty—and you couldn't face that.'

'No.'

Again, the one-word answer gave tacit agreement to what he had said, and was quietly spoken, but it was neither hesitant, nor holding regret.

'I could not have faced the consequences of marrying you. And so for that reason, whatever kind of marriage I had with Damian, I cannot—*do* not—regret it.'

Her expression changed.

'It's the only truthful answer I can give. I'm... I'm sorry I can't give you any other. And I'm sorry that I hurt you...that I killed the love you felt for me.' She took a breath. 'And I am glad, for your sake, that you no longer feel anything for me—'

She broke off, looked away, out of the window, over the rooftops of Paris.

There had been a bleakness in her voice just then that had been absent from the quiet, unhesitant way she'd told him she did not regret her marriage to Damian. But it was her last words that echoed inside Leandros's head. They were true—of course they were true. How could they be anything other than true?

And yet—

Are they still true? Do I feel nothing for her?

The question hung in his consciousness, wanting an answer—an answer he could not give.

For a moment he stood still, eyes resting on her averted face, on her fingers curved around the stem of the champagne flute she was holding. Then slowly, so very slowly, his hand reached out to touch the curve of her wrist...so lightly...so fleetingly.

'Things change, Eliana,' he said softly. 'They've changed already between us. They could change again.'

He let his hand fall away. He was conscious of the beat of his own heart. The silence between them. She did not turn back, so he could not see her face, but he saw her fingertips around the stem of her glass tighten. And her free hand moved to fold over the place where he had touched her so briefly—so gently.

Was she sheltering herself against his touch? Or sheltering the touch itself? How could he tell? How could he know?

How can I know anything about her, about what she feels? And why should I care?

He did not know that either. Knew only that somehow, now, he did care.

His own words to her echoed.

'Things change, Eliana. They've changed already between us. They could change again.'

Could they? Could they change again?

And do I want them to?

That was another unanswered question. So many unanswered questions...

So much confusion and complexity—how can I make sense of it all?

The sound of the doorbell was intrusive in the silence that had fallen between them. Was it welcome? Or the opposite? Whichever it was, he turned back into the room, pulling open the door to admit the butler and his minions.

The arrival of dinner needed to be attended to, and maybe he was glad of it. That exchange with Eliana had been too intense, going too deep into past and present. He needed respite from it—and maybe so did she.

She seemed glad to take her place at the table in their dining room while a resplendent meal was presented to them.

Leandros had specifically selected a menu that would enable their entrée—*boeuf bourguignon*—to be kept warm in chafing dishes, with chilled *tarte au citron* for dessert, so that he could dismiss the staff...not have them hover.

Yet the moment they were gone he felt silence threaten again. He dismissed it with resolve. He'd wanted an easier day, and wading into asking questions such as he had on the balcony was not conducive to that end. Now he wanted that sense of ease back again. Wanted the atmosphere lightened.

Wanted to feel again what he had felt during the day.

Companionable.

Deliberately, he raised his refilled champagne glass to Eliana across the table.

'Bon appetit,' he said. 'I hope our dinner is as delicious as you have said it sounds.'

He made his voice light, replacing his flute and picking up his fork to start to do justice to the beautifully layered vegetable terrine that was their first course.

'I'm not sure what all the layers are,' he pondered, 'except that one of them, judging by its colour, is definitely beetroot.'

'There's courgette in there somewhere,' Eliana answered, and he was glad that her tone of voice was as light as his. 'And perhaps asparagus?'

They went on identifying the multi-coloured, multi-textured layers. It was easy conversation, light and inconsequential. But it served its purpose. Lightened the atmosphere.

He glanced towards her. As ever, her beauty made his breath catch.

It comes to her naturally—she makes no effort, but it is there all the time.

Memory came—how struck he'd been when he'd first been courting her, wooing her, making her his own, by just how naturally beautiful she was. Unsophisticated, yes, unlike the females he usually ran with, but her beauty had been in her smile, her eyes, her sun-kissed hair… In the way she'd laughed, and dropped her gaze when he looked at her—not in a flirtatious way, or to entice him… Although sometimes he would catch her stealing a look at him from beneath her smoky lashes…a look of longing…

He'd liked that—had liked to bring the colour flushing to her soft cheeks when he'd paid her compliments, which she'd absorbed like a flower drinking in the warming rays of the sun…

I thought I'd found a woman different from any that I had known. One to fall in love with.

He hadn't intended to fall in love at all. It had not been on his agenda—but Eliana had changed all that. With her in his life he'd no longer wanted to play the field, hadn't been interested in the chic, sophisticated females he'd once focussed his attentions on. Eliana had swept him away—swept him totally away.

Until she'd walked away from him. Handed back his ring. Walked out of his life.

But now she's back in it. I've let her in. Thinking I knew why.

His gaze rested on her now, and he felt again the confusion he'd felt in the night, when he'd realised the truth about her marriage...felt again, even more intensely, what had passed between them out on the balcony just now.

What do I want of her? What do I want at all?

No answers came—or only one, to which he now returned.

He wanted to be with her as he had been today—easy, peaceable...companionable.

Nothing more than that.

Nothing less.

CHAPTER ELEVEN

THE WALL-HUNG TV blazed with a last burst of colour and declared *The End*. Robin Hood and his Maid Marian had just ridden off into their personal sunset. The choice of film had been mutual, and just right. A colourful swashbuckler, traditional Hollywood, as familiar as it was enjoyable.

Eliana stretched her legs from being curled up under her on the sofa. Beside her, but not too close, Leandros sat lounging back, long legs extended, crossed at the ankles, picking at the last of the *petits fours* on the coffee table.

He turned towards her.

Smilingly.

'Daft, but fun,' he said.

She gave a light laugh. 'Definitely,' she agreed.

Her gaze lingered on him a moment, eyes veiled, as if she was self-conscious suddenly, and then she reached for her wine glass. They had eaten a leisurely dinner, and had been finishing off the luscious dessert wine since they'd repaired to the sofa. The mood that had prevailed since their outing to Giverny still held, and Eliana was glad of it. Yet a sadness of sorts plucked at her. Leandros had wanted a different answer to the question he had put to her. Different from the one she had given him: that she would make the same choice again as she had six years ago.

I can't undo the past.

His voice echoed in her head. *'Things change, Eliana.'*

But the past did not change. What had been true then was still true. And her feelings too. Feelings she could never smother or deny, though they would only bring her yet more heartache in the end.

So be content with this—with what is here and now.

'Fancy watching anything else?' Leandros asked in an easy tone.

She gave a shake of her head, finishing the last of her sweet wine and getting to her feet.

'Time for bed,' she said lightly.

Did something flicker in his eyes? If it did, she discounted it. 'Separate bedrooms' he had said, and she knew he had said it out of concern for her, after the debacle of the night before. But that would not be. That would not be at all.

She gave a secret smile, but poignant. The past was gone. The future was impossible. Only the present was hers.

And that was what she would claim and give to him.

Give to us both.

And she would hold it in her heart against the long, empty years ahead, when Paris was over and done with and this precious time with Leandros would be nothing more than a memory...

Leandros clicked off the TV, his gaze following Eliana as she retreated to her bedroom. He did not want her to do so, but he had given his word.

Memory came. Tormentingly. He sought to hold it back. He would not—*must not*—recall the night before...recall the feel of her naked body beneath his, her eager mouth, the sensual white-out of his instantly inflamed passion, his desire...

The bedroom door shut behind her, and he got to his feet. Sitting beside her as they'd watched the ancient Hollywood film had been both good…and bad. Good to be so close to her—bad to be so close to her. She'd sat curled up, relaxed, her hair falling from its chignon, the soft drape of her dress shaping her breasts…

It had been hard to focus on the swashbuckling going on onscreen. Hard to think of her now, in her bedroom, removing her dress, loosening her hair…

He snatched up the coffee tray and the wine glasses, taking them through into the kitchen. Busying himself, he washed them up to give him something to do—something to stop him thinking about the rashness of promising Eliana 'separate bedrooms', even though that had been the only decent thing to do after the debacle of the previous night.

Leaving the cups and glasses on the draining board, he headed to his own room. He would take a shower—tonight he definitely would.

He did so, turning the temperature as low as was necessary—which was very low. He endured it as much as he could—it was a cure, but a punishing one. He stepped out of the cubicle, seized a towel, wrapping it around his hips, grateful for its warmth. He grabbed another one, patting his chest and shoulders dry, then reached for his toothbrush.

As he brushed his teeth he felt the same heaviness fill him that had assailed him on the balcony, when she'd told him what he knew with bitter truth he had wanted her not to say.

I wanted her to say she regretted marrying as she did… regretted rejecting me as she did. That she would never do so given a second chance. I wanted her to tell me that if she got that second chance she would choose me this time…

But she had said none of that.

He frowned at his own reflection. His jawline was darkening, his hair damp from the shower. His gaze at himself was interrogating.

But that was the past—and it is the present we have now.

His own words sounded again in his head. *'Things change—they can change again.'*

Could they?

And would I want them to?

And Eliana? Would she want them to? Last night she had come to him, just as he had told her he wanted her to, in passion and desire, answering his for her. Last night he had thought that enough—thought it all that he wanted of her. But now…?

His promise to her of 'separate bedrooms', of making no more demands of her, setting no expectations on her, had negated the very reason he had brought her here to Paris with him. Negated hers for being here.

It was a promise he would honour. But tonight, he knew, as he replaced his toothbrush, would be an ordeal.

For himself.

Heaviness still weighing him down, he cut the light above the sink, saw his bleak reflection vanish, and went back out into his bedroom.

Where Eliana was waiting for him in his bed.

She saw him stop short. Sudden doubt assailed her, then vanished. She lifted her hand to him. Her other hand was holding the quilt across her breasts. Her hair was loose on her bare shoulders.

She said his name. Her voice low and tender.

For a moment he did not move.

And then—

He was there, taking her hand, pressing it tight, coming down to sit beside her, his eyes pouring into hers. They were alight with urgency—and with doubt. Searching for her meaning.

'Is this what you want? Eliana—tell me. It must be what you want—only what you want. Or—'

She did not let him finish. His low, husky voice had been fraught, questioning. She lifted her other hand, placed a finger across his mouth. The movement made the quilt slip, exposing one breast, but she did not mind. How could she? She was here for him—and for herself.

For us both.

Her eyelids dipped and she raised her mouth to his, the hand that had touched his now cupping his cheek. It was rough to the touch, but she did not mind that either, smiled at it as she kissed him.

Not urgently, or on fire, but sweetly, softly—tenderly.

She drew back, her hand in his, pressing him back. She held his gaze again.

'This is our time, Leandros.' Her voice was soft and low and very, very certain. 'This time is ours...'

Again, for a moment he did not speak—not with his voice. But with his eyes... She felt her breath catch. Oh, with his eyes he said all that she wanted to hear.

'Eliana...' He breathed her name, and it seemed to her a blessing and a gift.

A redemption for all that she had done to him and the pain she had caused—to him, and to herself. She did not ask for forgiveness, only for this. For this coming together now, as they would have done so long ago.

This is our wedding night.

The words were in her head, and it seemed they were a gift and a blessing too.

And then there were no more words, only the sweetness of his kiss and all that came thereafter, as gently, tenderly, he lay her back and finally made her his own.

She was softness, she was sweetness, she was wonder. And a delight to savour and behold...to tenderly caress and to possess. But unhurriedly and carefully...oh, so carefully.

The flame between them was a gentle one, a slow-burning one, taking its time. For why should there be a rush? They had all night.

He had one focus only: that *this* time he would make amends. Last night there had been a desperate hunger, an urgency to assuage his needs and hers. Tonight he would be as gentle, as patient, as she desired—as he desired too. And with each trace of his lips, of his fingertips, with the smoothing of her sweet delights with his palms, from breasts to thighs, and all that lay between, he would give her the slow, sensuous pleasure that he was receiving from her in return.

This was passion—oh, this was passion, indeed. But slowed to a tempo that Leandros knew with every instinct he possessed was what this moment needed. What Eliana needed.

And what I need too.

Time—just time. So simple and so precious. As precious as the little sighs of pleasure that sounded in her throat as he drew from her, slowly and sensuously, the delight that he knew he could give her, felt her own body's response to his. Slowly and sensuously, he took her on that journey with each soft kiss, each languorous caress, taking his time, cupping her breasts that swelled to his touch, trailing his fingertips along the silken columns of her thighs, the delicate folds, drawing from her yet more low sighs of soft, melting pleasure.

She wound her arms loosely around his neck, gazing up at him. There was ardency in her gaze, invitation in her smile. And when he moved his body over hers that invitation was in her body too. Slowly, with infinite care, infinite patience, he eased into her, pausing, as his lips moved across hers tenderly and reassuringly, to let her body accommodate him.

He heard her sigh—with completion, with acceptance. Felt her enclose him, hold him, fold around him. Bring him to his own moment...

He lifted his mouth from hers. 'Eliana, I can't— I can't... hold back...'

Though he had known he must be infinitely gentle, now it was impossible to deny his body the fulfilment it sought when it had found so perfect a union with her, so absolute a fusion.

Her hands cradled the nape of his neck and she smiled at him.

'No more can I,' she said, and as if a bow had been re-leased she arched her spine, her fingers flexed into his nape. Her head was going back. Face transformed.

She cried out—but not with pain. Never that—never again. With an ecstasy that pierced him to the core he felt her convulse around him, and in that moment came his.

Fusion upon fusion, they held each other as their flesh became one. As they became one...

Eliana lay in Leandros's arms. It was the sweetest place to be in all the world. Her hand was splayed upon his chest, the other wound around his waist. Their thighs mingled, tangled. His arm curved along her spine, holding her close to him, his other cradled her head against his shoulder.

They did not speak. There was no need to. No need for words. Only for this moment, this time, held in each other's arms in the velvet darkness of the night.

So much filled her. So much she could not believe her heart could hold it all. It flowed from her, enveloping him, encompassing him, binding him to her.

For this moment. For this time. For now.

This now was everything to her. All the world and more.

She was in the arms of the man she loved.

But she must lose him again.

A cry of protest rose within her, silent and imploring.

But not yet—not yet. Grant me this time—this precious time—before I must break my heart again.

She had been granted time. That much had been given to her.

A week.

A week in which to live out a lifetime of her love for him.

'Time for our treats,' announced Leandros. 'Lunch was a long time ago!' He pointed to a nearby bench. 'What about that spot?'

'Perfect,' said Eliana. She looked around as they headed for the bench. 'I had no idea the Luxembourg gardens were so vast!' she exclaimed.

Everywhere there were vistas, a mix of formal gardens and more natural—even an orchard.

'Over sixteen hectares,' answered Leandros, quoting from the tourist guide.

They settled down on the bench at the edge of the gravelled pathway. Across the gardens they could hear the happy laughter and glee of children enjoying the rides and slides, and from their bench they could see the huge stone pond, where toy boats were being sailed.

Leandros undid the ribbons around the box of *patisserie* he'd been carefully carrying since they'd availed themselves of a convenient *boulangerie* after lunch. The good weather was holding, and he was glad, but autumn was on the way. The sun was not as warm, and the leaves of the trees in the gardens were visibly beginning to turn.

But for now it was pleasant—very pleasant indeed—to sit here, legs outstretched, crossed at the ankles, his feet in comfortable trainers for all the walking he and Eliana were doing as they made their daily explorations of the city.

Contentment filled him. How could it not?

He smiled at Eliana. She was wearing lightweight trousers in dark blue, and a lightweight knit with a vee neck that showed off the delicate sculpture of her neck. Her hair was caught back with a barrette, her make-up only lip gloss and mascara. Yet his breath caught at her beauty.

With so much more than her beauty.

She was leaning forward, lifting the lid of the cardboard box holding the *patisserie*.

'The *religieuse* for me,' she said decisively, helping herself to the choux and crème confection, sinking her teeth into it as she sat back to enjoy what France was so famous for.

'I'll take the *mille-feuille*,' Leandros said, and did so.

They consumed their indulgences companionably. But then they did everything companionably. And so much more than merely companionably...

As if the last six years had never been. As if this truly were our honeymoon—the one we should have had together.

Shadows flickered in his eyes.

But she hadn't wanted that—hadn't wanted a honeymoon with him.

So why now? This time with me?

He could not think it was for the reason he'd first put to her. Not any longer. How could it be? She'd refused to let him buy any more clothes for her. Refused, even more tellingly, when he'd stopped outside a jeweller's and invited her to tell him what she liked best in the display.

'But I want to get you something—a souvenir from Paris,' he'd said.

She'd only shaken her head, then taken his hand to continue their walk.

They were doing a lot of walking, seeing all the sights, and he was delighting in showing them to her—from the

Eiffel Tower to the Pantheon, from Napoleon's tomb to the
Arc de Triomphe. They'd wandered through the Tuileries
gardens and along the Champs-Elysées, strolled through the
Latin Quarter, stopping for coffee at the cafés made famous
by the French *philosophes* and intellectuals and artists, sam-
pling the rich bounty of Paris's art galleries... There was
so much to see...impossible to do it all in just one visit.

He'd said as much over dinner one evening, at the restaurant he'd taken her to—one of the most renowned in
Paris, to which she'd worn another of the evening gowns
he'd chosen for her in a rich vermilion. It had taken his
breath away when she'd emerged from her bedroom in all
her splendour. The bedroom that was now really only her
dressing room...serving no other purpose.

Because each night—each blissful night—she was his...
completely his. Ardent and passionate, her desire matching
his. Night after night.

'There is still so much to see,' he'd said to her that night
across the candlelit table. 'Too much for a single visit.'

Had it been the candlelight flickering on her face that
had made it look shadowed? She hadn't answered him, only
smiled and praised the wine, lifted her glass.

He'd lifted his, and tilted it to her. 'To our next visit,'
he had said.

Yet even as he'd said the words he'd wondered if he
should. Wondered again now, as they emptied the box of
patisserie between them.

This time with her—could it last? Should it last?

I wanted to bring her here to free myself of her.

Perhaps he should remember that...

He closed the empty box. The delights inside, those sweet
indulgences, were all gone. Consumed.

Eliana was getting to her feet, dusting the crumbs off her.

'My fingers are all sticky. I need to rinse them in the pond.'

His were as well, and he followed her, depositing the empty box in a bin, its purpose served. The water in the pond was cool as he dabbled his fingers, shaking them dry.

'You used to pick the nuts off the baklava—'

Eliana's reminder plucked at him. That time with her back then had been as sweet as this time now. But it had passed. This time would pass too.

Maybe I should just be content with what we have now and then let it go.

Just as he must let go the poisoned past between them, he must let Eliana go...slip out of his life.

He must move on from her.

But not quite yet.

He smiled as he looked down at her, perched on the stone edge of the pond, rinsing her fingers.

'How do you fancy seeing if we can hire a model yacht to race?' he invited.

Her answering laugh, and her smiling eyes meeting his, confirmed his thoughts.

No, not yet.

CHAPTER TWELVE

ELIANA'S PHONE WAS buzzing softly but insistently, waking her up. It was morning, but early still. As she groped for it the call went to voicemail—but the number was still displayed.

Immediately, she slid out of bed. Leandros was still asleep, and she was grateful. She hurried from the room, wanting the privacy of her own bedroom so she could hear the voicemail. But after she did, she set the phone down, sank down on the unused bed, consternation in her face.

Then, her breathing shallow and agitated, she got to her feet.

She needed to go—right now.

Leave Paris.

Leave Leandros.

Leave this brief happiness that had come so unexpectedly, had been so unlooked-for—which she had always known could only be brief and soon must end.

And now it had.

Leandros sat in his airline seat, his hands clenched over the armrests. His face was tight, expressionless. But behind the mask of his face a storm was taking place.

She had gone. Walked out on him. No explanation. No justification. No attempt at an excuse. Nothing.

Except a scrawled note.

Leandros, I have to get back to Thessaloniki.

The words stabbed in his head as the plane flew on above the clouds, heading south. Stabbed him—and mocked him. Just as the past had mocked him, was still mocking him now. It was happening again. She was walking out on him, walking away. Just as she had done before.

But this time—

Why? Why is she doing it again now? Six years ago she left me to marry money—but what is there for her in leaving me now? There is nothing for her in Thessaloniki—just the scraps from Jonas Makris's begrudging table!

He closed his eyes, his grip on the armrests of his seat tightening so that his knuckles were white with it. The rest of her words stabbed at him.

We knew from the start that Paris was only to set ourselves free from the past—nothing more.

Now the stab went deeper. Mocking him even more. Yes, his wanting to be free of her, to stop her haunting him, tormenting him, had been the reason he'd taken her to Paris. He'd wanted nothing else. But now—after those carefree, contented days with her, those incandescent nights with her…

Is that still what I want?

Her final words tolled in his head.

Nothing more.

His eyes flared open, bleak and empty. And those words tolled again.

Nothing more.

Each one was a stab to his throat.

Eliana was at the bank, her face set. She was going to have to raid her minuscule pot of savings, assiduously hoarded out of what had been left of her allowance and her earnings. With a grim expression, she made the payment she had gone there to make. Then headed back to her apartment. Not that she could afford to live even there now.

She felt a flicker of unease. What she was doing was risky—but she had no choice. Her finances demanded it.

Her mind flitted back, like a magnet seeking true north, to where it longed to go—where *she* longed to go. But that was barred to her now.

I took the 'now' that was offered to me knowing that it could not last. And now that 'now' is gone.

Regret mingled with guilt—a familiar toxic mix. But now it was not for the past of six years ago. It was for the past of only the day before yesterday. But there was nothing she could do about it. Only endure it. Endure it as she had before—six years ago and every year since then. And now once more.

This time it was more unbearable. More agonising.

To break her heart a second time...

The taxi pulled up outside the run-down apartment block and Leandros got out, his face set. Why had he come here? He should have stuck to writing Eliana out of his life— again. But after one sleepless night in Athens he had flown up to Thessaloniki.

Wanting answers.

She owes me that.

The words of the totally inadequate note she had left in- cised in his brain.

Why? Why did she have to come back? After what we had in Paris...

Someone was coming out of the block, and he used that opportunity to get into the shabby lobby. The elevator had a notice on it saying it was awaiting repairs—the same notice as last time—so he vaulted up the stairs, chipped and stained.

He gained Eliana's floor. Rapped on her door.

Demanding entrance.

Eliana paused frowningly in the act of closing her suitcase. The landlord's agent? Come to inspect the premises before she left?

She went to open the door, not wanting a confrontation, but steeling herself for one all the same.

It came—but not with the landlord's agent.

She gave a gasp.

Leandros strode in, turned. But not before he had seen the suitcase on her bed, the larger one already closed and standing by the door. He took in the stripped bed, the absence of any of her belongings. His eyes swept back to hers. Skewered them.

'Moving out?' he said.

His voice was calm, but it made a hollow inside her for all that.

He filled the room—filled so much more. She hung on to the door-jamb, just to give her strength. A strength that was ebbing away like ice on a hot stove, just as swiftly. Her mouth had dried, but she had to answer him.

'Yes,' she said.

His skewering gaze pinned her. The planes of his face were stark. Only once had she seem him thus—when she had slid his ring from his finger and walked out of his life.

'I… I have to go,' she said.

He frowned suddenly. 'You've been evicted?'

She shook her head. 'No… I'm just…just moving somewhere else.'

Weakness was flooding through her—and something quite different that had nothing to do with the dismay that was paralysing her. A longing so intense she felt faint with it. But it was a longing that had no place in her life.

'Where?' he demanded.

'Just…somewhere else.'

She knew there was evasion in her voice. He'd heard it, she could see. See it in the sudden icing of his gaze. The narrowing of his eyes. The starkness of his cheekbones.

'So tell me where.'

Her heart was thudding, her hand still splayed across the door-jamb, clinging to it for support.

'It doesn't matter where. Or why.'

He took a step towards her and she threw up a hand, as if to ward him off.

'Leandros, it doesn't *matter*! It doesn't matter where I'm going, or why. It isn't…it isn't anything to do with you.'

He stared at her. 'You say that to me,' he said slowly, 'after Paris?'

Her face contorted. 'Leandros—Paris was…was… Well, what it was…' How could she tell him what it had been to her? 'But it was never going to last—and you didn't want it to either.' She shut her eyes a moment, then sprang them open again. 'Oh, Leandros…' Her voice had changed… she heard anguish in it. 'I know why you took me there. I know the memory of what I did to you six years ago has haunted you—poisoned you. At first I thought that I owed you Paris, and I was prepared to go through with it. But then… Well—' she drew a ragged breath '—things changed. Maybe…' she half lifted a hand towards him, then let it drop away '…even healed,' she said. 'Or…or something like that. Whatever it was, it was…good.' Her voice dropped. 'But it could never have lasted. It just couldn't.'

'Did you not want it to?'

His voice was hollow, as if something had been emptied out of it.

He stepped towards her. 'Eliana, what happened in Paris—it *was* good! You know it was good. We made it good. I said to you that we could change, and we did—both of us!' His voice was vehement—urgent. 'Why lose it? Why walk away from it?'

How could she answer? It was impossible.

She took another ragged breath. 'I wish you hadn't come here…chasing after me. There's no point.'

'So where are you going? Why? And why do you not answer what I've asked you?'

She could see a nerve working in his cheek, the starkness in his face as she stayed silent.

Then suddenly, he gave an oath, his expression changing completely. 'You're going to someone else—'

There was no emotion in his voice, yet it chilled her to the core. Chilled her—and handed her what she desperately, despairingly, needed.

'Yes,' she said.

For one unendurable moment his eyes held hers, and in them was what she had seen only once before, on that unbearable day she'd handed him back his ring. Then, without a word, he walked past her.

Out of the apartment.

Out of her life—a second time.

She closed her eyes, hearing his hard, heavy footsteps on the stairs heading down. As hard and heavy as the hammer-blows of her heart. Slaying her.

Leandros was in his office, but he was not working. Work was impossible, though it was piling up. Over and over in his head he could hear a replay of his last exchange with Eliana.

'*You're going to someone else.*'

And her one-word answer.

'Yes.'

One word—one single word—and it damned her. Damned her to hell. But he didn't want her in hell. Hell was where *he* was—and seeing her again would be another circle of hell for him, another agony.

How could she be going to someone else? *How* could she be leaving him? After what they'd had in Paris?

After what we claimed for ourselves.

'Healing', she'd called it, and the word blazed in his head now. Yes, that was exactly, totally what it had been. He felt it now, the truth of it filling him.

I found her again—the woman I once loved.

But now he had lost her again.

Rebellion rose up in him.

Six years ago I let her leave me. I let money be more important to her than loving me. I let her do that. I didn't challenge it... I didn't fight her for it.

Because six years ago she hadn't been worth fighting for. But this time...

This time she is.

Whatever had happened to her in the dysfunctional marriage she'd made, she had changed. She must have changed. Or else why would she not have taken from him everything she could? All that he had originally promised her? She'd refused gifts of jewellery, left her couture wardrobe behind. Walked away with nothing of what he'd offered her when he'd told her he wanted her to go to Paris with him.

And what they'd had in Paris had been *good*.

Maybe I didn't understand what was happening to me—to us. Maybe I still wasn't sure what I wanted. But now—Now I won't lose it. I won't let it go, never to return.

He felt his hands clench into fists. *This* time he would not give up on her.

He stared, unseeing, across his office. Emotion was

churning inside him. Powerful. Insistent. Focussed on one goal only.

Eliana.

Getting her back.

Eliana was back at work, back to stacking shelves, back at the till, back to fetching and carrying. She wasn't working full-time any longer, but the wage she earned was still essential to her finances. The supermarket was farther away from where she was now based, and she was on the lookout for something closer. She wished she could find something better paid, but that was unlikely, given her lack of marketable skills.

She gave a sigh. No point wanting things that were impossible.

Like wanting Leandros.

No, she mustn't let her thoughts go there, or her memories. It was like pouring acid on an open wound.

I survived a broken heart six years ago—I can survive it again. I must.

Because there was no alternative. As before, she'd made her choice—and now she was living with it.

No point complaining or repining.

Numbly, mechanically, she went on stacking shelves.

Leandros frowned. This apartment block might be in a better street than the dump Eliana had lived in before, and it was in better condition—cleaner and well-kept—but it was not what he'd expected. Had she really taken up with someone who lived here?

But it was not where that someone lived that he cared about—it was that there was a 'someone else' at all.

How could she? How could she after what we had in Paris? Did it mean nothing to her?

His thoughts darkened as he walked into the lobby. Six years ago her time with him had meant nothing to her either...

He gave her name to the concierge—at least this block had one. The man frowned for a moment, then his face cleared.

'Second floor, apartment six—opposite the stairwell,' he said. 'Do you want me to phone?'

Leandros shook his head, vaulting up the stairs.

As he gained her floor he stopped dead. *What the hell was he doing?* He'd trekked here to fight for her—thinking that *this* time she was worth fighting for. But was he just fooling himself? Whatever had happened in Paris, she had still walked away from him as she had done before.

Six years ago he'd known who she'd left him for. And why.

Last time around I knew. This time around I don't need to.

Could not bear to.

That was the sorry truth of it.

He made to turn away. He could not face this. Could not bear it. Whatever she was doing in a place like this, whoever she was with, he didn't want to know.

She's gone—and I've lost her. Lost her just as I lost her before. I have to accept it.

He twisted round to head back down, get the hell out of here.

The sound of the door of the apartment facing the stairwell starting to open—the very door he'd been about to approach—made him pause. He turned back, not wanting to, but turning anyway. As he did so a gasp sounded.

Shock. Dismay.

Frozen in the open doorway was Eliana. And she was pushing a child's buggy.

* * *

Faintness drummed through Eliana. It could not be—she was imagining things, creating a mirage out of her own mind.

Her vision dimmed—then cleared.

He stepped up to her. Leandros. Out of nowhere.

'How…?' Her voice was as faint as the faintness drumming through her.

'A private investigator located you for me. Followed you back from the supermarket you work in.'

There was no expression in Leandros's voice. But she knew that shock must be going through him, as it was her. Knew why.

His eyes dropped from her to the buggy she was clinging to. To the infant within.

A single word broke from Leandros, and his eyes flashed back to her. 'Yours?'

There was nothing in his voice. And yet there was everything in it. She didn't answer. Could not. Desperation clawed in her head.

What to answer—? What to say—?

A voice called from inside the apartment.

'Who is it, Eliana?'

There was a note of fear in the voice, and she knew why. She turned her head, called back, wanting to reassure.

'It's all right—'

But a hand was closing over the handle of the buggy. Leandros had stepped forward, blocking her.

'Inside,' he said.

It was not a request or a suggestion.

Numbly, she drew back indoors. Her mind was in freefall—but how could it not be?

He followed her in. Looked past the narrow entrance hall into the living room beyond.

Incomprehension in his face.

* * *

Slowly…very slowly… Leandros took in what he was seeing. A living room with a dining table by the window, a little balcony beyond. The room was filled with old-fashioned furniture, sideboards and cupboards heavy with ornaments, pictures on the wall, a settee covered with a crochet throw, and another swathing a commodious armchair in which a grey-haired woman was sitting, a walking stick propped up beside her chair. Beyond the living room, Leandros could see a small galley kitchen.

The grey-haired woman was speaking, sounding both alarmed and confused. Her local Macedonian accent was distinct to his ears.

'Eliana, who is this? Why is he here?'

He turned his attention to the woman. 'I am a…a friend of Eliana's, *kyria*,' he said. 'I am sorry to disturb you—but I need to speak to Eliana.'

'She was about to take Miki to the park,' the elderly woman said.

'Miki?' Leandros echoed.

His eyes went back to the infant. Maybe two years old, or three—he didn't know much about the ages of small children. The little boy was looking at him with interest in his dark eyes.

'My grandson,' the woman said.

There was pride in her voice—and doting affection too.

'We can still go to the park, Ya-Ya.'

Eliana's voice made Leandros turn back to her. She was as white as a ghost, her hands tightly gripping the handle of the buggy.

She looked at Leandros.

He nodded. Absolutely nothing here made sense. But getting out of there did.

He gave a brief, perfunctory smile to the grey-haired

woman, just to be civil, and then he was turning back into the entrance lobby, reopening the front door that he had closed. Pointedly waiting for Eliana to precede him.

'We'll take the lift,' he said.

Eliana, her heart thudding as it had been from the moment her eyes had seen Leandros, sat on a bench in the little park that was only a street away from the apartment.

It was a pretty enough place, with mulberry trees for shade, pleasant paths, well-planted flower-beds, hibiscus shrubs, and an area of grass, dry and brown in this season after summer. There was a children's play area, with swings and slides, a little roundabout and a see-saw, and a few other attractions to appeal to small children. Miki was seated on one—a colourful pony perched on a strong steel spring, rocking himself happily backwards and forwards. Rubberised flooring meant that even falling off would not be painful.

Leandros sat down beside her.

Memory pierced. How they sat side by side that afternoon in the Luxembourg gardens, into which this little urban park would have fitted a score of times over, eating their *patisserie*, watching the Parisians and the tourists enjoying themselves.

'So talk,' said Leandros at her side.

His voice was grim. And, as before, it was not a request or an invitation.

For a moment she did not answer. Her eyes rested on the little boy, oblivious to the complications and currents swirling all around him.

'I take it he's yours.'

Leandros's voice was flat. Hard. As hard as stone. Things were starting to make sense—but darkly. Bleakly.

'But who the hell is his father? Because the woman in

that apartment is *not* Damian's mother! And besides—' He broke off. 'Damian was gay, so—'

He broke off again.

Eliana turned to look at him. He was frowning.

'But you were a virgin,' he said. 'So how—?'

He took a rasping breath.

'IVF might have got you pregnant by Damian, or by any other man, but to give birth and still be a virgin…? Is it even *possible*?' He lifted a hand, then dropped it like lead. 'Caesarean delivery?'

He gave a swift shake of his head in negation.

'But you have no scar.' His frown deepened. 'Maybe you used a surrogate? Because how the hell else—?'

It was time for her to speak. What else could she do now? Only the truth would answer him.

'Miki is not my son.' She spoke quietly, the words falling slowly from her lips. 'He is Damian's.'

She didn't look at Leandros, only at the little boy still rocking on his pony, humming away to himself.

'Damian was not gay, as you supposed,' she said, and she knew that now she had no choice but to tell all—to tell everything. 'And as I let you think. He was just in love with someone else. Miki's mother, Maria. He wanted to marry her, but she worked as a maid in his father's house— that was how they met. Jonas, as you know, is a self-made man—and he was ambitious, as many such men are, for his only son. His heir. The last thing he would have permitted was his son throwing himself away on a woman who worked as a maid. Someone from the same background he himself had climbed away from. He wanted better for his son. He wanted old money…the prestige of a "good family". Mine, as it happened.'

She swallowed.

'That was why he found Damian's marriage to me acceptable. Oh, he profited materially too, by buying up my poor father's debts and ending up with his house. But my real value to him was that I made a very "suitable" wife for Damian socially.'

Her gaze rested on Damian's little son.

'That was Damian's father's reason for wanting me to marry Damian. Mine…' her voice twisted '…you already know.'

She drew another breath—a difficult one.

'As for Damian… Well, it suited him too. Marriage to me meant he could continue his liaison with Maria, the woman he'd never be allowed to marry. She became pregnant…gave birth to Miki. Damian, of course, could never acknowledge him—never do anything but conceal his existence, conceal Maria's as well. As for me… I knew from the start and went along with it, what Damian wanted of me—being a smokescreen to hide Maria behind, and placating his father with a marriage that Jonas would welcome. We agreed to it before we married.'

Her voice changed.

'I pitied Damian…felt for him. His father ruled him with a rod of iron. Damian was cowed by him—he always had been. He had no money of his own—his father held the purse strings. If he'd left me for Maria his father would have cut him off penniless. So he just made the best of it—as did I.'

She paused again. Then finished the sad and sorry tale.

'Maria was in the car when Damian crashed it. They died together. Leaving Miki with only his widowed grandmother. And me.'

She looked at Leandros.

'I can't abandon him, Leandros. His grandmother is getting on—you saw that. And she isn't in the best of health either. She has her pension, but it isn't much. I… I give her as much as I can afford from the meagre allowance Jonas makes me as Damian's widow, but it doesn't go very far. It stretches so far as paying for a childminder for Miki, because his grandmother can't really cope on her own. And after Damian and Maria were killed, I... I steered clear. Not because I wanted to, but because—'

She took a sharp, incising breath.

'Leandros, Jonas must never learn of his grandson's existence! He's never suspected it, and it must stay that way! Thankfully, the ambulance crew at the scene of Damian's car crash got Maria out first—she was still alive, I discovered—and she was taken to the ER. She died en route. So far as Jonas knows there was no passenger with Damian. But if he learnt about Miki he'd get hold of him! He'd value him now, because—illegitimate or not, and despite who his mother was—he's all the progeny he's going to have! He'd use his wealth and influence to get custody...ensure Miki's grandmother never saw him again. It would be a hellish childhood for Miki! I know that from what Damian said about his own childhood, and I've seen for myself—experienced for myself—how Jonas treats people. Miki is much better off with Maria's mother, despite her age and her not being well off. She adores him, and for her... Well, he's all she's got now, with her daughter dead.'

She fell silent. The tale was so sad...so pitiful all round.

'Ellee!'

The sound of Miki finally tiring of riding the pony made her get to her feet.

She went over to him, lifted him off. 'What shall we do next?' she asked brightly. Fondly.

Spending more time with him had been the one clear bonus of moving in with his grandmother in order to save on her own rent, as she now had to do. She might only be

Miki's stepmother—or not even that—but he was growing in her affections. And she in his.

'Slide! Slide!' he cried out, and she laughed, taking his hand to make their way across to the smaller of the two slides.

She hefted him up to the top, holding him steady. 'Ready?'

'Slide! Slide!' he enthused again.

'Whee!' she said, sliding him down, holding him around the waist to keep him steady.

'Again! Again!' he cried.

She moved to heft him up again. He was quite a weight, at just gone three years old.

'Let me,' said another voice.

Leandros was walking towards them.

'Right, then, young man,' he said, and swung Miki back up to the top of the slide, copying Eliana's safety precautions as Miki glided gleefully to the bottom.

It took a while for him to get bored, but he did eventually, and progressed on to the roundabout, and then an infant swing with an encased seat to stop him falling off. Finally, the sandpit beckoned, and Eliana extracted a small plastic bucket and spade from under the buggy, settling him down with them in the sand. He got stuck in happily, fully absorbed.

Benches surrounded the sandpit, most filled with mothers watching their children in the sandpit, but one was unoccupied. She sat down on it, Leandros beside her.

He turned towards her.

'What do I say to you?' he said.

'What do I say to you?'

The words—as inane as they were inadequate—echoed in his head.

When she had so shockingly revealed her virginity he

hadn't known what to say to her. Nor did he know what to say now—with this even more shocking revelation.

That the 'someone else' she had gone to was Miki...

And that her marriage was a farce—a lie from the very start. A lie both she and Damian agreed to. And now she has taken responsibility for a child that is not hers. A child she will not abandon and is determined to care for—whatever it costs her. Even it costs her me...costs her what we found again in Paris.

His gaze went to the small boy, playing happily in the sand. He was a nice little lad—cheerful and sunny—and Leandros watched him happily and assiduously fill his bucket with sand, then chortle as he emptied it all out again, only to repeat the process industriously.

A thought came to him, poignant and powerful.

What if he'd been ours—Eliana's and mine?

They might easily have had a child that age by now... possibly another baby as well. His eyes went to Eliana, emotion snaking through him at what he had just thought. A sense of waste smote him.

How different our lives might have been from what they are.

She spoke now. 'There isn't really anything to say.'

Her voice was even, but he could hear a note of resignation in it. Or was it rather acceptance? Or both?

'It's just how things have panned out. We make our decisions in life, Leandros—and live with the consequences.'

She dropped her eyes, letting them go to where the little boy for whom she had shouldered a responsibility she should not have had to take on was innocently playing. A callous fate had imposed it on her.

'I can't abandon him,' she said again. 'Financially it's hard, but I'm just about managing.' She paused, glanced back at Leandros, then away again. 'The...the reason I left

Paris so abruptly...' he could hear a sense of strain in her voice '...was that Maria's mother, Agnetha, had phoned me in a panic. She'd had a letter from her landlord, raising her rent or threatening her with eviction. She was so upset and scared because it was beyond her means to find the extra money, and I knew I had to get back and help out.'

She drew breath and ploughed on.

'I was already completely stretched financially, and I had to raid my savings, such as they are, to find the extra rent due. I made the decision that I could only stay afloat if I gave up my own apartment and moved in with Agnetha. It's risky—because, as I said, I don't want there ever to be any association between the widow of Damian Makris and a small child. It might start gossip, questions, speculation... and that might filter back to Jonas.'

She gave a wan smile. 'Ironically, if he jumps to the same conclusion you did, it would keep Miki safer. Jonas would just think I'd cheated on Damian and had an affair with someone else and a secret baby. Of course he'd cut off my widow's allowance instantly, but at least he wouldn't get any suspicions about Miki's true parentage.'

She fell silent again. Then spoke once more.

'I've stopped sending him to the childminder, to save some money, and cut my own working hours down, so it's only mornings. My income is less, but it was only going on the childminder anyway. This way I can bring in a little more money, and Agnetha can manage half a day looking after Miki—at least for now. I take over at lunchtime. As I say, we're...we're just about managing...even with the rent hike.'

Frustration bit in Leandros. 'Eliana, you can't go on like this! It just isn't—'

A dozen terms for what it wasn't rang in his head, but he only picked one of them.

'Sustainable,' he said heavily. 'You can't live like this.'

She gave a little shrug. 'It's the best I can manage,' she said.

She took a breath and he felt, with a start, the lightest and briefest of touches on his wrist.

'Leandros, I'm sorry that you've found out about all of this. And I'm sorry I just walked out on you as I did in Paris. But I just didn't want you to get…well, *involved*, I guess. Sucked in.'

She got to her feet, looked down at him.

'I'd better get Miki home—Ya-Ya will have his tea ready. Don't…don't come with me. There's no point—truly.'

There was a sadness in her face that tugged at him.

'I've made my life, Leandros—and it is what it is. But…'

She took a breath, and something changed in her eyes that tugged at him even more.

'But I will always, always remember our time in Paris! I will treasure it dearly. I didn't think I would—I thought, originally, it was simply something I owed you, because of how I'd treated you when I broke our engagement and became the faithless fiancée you've always—justifiably—considered me. I knew the depth of your bitterness…your contempt for me…and how could I disagree with it, after treating you as I had? But then… Well, all that changed, didn't it? I don't really know why—and I don't deserve that it did. That you should have been so kind to me, like I said out on the balcony that evening. But I'm grateful…truly I am. So grateful for those wonderful days we had—'

She broke off, her face working suddenly, and then, as if with an immense effort of will, she cleared it. She bent down, in a sudden, swift gesture, and he felt her lips graze his cheek, as lightly as a feather.

Then she turned, headed towards Miki, crouched down beside him. He watched her speak to him, and saw the little boy nod, and let her pick up the bucket and spade. She took his hand, led him over to the buggy and settled him into it, and then wheeled it off towards the park's exit.

She did not look back.

Eliana made it through the evening, but it was hard. Agonisingly hard. With all her heart she wished Leandros had not found her as he had. What could it achieve? Nothing—only the agony of seeing him again, having him physically so close to her again for that short space of time.

But he was gone again—as he must be. As he must stay.

Six years ago their lives had diverged, at her instigation. In Paris they had briefly—fleetingly—come together again. She felt her heart turn over. Just enough for her to know the truth about her own feelings. Just enough for her to taste, for that brief time, the happiness that might have been hers had she not made the choices she had six years ago.

But now that time in Paris—that oasis of what might have been—had gone as well. Their lives had diverged again—for ever. And, yet again, she must live with the consequences of her choices.

When Miki was in bed, and Agnetha had settled in her chair to watch her TV programmes, Eliana slipped from the apartment, saying she would get some fresh air, be back within the hour. Agnetha had made no remark about the visitor who had arrived on their doorstep, but Eliana had seen apprehension in her face. So she had given the woman the reassurance she knew she needed to.

'Yes, Leandros is the man I went on holiday with,' she said. That was how she'd explained it—nothing more. 'We had a lovely time, but I won't be seeing him again. My place is here, with you and Miki. You have my word.'

She heard what she had promised echoing again in her head as she caught a bus to take her to the seafront. She wanted to go there—to walk along the promenade as she had walked that evening with Leandros, after he had walked back into her life.

How much had changed.

And how little.

She stood, leaning on the balustrade, looking out over the dark sea at the lights from the city playing over its waters, hearing the noise of traffic behind, the buzz of the city. So old a city...stretching way back into classical times... changing hands so often over the course of the centuries. So many lives lived here—and hers was just one more of them.

For a long while she stood, gazing out to sea. Leandros might still be here in the city, in whatever hotel he'd booked into, or he might have taken an evening shuttle to Athens. That was more likely. Flying away, out of her life. This time for ever.

A line from a film came to her. An old Hollywood film, like the one she and Leandros had watched in Paris together...

'*We'll always have Paris.*'

But Paris, for her, was all that she would have...

All she would have of Leandros.

Through the long empty years ahead.

CHAPTER THIRTEEN

LEANDROS WAS BUSY. Punishingly busy. He had a lot to get done. He had lawyers on speed dial, estate agents on speed dial, and a firm of specialist financial investigators on speed dial. He needed to get things done—and fast.

Impatience drove him. And urgency.

And a determination that seared through him like rods of steel.

He was moving forward on all fronts and he would get where he wanted to be. Needed to be.

His phone rang and he snatched it up off his desk in the office—once his father's office, now his. He was now heading the company that had brought him the wealth that his father had been so keen for him to not jeopardise...not to share with a wife whose main interest in his son was his money, his coming inheritance.

'Any news?' he demanded of the caller—an estate agent this time.

Two minutes later he replaced the receiver, a look of satisfaction on his face. That box was ticked. Good. Time to move on the next one.

He picked up his phone again, spoke to his PA in the outer office. 'I need an employment agency,' he said briskly. Then spelt out his requirements, hung up the phone again.

OK, so what next? Time to chase that damn lawyer

again—the one that specialised in family law. He needed
answers—reliable ones—and then to set bureaucracy in
motion.

So much to do.

He needed to move faster.

*I've wasted six years—I won't waste a day longer than
I have to.*

That was the promise he'd made to himself as he'd
watched Eliana walk away from him—for the third and
final time.

Psychiko—Paris—and now Thessaloniki.

It wasn't going to happen again.

He speed-dialled the lawyer, ready to make sure it
wouldn't.

*I said I'd fight for her—and that's what I'm doing. Be-
cause now I know that however venal the reason she left
me six years ago, this time it could not be more different.*

And because of that knowledge searing through him, he
would fight for her—and this time he would win.

*Because now I know with absolute certainty that my
whole life depends on it—my whole future.*

And Eliana's.

The woman he now knew, with that same absolute certainty, he could not live without.

Eliana was in the kitchen, washing up Miki's tea things.
Miki himself was snuggled up with his *ya-ya*, watching a cartoon with her. Eliana could hear their chuckles,
and it warmed her. This was what she had shaped her life
around—that orphaned little boy and his bereft grandmother, victims of a fate that had stripped Miki of his parents, his *ya-ya* of her only child.

I took this on—I must see it through.

The problem was brutal: lack of money. If she had more

money then she could move Miki and his grandmother out of the city—install them in a little house somewhere, with a garden, space for a growing boy. But there was no money for any of that—only just enough for keeping their heads above water as it was.

Would Leandros think her impoverished, penny-pinching life now her just desserts for what she'd done six years ago? He'd been shocked by Miki's existence, but would he think it was simply up to her to deal with it?

After all, he'd let her walk away—had made no attempt to come after her. Had simply accepted what she'd told him and left her to it.

She gave an inner sigh. She must not think about Leandros. He was gone from her life, and that was all there was to it. She had a life here to get on with—such as it was.

She put Miki's dried dishes away and fetched some vegetables from the fridge to make a start on supper. Her days were very much the same—a routine she was getting used to. She got on well enough with Miki's grandmother, though they had little in common other than Miki.

A sliver of apprehension went through her. Living here with Miki and Agnetha did increase the risk that word might somehow get back to Damian's father...

The sound of the doorbell made her jump, as if she had conjured up the very thing she feared. Frowning, she went back into the living room, glancing at Agnetha and Miki, still absorbed in watching their cartoon.

She unlocked the apartment door, pulling it open.

And stopped dead.

It was Leandros.

'Hello, Eliana.'

Leandros made his voice even, as if turning up on her doorstep was an unexceptional circumstance.

She was staring at him, her hand flying to her throat, shock on her face.

'May I come in?' he asked.

Numbly, she stood aside, and he walked in.

In the living room, he nodded politely to Miki's grandmother.

'Good evening—I am sorry to disturb you unexpectedly, but I would like to take Eliana out to dinner. I hope that will not inconvenience you?'

His entry had made both Miki and his grandmother look up. An expression of interest formed on Miki's face. And then recognition.

'That man,' he announced, pointing at Leandros.

Leandros smiled at him. 'Yes, that man who came to the park with you. You went on the slide.'

'Whee!' corroborated Miki happily.

Then he went back to watching his cartoon.

His grandmother, Leandros could see, was looking across at Eliana, an uncertain look on her face.

Then: 'You should go,' she said. 'I'll be fine with Miki.'

Leandros looked at Eliana. She was looking fraught.

'Please,' he said to her. 'I thought we might go back to that place we tried last time—the fish was good.'

She opened her mouth. 'I… I…'

'Good,' he said. 'That's settled.' He smiled. 'Do you want to get Miki to bed first? I can help if so.'

His smile encompassed Miki and his grandmother as well.

'I was about to cook dinner,' Eliana said.

Miki's grandmother shook her head. 'I'll have soup later on. You go. Go on—it will do you good.'

She sounded more encouraging now, though Leandros could see she was uneasy, and wondered why.

'It will indeed,' Leandros agreed smilingly.

He looked questioningly at Eliana.

She seemed to hesitate, as if she were trying to come up with another reason not to go with him. Then she simply turned round.

'I'll need a jacket,' she said.

She disappeared—presumably into her bedroom—and emerged a moment later with a short jacket. A cheap one, from a chain store, like the trousers and jumper she was wearing. Her hair was tied in a knot on the back of her head, and she wore no make-up.

Yet she is as beautiful as the moon and the stars...

His expression softened. 'Right, then, off we go.'

He bade Miki's grandmother a courteous goodbye, saying he would not keep Eliana out late, and let Eliana lead the way out of the apartment. She said not a word, and nor did he, as they went downstairs.

Out on the pavement the air was cool—autumn was reaching here too. The taxi he'd come in was waiting at the kerb, and he gave the driver their destination as he ushered Eliana into her seat, coming in after her. She sat looking out of the window, not speaking. He let her be.

The taxi gained the seafront and cruised down it till they reached the restaurant, then pulled up. Leandros hadn't made a reservation, but like last time they were early, and there were plenty of tables to choose from.

But that was the only resemblance to the last time they'd been there—that and Eliana's cheap clothes.

Because everything has changed since then—changed totally and for ever.

And now there was just one more change he must to achieve...

Eliana felt dazed and weak. What was Leandros doing here? And what was *she* doing here with him? Here in the very same place where he had asked her to come to Paris with him, after walking back into her life after six long years.

As she had that time, she went numbly along with the business of ordering. The fare was just as last time, and she ordered, without even thinking about it, what she'd had before. Leandros ordered a beer for himself, and table wine for them both, and mineral water. Bread was deposited in a wicker basket, and the waiter whisked off again.

Eliana started to pick at her bread.

What was happening? *Why?*

She lifted her head to Leandros, who was thanking the waiter as he returned with his beer and set down a carafe of red wine at the same time with her mineral water.

'Why are you here, Leandros? What is this about?'

Her tone was calm, which was odd, because inside she wasn't calm at all. Inside, emotions were ricocheting around inside her like random gunfire from every direction.

Leandros set down his beer, looked across at her. 'I've been busy,' he said.

She frowned. What did that mean?

'There was a lot to get done, but I think I've covered everything.' He paused, then spoke again. 'Starting, I think, with this.'

He reached inside his jacket pocket, drew out a long envelope and set it down in front of her.

'Open it,' he instructed.

The frown still on her face, she did so. Her hands seemed clumsy, her fingers making a hash of opening it neatly. She yanked out the thick paper inside, unfolded it. Stared.

Not understanding.

Not understanding at all.

'It's the deeds to your father's house,' Leandros said.

Her eyes flew to him, distended.

'I bought it from Jonas Makris,' he told her. 'Oh, he didn't know it was me—I used a proxy. A very eager proxy,' he said with a wry expression on his face. 'He offered him an absurdly high price—saying how he adored houses of that period and was determined to acquire it, whatever the cost. Jonas couldn't resist—though I did tussle him down from the price he thought he could get,' he said with a note of satisfaction audible in his voice. 'I made speed of the essence, and the transaction went through yesterday. So...' his voice changed '...there it is. Your father's house, back in the family.'

He paused, clearly seeing the shock, the incomprehension, in her face.

'It's yours, Eliana,' he said.

Her eyes distended again. Not with incomprehension now, but in disbelief—swiftly followed by the shaking of her head.

'No, of course it isn't! Of course it isn't mine! It's yours—*yours*, Leandros! *You* bought it, with *your* money—of course it's yours!'

It was his turn to shake his head. 'What would I want with a house like that? I've got a perfectly good one of my own in Psychiko. Left to me by my father.' His voice changed again. 'Just as *your* father, Eliana, should have left you his house.' A hardness entered his voice. 'And not expected you to marry a man like Damian Makris to stop him losing it!'

Eliana bit her lip. 'He didn't, Leandros. He didn't expect me to do it. Never. I married Damian of my own free will—it was my choice. I told you that.' Her voice dropped. 'Just as it was my choice to break my engagement to you to do so. My choice—mine alone.' There was a tightness in her voice as she looked at him. 'I married money, Leandros—and it was my choice to do so.'

'To save your father's house for him.' That edge was still in his voice. 'To save him from financial ruin.'

Her expression changed. 'But my marriage to Damian also kept me from poverty—just like you've always thrown at me. The poverty you've always said I could not have faced had your father disinherited you as he threatened.'

She lifted her chin as she spoke. She could make no defence against Leandros's accusation—his accusation six years ago and his accusation ever since.

A flash came in his eyes. Anger. Well, she deserved that. She always had.

But his anger was not for that reason.

'That,' he bit out, 'is not true.'

He reached for his beer, took a hefty swallow of it, set it back on the table with a thud. That flash in his eyes came again.

'I've thrown it at you time and time again! And it's never been true! Because if it were—if all you cared about was a luxury lifestyle—you wouldn't be living the life you're leading now. The life I found you living the first time I tracked you down to that dump you lived in. And you're facing poverty now, taking on Damian's child as you have—'

'I don't have much choice,' she replied.

She didn't want this conversation. There was no point to it—no point at all.

The flash was there again. Fiercer still.

'Yes, you do have a choice! You could leave Miki and his grandmother to fend for themselves. And if Jonas gets hold of his grandson, what is that to you?'

'I'll never do that—never!' There was vehemence in her voice.

'Exactly! And that proves my point. You could take the allowance Jonas makes you and keep it all for yourself.' His voice twisted. 'Keep all those damn clothes I bought you

in Paris! Head back to Athens, get out and about again—
find another husband or a lover. It doesn't matter which.
Your incredible beauty would guarantee you hit paydirt!'

Her face was paling, the blood draining from it. Dear
God, did he still think that of her?

His voice changed. 'But you won't. It's unthinkable to
you.' He took a razored breath. 'As unthinkable as you marrying Damian just to keep that luxe lifestyle for yourself.'
A laugh broke from him, harsh and humourless. 'Because
you didn't marry him for that reason at all, even though it
was what I told myself, and went on telling myself these
past six years. I wanted a reason to hate you, because you
no longer valued my love! And that hurt, Eliana—dear
God, it hurt! I saw you as pampered and cosseted by your
father—overprotected. But it was the other way round—
that's what I've finally realised! It was you protecting your
father. That's why you married Damian—to protect your
father, to let him see out his days in the house he loved,
to escape the financial ruin he was facing at least for his
lifetime. You were landed with it after his death instead.
Just like your husband landed you with the son he was too
scared to claim for himself!'

'Don't blame them!' Her cry came from the heart. 'Don't
blame Damian—please don't! He was so cowed by his father—so scared of him. And my father just wasn't good with
money. Those with inherited money often aren't good—they
weren't the ones who made it, and they don't know how to
manage it. He…he did his best. But he just…well, got into
a mess. And after my mother died he was so devastated…'

Leandros was looking at her. 'I thought you cosseted…
overprotected by a doting father. But I'll say it again: it was
the other way round—wasn't it, Eliana?'

She looked away. The truth was hard to face—she had
loved her father so dearly…

'He was a good man—a kind man—but…but unworldly. He didn't even see how Damian's father was netting him, getting control over what happened to the house. And the stress of losing all his money had already given him one stroke…'

Her gaze dropped to where the deeds to the villa lay on the table in front of her.

'I'm glad,' she said slowly, sadly, 'that he never realised he was going to lose the house when he died…that it wouldn't come to me.'

She heard Leandros speak. 'But now it has.'

Her eyes flashed up. 'You know I can't possibly accept it! How could I? And what possible reason could you have for giving it to me?'

There was a veiling of his eyes. Yet they still rested on her like weights.

'Do you not know, Eliana? Do you really not know?'

His words fell into silence. Around her she could hear noise from the kitchen, hear the waiter greeting the other diners starting to arrive, conversations beginning.

Could hear, inside her, the thudding of her heart. Which was like a hammer. Drumming in her pulse.

'I want it,' he spoke slowly and clearly, for all the veiling in his eyes, 'to be my wedding present to you, Eliana.'

The drumming was deafening…drowning out everything. Making her feel faint. Making the room come and go around her.

She felt her hand taken, lifted. Heard Leandros speak again, his voice low. And what was in it was an intensity that broke her apart.

'Six years ago you walked away from me, turned me down. This time—' his fingers around hers spasmed '—don't. Just…don't. Don't turn me down again.' He paused, then spoke again, his voice husky, as if each word were painful. 'I couldn't bear it.'

Her face worked. Emotion was storming up in her, storming through the drumming of her blood. Leandros was speaking again, his words breaking through the deafening drumming of her blood, reaching for her. Finding her. Emotion was filling his words...so much emotion...

'We found each other again in Paris. Don't— Eliana *don't* let us lose each other again! When you walked out on me that second time, it was like...it was like a knife in my throat. And I knew...*knew*...that what we'd first had, all those years ago, was there again.' His voice dropped. 'Maybe it had never gone away. Just been suffocated by my bitterness...'

She turned her fingers in his. Then she spoke, her voice low and halting—and painful.

'I hurt you. I hurt you and I know I did. And I have never, for a single day, forgiven myself. I told you in Paris that, given a second chance, I'd make the same choice again— marry Damian. Because nothing would have been different if that second chance had come. If I hadn't married Damian my father would still have been facing a financial ruin I could not have borne to impose on him, and—'

She stopped.

His expression had changed. Arrested.

'And what?' There was an edge in his voice, but the blade was not aimed at her.

She shut her eyes. That drumming was still in her ears, her heart, her pulse.

'And your father would still have been threatening to disinherit you if you married me,' she said.

Her eyes flew open. Suddenly it was her hand clenching his, crushing it with her intensity.

'Leandros, did you never think how I felt when he told me that? Told me you'd be penniless if you married me? Dear God, Leandros, I *loved* you! How could I possibly

have gone on with marrying you knowing it would estrange
you from your father? Strip you of your inheritance? How
could I have done that to you?'

He was staring at her. She wanted to cry out—cry out
the dismay she'd felt when his father had made it so crystal-
clear to her what marrying his son would do to Leandros.

'So I didn't, Leandros. I didn't do it to you. I told you
I didn't want to marry you any longer and I let you say...
let you say...'

'Let me call you what I did. Venal and luxury-loving—
another Manon.' His voice was hollow. Shaken.

'It was better that you did that. Better that you hated
and despised me than felt I was only marrying Damian to
protect my father. If you hated and despised me you could
move on—set me aside.'

He let go her hand and it felt cold suddenly. But not as
cold as the chill that filled her as he spoke again. Slowly,
heavily. As if a weight were on his chest.

He drew a breath—a razored one. 'My father only said
that to test you. He'd warned me ever since I was a teenager that there would be women out there whose interest
would not be in me, but my family's wealth. He'd told me
he would test any woman I wanted to marry. Test her to see
what her reaction was. And I—I agreed with it.'

His voice grew heavier yet.

'I told myself that your rejection of me justified that test,
justified his suspicions—proved that they were not ground-
less. He told me that your father was in financial difficulties,
that your marrying me would be a good way out of them.
And when you walked out on me I thought he was right.
And then, when your engagement to Damian Makris was
announced, I knew it for certain. Money, and only money,
was your reason for marrying—marrying anyone at all.'

He reached for his beer, his fingers indenting around

the glass such that the tips whitened. He knocked back the rest of it. Placed the empty glass back on the table. Eyes spearing hers.

'I have never,' he said, 'been more wrong in my life.'

He passed a hand over his brow, as if in a weariness very profound.

'I screwed it up. I screwed it up so totally, so completely. And if I hadn't—if I'd trusted you...trusted the love I knew you felt for me—I would have refused to believe your reasons for leaving me. Challenged them—demolished them somehow. I would have—*should* have—realised why you were saying those things to me.'

She shook her head. 'But I still wouldn't have married you if it had meant your disinheritance, your estrangement from your father.'

He thudded his hand down on the table. 'But it wouldn't have! I told you—he was just testing you, that's all! If you'd stuck by me, told me you didn't care if I were rich or poor, then he—and I—would have known that it was me you loved, not the Kastellanos money! Oh, God, Eliana, we'd have bailed out your father—rescued him—and then you and I...' his voice was raw '...we would have spent these last six years together—as man and wife. The way we should have done if I hadn't screwed it up. The way...'

His voice changed, and he reached for her hand again, seizing it as if it were a treasure that was about to slip away, out of his grasp.

'The way we still can.'

That razored breath came again.

'Marry me, Eliana—marry me this time around. With all the past cleared out of the way! Paris proved it to us both!'

His voice dropped, filled now with an intensity that reached into her very being.

'It proved to me that I have never, never stopped loving

you. I tried to—tried to kill it, poison it, defile it. But in Paris it broke free of all that. Even if I still hadn't realised it, every night with you proved it—every day! And if— oh, dear God—*if*, my most beloved Eliana, in that heart of yours which has made you make such sacrifices, you can find a grain, a seed, a crumb of what you once felt for me, then… Oh, then I will spend all my life—*all my life!*— growing it in you.'

Her vision was clouding. There was an upwelling within her that was unstoppable.

'You don't have to do that, Leandros,' she said. Her voice was almost a whisper, broken in its intensity. 'Because it's there—it's always been there. Always! I thought it had gone—told myself that the only reason I'd agreed to go to Paris with you was because I owed it to you after all I'd done to you. But it was a lie! Oh, it was a lie. And when… when we came together, in each other's arms, then I knew what the truth was. I was with you, in your arms, for one reason only—because I still loved you. I love you and I always will, Leandros… Always and always and always…'

Her vision had gone completely. Tears were running down her cheeks. Her heart was turning over and over within her.

She clutched at his hand and he lifted it—lifted it to his lips, crushing it with his kiss. She gazed at him with her obliterated vision, tears still streaming. Her heart overflowing even more than her eyes.

A discreet cough sounded beside her. She looked dimly in its direction. Their waiter was silently offering her a stack of paper serviettes. She gave a laugh—a broken, emotional sound—and grabbed them, using one, then two and three, because her tears would not stop. They would not stop for there were six long years of tears to shed…

She heard Leandros speak—but not to her. He was addressing the waiter.

'I think,' he was saying, 'that she's giving me a positive answer to my marriage proposal…'

The waiter was nodding. 'Oh, quite definitely. My wife cried all day when I asked her to marry me! It's their way of showing happiness, you know,' he said kindly.

He disappeared, and Eliana went on crying. She could not stop. Leandros was crushing her hand, and she was clinging to it. Clinging to it as if were life itself. Which to her it was.

Then the waiter was there again, a bottle in his hand.

'Compliments of the house, the chef says. He's the owner, so what he says goes.'

He put the bottle on the table. It was sparkling wine, a popular Greek domestic variety, and he was removing the cage, then easing the cork. He poured them two glasses—wine glasses, meant for the wine in the carafe. But that was fine by her, because everything was fine by her—everything…

'Congratulations!' said the waiter, and disappeared again.

Leandros was picking up his glass, tapping it against hers. So she picked hers up as well.

'To us,' he said. 'And to you, Eliana, the heart of my heart, whom I let go and have grieved for ever since. And now I claim you again—with all my heart.'

He clinked his glass against hers again and shakily, tearfully, she raised hers to her lips.

'To us,' she echoed.

For finally, after six anguished years, there was an 'us'. It was finally true.

And now it always would be.

Always.

Hand in hand, they strolled along the wide Thessaloniki seafront. They were not the only ones to do so, but to each other only they existed. A great peace filled Leandros. A peace of the heart, and of the mind, and of the soul itself.

Regret filled him, yes, and he knew it always would—for what he'd done six years ago, to himself and Eliana. Condemning them to the wasted years between. And yet for all that, far more overwhelming was the thankfulness that poured through him.

He paused, turning Eliana towards him now.

'There's a line somewhere in Shakespeare's *Othello*, about how Othello "threw a pearl away"—and that is what I did. I threw you away...let you leave me without a fight... because I did not trust you—did not trust the love I *knew* you felt for me.'

He drew a breath, his eyes holding hers. They would never let her go again. 'But I will trust it for ever now—and you, my heart, my love, can trust for ever, and for all eternity, my love for you.'

In the lamplight, he could see tears welling in her eyes, and he bent to kiss them away. Then he kissed her mouth as well. She slipped her hand from his, but only to wind it around his waist, strong, possessive.

His hands went to her shoulders. He lifted his mouth away, his eyes still pouring into hers. 'Forgive me.'

His voice was low and husky. His eyes were saying all that that brief plea could not.

A cry broke from her, and her arms tightened around his waist.

'Oh, my dearest, dearest one—we've been given each other again, and that is a gift past any price.' A crooked smile curved her lips. 'Even that of any pearl...'

He gave a laugh, releasing her shoulders. 'You shall have pearls and rubies and diamonds and emeralds and sapphires and—'

She kissed him, and it silenced him. Then she spoke again.

'Leandros...money—the want of it, the fear of it—drove

us apart. With all my heart—with *all* my heart—I wish it had not been so. Had you been a poor man six years ago, and had my father always been poor, such that there would have been no call for me to protect him as I felt I had to do, then *nothing* would have stopped me marrying you. Believe me, I beg of you, that is the truth.'

It was his turn to kiss her, so he did. Gently and tenderly.

'Always,' he said.

He smiled down at her lovingly. Then his smile turned rueful.

'How I wish,' he said, 'that I hadn't promised Miki's grandmother I wouldn't keep you out late. All I want to do now…' his voice was husky, and she knew why '…is whisk you off to my hotel room and make passionate love to you until dawn breaks.'

She gave a laugh, her hands tightening around him. 'Me too,' she said. 'But first I must get back, sit down with Agnetha and talk with her.' Her expression changed. 'Are you sure, Leandros, that you're happy with what you told me at the restaurant? About your plans for how we should settle matters?'

He kissed the tip of her nose—it was safer than kissing her lips, given that he could not, alas, whisk her back to his hotel room.

'Absolutely. It will work out perfectly for all of us.' A thought struck him. 'Shall we take her and Miki out to lunch tomorrow and tell her together? We both know a good local fish restaurant here—and after our free bottle of fizz, I think we owe them some more custom.'

She laughed again. 'But you insisted they put it on the bill—*and* left a huge tip too!'

'Well, happiness makes you do things like that,' he answered.

He would have bought a hundred bottles of domestic

sparkling wine if it would have given him even a fraction
of a fraction of the happiness that was possessing his whole
being now.

He lifted her hands away from his waist—that was safer
too…not to have her crushed against him. He slipped his
hand into hers instead. Started walking forward again,
along the seafront.

How long it had taken for him to arrive here—thanks
to his own blindness and lack of trust, his fear and bitterness. But now he was here, holding the hand of the woman
he loved—the woman he had always loved, would always
love, till the last breath in his body and beyond—and no
power in heaven or earth was going to separate them again.

'My Eliana,' he said, pausing to kiss her one more time.

And his name was breathed by her in turn, with all the
love in it that was in him for her…sighed in the gentle
breath of the soft breeze lifting off the night-dark sea as
they walked forward again, hand in hand, into the future
that awaited them—waited them to possess it together.

EPILOGUE

ELIANA SAT BACK on the sun lounger. Leandros's was drawn up beside her, and both were shaded by a parasol against the warm early-summer sun. A little way away Miki was sitting in the shallow paddling pool that had now been added to the villa's main pool. He was perfectly content, splashing away, playing with his fleet of colourful plastic boats, chatting to them.

Eliana smiled to see him. He was happy here—and so was his beloved *ya-ya*. Both had made the transition to her father's villa—now hers and Leandros's out-of-city home where they came for weekends.

They often invited guests like Chloe and her new husband, Andreas—Chloe had been delighted at her reconciliation with Leandros.

Miki and his *ya-ya* lived in the little lodge where her father's housekeeper had once lived. Keeping them company was Sophie, who combined the roles of nanny for Miki and home help for his grandmother.

Hiring Sophie had been part of what had kept Leandros so busy before he'd descended on Eliana in Thessaloniki to lift her from that life into the life he wanted for her—as his beloved and adored wife. And as Eliana wanted Leandros for her beloved and adored husband, it suited them both.

And there was more that had kept Leandros busy then, which was bearing fruit now. Beyond the hiring of Sophie, and the repurchasing of Eliana's father's villa, his lawyer and his specialist financial investigator had been busy.

His lawyer had set in train Miki's grandmother's claim for formal adoption—which had gone through, with Eliana and Leandros named as guardians. Now Miki, Eliana knew with relief, would be safe from Damian's father, should he ever discover he had a grandson.

As for the financial investigator—Leandros had told her what he had found out.

'However closely Jonas had controlled Damian, it seemed odd to me that, with his having been so tragically killed in a car crash, there had not been some kind of life insurance pay-out. Well, there had—and I've been given proof of it. And proof of something more. The beneficiary, Eliana, was not Damian's father. It was you—his wife. His widow. It's a generous sum—a very generous one. Jonas kept it from you, but you have the legal claim on it—you can get it back.'

She had. But not for herself.

'This is for Miki,' she'd told Leandros. 'His father's legacy. Invest it for me, make it grow, and it will be his inheritance—set him on his way when he's grown.'

She had been glad to do it—it had been the right thing to do.

For herself she had so much.

I have everything—I have Leandros. He is all I could ever want—rich, poor, or anything in between. Because now he is mine.

And she was his—now and for ever...for ever and now.

Her gaze went to him, the man she loved with all her heart and soul and always had.

He felt her gaze upon him and looked across at her.

'It will be Miki's birthday soon,' he mused. 'Four years old.'

He paused. Let his eyes rest on Eliana. There was speculation in them, and something more—something that made her heart turn over. As it so often did whenever he looked at her for any reason at all.

'It could be time,' he said slowly, 'for him to have a step-brother or stepsister. Sadly, he'll always be an only child—but we can provide him with step-siblings. He'd like that.'

She reached for his hand. 'He would,' she said, 'and so would I—and so would you. This house cries out for chil-dren—and I was so very happy here as a child.'

Leandros lifted her hand and casually bestowed a kiss upon it. 'Then it's settled,' he said. 'One stepbrother or stepsister coming up—the moment nature can provide it.'

Eliana laced her fingers through his, letting her thumb stroke languorously across his palm.

'Nature might need a helping hand,' she said lazily, sug-gestively. 'A romantic setting might do the trick. What do you think?'

She eyed Leandros. He took the bait, just as she knew he would. They ran in harmony and always would.

'Romantic setting, hmm…? Let me think…' He furrowed his brow. 'Call me predictable,' he ventured, 'but how does Paris strike you for romance?'

She gave a soft laugh. It had been their planned desti-nation six years go, but they had never made it there. And then it had been the place where, miraculously, all the bit-terness between them had been dissolved. And after that, just before Christmas, when the air had been crisp and cold, with chestnuts being roasted on braziers in the street and Christmas markets festooned with decorations, and all the great edifices of the city illuminated nightly, Paris had been where they had gone for their true honeymoon.

And now it would be their destination again.

'Paris it is,' she said contentedly.

And Leandros laughed and kissed her hand again.

Later on, when midnight approached and they retired to their bedroom and their bed, he kissed her all over—and then more than kissed her.

Afterwards, as they lay in each other's arms, heart against heart, he cradled her.

'Might as well get into practice for Paris,' he said.

And that, thought Eliana, as sleep drifted over her and she fell, as she always did in his arms, into the sweetest dreams, was an excellent idea...

* * * * *

Were you blown away
by Greek's Temporary Cinderella?

Then don't miss out on these other passion-fueled stories
by Julia James!

Destitute Until the Italian's Diamond
The Cost of Cinderella's Confession
Reclaimed by His Billion-Dollar Ring
Contracted as the Italian's Bride
The Heir She Kept from the Billionaire

Available now!

PREGNANT
BEFORE THE
PROPOSAL

CLARE CONNELLY

MILLS & BOON

To Megan Haslam,
who commissioned my first Mills & Boon
and has been the most incredible partner ever since.

We've worked together on more than forty books
and I have adored the process each and every time,
and learned so, so much from your
generously shared wisdom.

Thank you for always seeing the essence of the
stories I wanted to tell, and helping me to
carve that out better, tighter, more emotionally.

You are a superstar!

CHAPTER ONE

LIBBY CURSED UNDER her breath at the unmistakable and unexpected sensation of the luxury yacht *moving*. Not moving in the gentle, bob-bob-bob way it was supposed to whilst moored at the marina, but rather like a bull at a gate, out of the dock, at high speed.

She stood, then almost fell, as the boat veered hard left.

Removing one of her yellow gloves, Libby placed it, along with the microfibre cloth she'd been using to dust beneath the Spanish Revival desk in the centre of the luxuriously appointed office, down on the floor and planted her feet a little wider.

They were *not* supposed to be moving.

At least, not while she was on board.

Her eyes flew to the clock across the room.

Her cleaning shift had another hour to go and Libby was supposed to be completely alone. Only she wasn't. When she'd come onboard, it had been to discover that the owner of the craft, whom she'd been told would be at an event in the city, was actually *in situ*, all swarthy, brooding billionaire.

It hadn't bothered Libby *per se*, though she generally preferred solitude—the habit of a lifetime was hard to shake.

Now, she realised there was someone else. Or many someone elses.

Outside the corridor of the office, she could hear raised voices. Shouting. Her ears pricked up, listening to the foreign language. Spanish? Italian?

She whirled around, looking for somewhere to hide, something to grab to defend herself with if necessary. She grabbed a paperweight then ran behind the desk, to hide beneath it. Many were the times in Libby Langham's twenty-six years when she'd wished for a few extra inches, but this was not one of them. The space wasn't huge and yet it easily accommodated her petite frame.

With great effort she stilled her breath, and though she was no longer a five-year-old with a penchant for playing hide and seek, she clenched her eyes shut, willing away whatever dangers might come her way.

The door burst open. More shouting—the voices of several men. Then the sound of skin connecting with skin and the slamming of the door.

She kept her eyes squeezed shut, the paperweight in her hand heavy and smooth, somehow comforting, and she waited, listening.

Footsteps.

Heavy breathing.

A curse rang through the air, gruff and hoarse, the language foreign, and yet she could easily discern it was a swearword from the harsh inflection.

Fear rose in her chest like a tidal wave, threatening to devour her.

She heard pacing, another expulsion of breath, and then a rasped, accented voice commanded, 'You can come out of there now.'

Her crystal blue eyes opened in alarm but naturally she

stayed where she was, the fingers of one hand crossing in the hope of good luck.

'You're the cleaner, *si*?'

Her heart sank, but at the same time something like relief flooded her. This was the owner of the boat; she was almost sure of it. She didn't know his name—the company had simply given her the address and hourly rate—but he'd nodded a greeting when she'd come onboard, said a curt 'hello', before returning to his work. His voice sounded close enough to the same.

She'd wondered at the time if it was some kind of Hollywood heavyweight—not unheard of in this uber luxe Sydney marina. He certainly had the looks of a film star. Though he was rough around the edges, she mused, not at all styled and primped. There was a rawness to him that was almost primal, that—

'Do you speak English?'

Her train of thought was interrupted by his abrupt query.

With shaking legs, Libby pushed up from under the desk, wiping her un-gloved hand down the front of her uniform as she scanned the room quickly.

Yes. It was the same man she'd seen when she came aboard a couple of hours earlier. He was formally dressed for being on a yacht—in suit trousers and a white button-down shirt that was pushed up to the elbows. His shoes were gleaming.

'We have a situation,' he said darkly, crossing his arms over his chest.

'So I gathered.' She was pleased to have finally been able to locate her voice. Her tongue darted out, licking her lower lip. 'What's happening?'

'Four men have taken over the—' he paused as the

yacht lurched quickly and the man's eyes swept shut '—boat,' he finished. 'Though God only knows what will be left of it when they are finished.' His nostrils flared with indignation.

'You're hurt,' she said, just realising that his cheek was bruised.

The man lifted his fingers, absent-mindedly tracing the line of his cheekbone. 'It's not important.'

She bit down on her lip. 'Do you need something?'

His brow furrowed and his eyes—a deep, dark grey—regarded her with a hint of mockery. 'Do you happen to have an ice pack in your pockets?'

'Well, no,' she finished lamely, cheeks heating at having been caught out. 'I just—'

'I'm fine,' he interrupted, reaching down and scooping up her glove and cloth. 'And next time you want to hide, you should take all the evidence with you.' He handed them to her.

Libby winced, feeling stupid, which she hated more than anything. How many stepfathers had made her feel like a fool? Some had simply ignored her; others had tolerated her with obvious impatience. Those men had been bad enough. But there were the ones who'd been genuinely unkind, who'd seemed to delight in berating Libby, in pointing out her every mistake, just because she was thoughtful and considered and liked to know what she was talking about before she spoke.

Spinning around to hide her expression, she walked a little away from him. 'Have you tried calling for help?'

'They took my phone, naturally. But you—'

'Yes, I have one,' she said, fumbling in her pocket and removing it. 'No signal.'

'It doesn't matter. The emergency number will work, it routes through satellite. Give it to me.'

It didn't even occur to her to argue. The man had such a natural authority, it was easy to believe that he could somehow make everything better.

She watched as he called, her eyes flitting every now and again to the locked door, ears straining for any noise that might indicate the pirates were returning.

He spoke with easy command, describing the boat to the last detail, plus his best guess of their current position and likely destination. He also described the four assailants, from their approximate ages to heights, plus his own location on the boat.

'I am here with someone—a cleaner.' Covering the mouthpiece, 'What is your name?'

'Libby.' She cleared her throat. 'Libby Langham.'

'And is there any family you need contacted?'

She blanched, shaking her head. No family. Not for Libby. She had been alone a long time; she was used to it. And if her mother's string of failed relationships had taught her anything, it was that being alone was preferable to the never-ending cycle of fast love and traumatic breakups. She might have been lonely, but at least she wasn't hurting.

His eyes skimmed her face for a moment, sending her stomach dropping to the floor, and then he finished the call. 'I will attempt to contain the situation before you arrive—'

Evidently, whoever was on the other end of the call didn't think that was such a great idea, but the man—Raul, he'd said his name at the start of the conversation, Libby remembered—was not to be dissuaded.

'Then you had better send help swiftly.'

He disconnected the call but held the phone in the palm of his hand, contemplating.

'What did they say?' she asked, fidgeting anxiously.

'They're sending police.' He paced the room. 'This is not the first boat theft in the area—which is something the marina should have mentioned, don't you think?'

Libby grimaced. 'It would have been nice.'

'You work here. Have you experienced this?'

She laughed, though it wasn't funny. 'Being hijacked at high speed? No. But we've literally just taken over the contract for the marina. This is only my second job on a boat,' she said, aware that she was babbling.

His intelligent eyes scanned the surroundings, assessing. 'I'm going to go out there,' he said, moving across the room, twisting the doorknob and confirming that it was locked.

'No way. That's madness.'

He arched a brow.

'You have no idea if they're armed, nor what they're capable of. The police are on their way. Just…wait it out.'

His nostrils flared. 'I was caught unawares before, but I will not be again. You stay here.'

She swallowed past a lump in her throat. 'I'm not going to let you go and take on all the risk.'

'It's my boat,' he pointed out. 'You're just caught in the crosshairs.'

'Yes, but I *am* caught in the crosshairs, so don't do anything stupid.'

'They are just kids,' he snapped. 'Idiotic, stupid children. I know, because I was one once. Don't worry. I can handle myself.'

She shook her head, wondering why she *was* so worried. After all, it was his life, his choice to do whatever he wanted with it.

'Fine, but I'm going with you,' she said boldly, earning a sharp laugh of derision.

'Very brave, Libby Langham, but I suspect you'd quickly become a liability.'

'I'm tougher than I look,' she responded, smarting from his retort. Little did he know, she'd had to toughen up from a young age.

His nostrils flared. 'Stay here.'

'No way. If you go, I'm going.'

He glared at her.

'How are you going to get out, anyway?' she pushed. 'The door's locked.'

He threw her a look. 'I'm sure I can deal with that.'

'So you're going to what? Kick it down?'

He arched a brow. 'Don't think I can?'

She shook her head. 'What if they're on the other side?'

'Then you'd better grab your paperweight again,' he said, half mocking. 'How good is your aim?'

She was tempted to ask him to stay still and she'd let him know, but her nerves were stretched to breaking point.

'I'm serious,' she said quietly. 'What's your plan? Just to go all Rambo on them?'

'Why not?'

She eyed him consideringly. He definitely had the physique of someone who could handle themselves and for all she knew, he had the skills too.

'What are your chances?'

He surprised her then by pacing across the room and stopping right in front of her. 'Let's just say I never back away from a challenge.'

'What does that mean?' she murmured. Up close, she

was aware of the way his eyes were more than just grey, they were almost silver or gold, with specks of luminescence made all the more noticeable by his thick, dark lashes, which seemed to form perfect frames.

'My chances are good, Libby. But they're better if you stay here.'

'Don't count on it,' she muttered and, though she was afraid, she knew there was no way she was going to remain hidden in the office while he went and put his life on the line.

The boat jerked hard to the left, knocking them both a little off-balance. Libby might have fallen altogether if Raul hadn't pressed out his hand and caught her elbow, steadying her, holding her just long enough to make sure she was safe. But it was more than long enough.

Heat radiated through her skin, over her body, adrenalin firing in her veins.

'Let's do this,' she said with a nod, gaze darting towards the door.

His eyes narrowed, inspecting hers. 'On one condition.'
She waited.

'Do exactly as I say. And stay behind me.'

'That's two.'

He shook his head. 'Don't make me regret this.'

'You *should* regret this,' she said. 'You have no idea—'

'We could both be dead before the police get here, the way they're steering this thing,' he pointed out. 'You think being down here and waiting for help makes us any safer?'

She bit into her lower lip, shaking her head. 'I guess not.'

'Good. So?'

'Fine,' she agreed, though she crossed her fingers behind her back. She'd do whatever she needed to in the moment, and if Raul didn't like it he'd just have to lump it.

It was obvious that he still had some misgivings but, to his credit, he silenced them, moving to the door, giving it a shake once more, then leaning closer, listening for any noises beyond. He crouched down, eyes lined up with the small gap between the carpet and the timber. It was strange to notice something so superficial in a moment such as that, but Libby couldn't help the way her eyes dropped to his bottom and lingered there, her mouth suddenly dry as she appreciated the strength of his haunches, and his overtly masculine form.

'See anything?' she asked, close to his feet, voice surprisingly thin.

'Nothing,' he confirmed.

'Okay, good.' She quickly looked away, blinking to clear her mind of the imagery of his rear end. 'That's good, right?'

He stood, tilting a look at her. 'Yes, it's good. Stand back.'

She did as he said, taking a few paces away from the door, relieved to put some space between them.

Raul turned to her. 'I don't know where they are—obviously, at least one of them is on the deck, perhaps all. Perhaps they'll hear the door opening. Be prepared for anything, got it?'

She nodded, nerves making it impossible to speak.

'Got your paperweight?'

She pulled a face. 'Are you making fun of me?'

'On the contrary, it's an excellent weapon. Keep it, in case you need to defend yourself.'

Her eyes widened. 'Do you think—'

'I don't know,' he said sharply. 'If you would prefer to stay here and let me handle this, I would welcome that choice.'

'No,' she demurred, reaching for the paperweight, then returning to the middle of the room.

He frowned, turned his attention back to the door, and ran at it, kicking his leg at the last moment, with the skill and precision of a man who might have done so every day of his life.

The door splintered a little at the frame, but it gave quickly and easily. Raul moved fast, his hand catching the door even as he dropped his foot to the floor, to prevent it from slamming loudly against the wall.

Then, needlessly, he turned back to Libby, lifting a finger to his lips to remind her to be quiet.

With a pulse that was racing so hard she could hardly think straight, she fell into step behind him. At the end of the corridor, he lifted his finger to his lips again, before pulling open a door beneath the steps.

She looked around anxiously as he disappeared inside.

A moment later, he returned with some orange rope and nets.

'Let me guess,' she hissed. 'You were a Boy Scout in another life.'

His smirk did something funny to her stomach. 'Not quite. Ready?'

She nodded, though how could she be? She had no idea what was coming next.

'Wait for my signal,' he murmured, climbing the steps stealthily. At the top, he slowed, looked around, climbed higher, until he'd disappeared altogether, then his hand appeared, gesturing for her to follow.

She did, swallowed, stumbling on one step and wincing at the noise, waiting to make sure nothing happened because of it. But the engine was too loud, and the waves were crashing against the side of the boat; there was no way they'd be heard.

They emerged onto the back of the deck.

'They're together,' he said. 'We have the element of surprise. Plus,' he said, glancing through the windows before crouching down, 'they look drunk.'

She nodded. 'You're sure you don't want to just wait?'

The boat turned hard right, and Libby opened her mouth to squeal because it tipped at such an angle she genuinely thought they might capsize. It was only Raul's hand—broad and capable, warm and strong—over her mouth that silenced her.

She stared into his eyes—eyes that were loaded with warning and confidence, that told her to be quiet, all would be well—and she found herself, weirdly, believing in him.

'We can't wait,' he said. 'Believe me when I tell you: we'll be doing them a favour too. They evidently have a death wish.'

She lifted her head the smallest amount so she could see inside the windows, and realised that Raul had been right. They were little more than teenagers. Raul and Libby had a moral imperative to save them from themselves.

She eyed the paperweight sceptically; she'd be unlikely to use it.

'Keep it,' he said, as if reading her thoughts. 'Just in case.'

And then he smiled. A smile that was dazzling and beautiful and which somehow managed to assuage all her doubts and anxieties. 'Follow me.'

In that moment she was pretty sure she'd follow him into the very fires of hell if he asked it of her...

CHAPTER TWO

HE WAS LIKE a hurricane, a phenomenon of strength and precision that came almost entirely out of nowhere, bursting into the control room of his mega yacht as though he'd been born fighting. There were four men and only one Raul, but Raul went for the biggest teenager, clearly the ringleader, shoving him away from the controls and standing with his legs braced, eyeing up the group, who looked shocked and, yes, drunk.

'Right—' he spoke with stern command '—get over there.'

The oldest, rubbing his shoulder, where it had connected with the wall, glared back. 'Who's gonna make us?'

'Believe me, you don't want the answer to that question.' His accent grew thicker. 'I am giving you a chance to end this peacefully,' he said, reaching behind them and bringing the boat to a halt. Libby saw him remove the key and slip it in his pocket.

Clever.

The feeling of stillness after such a chaotic and wild ride was a huge relief. She held her ground, wary and watchful but oddly not feeling in any danger.

Raul just seemed so completely in control, it was mesmerising.

'Yeah, well, you're outnumbered,' one of the smaller

teens said, bravely approaching Raul. 'Come on, we can take him.'

'I wouldn't bet on it,' Raul replied, and when the teen lifted his fist and attempted to land another punch, Raul caught it, twisting it quickly and sharply up the boy's back.

'Stay back,' he warned another of the group, who'd made to move closer. Then, turning to Libby, 'Come here, please.'

It took her a moment to galvanise her feet into action, but after a small pause, she skirted around the edge of the group towards Raul.

'Take the rope. Tie this one up.'

She nodded, moving as quickly as she could with fingers that were shaking, while Raul continued to restrain the teen's hands and stare down the rest of the thieves, who were clearly running out of fight.

'We didn't know you'd be on board,' the fourth one to speak muttered. 'It was meant to be empty.'

'My plans changed,' Raul snapped. 'But, either way, this was not an open invitation for you to take my boat and almost destroy it.'

'We didn't—'

He glared at the ringleader. 'Enough. Go and sit down against the wall, hands behind your back.'

Libby's pulse was racing in her ears. Was it really possible this could be over so easily?

Apparently not. At the exact moment she began to relax, one of the smaller teens lunged towards her, grabbing her around the neck, and she startled and might have screamed, except she had Raul's warning in her mind that she would be a liability and she didn't want to prove him right.

And so she thought quickly, stomped her foot down onto

the boy's toes as hard as she could, then lifted her knee and connected it with a sensitive part of his anatomy. He dropped to the ground, curled into a ball.

'Effective technique,' Raul drawled with approval. 'Anyone else want a lesson from Libby?'

'We didn't know you'd be on board,' the ringleader said again.

'And how exactly did you become privy to his schedule?' Libby demanded, emboldened by her success in subduing the would-be attacker.

'I—'

'Shut up, Jerry,' the smallest of the group shouted.

Raul's eyes locked onto Libby's with something like admiration.

'Let me guess. One of you has a friend who works at the marina.' Her eyes widened. 'Or for the cleaning contractor!' she said, snapping her fingers. 'Of course. How else would you know anything about the boat owner's commitments?'

Raul moved then to subdue the third boy, tying his hands easily before moving to the fourth. 'Sit down,' he commanded. 'And don't say anything.'

Turning back to Libby, he murmured, 'Watch them.' Then, more quietly, 'Are you okay?'

She nodded, and she was, though she could feel the start of her adrenalin turning into something else, her throat thickening with emotion at what had just happened.

Raul inserted the key into the boat and thrummed the engine to life. A moment later, they were cruising back towards the marina—at high speed, but with absolute safety and command. Libby tried not to take her eyes off the delinquents, but every now and again she sneaked a glance at Raul and felt her pulse wobble.

* * *

He'd gone into survival mode. The same strengths and instincts that had kept him alive on the streets of Spain as a runaway street kid had thundered to life once more, fine-tuning his responses so that he acted purely with one objective in mind: survival. Not just his own survival, but Libby's too.

The yacht under his control once more, the gang subdued and contrite-looking, Raul allowed himself to glance once in Libby's direction, noticing things he'd been too under pressure to conceive of at the time.

From her shimmering blonde hair to icy blue eyes, petite frame and honey-gold skin, full and pouting lips, and natural athleticism—which he'd witnessed for himself as she'd prepared to go toe to toe with the teen who'd attacked her.

Her eyes lifted to his and caught him staring. He smiled slowly, a quirk of his mouth. Her lips parted, showing a full, perfect circle, and he felt something tighten in his groin.

Adrenalin of a wholly different nature fired to life. He recognised it well.

The thrill of victory, of survival, made him feel more alive than almost anything else.

It was a thrill he remembered. Now his victories tended to be in the boardroom rather than on the streets. At first, that had been thrilling, but in recent years he'd become complacent even with his biggest corporate wins.

'We just thought—'

Raul turned his attention back to one of the teens, a stab of sympathy shifting through him.

'You didn't think,' he said quietly. 'You tried to take what you wanted, and you could have all got yourselves killed in the process.'

The teen dropped his head.

The marina was in view now, complete with flashing lights, indicating the water police were in action. He pulled the yacht towards a pontoon, concentrating on the manoeuvre as well as on the teens.

As soon as the boat came to a stop there was the sound of thudding boots on the deck and then police were bursting into the control room, sweeping it with loud noises, guns held.

'I am the owner,' Raul announced, palms lifted. 'This is my boat.'

Libby, he saw, echoed his gesture, lifting her hands.

'These are the four you're after.'

'Do you have some identification, sir?' the more senior of the officers queried.

Raul reached into his pocket and removed a slimline wallet, from which he brandished a driving licence. The officer took it, looking from Raul to the photograph then nodding.

'And you?' He turned to Libby.

'She's with me,' Raul said, surprised at the possessive heat that stole through him. Then again, Libby had stood shoulder to shoulder with him in the midst of whatever danger might have befallen him. Naturally he felt a connection with her.

'Righto. Take 'em out,' the officer said with a nod. 'I'll need you to make a statement. Do you require medical attention?'

'He was punched,' Libby said, and Raul almost laughed at her concern.

'I'm reasonably sure I'll survive though,' he drawled, moving closer to her unconsciously. 'Are you okay?'

She nodded once.

'So you're happy to make a statement now?'

Raul looked down at Libby. She was shaking. Predictably, shock was setting in.

'A brief statement,' he said with a nod. 'And by brief, I mean five minutes. I can provide more tomorrow.'

The officer opened his mouth as if to argue but then he nodded. 'Of course.' He pulled out his notepad and asked for the bare outline of events. Raul detailed what had happened. Libby nodded. It was over quickly. The officer handed Raul his card. 'If you remember anything else, give me a call.'

Raul's eyes glittered. 'Count on it.'

As quickly as it had begun, it was over. The officers left, the sirens stopped, and they were alone. Libby's adrenalin had completely evaporated now and she found herself shaking from head to toe.

'I...should go,' she said, turning to Raul, frowning, because it had truly been the strangest afternoon of her life.

'No, I forbid it,' Raul responded, his lips twisting in a half-smile, yet his voice was deathly serious. 'Sit.' He guided her into the captain's chair then disappeared, returning a moment later with a blanket, which he wrapped around her shoulders, before leaving once more.

When he came back it was with a tumbler of Scotch. 'Drink this.'

Libby wrinkled her nose. 'I'm not really one for hard liquor.'

'Desperate times,' he said, with a quiet gentleness to his voice.

Her gaze was drawn to his and something exploded in her chest. It was the strangest feeling! As though something in the very depths of her soul recognised something within him, calling to her, making her trust him implicitly.

She reached out, taking the Scotch, eyes latching onto his and holding as she lifted the tumbler to her lips and tasted it. Shuddering a little, she let the liquid touch her tongue, discovering there was something pleasing about it after all, something steadying to her nerves. She scrunched up her face and drank the rest, then coughed as it hit her palate like a Molotov cocktail.

'Okay?' He patted her back as he asked, crouching down beside her, and this time, when their eyes met, everything inside her seemed to jolt into place. She was floating and flying all at once. Her bones seemed to turn to jelly.

She nodded, but she was shaking. From the terror of what had just happened? Or from something else?

Strangely, she hadn't been afraid. Not once they'd entered the room and she'd seen how in control Raul was. He'd made it all seem fine. Somehow, she'd just known he would triumph. He had a quality; there was something inherently trustworthy about him, something Libby had never really experienced first-hand in a man. Not her father, whom she'd never known, not any of the men her mother had dated, and not her first—and only—boyfriend.

She stared at Raul because it was impossible to look away.

'I feel—' she said, pressing a hand to the middle of her chest, frowning as she searched for the right word.

His eyes were shuttered, impossible to read. But something was bubbling up inside Libby. An awakening, something that was vitally important. It caught her completely off-guard because it ran contrary to all of her usual instincts. Having seen the way her mother flung herself headlong into romantic entanglements, Libby had very,

very carefully always been the exact opposite. Oh, she wanted love, she craved it in many ways, but not like her mother had. When Libby fell in love it would be for keeps, with the right kind of man. Someone kind and gentle who wouldn't hurt her. She'd certainly never give in to something as superficial and unreliable as physical chemistry!

Yet now she felt desire running through her like a current, sucking her along with it, hypnotising her and seducing her, making her want to act on these impulses despite her better judgement. Was this what it had been like for her mother?

'Raul,' she said desperately, moving her hand from her own chest to his. 'You were incredible.' She heard the awe in her voice, the admiration, wondered if she should contain it, act cool or something. But she couldn't. 'I feel more alive than I've ever felt,' she said, smiling, and when his gaze dropped to her mouth she was propelled forward. There was an inevitability to it, a sense of rightness, and before she could overthink it and listen to the warning instincts that had kept her safe from heartbreak all these years, she brushed her lips to his, seeking connection.

She'd half-expected him to pull back. She felt him stiffen and knew he hadn't been anticipating her action. She hovered there, lips pressed to his, but not deepening the kiss, just breathing him in, wondering if she'd just made a colossal, embarrassing mistake.

But then, as if the same inevitability was driving Raul, suddenly he was kissing her too, with a visceral growl ripped from his chest, a hand coming to cup behind her head, holding her there for his pleasure, his tongue rolling hers, his lips commanding, demanding, perfection. They moved as one, her standing, or being pulled to standing, by Raul, his hands drawing her closer, into his chest, which was broad and rugged, and through which she could feel his heart beating rapidly.

It was like the bursting of a dam.

The tension and the danger of the preceding thirty minutes had accumulated to form a ground swell of need that was threatening to devour Libby, but in Raul there was salvation, there was relief.

His hands moved deftly, removing her clothing, and she didn't question how out of character this was, how strange; she simply went with the flow, surrendering to a moment that was so much bigger than her.

His chest was bare beneath her hands; she realised she'd done that, shucking his shirt then moving to his trousers, which he stepped out of at the same time she pushed at them. There was desperation in their movements and now they knelt in unison, then his body was over hers, hungry, urgent, his mouth demanding, his hands roaming her skin, touching every inch of her, worshipping her breasts until she could hardly breathe, his mouth following his fingers, chasing his kisses. She felt as though everything was spinning too fast, like she couldn't focus on anything beyond this.

But then he was moving, his body gone, and confusion swamped her. She pushed up on her elbows, watching as he unfolded his wallet, removed a condom and pressed it over his length.

Her eyes widened, because he was huge and she hadn't done this in a long time, and even then only a few times, and hadn't really enjoyed it, so in the midst of the inevitability of this, something sharp jabbed her consciousness, making her doubt.

She should stop this.

She wasn't her mother.

She'd learned her lessons all too well.

Except she hadn't, apparently, because she was burning up with need and desire and her brain refused to listen. Raul came back to her, and so did her certainty, her need, pushing everything else away, so when he separated her legs with his knee she felt only excitement. Then he was pushing into her and she was crying out with a surge of something she'd never known before, as all the life-affirming feelings of relief, adrenalin, need and power thrilled in her veins. He kissed her as he moved and she wrapped her legs around his waist, the sublime perfection of this moment somehow totally appropriate after the strange detour her day had already taken. Later, she'd probably wonder what had come over her, but for now, all Libby could do was lie there and enjoy the best pleasure she'd ever known…

'Well,' he drawled, moving away from her with true regret but knowing he needed to put some distance between them if he were to have any hope of regaining his sanity. 'That was unexpected.'

To his relief, Libby smiled. A slow, sensual smile. 'Which part? The boat being stolen, or the sex?'

Amusement flickered in the pit of his belly. 'Both.'

'Agreed.' She looked around the control room, her lips turning down as the wild tangle of their clothes became evident.

'I think in the heat of the moment—'

'The relief of having survived,' she agreed, nodding.

He was glad she was being so sensible, that she saw things as he did, so why was there also a hint of frustration that she was so quick to dismiss this?

Raul was flying out of the country the next day, it

wasn't as though he could offer her anything more, not like he would want to, anyway.

'It was all...surreal,' she said with a lift of her brows.

'But wonderful,' he murmured, pulling on his shorts and crouching down. 'The second part, anyway.'

Heat flushed her cheeks, a sweet innocence that made him wonder how often she did this sort of thing. She hadn't been a virgin, but there was something about her totally unguarded responses that made him wonder...

He shut down the thoughts.

He didn't wonder about the women he slept with. He didn't postulate on their private lives. He had sex, and he moved on.

'Are you okay?'

She nodded, expelling a soft sigh.

'I mean after the whole boat hijacking incident. No injuries?'

She shook her head.

'Sometimes, these things can build as a trauma inside of you. If you should find you experience this, and need help, I want you to let me know.'

Her eyes widened. 'I'm sure I'll be fine,' she mumbled.

'I am too. Nonetheless...' He moved to his wallet, ignoring the other condom in there with great willpower. 'Here's my card.'

She took it without looking down. 'Thanks.'

He nodded once, feeling that at least he'd done his duty there. 'Suffice it to say, I'll cover any expenses. Therapy, whatever you need.'

She laughed then. 'Raul, it's fine. I'm fine.' She stood, retrieving her underwear, dressing with a litheness of movement that made his mouth dry. She was so effortlessly graceful, she was beautiful to watch.

He frowned. 'Would you care to have dinner with me?'

Her eyes widened as though it was the last thing she'd been expecting him to say. And wasn't that true for him too? Dinner? After sex?

He could only put the uncharacteristic offer down to the bizarre day he'd had.

'It's too early for dinner,' she pointed out, waving a hand towards the sky. She was right. It probably wasn't even six yet. 'And I'm not hungry.' She finished dressing. 'I'll just get my things and go.'

After the storm came the calm, and in that calm she had space to freak out, just a little, at what had happened. While sleeping with Raul had been incredible, it had also been totally unlike Libby, and she found herself jangling with nerves and needing some space to be alone.

The idea of sharing dinner with him made something ache in the pit of her stomach. She couldn't say why, only that she felt his gravitational pull and saw danger in it, a danger that surprised her with its intensity, because a moment ago she'd been thinking that he was safety and trust personified.

Frustrated with her ambivalence and lack of clarity, she pushed a bright smile to her face, hoping it radiated with a confidence she was far from feeling.

'Well, it was…nice…if somewhat strange, to meet you,' she said, and she held out her hand. It might have seemed like an odd thing to do, having just slept with him on the floor of his boat, but Libby needed to reassert herself as a confident, sensible woman—the exact opposite of her mother in every way.

'You too, Libby Langham.' He took her hand and a shiver ran all the way from her fingertips to her heart, making her tremble. She quickly pulled her hand away and spun before he could see it. She needed to get out of there.

'You can't be serious?' The police detective regarded Raul as though he'd sprouted three heads.

'Why not?' Raul didn't move, not even a little. He held his expression, his stance and, most of all, his mettle.

'Well, it's just...unusual, that's all. I mean, they tried to steal a multi-million-dollar boat from you,' the detective pointed out, drawing a hand through his hair before gesturing towards Raul's face. 'Clocked you on the cheek. And you're offering to pay their school fees?'

'I'm offering whatever assistance they need,' he confirmed with a nod. 'I would like you to arrange a meeting with their parents for this afternoon.' He flicked a glance at his watch. He'd be flying out later tonight, so there was limited time in which to wrap this up. But having grown up poor and on the streets, Raul had also done things in his youth of which he was ashamed. He knew how easy it was to take a wrong turn in life, to make a mistake, particularly when no one believed you were capable of more. It was because of one couple's act of faith in him that Raul's life had forked in a better direction, and it was for them that he now tried to offer hope when he could to other children in similar situations to what his own had once been.

'These boys have been in and out of trouble most of their lives,' the detective repeated incredulously.

'All the more reason to try something new. Arrange the meeting—if they want help, I'm going to give it.'

He left the police station, satisfied with the steps he was planning to take for the youths, knowing it was the right thing to do. And yet there was a sense of impatience in his belly too, a feeling of wanting more.

Of wanting Libby.

His mind flashed back to the boat, to their time together, and he closed his eyes for a moment as a wave of desire washed over him, remembered pleasure holding him completely in its thrall, and then he was moving, determinedly pushing the whole experience from his mind and focusing on his next destination, his next conquest, his next challenge. Raul didn't look back, he didn't do repeat experiences and, most importantly, he didn't stick around anywhere—or anyone—long enough to get attached.

CHAPTER THREE

Three months later

IT WAS A miracle she'd even kept the business card, because Lord knew she'd had no intention of calling Raul for help. Perhaps it had been a sort of talisman, proof that she hadn't imagined the whole thing. Yet she hadn't looked at it again. She'd placed the card into her wallet and then ignored it.

Every time she'd gone to pay for something, her fingers might have glanced over the edges of the thing, but she'd never once weakened and removed it, looked at it and invoked an image of Raul Ortega. Then again, she hardly needed a business card for that.

He was burned into her brain in a way she found quite frustrating, given the brevity of their acquaintance. She only had to close her eyes to see his, to remember the way he'd felt, smelled, tasted…

And now, she thought, with a whole heap of butterflies terrorising her belly, what was she to do?

She glanced down at her lap, to the white stick with two bright pink lines, and felt a desperate sense of panicked disbelief rising inside of her.

Pregnant!

How could it be?

They'd used protection!

It had only happened once!

They barely even knew each other!

It was… She shook her head. Inevitable?

Even as she thought it, she knew it was stupid, and wrong. Nothing about this should have been inevitable. It shouldn't have happened.

She groaned, pressing her head back against the threadbare sofa cushions, tears filling her eyes even as a protective hand shifted to cover her still-flat stomach.

It was history repeating herself, she thought with a groan. Libby had been an accident too. She'd been raised by a single mother, had never known nor met her father. She'd never even been sure her mother knew who he was. If she had, the older woman had scrupulously avoided revealing that to Libby.

She patted her stomach, the connection she felt to the burgeoning life unmistakable and immediate. It was something she'd never really felt before.

She'd loved her mother, almost out of a sense of obligation. Children loved their parents—that's just how it was. Only they'd never been close, and now that Libby looked back she recognised that she'd been the responsible person of the household for almost as long as she could remember. Grocery shopping and meal preparations had mostly fallen to her, so too the cleaning. Between school and those domestic duties, Libby had been too tired for a normal teenage experience, and as for thoughts of university…? No way. It wouldn't have been possible.

And now, just when she felt like her life was stabilising, she was looking down the barrel of single parenthood, with no possible support network, no safety net.

Just like her mother had been, she realised with a groan. After all her best endeavours to be *different*, to make different choices, to live a different life, here she was facing the exact same predicament.

It horrified her.

Libby wrapped her arms around her chest, shivering despite the warmth of the day, then flicked another glance at Raul's business card.

She was terrified to tell him, terrified not to tell him: she was simply terrified in every way.

New York glittered like a million stars, bright and beautiful, but Raul barely saw it. He'd sworn he'd never take things like this for granted. Not when he was working his ass off to get ahead, not when he was on his way up. But success and wealth were impossible not to become accustomed to, and after almost a decade as a billionaire, nowadays, Raul didn't tend to see the opulence and rare privilege afforded to him.

The stunning vista was simply a backdrop to the work he was doing, and he had more interest in his computer screen than the Empire State Building.

When his phone began to ring, he was tempted to ignore it, except it was his most private line, the number he gave out only rarely.

If someone was calling him on this number, it was important.

He reached for the receiver, cradling it beneath his chin. 'Ortega,' he grunted into the phone, eyes still lingering on the screen.

Outside, it had begun to snow, little drifts of white dancing in front of the window, but he didn't notice. If he'd moved to the glass and looked all the way down, if he'd been able to see so far beneath him, it would have been to appreciate the looks of wonder on children's faces, delight all 'round.

'Hello?' he prompted, impatient now. He had until mid-night to file these documents; he didn't intend to miss the window.

'Erm, hi.' The voice was soft and familiar, even though he couldn't immediately place it. Yet his body reacted, his gut tightening, something popping in the depths of his belly.

'Who is this?' he asked, guarded. Anyone who could make him react so instinctively deserved his wariness.

Silence.

Heavy breathing.

He gripped the phone more tightly, but then there was simply a dial tone.

Whoever it was had hung up.

Now he did stand, jack-knifing out of his chair and striding towards the window, standing with legs wide and hands in his pockets, staring out, not seeing. A sense of unease slipped through him, as though he'd just missed something, or someone, important.

Libby knew she was being a coward, but hearing his voice again had flooded her with such a ball of tension she could hardly think straight, much less speak.

On the day they'd met, she'd been blown away by his sense of command and authority. But those same things had flown down the phone line when she'd called him, and they'd knocked her sideways.

She couldn't help but feel that she was about to throw a bomb into his life, and all that natural authority would be turned on her. She needed to form a more definitive plan first, so that when she did tell him about the baby, and he asked what she wanted to do, she could respond with a degree of certainty.

* * *

It was in the small hours of the morning that the answer came to him.

Strangely, it wasn't so much her voice as the husky little breaths she'd exhaled into the phone line. They'd been familiar in a primal way, triggering a sense memory that had lain dormant for months. But once back in the privacy of his home, naked in his bed, he remembered, and a hot flash spread through his body as every cell reverberated with surprise. Surprise at the pleasure he'd felt at hearing her voice, at the knowledge that she'd called him after all.

And then concern. Because if she was calling him, surely it meant something was wrong.

When he reflected on the details of the day, contemplated how traumatic it must have been for Libby, he knew he needed to make sure she was okay. He should have done so before now, he realised with a sense of shame, only he'd never taken her phone number, he'd simply given her his.

And she'd used it.

No longer tired, despite the fact he'd been up since early the previous morning, he pushed back the sheet and began to make plans, setting things in motion so that he could assure himself Libby hadn't suffered as a result of that day...

So the morning sickness wasn't just for mornings, Libby thought with a shake of her head as she gingerly straightened and stared at her reflection in the bathroom mirror. Having battled nausea all day, finding her appetite almost non-existent, she'd forced herself to eat a piece of Vegemite toast when she got home from work, simply because she figured she had to have something for the sake of the baby, but it hadn't settled her tummy as she'd hoped.

Quite the opposite.

The only silver lining was that she felt marginally better now, having showered and changed into a singlet top and floaty skirt. She was well enough, finally, to contemplate a cup of tea. Moving to her kitchen, she flicked the kettle to life and stood, waiting for it to boil, eyes on the view beyond the kitchen window. At first glance, it was hardly inspiring. Just a brick wall to the neighbouring building. But it was the details that made Libby's heart lighten. The bougainvillea that clung to the sides, bursting with green leaves and bright pink flowers, the graffiti someone had done a few months back, a picture of a puppy dog in a hot-air balloon, and the way one of the residents had artfully strung their laundry from their window to a back fence, surely in contravention of some building code or other, but from where Libby stood, the sight of the summery linen clothes drying on the line was like a still-life painting.

The kettle flicked off and she splashed boiling water into the cup, watching as the colour seeped from the bag and into the tea, stifling a yawn. She was always tired at the moment, though doing double shifts at work every day for the last week hardly helped matters.

Nonetheless, Libby was abundantly conscious of the ticking time bomb of her pregnancy. She needed to start saving—and fast—if she was going to be able to take off a few months when the baby came.

And then what?

Her mind began to spin so fast she felt giddy.

She needed to find a job she could do from home, that much was clear. Cleaning for the agency was off the cards. She could take in ironing—another skill she possessed in abundance—but the idea was anathema to Libby. While she *could* iron, she hated it, and knew she'd turn to that only as a last resort.

So what else was there?

She flicked a glance over her shoulder at the fridge, where the pamphlet for the local adult education campus was printed. She'd circled the bookkeeping diploma months ago, even before she'd met Raul and shared that one fateful afternoon with him, but the idea of undertaking night school and picking up that skill was both terrifying and somehow imperative.

Could she do it? Libby bit down on her lip, pressing a hand to her belly.

The truth was, she didn't know. She'd never had the luxury of pushing herself academically. Her mother had wanted her to drop out of school in grade ten, so she could start 'contributing' to the household financially. Libby had held fast though. There weren't many things she'd been willing to go into bat for, but graduating high school was one of them. It had been exhausting and stressful, and she knew deep down that she could have got much better grades if she'd been allowed to study at night, but she'd had to content herself with passing.

But now? What was stopping her from enrolling in a course? True, it would be exhausting, but at least she'd have a sense of accomplishment, and the prospect of being able to support her child.

She pulled the milk from the fridge and added a splash to her tea, but midway through returning the bottle there was a sharp knock on her door. Her heart started at the unexpected interruption and she glanced out of the kitchen window, but whoever it was had moved into the alcove, shielding them from sight.

Desperate for her tea, she took a quick sip, exclaiming a little when it scalded her tongue, then moved through the small apartment to the door, wrenching it inwards with a polite smile on her face…

Which immediately dropped at the sight of Raul Ortega on the other side.

Her lips parted and everything went wonky in her mind. Libby's eyes seemed to fill with bright, radiant light.

'Raul,' she breathed out, gripping the door more tightly, needing it for strength and support. 'What are you doing here?' she whispered, blinking quickly. Was she imagining this?

'You called,' he responded, and Libby's heartrate ratcheted up.

'Oh…' she mumbled, her tummy twisting painfully.

'I presumed you needed something.'

Anxiety burst through her. He wasn't supposed to be here! This wasn't a conversation she wanted to have face to face. Or at all, if she could help it. Except she'd known, almost as soon as she'd discovered her pregnancy, that she wouldn't keep her child from his or her father, nor the father from her child. While Libby intended to be the primary caregiver, she would never stand in the way of the formation of such an important, foundational relationship.

So of course she *had* to tell him, and she had fully intended to, when the time was right. She just needed to build her courage up.

Except he was standing right in front of her, staring at her, lips pursed with a hint of impatience, and all the air whooshed right out of her lungs.

'Raul,' she said, as though it were a lifeline. As though by repeating his name everything might start to make sense.

But it didn't.

Had he come to Sydney just because she'd called? Or

had he already been here? Surely the latter. There was no way he would have flown to Australia on the back of a ten-second call that essentially amounted to a prank.

Was it possible they'd been in the same city for weeks, months, and not known that a new life was forming of their inadvertent creation?

Sweat began to bead on the top of Libby's lip. She thought longingly of her tea.

'Why did you call?'

It was so imperious, so demanding. Just like she'd known him to be, only then his commanding nature had all been focused on the delinquent boys who'd stolen his yacht.

'I—' She darted her tongue out, licked her lower lip. Libby had never felt more terrified in her life. Strange, when she'd been mentally gearing herself up for this conversation for over a week. As Raul's eyes dropped to her mouth and chased her tongue, though, something began to fizz in her belly then spread to her bloodstream, filling her with a tangle of emotions she couldn't fathom.

She sucked in a deep breath, tried to steady her nerves. 'You'd better come in,' she said, aiming for decisive and coming off loaded with dread. She cleared her throat. 'This…won't take long.'

His brow furrowed and he jammed his hands into his pockets, but he nodded once, curtly.

Curtly!

Her stomach dropped to her toes. She spun on her heel and moved inside her apartment, immediately ashamed of how shabby and small it was, aware of how it must look to his eyes. It had come partially furnished, so the sofa and small table weren't hers. She'd done her best to brighten up the place, covering the card table with colourful fabric and the sofa with a blanket she'd bought at an op shop, but it was, nonetheless, unmistakably cheap.

Not that she had any reason to apologise for her financial circumstances. If anything, Libby was proud of how she'd pulled herself up by the bootstraps. But Raul was... different...to anyone she'd ever known. Somehow, she didn't want him seeing her through this filter.

'I've just made a cup of tea. Would you like something to drink?' she asked nervously, pacing into the kitchen and wrapping her hands around the mug.

'No, thank you.' His frown deepened. 'How are you?'

'Fine,' she lied. 'Just fine. And you?'

He paused. 'Yes, also fine.'

But this was a disaster! Everything felt so strained and different to how it had been on the boat. Then adrenalin and adventure had been a great equaliser. She'd been emboldened by their shared experience, made brave and powerful by what they'd been through and how she'd shown her strength. Now her stomach was in knots and she had no idea how she could possibly get through the next few minutes. Only she knew she had to—somehow.

'Why did you call me, Libby?' he asked again, propping one hip against her kitchen counter.

The kitchen also showed signs of disrepair, but it was Libby's favourite room of the house, for the view it had of the beautiful bougainvillea and the way she'd brightly accessorised it so every surface popped with colour.

Drawing as much comfort from her surroundings as she possibly could, Libby sucked in a deep breath. 'I... thought you should know...' she began, then sipped her tea quickly. It had cooled down just enough to be palatable without burning.

'Yes?'

Her teeth pressed into her lip. 'God, this is way harder than it should be,' she said on a humourless laugh. If only he knew how much this was her worst nightmare. Not being pregnant, but all the circumstances surrounding it.

'Libby, are you okay?'

'No,' she groaned, placing her tea on the bench. 'Not really.' She frowned. 'And yes, at the same time.'

'That makes no sense.'

'I know,' she said softly, sucking in a deep breath. 'The thing is...' She stared at her tea rather than into his eyes, which were too perceptive, too inquisitive. Too *everything*. 'The thing is,' she started again. 'That day...'

Silence fell, except for the ticking of the clock, which sat on the kitchen bench. Strange, she'd never really noticed how imperious and loud it was before. Every second cranked noisily past.

'Raul, I'm pregnant,' she said finally, the words, now she'd committed to saying them, rushing out of her. 'Three and a half months pregnant, in fact. You're the father.'

CHAPTER FOUR

RAUL HAD OFTEN heard the expression 'the bottom fell out of someone's world', and he'd always thought it to be a slightly indulgent concept. He'd experienced many shocks in his life, many turns of event which had required him to dig deep and find his inner strength and determination, but he'd never once believed the bottom could fall out of his world.

Until that moment, when everything in his life lost its familiar shape and context, even his own self.

The universe shifted.

No! he wanted to shout. He wanted to reject her statement with every cell in his body. He wanted to pull apart the universe with his bare hands and shake this reality away. He *couldn't* be a father. Not to anyone. He couldn't be anything to anyone. He was a loner. Born that way, raised that way, he was better on his own.

His breathing grew rough and he stared at Libby, as if just by looking at her he could undo the words she'd spoken, or make better sense of them. As if by staring at her he could make sense of anything.

Her head was bent and the sun sliced through the kitchen, bathing her head in gold, like a halo. His eyes dropped of their own accord to her stomach. It was flat and neat, just as he remembered from that afternoon. She was naturally slim, but as he lifted his gaze back to her face his attention lingered on her breasts. Was he imagining them to be more rounded than they had been then? Was that proof of her assertion?

Was there any likelihood this wasn't true?

Why would she lie?

He'd used a condom, but that wasn't foolproof. He lifted a hand to his jaw, rubbing it across his chin, staring straight ahead without speaking. He'd been knocked sideways by her statement, but now his brain was clicking back into gear, spinning furiously fast in an attempt to analyse this properly.

She was clearly poor.

Her choice of occupation was hardly well paid, and her apartment was further proof that her means were stretched. Pregnancy might seem like a way to get some extra cash. Was that her end game?

Not that she'd planned this, of course. How could she have? The entire thing was spontaneous, brought on by the dramatic events of that day. He'd ensured, as he always did, that protection was used. He didn't ask if she was on contraception, he'd simply assumed a woman of her age would be, but that was obviously a stupid miscalculation.

'I see,' he said eventually, the words flattened of any emotion, even when he felt this news in the very core of his being.

Her head remained lowered, eyes shielded from him.

His brain whirled even as his body was in the midst of a classic fight or flight response.

Raul's instincts were shaped by his own experiences, but he would not betray them until he understood Libby's intentions, until he understood himself better too. A baby was just about the worst thing that could happen to him—

he'd never wanted children—and yet…even as he knew that to be true, there was something about this news that was punching him hard in the gut, making him fight for the child he'd never even wanted.

'And?' he asked, waiting with the appearance of patience.

Her eyes finally lifted, met his, and something jolted inside of his gut.

This was the mother of his child. They barely knew one another, yet here she was, standing in front of him with the face of an angel, telling him they'd made a baby together. A primal, fierce possessiveness fired in his blood.

'I never knew my dad,' she said, lips pulling to the side. 'I didn't even know his name.' Her brow crinkled as she contemplated that. 'I don't need you to be involved. I don't need you for anything,' she added, tilting her chin defiantly. 'But I did think you deserved to know. And our child will know about you too. Whatever capacity you choose to be in their life is up to you, and them, when they're old enough to decide.'

For the second time in as many minutes, the bottom fell out of his world.

It was a new sensation and he didn't like it at all.

She'd started the conversation with such uncertainty but, having made her pronouncement, she'd really taken the bull by the horns. Could she have any idea how deeply unsettling her description was to Raul?

Of course not. How could she?

He was being forced to grapple, at lightning speed, with something he hated the idea of yet now had to accept as reality. She was, on the one hand, offering him a way out. He could provide her with money so she could live comfortably and raise this baby without him.

But not wanting a child was not the same thing as being

willing to ignore his own child, now that it was a reality rather than a theoretical scenario. The very idea was anathema to Raul, and he didn't have to be a psychotherapist to understand why.

No one had fought for him. No one had protected him. And no child of his would experience what he had—not while he had breath in his lungs.

'You are suggesting that you will raise the child by yourself?' He heard the derision in his voice and knew it was the wrong approach, but his emotions were moving beyond his control.

'Why not?' she asked, crossing her arms over her chest. His eyes dropped to her breasts before he could control the reaction. When he looked at her face once more he saw pink in her cheeks and something stirred in his groin.

He forced himself to hold her gaze. 'What will you do for money, Libby?' he pushed, waiting to see how she answered that. Did she see him as a meal ticket? If so, this was her chance.

Obviously, he intended to financially support his child, but it was strangely important to him to understand more about Libby. She was such an unknown quantity. She'd crashed into—and out of—his life in the most volatile, stunning way, so sometimes he'd wondered if he'd dreamed the whole encounter. They'd come together like magic and motion and then she'd left, and that had been that. The end. He knew nothing about her, and he wanted to. Not because of who she was as a woman, he told himself, but because she was to become the mother to his child.

'I've got some ideas,' she said, drawing his focus back to the conversation. 'I'm still working out the details, but don't worry,' she said with a hint of disdain. 'I'm not planning on taking a cent from you, Raul; this isn't a shakedown.'

He stared at her, embarrassed to have been seen through, and even more so because it made him seem ungenerous and irresponsible—he was neither. He'd hated the idea of Libby using him to secure some kind of payday, but it had never occurred to him *not* to contribute financially. The problem was, he wanted more than just to hand over cash every month.

'You need money,' he said, 'and obviously I will provide it.'

She closed her eyes, grimacing. 'I don't want that.'

'Why not?' he asked, fascinated by her response.

She lifted her slender shoulders in a shrug. 'I just… I know I can do this,' she said.

'You also know I am a very wealthy man,' he pushed, still trying to get her measure.

'Yes.'

'Do you imagine I would leave you here, struggling in squalor, raising a child I helped make?'

'I—' She looked around, her cheeks bright red now, and tears filmed her eyes. His gut twisted sharply with regret. Squalor might have been pushing it. Libby's apartment was down at heel but it was obvious she'd taken a lot of effort to make it bright and happy.

But this wasn't the time to backpedal. He had to make her see sense.

'I have never wanted children,' he said quietly.

She glanced at him, lips tight. 'You don't need to have anything to do with our baby—'

'That is no longer an option.'

Her eyes widened.

'I didn't plan this. I'm fastidious about protection for precisely this reason; I don't take any chances. Yet here we are.' He frowned, an idea occurring to him out of nowhere. An idea he hated with every part of himself and yet it formed with such clarity in his mind, he knew it was the only solution. His gut sank like a lead balloon. 'Are you absolutely certain about this?'

She spun away from him, reaching into a drawer and removing an envelope. She hesitated a moment, then slid it across to him. He took it, peeled the triangle back and removed a small, square picture. Grainy, but recognisable enough.

An ultrasound photo. His child. He stared at it, waiting to feel that magical emotion people talked about in moments such as this, waiting to feel a rush of love for the blurry, blob-like thing, but all he was conscious of was a need to move all the pieces into alignment so he could protect this child, as no one had protected him. That wasn't love, it was responsibility.

'I had a scan to confirm it,' she explained. 'I'm definitely pregnant. Sorry.'

He handed the picture back without looking at it again. 'It's not your fault.'

She winced. 'Still, it's not ideal.'

'No,' he agreed. 'It's far from it. But we can't change it now. So, let's make a plan.'

Let's make a plan.

Did he have any idea how comforting that statement was? Libby had spent the last two weeks feeling like she was going to be totally alone in this, and here was Raul, offering to take her hand in his, at least in terms of working out what to do next, and she could have wept with relief.

The feeling did not last long.

'I did not know my father either, Libby. Nor my mother. I have only a few very vague memories.' He frowned.

'You and I have one vital thing in common,' he said with steel in his voice. She waited, breath held, even as questions spawned in her mind about his upbringing. 'We both know the particular insecurity that comes from a less than ideal childhood.'

She closed her eyes on a wave of recognition. Hadn't it been the first pledge she'd made to this baby, when she'd learned of their existence? That she would shield them from the pain and uncertainty she'd lived with?

'I will not allow history to repeat itself. Not for either of us.' His nostrils flared on the statement and she heard the determination in his tone.

'I feel the same way,' she murmured. 'It's why I wanted to tell you.'

'You wanted to give me the option of involvement,' he said, brushing past her acknowledgement, 'because your father and you didn't have that. But it's not enough, Libby. Not by a long shot.'

She pressed her back against the kitchen bench, needing strength. Her tea was tepid now; she took a sip anyway. 'What are you suggesting?'

Silence fell. The ticking of the clock took on an almost ominous tone.

'There is only one solution.' His voice was flat, devoid of all feeling and warmth. She stared at him, waiting for the penny to drop, because Libby could see no option beyond the one she'd suggested. Unless he intended to fight her for custody? She blanched at the very idea.

'Raul,' she mumbled. 'You can't mean to try to take the baby from me?' She trembled from head to foot. 'I know I don't have your resources, but I will do everything I can to be the best mother possible to our child. You can't—'

'That is not my intent.' He spoke quickly, immediately dismissing the idea.

She didn't feel the wave of relief she'd anticipated. She was on tenterhooks, waiting for him to say whatever was cogitating behind those intelligent eyes of his.

'I want to raise my child.'

Libby's heart stammered.

'I want to be in their life every day, not just occasionally, and I presume you feel the same way.'

She nodded, not trusting her voice to speak.

'Then the solution is obvious, and simple.' His tone was bland but she saw the look in his eyes. It was a look of sheer disbelief. 'We'll get married.'

Libby almost passed out. Her heart skipped a thousand beats and her eyes flashed with white.

'No.' She lifted a hand to her lips, pressing it there.

Something precious she'd nurtured inside of herself since she was a girl was being strangled by his cold, pragmatic suggestion. The little girl who'd hidden in her room and read romantic fairy tales to escape the reality of her life, who'd promised herself that one day she'd make all her own fairy tales come true, had never given up on the idea of real, all-consuming love. Of finding the kind of man who was like a modern-day Prince Charming, who'd love her with all that he was, for all time. She'd hated the way her mother had gone through partners. It had made Libby all the more determined to believe in *true* love. In the idea of finding that one perfect person who was destined for her, and she'd been holding out for them all this time.

A cold marriage for the sake of a child, in the twenty-first century, was a death knell to all those hopes and dreams.

'I can't,' she whispered.

'Marriage is the last thing I want as well,' he responded, and hurt lashed her. She turned away from him then, looking out of the window and finding no pleasure remained in the view.

'We don't even know each other.'

'That's less important than being married before the baby arrives.' He spoke as though it were a foregone conclusion. 'You will be supported in every way,' he said, ignoring the fact she hadn't accepted his proposal. 'You will live in my home, have true financial stability and comfort. You will not have to work unless you want to—you can be a full-time mother, if that is your wish. This is not a jail sentence, but a gift of freedom. Our marriage can give you wings, can't you see that?'

'Marriage to a virtual stranger? Freedom?' she repeated, incredulous, turning to face him then wishing she hadn't when the sight of him made her central nervous system go into overdrive. Even now, feeling as she did, totally on edge and laced with panic, she was all too aware of him as a man, and that terrified her. 'How can you say that?'

'What will your life be like if you do not accept?'

'I'll manage,' she promised defiantly.

'And what about our child's life?' he pushed, moving closer, looking down at her with cool eyes, appraising her every gesture so she felt totally seen and vulnerable. 'Do you really think you can offer them enough?'

Her lips parted; it was a low blow. 'Of *course*.' But was she so sure of that? Hadn't it been the biggest problem she'd been trying to solve, since finding out she was pregnant? Her voice trembled. 'I will love this child enough to give them anything.'

'Evidently not,' he said quietly.

'What's that supposed to mean?'

'I am offering them everything—and you are choosing not to take it.'

Libby's eyes widened.

'This is not about you,' he continued, and shame curdled in her belly. 'I am not offering to marry you as a man offers for a woman. This is a sacrifice we would both be making, for the sake of our child. Is there any better reason to sacrifice, Libby?'

Did he have any idea how badly he was twisting the knife in her heart? Not because she felt anything for Raul, but because her longest-held dream was of being loved, really loved. On her loneliest nights, she'd consoled herself with visions of her future. Nothing special or glamorous— a very ordinary, happy life, in a nice simple cottage with a garden and an apple tree, a white timber fence with nasturtiums scrambling along it, sunlight dappling the thick, lush lawn, perfect for picnics, and most of all—love and laughter. Chubby little children whose hands would seek hers, and a husband who'd wrap his arms around her waist and draw her to him, their hearts in lockstep, always.

She expelled a soft sigh. It was a fantasy. A childish dream.

Maybe Raul was right... Maybe she needed to grow up and accept the reality of this. Fairy tales were for children; there were more important considerations here. In marrying Raul, Libby would be giving up on the idea of romantic love, of meeting her soulmate and losing her head to them. But there were other kinds of love that were just as important, and the love she already felt for her child, and knew they'd feel for her, was enough to start stitching her heart back together again. She could still know the contentment of a little hand in hers, of a toddler in her lap for reading time, of goodnight cuddles and kisses…all of the things she'd never had enough of.

Raul was right: marriage to him was a sacrifice, but she would make it, for the baby. But it would need to be the right kind of marriage, a partnership at least. If love wouldn't be part of the picture, she had to know there would at least be teamwork. They were going to be parents together, after all.

'Obviously, financially, you can offer us the world,' she said, running her hand over her stomach, pausing when his eyes followed the gesture and flared. Her heart trembled and when she spoke, her voice was unsteady. 'But I would need more, if I were to go along with this.'

His dark brows lifted, surprise showed in the depths of his grey eyes before he concealed it. 'What are your conditions?'

It was like he'd been expecting it, she thought, then realised he probably had. Raul Ortega was used to negotiations, and this was no different. He wasn't taking over a company now though, but her life, and she had to be just as pragmatic and sensible as he would be if their positions were reversed.

'I would want everything in writing before we got married,' she said, lips pulling to the side.

'A prenuptial agreement?' he prompted.

'Yes, exactly,' she agreed quickly. 'If something happened, and it might—we don't know each other well enough to just trust blindly—and our marriage ended, and even ended badly, I would need to know that I would continue to be…looked after. That our baby would be looked after.'

His nostrils flared and the look on his face showed how

offended he was by her suggestion. Tone stiff, he said curtly, 'Naturally.'

'I beg your pardon, but it's not "natural",' she insisted. 'Plenty of women get the raw end of the deal, particularly in marriages like this—where one person enters into it with so much more.'

He crossed his arms over his chest. 'I will ensure you are taken care of, no matter what.'

She bit into her lower lip. 'It's not for my sake but the baby's,' she said, troubled by these negotiations even when she acknowledged their necessity. 'There should be a trust fund or something, set up for them. You don't know how you'll feel in five years, or ten, nor whom you might end up married to next and what they might ask you to do. I want this child's future to be inviolable if I do this.'

'A moment ago you were prepared to give up any claim whatsoever to my wealth,' he pointed out.

'Yes.' She nodded. 'But if I marry you, our baby will get used to living a certain way. I don't want him or her to have to face the prospect of losing that. Stability is important.'

'Fine.'

She couldn't tell if he believed her point was valid, but she took his agreement regardless.

'Describe what our marriage will be like,' she said after a beat, heat blooming in her cheeks.

'In what context?'

He was really going to make this awkward for her, wasn't he?

'Obviously, it won't be a real marriage, in the sense of… sex.' She stumbled over the last word in her statement. 'Contrary to whatever opinion you might have formed of me after that day, I'm not generally into meaningless encounters.'

A muscle throbbed in his jaw but otherwise he didn't react.

'You, on the other hand,' she continued a little breathily, 'presumably are.'

He lifted one thick dark brow and even though his expression didn't change she had the strangest feeling he was laughing at her.

'Go on.'

'I wouldn't expect that to change—' she sniffed '—but I would require your absolute discretion.'

His eyes narrowed almost imperceptibly.

'There are more kinds of insecurity than financial to worry about. I wouldn't want our child to suspect our marriage was anything other than…happy.'

'Fine.'

'To which end, we would both need to agree to treat one another with respect,' she said, thinking quickly. 'And to get to know one another well enough to be…' She searched for the right word.

'Friends?' he prompted, but his voice was loaded with cynicism.

'What's wrong with that?'

Raul looked at her for a long time, so long that Libby's chest felt as though it were going to explode from the pressure being exerted on her.

'We will get to know each other,' he said finally. 'Within reason.'

She frowned. 'What does that mean?'

'This is not an audition for a real marriage,' he said coldly. 'While we should be respectful and even *friendly*, it is important not to ever lose sight of why we are doing this. I will not fall in love with you, Libby, so please be realistic in your expectations. This is only for our child, okay?'

Her lips parted on a groundswell of shock. 'Wow, ego much?'

His eyes shuttered, concealing his feelings from her. 'I am simply being honest—which is, in my opinion, an important prerequisite for this.'

'Fine,' she agreed, knowing she should have been grateful for his truthfulness, even when it cut her to the quick. It was just such a bald, frank assessment, another dropping of the guillotine on those childish hopes. But she wasn't stupid enough to put those dreams into Raul's hands, anyway! So what difference did it make if he was pronouncing they would always be loveless?

'I presume the same conditions imposed upon me would apply to you as well? If you were to take a lover, it would be with the utmost caution to avoid discovery.'

'Of course,' Libby said, rolling her eyes. 'But you really don't need to worry about that. I'm not exactly a highly sexed person,' she said, 'which makes the irony of this just all the more ridiculous.'

He was quiet. It was the only explanation for why Libby kept speaking, as if nervously filling the void.

'To think, the first time I have sex with anyone in three years I fall pregnant.' She groaned. 'I swear the fates are laughing at us, Raul.'

CHAPTER FIVE

HE TRIED NOT to wonder about that. He definitely didn't ask. But how could he fail to be curious about why a woman who was so sensual and passionate hadn't had sex in such a long time?

It was not the most important thing in that moment though, so he pushed it aside.

'Be that as it may,' he said with a tone of resignation. 'Here we are.'

'Yes, here we are.' She stared up at him, as if looking for an answer he didn't know how to give. An assurance. But he was all out of promises. Raul was moving into fresh new territory, and he wasn't going to pretend otherwise. 'Which brings me to my next point,' she said slowly.

'There's more?'

Libby rolled her eyes. 'We're talking about a marriage. Don't you think it's wise to go through more than a couple of details?'

She had a point, but Raul believed they would make it work however they had to. He knew all he needed on that score: they both cared about this child more than they did their own wishes. It was his only concern.

'What else?' he prompted.

'Where we'll live, for starters.'

'My headquarters are in New York.'

Her throat shifted as she swallowed. 'New York?' she said softly. 'For real?'

He scanned her features. 'You don't like it?'

'I've never been,' she replied. 'I've never been anywhere. I can't just move to New York.'

'Why not? What's holding you here?'

She looked around.

'Do you have family? A support network?'

'I have friends,' she said, but weakly.

He expelled a breath. 'We can move back, if you don't like New York. For now, though, it's how it has to be. I cannot uproot my business at the drop of a hat and relocate to Sydney.'

'You mean you don't want to,' she said stubbornly.

'I am prepared to make all sorts of accommodations for this child; I am asking you to meet me halfway.'

'New York is the other side of the world, that's not halfway.' Her expression was belligerent, but he could see she was waning on this point. 'I don't even have a passport.'

Raul's brows flexed as he processed her statement. It was totally antithetical to him—he who travelled at the drop of a hat, drawn to his business interests all over the world. But he could see the vulnerability in her face at having made the admission and didn't want to exacerbate it.

'No problem. My assistant will arrange it.'

Libby's jaw dropped. 'Just like that?'

'You will likely have to fly to Canberra to expedite matters. Justine will arrange it.'

'Your assistant?'

'Yes.' He nodded once. 'Is there anything else?'

She shook her head, and she looked so lost, as though she was a little girl, stranded in a storm, that he felt the strangest compulsion to reach out and draw her into a hug, to stroke her back and promise her everything would be okay.

But Raul didn't really believe in those assurances.

He wanted, more than anything, to make their child's life perfect, but he wasn't stupid enough to promise any such thing. Life had a way of pulling the rug out from under you. It was better to brace for that, at all times, than live in a fool's paradise.

So he simply said, 'I'll see to the paperwork. You handle the passport. Deal?'

And, just like that, a week later, Libby was sitting onboard Raul's private jet, staring at a thick wad of papers, highlighter and pen in hand as though they were her sword and shield.

He'd engaged a law firm to advise her, but Libby wasn't going to leave things to chance. Trust didn't come easily for her, and she wasn't going to be stupid about something as important as her child's future.

So she sat, legs curled up beneath her on the enormous armchair, carefully reading the prenuptial agreement line by line, annotating where necessary, making notes of any queries she had.

The first few pages dealt expressly with the financial arrangements and custodial expectations. The amount Raul had suggested putting in trust for their child made Libby's eyes water. She felt a rush of compunction to imagine he thought she had any expectation of him setting aside quite so much. She'd simply meant *enough*. Enough for their child to never have to worry as she'd always worried. Enough to know they were financially secure, come what may.

Raul had made their unborn baby a multimillionaire even before they'd drawn breath.

By page five, they were onto a matter that made Libby blush for a whole other reason.

Extramarital considerations

She read the stipulations with a pulse that was thready and uneven.

It was everything they'd agreed, and then a little extra. In addition to the requirement that any extramarital relationships be kept completely discreet was the requirement that the spouse would be notified, to avoid potential awkwardness.

Libby couldn't believe she was actually contemplating signing a document like this. It made a mockery of everything she had ever believed about marriage!

'Good evening, ma'am.' A steward approached her, male, with blond hair and a broad smile. His accent was American. 'Would you care for some refreshments?'

Libby quickly shut the contract, mortified to think he might have seen even a hint of what was written on the page.

'Um...' she said, aware of not just the steward but also Raul. Though he sat further down the cabin, and she wasn't even looking at him, she felt his eyes on her. She knew he was watching.

Her pulse ratcheted up.

'I can bring you a menu,' he offered.

'Okay,' she agreed, fidgeting with her fingers. 'Thank you,' she added, forcing herself to smile.

Morning sickness, as pervasive and never-ending as it had been a few weeks ago, seemed to have given her a temporary reprieve and, if anything, Libby was hungry *all the time.* She found the cravings to be the strangest thing: she'd gone from enjoying reasonably simple foods to wanting to try things she'd never heard of. Inwardly, she couldn't help smiling as she imagined her baby's strong will already in evidence.

She stroked her stomach absentmindedly, staring out of the window at the jet-black sky as the plane cut its way across the globe.

A moment later, the steward was back, handing Libby a menu that was identical in branding to Raul's business card. She scanned it quickly, bypassing the savoury selection and landing instead on pancakes with bacon and a cup of tea.

'Won't take me long,' the steward said with another charming grin as he disappeared from the cabin.

Libby was not alone for long. Raul strode towards her, and every single one of Libby's senses went onto high alert as he took the seat opposite her, his long legs spread wide, his body the last word in relaxed athleticism. So why did his proximity have the opposite impact on her?

Every time they went a stretch without seeing one another, she forgot. She forgot how big and strong and *masculine* he was. How just being near him called to some ancient part of her, making her want to throw caution to the wind, just as she'd done on the boat. She'd put it down to the heat of the moment, the relief and the drama, but what was her excuse now?

Hormones?

She suppressed a grimace, turning to look out the window once more.

'How are you finding it?'

'Mortifying,' she answered honestly. 'I cannot believe you had a lawyer draft this.'

'Why?'

'Because it's so...*personal*,' she spluttered.

'They act for me in the strictest confidence,' he assured her. 'This document is completely private.'

'It's not that,' she said with a shake of her head. 'Doesn't it embarrass you that they think this is what our marriage is about?' She lifted the contract higher.

'It is what our marriage is about,' he said without a hint of shame. 'Besides which, I do not particularly care what my legal team thinks about my private life.'

Libby's eyes narrowed. 'I bet you don't care what anyone thinks,' she said, wishing on all the stars in the heaven that she knew just a little more about the man she was metaphorically getting into bed with.

'Not particularly,' he said with a shrug.

The steward returned with a cup of tea. Libby thanked him but made no effort to lift it off the table.

'It is my experience that people will generally think what they want whether you like their opinion or not. Worrying about it is therefore somewhat futile.'

Her lips twisted into the ghost of a smile. 'I suppose you're right,' she said, wondering at his innate confidence, and where it came from. Except it went beyond confidence. There was an air of such self-reliance that now Libby did wonder about his life, his childhood, his experiences. What had happened to shape him into the man he was today?

'You said you didn't really know your parents,' she murmured, placing the contract aside and giving him her full attention—or at least, finally showing that he already had it. 'Who raised you?'

Was she imagining the slight pause? The shift in his features?

'I was in foster care,' he responded crisply. It was an open-ended answer. She had no personal experience with the foster system, but she'd heard and read enough to know that some people didn't fare too well with it, while others did. She supposed it was down to the luck of the draw.

'And?'

His expression didn't change. 'And at fifteen, I ran away,' he said matter-of-factly. 'I decided I'd had enough of being parented, and wanted to take my chances on the streets.'

'You did?'

He nodded once.

'I can't even imagine...' she said softly.

He looked at her long and hard and Libby's mouth was suddenly as dry as dust.

'Can't you?'

Her eyes widened. How could he possibly know about her childhood?

'Why do I find that hard to believe?' he pushed.

She shook her head. 'I don't know.'

'Perhaps it's because I see something in you, Libby, something that is broken in all the same ways I was.' He ran his gaze over her features, slow and deliberate, as if he was tasting her. 'Am I wrong?'

Her lips parted. He wasn't wrong, but she'd always thought she hid her pain so well. She tried. Her childhood had been difficult, emotionally draining, hurtful. She carried those wounds to this day, yes, but Libby had sworn she wouldn't be defined by them. Where she felt pain, she acted with love. She smiled when her heart hurt. She was determined to respond to whatever darkness had been in her life with pure light. To hope for lasting love even when her mother had demonstrated again and again how unlikely that was.

That Raul had seen beyond her façade scared Libby to death.

'I don't think we'd be entering into this marriage if we hadn't both experienced a rough start to life,' she said uneasily.

'Which means?'

He was asking for specifics and Libby knew it was only fair that she should give them. After all, he had. At least, a brief enough outline for her to gain more of an under-standing of him.

'My mother was single,' Libby said, sipping her tea, forcing herself to meet Raul's eyes. 'Except when she wasn't. The only thing is, she never met a man she wanted to be with for more than a few months.' Libby rushed through the explanation. 'I had a lot of stepdads,' she added with a grimace.

Raul was very still across from her, his eyes glittering when they met hers with a hardness that took her breath away. 'It takes a lot more than biology to be a good parent.'

She nodded her agreement. She'd seen that first-hand.

'Libby.' His voice was gruff, deep. 'What we're doing here, *this* is who we are. We will do right by our child, in a way no one ever did for us.' The determination in his voice, the pride, took her breath away.

Tears sparkled on her lashes as she nodded, not sure she could trust her voice to speak.

'This is all that matters,' he said quietly.

Libby knew then that they'd made the right decision. This was all about their baby, and always would be.

He had been careful not to touch her as they entered the lift to his penthouse. He'd been careful not to touch her since collecting her from her place in Sydney, and a strange swelling of something had begun to stretch in his chest.

Protectiveness.

It was the sight of Libby with her bashed-up old suit-case and a look in her eyes that was pure determination and strength. As if to say, 'Show me everything you've got; I'm ready for it.'

She was a fighter. He recognised that quality; he understood it. He didn't doubt she could take care of herself, and their child.

But she didn't have to.

Raul hadn't wanted this. It was the antithesis of what he wanted, in fact, and yet here he was, ready to protect the mother of his child with his life.

Despite her air of strength, he felt her nervousness, her anxieties about the step she was taking away from the familiar, and he'd wanted to reach across and put a hand on her knee as the car had pulled out from the kerb.

But he hadn't.

Just as he hadn't put his hand in the small of her back to guide her up the stairs when they'd reached his plane. Nor had he reached out and placed his hand over hers when they'd spoken on the plane and realised how similar their goal was, to protect their child from the sort of childhood they'd had. But he'd wanted to.

The longer he'd sat opposite Libby, watching as she flicked through the document and then fell asleep, high-lighter with the lid off, small body curled up in the too-big armchair—they'd never felt too big for him—his fingers had tingled with a want to simply feel. Just one stroke of her soft cheek, to remind himself...to remember.

The air in the lift hummed with a sultry, seductive pulse, urging him to move closer to her. To brush against her, almost as if by accident. But there was a warning there too, because he suspected whatever incendiary spark had flared between them on the boat was still ignited, and they'd be all kinds of stupid to let it burn out of control.

If there wasn't a child involved.

If they weren't getting married.

But this was a serious, lifelong commitment to do right by their infant. He wouldn't let biological impulses complicate everything, so he stood firm on the other side of the lift, staring straight ahead, barely breathing until the doors opened and he waited for the release of the pent-up tension, the energy.

The relief didn't come.

Grinding his teeth, he stood at the doors to the lift, holding his hand across them and waiting for Libby to precede him.

Her eyes flashed nervously to his then looked straight ahead.

'Oh,' she murmured, lips parting.

The lift opened directly into the foyer of his apartment—a large space that was decorated as it had been when he'd bought the place, all in beige and white, with a big mirror above a hallstand that had a decorative bowl and nothing else.

Raul lived a minimalistic life, despite his wealth. He'd learned as a teenager to need only a few small things, to be ready to leave at any point. He hadn't consciously kept that habit but, now that he thought about it, he had very little connection to anything in his apartment. There were only a few things in here he'd want to take if he left. Which was why it had been easy to buy the place and keep it basically as it had been.

'You can change anything you don't like,' he said, stepping out into the foyer and placing his keys and wallet in the bowl, then turning back to her. But Libby had already stepped away from him, was moving deeper into the penthouse, one hand lifted to her lips as she stared at the double height room beyond the foyer. He tried to see it through her eyes. Through the eyes of the teenager he'd once been, so poor he hadn't eaten for days, sleeping in an alleyway that reeked of urine and sweat.

It was magnificent, objectively speaking. The penthouse had been made of two full storeys of apartments, combined by the previous owners. The floor-to-ceiling windows offered panoramic views of Manhattan, and there was a deep balcony with a spa beyond the kitchen.

'We can't raise a baby here,' she said, turning to look at him, and instead of there being admiration in her features, he registered abject horror.

He frowned. 'You don't like it?'

She looked around again, as if she might see something else in the apartment she'd missed on first inspection. 'It's not that.' She shook her head. 'It's…just…so…'

He waited, curious as to what word she would choose.

'A baby couldn't relax here,' she said then laughed softly, nervously. 'I couldn't relax here. My God, Raul, this is—' She bit down nervously on her lower lip, and that same protective urge fired in his gut. To hell with it.

He closed the distance between them and put his hand on her upper arm. A gesture designed purely to reassure and comfort, nothing more, and yet damn it if his fingertips didn't spark the second he touched her. She expelled a sharp breath and her eyes lifted to his, so he felt the world tipping sideways in a way he immediately wanted to fight.

'It's just a place to live.'

'But it's not a home,' she said urgently, swallowing, and he felt her tremble like a little bird. His gut twisted. What did he know about home? He'd never had one. 'Not like I've always wanted to raise a child in.'

Raul had bought the place because it was a good investment and he could afford it. A divorce had meant it was being sold for under market value; he acted quickly to secure it and he hadn't regretted the purchase since. But he had no emotional ties to the place.

'Okay, we'll find somewhere else.'

Her laugh now was a little manic. 'Just like that?'

'Why not?'

Libby shook her head, wrapping her arms around her torso. He didn't drop his hand. He hoped his touch was reassuring to her in some way, even when it was unsettling to him. 'It's fine. I'll get used to it.'

But Raul didn't like the tone of her voice—anxious and concerned. His thumb stroked her arm gently. 'Hey.' He drew her face to his. She stared up at him, eyes wide, looking for something in the depths of his expression, but he didn't know what. 'We will make this work.'

It was a promise he made to the both of them, something they both needed in that moment, to hear, and believe.

CHAPTER SIX

A WEEK AFTER moving to New York, Libby had to admit her fears had been baseless. Her worries about how she and Raul would make this work, her concern that their sexual chemistry would make any kind of cohabiting situation untenable, had evaporated in the face of the fact they barely saw one another.

Raul worked long hours. So long she had begun to wonder how he functioned—even to worry a little, because how could a person sustain themselves when working so hard? And when he was home, or rather in the sky palace, as she'd started thinking of it, it was more than large enough to accommodate the pair of them without them needing to interact. Libby had her own spacious bedroom, balcony and bathroom, and she tended to eat dinner alone, hours before Raul returned. Her days were long and solitary, but Libby refused to give into the temptation to feel sorry for herself.

While this was far from her ideal situation, there was plenty to be thankful for, and excited about. She focused on the baby and on exploring this enormous, exciting city. She certainly didn't think about the dreams she'd always cherished, and about how far her arrangement with Raul was from the safety and security of the real, loving marriage she'd wanted since she was a little girl.

Raul's apartment was on the Upper East Side, and Libby discovered she was an easy stroll from many of the sights she'd seen in movies and on TV. From famous restaurants and grocery stores to museums, galleries, Central Park, and just the streets themselves, she kept herself busy by walking for miles and miles each day. It was admittedly far colder than Libby had ever thought possible, and frequently she'd been caught out in the snow, but on the first day in town she'd found a department store and bought a discount puffer coat that zipped up from the knees to the collar. It was like wearing a blanket, and when combined with gloves and a beanie, she was warm enough to walk and walk.

It made her tired though—pregnancy was exhausting, anyway—but she was always glad to be tuckered out at the end of the day and ready to flop into bed. Sleep came easily most of the time, meaning she didn't lie awake, staring at the ceiling, wondering about Raul, and this bizarre arrangement of theirs.

And so one morning, eight days after arriving in America, Libby woke and looked out at the crisp blue sky and contemplated which direction she'd strike out in, where she might go, what she might see. She didn't think about Raul, she didn't think about their baby, she just focused on keeping herself busy, day by day, until one day, this all felt normal.

She made herself a piece of toast for breakfast, eyeing her Vegemite jar with a hint of concern. It was already half empty.

'Morning.'

Libby startled, almost dropping her tea into the sink, as her gaze jerked across the room to find Raul standing there, arms crossed, legs wide, watching her.

Her mouth went dry and her heart began to pound; her lips parted on a quick sigh. The temptation to cross the room and touch him was totally unwelcome. She mentally planted her feet to the ground, refusing to surrender to the sudden desire.

'Hi,' she said unevenly. 'What are you doing here?'

His expression was quizzical. 'In my home?'

She rolled her eyes. 'You know what I mean.' Forcing herself to act normal, or try to seem normal, she lifted a piece of toast to her lips, took a small bite, chewed, struggled to swallow. 'You're usually long gone by now.'

His eyes flickered over her face. 'We have to sign the paperwork,' he said, reaching for the tie that was hanging loose either side of his chest and beginning to draw it together. His fingers were nimble and deft, working the silk until it formed a perfect knot at his throat. She was transfixed by the simple, mechanical gesture. He obviously performed the task often, and yet there was something about his confident motions that made her skin lift in goosebumps.

'Oh.' Libby's heart thudded against her chest. 'Now?'

'As soon as possible. Have your lawyers looked it over?'

She shook her head, took another bite of toast to buy time, aiming for casual nonchalance. 'I wanted to read it through first.'

He looked at her expectantly.

'I'll do it today,' she promised, looking longingly towards the outside world, thinking of the walk she'd been planning on.

'Okay. Let's discuss it tonight. Dinner?'

Libby's eyes strayed back to Raul's face, surprise in her features. 'Oh.' She dusted crumbs from the side of her lips. 'I mean... Sure,' she heard herself agree, even when inwardly she wanted to run from the idea of dinner with Raul, discussing the contract for their marriage.

But wasn't she the one who'd insisted on all of this?

On a proper prenuptial agreement, on them trying to form a relationship that had some kind of semblance to civility and friendship? They couldn't do that by never being in the same room.

'Okay,' she said with more confidence. 'I'll cook.'

He looked as though she'd suggested an afternoon sky-dive. 'Please don't bother. I'll organise something.'

'It's no trouble,' Libby promised. 'I like to cook, really.'

'It wasn't my intention to put you out.'

Libby expelled a breath and then laughed unsteadily. 'Raul, if we're going to do this, we have to start acting more normally. We're going to be raising a child together. I'm going to cook meals—I *like* to cook. It isn't a big deal.'

He nodded slowly, still looking far from convinced. 'If you're sure.'

'I am.' She felt strange. This was the closest they'd come to normal domesticity—him here, in the mornings, putting on a tie, talking about something they needed to do together, planning for dinner.

'Any food allergies?' she asked as he reached for his jacket and pulled it on.

Raul's laugh was a single bark, but it spread through her body like wildfire and then she was grinning too. This man probably had the constitution of a lion. 'I like food,' he said, walking to the door. 'All food, and lots of it.'

'Got it,' she murmured, taking another bite of toast. 'Make loads.'

He shot her a smile as he opened the door and her heart jettisoned from her chest and into her throat. Something like panic slicked her palms. 'See you tonight, Libby.'

* * *

By the time Libby had made her way to the amazing grocery store on the west side of the park and perused the aisles and deli counter, decided what she was going to make then bought the ingredients, she was too laden to make it home on foot, so she had her first experience of a New York City cab—which she loved, and she and the driver made conversation the whole way around the park and up Fifth Avenue. She paid with cash and her dwindling supply put her in mind of how pressing her financial situation was. She knew it was a conversation she had to have with Raul.

After all, she had no employment prospects in New York as she wasn't legally able to work, and there was still rent to cover on her apartment back home. She'd made the decision to continue her tenancy, because it seemed too permanent to get rid of the flat just yet. She wasn't ready.

But the walls were closing in on her. She felt the financial insecurity pinching her, just as it always had as a child. Since leaving school, she'd been determined to stand on her own two feet. To work just as hard as she could to make sure she'd never have to worry about money ever again. Yet here she was, in a gilded cage, without her own financial security, and it scared her, even when she knew somehow that Raul would never see her go hungry. That wasn't quite the same thing as being in control of your own financial destiny, but there was nothing she could do about that for now. Once the baby was born she'd make it a priority to find a way to stand—at least a little—on her own.

Back in the apartment, she set dinner cooking then made a tea and sat down with the contracts, opening them to the last page she'd read on the flight over, and flushed to the roots of her hair.

To see the intimate details of their marriage written in such stark detail did something funny to her pulse, just as it had on the plane. She knew she should be glad that it was all there in black and white, but she couldn't help the hot flush that ran over her skin as she contemplated the sort of marriage they were negotiating, that two teams of lawyers would be aware of.

It all just felt so…depressing.

She sighed, turning the page, focusing on the next section. Schooling. She read with interest the provisions laid out by Raul—all very reasonable. They were to have equal say in the choice of school, and where they could not find agreement he'd selected a family counselling service to offer mediation. Libby turned the page, continued to read.

The next heading was: *In the Event of Both Parents' Deaths*. She blanched a little, the thought one that hadn't occurred to her. Her grip on the pen tightened, because the all-consuming love she already felt for their unborn child made her reticent to even contemplate such an event—the idea of their baby being flotsam in the world, with no one to love him or her, filled her with despair.

In preparation for the unlikely event of both parents' deaths, a suitable guardian will be nominated and agreed upon by both parents prior to the child's birth.

Libby's heart stammered. A suitable guardian?

She felt queasy at the idea of not being able to raise her own child, but of course it was something to consider, an important point to tick off. It wasn't likely to come to pass but, given Raul's upbringing, it made sense he'd want to know they'd made an effort to mitigate any eventuality.

She turned the page quickly: *In the Event of Divorce*.

And there it was, in black and white. The reality of what

they'd do if their shotgun marriage failed. Heart thumping, she skimmed the page first, then returned to the top
and read it properly.

The document set out terms requiring them to live no
more than three miles apart, to share custody fifty per cent
per parent, and to mutually agree to any other caretak-
ing arrangements. It was all very reasonable. So reasonable that, for a brief moment, Libby contemplated taking
the deal.

After all, they were terms she could almost live with.

Almost, but not quite.

Sharing her baby? Not having them with her half of the
time, but rather sending them to live with Raul. She shuddered. Perhaps there would come a point when she'd be
prepared for that, but it was not now, not yet. Not before
they'd even given this a proper try.

She pushed the contracts aside and returned to the
kitchen, trying not to think about the contingencies they
were making a plan for. All Libby wanted to focus on
was her baby.

'Where did you learn to cook?' he asked, shovelling a third
serving of lamb onto his plate along with mashed chick-
peas and some greens. Libby stared at him, aghast. It had
been delicious and tender, but surely he'd had enough?

'Um…' she said, momentarily not computing his question because she was so caught up in his appetite. 'I suppose I cooked a lot, growing up.'

He waited for her to continue, lifting a fork of dinner to
his lips. She was mesmerised. Not just by his appetite but
by everything about him. The entire experience of having him come home from work, place his leather laptop
bag down on a kitchen stool, drape his jacket nearby, roll

up his shirtsleeves to reveal two tanned forearms, remove his tie, flick open his shirt... It had all been so...intimate.

She glanced away from him, the word catching her by surprise.

They were *not* intimate. They'd slept together once, and they were having a baby, but there was nothing close nor personal about their dynamic, even when they were sitting opposite one another, sharing a meal.

'As a hobby?' he asked, though there was something in the depths of his grey eyes that showed he perceived more than he was revealing. That he already suspected the answer to that question.

She shook her head slowly. 'It was one of my jobs.'

He was quiet as he contemplated that. 'One of?'

'I helped run the house,' she said, pressing her fork around her plate, manoeuvring a piece of broccolini from one side to the other. 'My mother wasn't much for housework, but she expected things to be just so. She liked nice food, said it was our job to provide a good meal for the man of the house.' Libby couldn't help rolling her eyes. 'She was old-fashioned like that.'

Raul made a noise of disapproval.

'Besides which, I like food too, and it was either learn to cook or eat very badly, so I learned.'

'How?'

'I watched tutorials on the internet,' she said. 'I had to get creative. We couldn't afford a lot of the ingredients, so I'd take a meal and work out how I could do something similar for a fraction of the cost. There was a lot of pasta and rice substitution,' she said with a tight smile.

Raul's eyes narrowed; sympathy softened the edges of his mouth.

She cleared her throat. 'But I liked it,' she said, because

the last thing she wanted was for him to feel sorry for her. 'I got a sense of satisfaction out of what I could make. I enjoyed shopping, preparing, and discovering that whatever I'd cooked was actually pretty damned good. Most of the time.' She wrinkled her nose. 'There were also some disasters.'

His laugh was soft, warming. She liked the sound of it.

'When did you move out?' he asked, eyes heavy on her face.

'My mother left me, actually,' Libby said. 'I was nineteen. She'd started living with a new guy a few months before. He got a job in Brisbane, and I came home from work one day to find the place empty except for my bed.'

'Charming,' Raul muttered.

Libby made a sound of agreement. 'I was an adult.' She shrugged, trying not to focus on the feeling of betrayal and hurt. 'It's not like I was too young to manage. I coped.' Her chin tilted and she felt the look in his eyes, the emotions there, and wished he'd stop looking at her with so much pity, or something.

'How did you cope?'

'I was already working,' she pointed out. 'I just had to find somewhere smaller, cheaper, work a bit more.'

He made another noise. 'Always as a cleaner?'

'Actually,' she said wistfully, 'I got a job as a kitchen hand at first. I had big dreams of applying for an apprenticeship, becoming a chef.'

'Why didn't you?'

'I couldn't afford it,' she said with a shake of her head.

'The degree?'

'No. The apprentice salary was so low, and I wouldn't have been able to work as many hours and study. It just wasn't tenable. I always told myself "one day", but then life just gets away from you sometimes, doesn't it?' she remarked quietly. 'I'm twenty-six years old. It was just a pipedream, anyway.'

His brows drew together and Libby shook her head.

'Please stop looking at me like that.'

'Like what?'

'As though you feel sorry for me. I hate it.'

Surprise showed on his face for a moment, before he contained it. 'I think you got the raw end of the deal,' he said after a beat.

'But so do lots of people. I'm happy, Raul. Really, I am. I like my life and I liked my job. It's not what I dreamed of, but I make it work.'

'I'm sure you do.' His voice and expression were now even more unsettling than the pity he'd shown a moment earlier, because Libby heard admiration in his tone and it pulled at something deep inside her, something she pre-ferred to keep locked away completely. 'Is your mother still in Brisbane?'

Libby shook her head. 'She passed away a few years ago.'

Raul's eyes glittered as he waited for Libby to express an answering emotion to that statement.

'I was sad I didn't get to see her again, before she died. I often wondered if she regretted…well, lots of things,' Libby said with a humourless smile. 'I wonder, sometimes, if she missed me.'

'Your mother sounds like a selfish woman.'

It was a fair assessment. 'In many ways, yes, she was.'

'It's unlikely that someone like her is capable of feel-ing regret. I'm sorry.'

Libby laughed then, a soft sound of surprise. 'Don't be. I appreciate honesty.'

'I know you do,' he said quietly, then, to lighten the mood, pointed to his plate. 'This is honestly one of the best meals I've ever eaten. Thank you for making it for me, Libby.'

Warm pleasure flooded her veins and Libby smiled across at him, already wondering what she might cook next. But that was a silly thought. A red herring. They weren't a couple, and this wasn't the beginning of some kind of happy domestic relationship. It was nothing like the dreams she'd cherished—where she'd meet someone who swept her off her feet for real, not like her mother's silly, unstable relationships.

Despite the fact Raul was charming and Libby had enjoyed sharing a meal with him, she knew she couldn't lose sight of what they were doing.

It wasn't until Raul had cleared the table, and Libby had made some hot drinks and put out a tray of biscuits, that they got around to discussing the finer points of the contract. Libby was quick to admit to Raul how thorough he'd been.

'It's what I do,' he said, dismissing her praise.

'Write contracts?' she asked, curling her legs up beneath her on the sofa, one hand wrapped around her cup of tea.

'Make agreements,' he clarified, tapping his pen against the papers. 'Did you want to make any changes?'

She shook her head. 'I haven't sent it to the lawyers you hired for me yet. I don't really see that I need to.'

'You should,' Raul murmured. 'For additional protection.'

'From you?' she asked, genuinely surprised.

He nodded. 'It's always a good idea to get outside advice.'

'It seems pretty simple to me, but okay. I'll email it to-night.'

His eyes met hers, holding, appraising. 'We should discuss dates.'

Libby's first thought was a misunderstanding. She thought for a moment he was implying they should *go* on a date, in a romantic sense, and everything got wonky and strange, before sanity reasserted itself and she realised he meant the dates on a calendar. 'For what?'

'The wedding,' he said. 'I thought, given the practical nature of our marriage, we could go to a registry office for the wedding itself. But you may have other ideas.'

'I—' Libby stared at him, the wedding something she'd given startlingly little thought to. 'No, a registry office is fine by me too. Why dress up what we're doing?' she added. 'It's little more than a contractual agreement, right?'

'Yes,' he responded, scanning her face. 'That bothers you?'

Libby's eyes widened. She didn't bother to deny it, but nor did she want to admit how *much* the nature of this marriage bothered her. What she'd wanted for herself no longer mattered; she was going to become a mother. This baby would always come first for Libby. 'It's just... I know so little about you,' she said after a beat. 'To be getting married to a virtual stranger, having a baby with him... it's a lot.'

He appeared to relax back in his chair. 'What would you like to know?'

She laughed at the unexpectedness of that, and his grin pulled at her belly. She looked away, sipping her tea. 'Where are you from?'

'Spain.'

'More specifically?'

'Madrid.'

'When did you leave?'

'When I was twenty-one.'

'Do you ever go back?'

'Yes.'

'Often?'

'As required.'

She rolled her eyes. He was answering her questions but it felt a little like pulling teeth. She persisted.

'Do you ever want to live there again?'

His shrug was indolent. 'Who knows?'

She laughed despite herself.

'That's funny?'

'You don't strike me as a free spirit.'

He grinned. 'I go where I need to.'

'What constitutes need?'

'Work,' he said immediately, sipping his coffee.

'So that's what brought you to New York?'

'Yes.'

'Why New York?'

'The first global company I acquired was based here. I bought the building with the company. It just made sense.'

Her eyes widened. 'The whole building?'

His smile was slow to spread. 'Yes.'

'Just how rich are you, Raul?'

His laugh was low and gruff. 'I've lost count.'

'Whereas I have spent the last however many years knowing down to the last cent what's in my bank account,' she volleyed back with a small shake of her head.

'Speaking of which—' He stood, moving to the kitchen, where his jacket had been discarded, and removed his wallet. He walked towards her. 'This is for you.'

She took what he was offering without looking, but when she drew the item closer, she saw it was a credit card, with her name on it.

'Oh.' Her cheeks flushed. She wished she could say she didn't need it, that she could decline, but the reality was, she would need his financial support. That was part of the deal they'd made.

'What's wrong?' he asked, crouching down in front of her, staring at her in that way he had, as if unpicking every little piece of her.

'It's just… I've worked and earned for a long time. It's going to take some getting used to, just accepting money from you.'

'I respect that,' he murmured. 'This can be temporary, Libby. Once the baby is born, when you're ready, you can go back to work, or study, whatever you'd like. Don't overthink it.' He reached out then, almost as if against his judgement, and put a hand on her knee. 'We both know I can afford it.'

Libby's heart raced as she placed the credit card on the end table and forced a smile to her face. It would be different if they were in a real relationship, a real marriage. Then she'd have no trouble considering whatever was Raul's to be hers, and vice versa—such as it was.

'You'll need to come by the bank to sign some papers this week—to do with the trust funds I've set up.'

'Oh, when shall we go?' she asked, factoring that into her busy schedule of wandering the streets.

'You won't need me,' he said, standing and returning to his own seat. 'Justine can schedule it at your convenience.'

'Great,' she said, over-bright, feeling like a fool for expecting him to accompany her. Silence fell, but it was a heavy silence, at least, for Libby. She was aware of too much. Of what she'd learned about Raul and what she still didn't know, of the disparity in their finances and general life experiences and, most of all, her awareness of him as a man, which was making it hard to think with the objectivity she suspected she needed.

'I have also made enquiries about an obstetrics team,' he said, leaning forward, elbows resting on his thighs.

Libby's mouth formed a perfect O. 'You have?'

'You're pregnant, remember?' he drawled, face deadpan, but she smiled anyway.

'That's right, I'd forgotten,' she joked, patting her stomach. In the last couple of days she'd *felt* different, a little softer, and her jeans had become harder to button up, so she'd taken to wearing them with just the zip in place. 'But isn't there just a local hospital or something I can go to?'

'This is better.'

Libby dipped her head to hide a smile. She wasn't about to argue. If he wanted to pay for the best medical care money could buy, who was she to disagree? But...

'A whole obstetrics team?' she said after a beat, recollecting his phrasing.

'A nurse, midwife, two obstetricians—'

'Two?'

'In case one is unavailable.'

She laughed. 'Raul, we have no reason to think there are going to be any complications with my delivery. I'm young and healthy.'

'Nonetheless, why take chances?'

'Okay,' she said softly. 'We'll do it your way.'

'Thank you,' he said, and Libby's eyes lifted to his face at the unexpected expression of gratitude.

Was this how it would be between them? Discussion, agreement, compromise, gratitude? It wasn't a happily-ever-after love match, but it still felt pretty heartwarming for someone like Libby, who'd never known the pleasure that could come from mutual respect.

She returned his smile, even as she kept a firm grip on her heart and mind. He was charming, but she wouldn't allow herself to be charmed. 'You're welcome.'

CHAPTER SEVEN

RAUL KNEW SHE was pregnant. He believed her. He'd seen the sonogram image for himself. And yet, being here in the obstetrics clinic with a wand pressed to Libby's stomach and a gloopy grey and white image on the screen, listening to the sound of their baby's heartbeat in the air, Raul found it almost impossible to breathe. He stared at the screen—their baby—and was suddenly on the verge of a panic attack.

At least, he presumed it to be that—he'd never known this feeling before.

His vision filled with white and his lungs burned as though he'd run a marathon. And inside his mind he shouted every curse word he knew.

How the hell could he do this?

He couldn't be a father. He couldn't be a parent. What the hell did he know about raising someone? About taking care of another person? He'd made it his mission in life to care only for himself, to keep everyone else at a distance, and now he was looking at a tiny little life that would be *his*. His responsibility, his burden, his duty, his to care for and nurture and influence.

He swallowed, desperately needing moisture to return to his mouth and breath to reinflate his lungs.

'Raul?' Libby was looking up at him, her face showing concern. 'Are you okay?'

He tried to smile but suspected it was more of a grimace. Libby blinked, but not before he'd seen the hurt in her eyes.

He was messing everything up. He reached down and squeezed her hand, her need for reassurance in that moment trumping everything else. She didn't look up at him; her attention was focused on the screen.

He was ruining everything. God, he needed to pull himself together.

'Well?' He spoke more curtly than he'd intended. 'Is the baby healthy?'

The doctor's smile was practised. 'Everything here looks fine,' he assured them. 'I can see arms, legs, a heart.' He pulled the wand away from Libby's stomach. 'We'll do another scan in a few weeks.'

'Why?' Raul asked swiftly. 'Do you suspect something's wrong?'

'No,' the obstetrician said, running a hand through his hair. 'It's standard procedure, to investigate the organs. Today, we'll take some bloods, run a few more tests, but I haven't seen anything that concerns me.'

The obstetrician handed Libby a paper towel, which she used to wipe her belly, then she gingerly replaced her shirt. Raul's eyes clung to her stomach, the soft roundedness there hinting at what was to come, and something stole over him, a tingling sensation in the pit of his gut that ran like waves through his whole body.

Almost as soon as she'd told him about the baby he'd felt a primal rush of connection, a need to protect and provide for, and he felt that again now. This was *his* baby. Libby was to be *his* wife. Only he had no idea how to be a husband or a father. He had no idea how to be anything to anyone. He hated the thought of being relied on, even as he knew it had to be this way. But inside, Raul felt as though he was drowning; he wanted, for the first time in his life, to run as far away as he could from a challenge.

Libby desperately didn't want to take it personally, but the hour spent in the obstetrician's office had been one of the most emotionally complex of her life. On the one hand, there was the rush of hearing their baby's heartbeat, of seeing the little person on screen once more, of being reassured by the obstetrician that everything was developing as it should be. These things made Libby's heart warm and her soul glow. But then there was Raul, who'd spent the entire appointment looking as though he was being dragged through the very fires of hell, who'd made it obvious at every point that he didn't want to be there.

So why had he even come?

They left the health clinic with her nervous system rioting. She took several deep breaths, told herself to calm down, that it didn't matter what Raul felt or thought, that they were having an unplanned baby and naturally it was a complicated thing for each of them to navigate. But at the same time, she was angry. Angry in a way that fired the blood in her veins and made her temperature soar, angry in a way that put pink in her cheeks and caused her hands to tremble, so when they reached his car he asked, 'Are you okay?'

Libby shot him a look, contemplated answering honestly, but instead responded with, 'Why wouldn't I be?'

He frowned, unconvinced, but didn't say anything else. They rode back to his apartment in silence, with Libby looking out of the window, waiting for a sense of calm that didn't come.

He spoke once they entered the lift. 'Libby.'

She didn't look at him.

'What's going on?'

She expelled a shaky breath. 'Nothing.'

'Obviously that's not true.'

The doors pinged open into his apartment. She stepped inside, removing her shoes before moving through to the palatial living area. It was so exquisitely beautiful and, for some reason, it was the stunning opulence of the room that made her reach tipping point, and suddenly, her eyes sparkled with unshed tears.

'Libby?' His voice was a growl. She clung to her anger, rather than the swamping sensation of sadness threatening to devour her. But when she thought of what this experience was supposed to be like, what it would have been like if she were going through this with a true partner, she was thrown into a state of despair that was totally uncharacteristic for her.

'It's nothing,' she said as a tear slid down her cheek.

He was quiet. Perhaps if he'd pushed her again, she would have clammed up, refused to speak, but the palpating silence dragged words from her almost against her will.

'I wish you hadn't come,' she said quietly, and with relief, because it felt good to be honest with him.

Raul was very still, his expression impassive. 'To the appointment just now?'

She nodded. 'You couldn't have made it any plainer how much you didn't want to be there, how miserable you are about this whole thing. And I get it. You didn't want this, but it's happening, we're having a baby, and I don't want to be made to feel as though I'm ruining your life. Especially not in moments like that, when I should be able to just enjoy the experience.' She sucked in a breath, on a roll now. 'This isn't what I wanted for my life either, you know, but we're having a baby, and even when the circumstances aren't ideal, I'm still excited, I still want to make the most of each day of this pregnancy.' She angled her face away, unable to meet his eyes any more.

'You're right.' His admission surprised her. 'I didn't handle that well.'

She bit into her lip. 'You just shouldn't come to any more appointments.'

'That's not what I want.'

'Yeah, and I don't want to feel like I'm ruining your life,' she repeated, turning back to face him. 'It's not fair.'

'No, it's not.' He was quiet, still, and she felt like he was going to say something, but a moment later he nodded. 'If you don't want me there again, I won't come.'

Libby's heart did a strange, convulsive twist. The moment he said it, she realised it was the opposite of what she actually wanted: Raul by her side, *happy* about the baby. How unrealistic and pathetic! No matter how hard she tried, the optimist in Libby was struggling to accept the limitations of their arrangement. But she knew she had to, for her own sake. It was the only way she could do this.

Raul moved towards the lift with a steady gait, pausing once he'd pressed the button and the doors had pinged open. 'I'll see you tonight.'

Libby turned away from him, closing her eyes on a wave of sadness, and remorse. She wished now that she hadn't said anything. It had been futile and unnecessary. He was entitled to his feelings, just as she was hers.

But a moment later she heard footsteps and realised he hadn't left.

'This is hard for me,' he said, and when she turned to look at him, his features bore a mask of tension. She swallowed past a lump in her throat. 'I didn't know my parents. I did not have a good experience in the foster system. The streets were... You can imagine.' He ran a hand over the back of his neck, the action drawing her attention to the tightness in his frame. 'I have been alone a long time. I thought I would always be alone.' He paused, eyes boring into hers. 'I have no idea how to do any of this.' He gestured from himself to Libby. 'I panicked today.'

His raw honesty made her feel something she hadn't expected, something softening in her core. She didn't know why, but she nodded slowly, and he took that as encouragement or a prompt to continue, because he said, 'I am used to knowing exactly how to do what I need, in every situation. I am used to being in control, to running all aspects of my life.'

Libby expelled a soft breath. 'You can't control this,' she said gently. 'I get it; that's scary.'

A muscle throbbed in his jaw. 'I felt good things today too, Libby. Seeing our baby, hearing their heart beating.' He pressed a hand to his chest. 'I felt it. I just...didn't want to.'

More tears sparkled on Libby's lashes, but these were tears of relief.

'You have not ruined my life.'

She closed her eyes, surprised by how badly she needed to hear that, and by how much she wanted to understand Raul and his reactions.

'I'm sorry I got mad with you,' she said gently. 'I was scared too.'

His brows drew together, and she thought he might have been about to reject her assessment, but then he moved closer, pressing his thumb to her chin, tilting her face towards his. 'You're going to be a great mother.'

She blinked up at him, heart in her throat. 'How do you know?'

'Look at what you're already doing for our baby,' he said, stroking her cheek. Libby's stomach twisted. Did he understand how much she wanted this reassurance? To believe she'd be different to her own selfish mother? 'I'm sorry I upset you,' he said. 'I was thoughtless.'

She shook her head, silently denying his statement. 'This is unchartered territory for both of us. Let's just... agree to talk things through, when it gets tough. No matter what, we want what's best for the baby. That's all that matters.'

'Yes,' he said quietly, his voice low and raspy, and suddenly, Libby wasn't aware of their conversation or what had upset her, or even of the baby. Every fibre of her soul was focused on the man in front of her, standing so close that if she exhaled heavily, her breasts would brush his chest. She was aware of the feeling of his fingertips against her skin, his touch light, intended to be calming, but it was having the opposite effect on her frazzled nerves.

She blinked up at him and found herself in a time warp, the last few months evaporating in a deep well, sinking her back to the boat, that moment of connection, to how easy it had been when so overcome by the powerful emotions of survival to reach out and touch him, to feel and connect on a totally immersive level.

Raul's eyes were hooded, hard to read, but they dropped to her lips and stayed there, so Libby's pulse grew fast and erratic and she wondered if he could feel it somehow through her skin, if he could sense her response to him. Was he feeling it too?

She lifted her hand to his wrist, wrapped it around, fingers brushing his pulse point, but her own was too chaotic to make sense of his.

'Libby,' he murmured, frowning, his gaze moving to hers, probing her eyes as if he could read answers there, as if he could understand something important in the depths of her pupils.

'We shouldn't do this,' she said, even as she swayed forward, her body brushing his, and she felt the hiss of air escaping his lips, felt his chest jolt as he sucked in, and then his other hand was at her back, holding her right where she was, pressed to him, no more than a hair's breadth between their bodies. This was stupid and complicated, but it was also simple and right. What a strange and contradictory way to describe their situation, she thought as she lifted up onto the tips of her toes, her eyes holding his without fear.

His hand at her back moved higher, then lower, stroking her through the soft wool of her jumper, sending thousands of shockwaves through Libby, making her whole body reverberate with pleasure and awareness. Then he kissed her, slowly, gently, just the lightest brushing of his lips to hers at first, but that didn't matter.

The smallest spark can still ignite a forest, and the lightest touch of Raul's lips to Libby's was enough to remind them both of the heat that had burned between them that afternoon.

Raul groaned low in his throat and then... There was nothing light about his kiss, it was white-hot with a frantic need that turned her bones to mush and made her body tingle all over. Thought was no longer possible; she was simply a physical being, existing purely for this, for Raul.

Her hands pushed at his shirt, lifting it from the waist-
band of his trousers, fumbling with the buttons, yet per-
sisting until they were undone and she could push it from
his body, and then her fingertips roamed his flesh with
impunity, touching him as she'd been desperate to do, she
acknowledged only to herself, since that afternoon, when
her dreams had been filled with memories she thought
she'd never have the chance to relive.

He groaned again as her touch ran over his chest and
to his shoulders, then her hands wrapped around his neck
so her breasts were pressed to his torso and even through
the fabric she wore her nipples grew taut and sensitive,
tingling almost painfully.

He said her name like a curse but didn't break the kiss.
Instead, he reached down and lifted Libby, wrapping her
legs around his waist, carrying her easily through the penthouse, down the corridor and turning right, not left, taking her to his room rather than hers.

Inside, it was similar to Libby's, only bigger, with a more
masculine décor—a huge bed sat in the centre, and at the
sight of it, Libby's pulse went totally haywire, but there was
no time to question this. Not when Raul was kissing her
as though his life depended on it, not when he placed her
on the ground and began to remove her clothes, not when
his hands were worshipping her body, running over her,
touching her, teasing her, tempting her, making it impossible to imagine a world in which they didn't come together.

'You are so beautiful,' he grunted, shaking his head
with the appearance of disbelief as he removed the rest of
his own clothes, rendering them both naked in the privacy
of his bedroom. She wasn't nervous. It was as if she'd been
preparing for this her whole life, as if there was nothing
more vital or important.

'So are you,' she said honestly, artlessly, reaching out a hand, wanting to touch him again. He stepped forward, his Adam's apple jolting visibly as he swallowed. Libby touched the centre of his chest first and felt his breath draw inwards, then ran her fingers lower, down towards a dark arrow of hair that drew her to his manhood. Trembling a little, she let her fingers brush him, felt him jerk, and a rush of power made her smile.

'This is madness,' he said, eyes glittering when they met hers.

'I know. We really shouldn't.'

He nodded, standing still.

'Not after this.' She tilted her head, challenging him. 'Not again.'

He laughed softly, relief obvious in his features. 'You have yourself a deal,' he said with a nod, and then he was lifting her, carrying her to the bed, laying her down and kissing Libby with all the passion and promise she remembered, with everything she'd been craving and needing, and suddenly it didn't matter that their marriage was only a shadow of what she wanted. When he could make her feel like this, when there was pleasure as rich and as absorbing as Raul created, Libby cared for nothing else. This would be enough: it would have to be.

CHAPTER EIGHT

'CAN YOU MEET me in an hour?'

Libby's gaze shifted to the clock on the oven. 'Meet you where?'

He named a world-famous jeweller with a store on Fifth Avenue.

'Oh.' Libby's pulse trembled, not just because of the mention of a jeweller, but because the sound of Raul's voice alone had been enough to have that effect on her ever since they'd slept together the day before. They'd agreed it would be a one-off, so she wasn't stupid enough to be thinking about a repeat performance. At least, not consciously. But if she'd thought having sex with Raul would cure her of her cravings, she'd been wrong. If anything, it only stoked them further.

'Libby?'

She'd let her mind wander, and forced herself to focus now.

'I guess. But why?'

'You'll see.' He disconnected the call, leaving Libby frowning, holding the cell phone to her ear, staring out over a wintry Manhattan afternoon.

It was dark when her cab pulled up at the address she'd been given, the early sunsets par for the course at this time of year, and a hint of snow had started to fall, so Libby allowed herself a moment to stand and hold up her hands, catching some flakes in her gloves, smiling as she brought it near enough to her face to see the tiny little crystals.

'Beautiful,' she murmured to no one in particular, caught in the midst of a bustling group of people making their way down the street with little regard for the Australian who was enjoying her first real winter. Libby was so captivated by the glorious sight that she didn't notice Raul, standing by the door to the shop, his eyes having landed on her the moment she exited the taxi with unconscious grace.

Libby smiled to herself then dusted off her hands, preparing to move inside the shop, until a movement alerted her to Raul's presence. Her heart slammed into her ribs. She forced a smile but she was self-conscious suddenly, embarrassed by her childlike love for the phenomenon of snow.

'I'm not used to it,' she explained with a lift of her shoulders as she approached him.

His eyes skimmed her features. 'I remember my first winter here. It was a shock to the system.'

'But so wonderful,' Libby said on a happy sigh. 'I think it's gloriously beautiful.'

He lifted a brow and then surprised them both by laughing. 'Has anyone ever told you you're the most optimistic person they've ever met?'

Heat burned in Libby's cheeks. 'No, actually.'

'Well, I'm sure they've thought it. Are you ready?'

'What for, exactly?'

He put a hand at Libby's lower back, shepherding her through the large revolving door. 'To choose your ring.'

Libby stopped walking in the middle of the spinning

door, only to receive a bump on the bottom as the glass kept rotating.

'Oh. Can't you just pick something? Something simple,' she added.

'I don't know you well enough to know what you'd like,' he pointed out. 'And as you'll be wearing it every day for a long time, it should be something you don't hate, right?'

Every day for a long time. Not, she noticed, *for ever.* Because once their child was old enough, they'd be able to dispense with this ruse and go their separate ways, and she was sure they were both looking forward to that.

Libby forced a tight smile. 'Okay. Let's just have a casual look around.'

Only Raul didn't do anything casually, and the name Raul Ortega clearly opened the kinds of doors Libby had never even known existed. Far from being allowed to 'look around', they were greeted by a personal concierge, who insisted on taking them to a private room to view rings in comfort. Not only were they placed side by side on a small sofa so their thighs brushed the whole time, they were brought a trolley stacked with food and drinks then left completely alone whilst the staff assembled several boxes of beautiful rings.

Libby found the silence stretched her nerves almost to breaking point. It was the closest they'd been since making love and her heart was ramming against her chest in a way she wasn't sure was entirely safe. But the more she thought about Raul, about the things he'd said yesterday, his childhood, and reflected on the way he'd been when he saw the sonogram, the more she knew he was quicksand. He was the definition of emotionally distant, and the last thing she should do was let herself get swept up in the crazy, red-hot passion that sparked between them.

'About yesterday,' Libby finally said, figuring it was better to address the elephant in the room.

Beside her, Raul stiffened. 'I know. It shouldn't have happened.' He turned to face her, and Libby's stomach was suddenly hollow. 'We'll be more careful from now on.'

It was exactly what Libby had been going to say, but hearing it from Raul did something strange to her insides, and made her breathing strain. Before she could figure out how to respond, a woman walked in with two display cases of rings, and from then on it was impossible to talk about anything except the clarity of diamonds.

Raul had always run.

As a boy he'd loved the freedom, the feeling of wind in his hair, the strength in his legs, the burning in his lungs. He'd been carted from foster home to foster home, each situation offering new challenges and dangers, but always he'd had his own strength and speed. He'd slipped out of bed early most mornings, before anyone else woke, and he would run as far and fast as he could. It hadn't mattered to him that the streets weren't always safe; that had added to the thrill. Danger couldn't catch him; he'd outrun it.

When he'd left the foster system for good and wound up living rough, he'd run even when his belly had been so empty the exercise had cost him vital energy. He'd run because it was an inherent part of him—to know he could take himself wherever he needed to go, whenever necessary.

Running was a habit for Raul, and it was also where he did his best thinking, taking whatever problem he faced at that point in time and untangling the knots until it made sense to him. Usually, he focused on business, his mind effortlessly trawling over his current circumstances, reorganising the pieces, shuffling, until he happened upon a solution.

This morning, as the sun was just starting to hint its golden promise over the city, he found his mind singularly turned to Libby. Only each step he took brought him closer to confusion, not clarity, so he ran harder, faster, waiting for something to loosen in his mind, to offer comprehension, an understanding of their situation.

He was attracted to her.

And she was attracted to him.

So what?

He'd been attracted to women before. He'd slept with women. This wasn't new, for either of them. The only difference was that his baby was growing inside of her and, despite the fact he'd sworn he'd never have a family, he couldn't help but feel a biological connection to that child and, by extension, to Libby.

That was why this felt different, he realised as he hit the six-mile mark. It wasn't about them *per se*, but the fact they were going to be co-parenting. It was an intimate relationship regardless of the reality of their situation: that they barely knew one another.

Sleeping together didn't mean anything. It was an itch they'd scratched. And despite what they'd said, he suspected they'd scratch it again when they wanted to. That didn't have to be complicated. It didn't have to change anything.

And yet surely it was smarter to keep things in their own clear lane.

They were getting married for the sake of this baby. They were going to be living together, raising a child together. Just the thought of that made Raul's throat constrict with panic. So much so, he had to stop running a moment, pressing his hands to his hips and sucking in big bursts of cold morning air.

He didn't want this, he thought with a groan. He didn't want to be tied to anyone.

He was a runner. He ran. He ran whenever he wanted or needed to. He didn't have belongings he cared enough about to lose. He didn't have people he cared enough about to lose. He couldn't care about a child or a wife. He couldn't.

And yet, what choice did he have? He was about to become a father—it was a sacred role, one he knew he would fulfil because he'd experienced only absence there. In his heart, where he might have turned to find love and strength built from generations of support, he knew nothing. It was a void he would never pass on to his child. He had to be in their life; this was the only option.

He was terrified of the steps he was taking, terrified of a future tethered to anyone, and somehow Libby made that all the more frightening, yet he knew he had to act fast, to make this happen.

For even though he was afraid and acknowledged this to be the last thing he wanted, at the same time he also understood he wouldn't breathe easily until Libby was officially his wife and their commitment to this child was formalised.

And there it was. The clarity he'd sought.

Many times in Raul's life he'd been afraid and yet he'd acted. If anything, the fear made him more determined: he wouldn't be cowed by it. He'd been afraid to turn up at each new foster home, afraid of the new rules, the new people, the new environments, the new schools. Afraid and yet determined never to show it: he conquered fear and doubt with strength and courage, and he would do so again.

Running once more, he began to formulate a plan, meeting the uncertainty of his heart with black and white steps of determination and action.

That, after all, was Raul's way.

Libby read the email with a strange heaving in her chest.

Libby
The wedding will take place on Friday at two p.m., after which we'll have a late lunch to celebrate.
R

She read it again, frowning now, her heart pounding against her ribs.

The wedding will take place on Friday at two p.m.

There was no mention of how she'd get to the wedding, no mention of a honeymoon, no mention of any of the specifics that she wanted to know. But what he had mentioned was enough to send her pulse into total disarray.

Friday was only two days away.

Two days!

She knew they were getting married quickly, but foolishly hadn't expected it would happen so soon. And yet, wasn't that the whole point of this? He'd taken her to buy a wedding ring; that had clearly been a forerunner to the event itself.

...after which we'll have a late lunch to celebrate.

Celebrate what? Their sham wedding?

Her lips pulled to the side as she felt a familiar emptiness in her heart, the pain of knowing how far removed their wedding and marriage were from what she'd always wanted. But she forced herself to ignore it. This wasn't about her. She'd already grappled with the sacrifice she was making, and why.

For their baby, she'd do this. She'd make it work. And she refused to feel sad about it—there was just no point in lamenting what she could never have. She'd have to find a different kind of fairy tale, and she suspected that would begin and end with the love she felt for the little person growing inside her belly.

He arrived late that night, and Libby was already asleep; Raul left early the next morning, and so on and so forth, so on the morning of their wedding she awoke with a strange sense of absence warring with anticipation in the pit of her stomach.

She was getting married today, to a man she hadn't seen nor spoken to in days, and despite the pragmatic circumstances behind their union, her stomach was filled with butterflies and she couldn't help the hum in her bloodstream as she dressed with care for the ceremony.

It was not in a church.

She wouldn't carry a long, trailing bouquet like Queen Elizabeth's—the flowers she'd always fantasised about—but that didn't matter. She was focusing beyond the wedding, on the marriage, and the baby. Once this formality was dealt with, she could start giving her attention to setting up Raul's apartment for the arrival of their child.

It would feel real then.

Important to start preparing, decorating a nursery, buying clothes, getting ready for the reality of parenthood. There'd be childbirth classes too, and playgroups she could join.

Libby found great solace in turning her mind to those practical, baby-led plans, and she thought purely of their child as she dressed for the wedding.

She'd chosen a simple outfit, befitting the simple ceremony they'd be having, and at one o'clock she was preparing to go downstairs and hail a cab when the lift to the penthouse opened and Raul strode in, wearing a jet-black tuxedo with a snow-white shirt.

He was the last person Libby expected to see: in fact, she'd thought she wouldn't see him for another hour, and not here but at the office where their wedding was to take place, and so her jaw dropped and her eyes widened.

'You're not supposed to be here,' she blurted out. 'It's bad luck.'

His look was one of pure cynicism. 'I think that horse has bolted, don't you?'

She didn't need reminding, on their wedding day, of all days, that he found the whole situation unlucky. Libby's response was a tight smile. 'I presumed we'd be meeting there.'

'I brought you these.'

It was then that Libby noticed he was carrying a crisp white bag. She frowned, walking towards him, and when he extended it, she saw a bouquet of white roses inside, with baby's breath poked in between. The bouquet was held together with a cream ribbon made of wide satin and pinned down the seam with pearls.

'Oh,' she said, staring at it, her mouth dry. It wasn't what she had imagined and yet somehow it was lovely, and all the more so because he'd thought to arrange it for her. 'Thank you.'

He nodded. 'The photographer will meet us there.'

'Photographer?' she repeated, the detail yet another she'd presumed would be absent.

'For wedding photos.'

She rolled her eyes. 'I know what photographers do. I just didn't think we'd have one.'

'It's the done thing, isn't it?'

'Maybe for real weddings, but do either of us really want to remember this day?'

His eyes narrowed imperceptibly and a muscle jerked in his jaw. 'It's not for us. Our son or daughter will appreciate seeing a photo in the future, I'm sure.'

'Right,' she agreed. This ruse was all for the baby. 'Good thinking.'

'Do you need to eat anything before we go?'

She shook her head. 'I couldn't possibly.' Libby bit down on her lip. 'I'm filled with butterflies.'

He lifted a brow.

'Nerves,' she clarified.

'Why would you be nervous?'

'Because I'm getting married, and to someone I don't know particularly well,' she pointed out. 'It's weird and strange and even though I know this isn't a real marriage, I still feel like I'm about to do something momentous and important.' She shrugged. 'Aren't you?'

'Nervous?'

She nodded once.

'No.'

'Really? Not even a little?'

His eyes skimmed her face. 'You'll feel better when it's over.'

She grimaced. 'Like having a tooth pulled?'

His lips flicked in an unexpected smile. 'Exactly.'

'But no lidocaine.'

'It'll be mostly harmless. Over within minutes.'

She nodded, wishing the knots in her tummy would straighten out. Wishing that he understood the lack of fanfare was all part of the broader problem. She pressed a hand to her belly, not to feel the little life there but in the hope of straightening out her anxiety, and instead felt worse.

'Okay,' she said a little unevenly. 'Let's do this.'

The whole thing was surreal. She felt as though she were living in a sort of dream as they descended in the lift to the street level, where a limousine was waiting. They rode side by side and in silence to the hall. Confetti and rose petals were strewn on the steps, remnants of other marriages, presumably happier, more genuine matches.

Libby ignored the sight of it, ignored the pulling in her belly, ignored, most of all, the feeling that this was all so very, very wrong. It was for the baby, she kept reminding herself as she walked up the steps at Raul's side, into the beautiful old building with marble floors and wood panelling.

A simple sign pointed towards the *Register Office for Civil Unions*.

'I guess that's us,' she said, blinking up at Raul, wondering if she was waiting for him to change his mind, to say this wasn't their best idea, that they could wait.

But he didn't. He nodded once, his lips a grim line in his face, and she knew he was feeling as ambivalent about this as she was, even though he wouldn't admit it.

He put a hand against the base of her spine and, despite her anxiety, Libby trembled, her body surging in response and awareness, which she bitterly resented. How could she feel such contradictory emotions?

The hall was long and brightly lit, by windows on one side and electric bulbs overhead. Libby walked beside Raul, one foot in front of the other, until they reached a wooden door. Their names were on a printed piece of paper stuck to a noticeboard out front.

Two p.m. Ortega & Langham.

Libby's pulse was thready. She sucked in a deep breath, found it impossible to look at Raul, so stared at the wood grain of the door until she had practically memorised the pattern. Finally, a moment after two p.m., the doors opened and a young couple stepped out, a woman with bright red hair and a man wearing a kilt. They were too busy embracing, laughing, to notice Raul and Libby, and she was glad. She didn't want anyone to see her in that moment, the pallor of her skin, the slight trembling of her body— she was sure she must look like the most unexcited bride there'd ever been.

Only, even in that state of mind, Libby found herself trying to focus on the positives. To ignore her nerves and see the beauty of the room they were shepherded into, and the gift she was giving her child by marrying Raul. She wasn't old-fashioned enough to believe this was the only way to raise a little person; of course she didn't. But for Libby, having grown up with such insecurity in her life, she knew that for *her* it was the right choice. She wanted to give this child the world, and Raul could make that happen. Not just because he was wealthy beyond belief, but because in this one vital area they were in complete agreement. Nothing mattered more than their baby's future, their baby's security, their baby's happiness.

The ceremony was swift. Raul and Libby took turns repeating their vows, then exchanged rings. Libby was surprised Raul had one for himself. She hadn't even thought he would want to wear a ring, and yet when the time came he produced a simple band from his pocket, placed it in her palm, then waited, hand outstretched, for her to slide it onto his finger. Her own fingers trembled as she did so, and it took her a few turns, but Raul waited with no expression on his face as she performed the act, binding them, in the eyes of the law, 'till death do us part'.

It was an indication of Libby's mindset that she hadn't even thought of the conclusion of the ceremony until the moment was upon them. As the celebrant said, 'Congratulations, you may now kiss the bride,' Libby's heart jolted and she turned to Raul, wide-eyed, blinking up at him with consternation.

She wasn't prepared for this.

She felt too vulnerable, as though she didn't have her armour in place; she felt that she needed time to adjust to being married before having to kiss him, and yet it was a formality, part and parcel of the ruse they'd just completed. She stood there, too aware of every breath in her body, every throb of her heart, every pulse of her blood, every organ, every thought, every memory; it was all there, evoked inside Libby, swirling like a tornado, obliterating consciousness and time.

Raul moved slowly, his hand coming around her back, drawing her to him, as if giving her time to demur, to tell him to stop.

She didn't. She was very still, totally passive, waiting, heart on edge.

His other hand came to her face, tilted her chin towards him, and then his head bent slowly, cautiously, his eyes closing so his lashes formed two thick, dark fans against his cheeks right before his mouth claimed hers and she moaned softly as a rush of feelings overcame her.

Anxiety was gone. Nervousness and uncertainty disappeared.

Every little piece of her that had been shaky and on edge locked hard into place, so she was Libby again, but not as she'd ever been before. She was like a butterfly emerging from a chrysalis, no longer Libby Langham but Libby Ortega—different, beautiful, strong, married and a mother-to-be. These thoughts were blades cutting through the back of her mind without her awareness. All Libby could feel was the rightness of this kiss, the warmth of his hand on her back, the pleasure of his touch at her cheek, the flicking of his tongue against hers, a delicious, tempting, sinful dance that was laced with promise and anticipation.

She was lost, utterly, and she knew she should fight that, that she should do whatever she could to hold onto herself in all this madness, but being lost to Raul was one of the best things she'd ever felt, and on her wedding day, of all days, shouldn't Libby allow herself that one little indulgence?

CHAPTER NINE

RAUL PULLED AWAY for a moment, staring down at Libby as though he'd never seen her before, as though he'd never seen a flesh and blood woman in his life, his eyes sweeping across her face, trying to make sense of it, but even then there was a magnetic pull towards her that dominated all else, and suddenly he was kissing her again, his mouth on hers more demanding, more urgent, reminding him of the first cataclysmic time they'd touched. He'd put it down to adrenalin then, and maybe the same excuse applied now— their wedding day was not a moment without emotion for either of them, despite the nature of their union. Whatever the reason, he wanted to kiss her. He didn't question that want, he simply drew her into his arms and took what she was offering, with no thought of where they were nor how out of step this was with their marriage.

It didn't *feel* out of step.

It felt like exactly what he should be doing, and she tasted so sweet, like vanilla and strawberries, so he wanted more and more of her. Her dress was a simple silk with a white faux fur coat. She was a sensory explosion, all soft and textural beneath his touch.

He suddenly wanted to be anywhere but here, in a room in a courthouse, being married by some strange officiant. As if on cue, the man cleared his throat, perhaps more than once, but it took a moment for Raul to hear, to recollect himself and pull away from Libby, to stare down at her with an expression more like the impassive mask he should have been wearing.

'Thank you,' he said, not sure if he was speaking to Libby or the celebrant, but extending a hand in the celebrant's direction belatedly.

'Congratulations.' The man grinned, gesturing to the door. 'If you'll head out there, Rowena will see to the paperwork.'

In his peripheral vision, Raul saw Libby's tight nod of her head, and a single glance in her direction showed the dazed and confused look on her face. Something tightened inside of him. He had to get control of this. He had to manage things better.

As they signed the certificate of marriage, the photographer Raul's assistant had organised took pictures and Raul made a point of smiling, remembering the whole purpose of this was to have something to show their child when they were older. Perhaps they'd even print one of the pictures and hang it on a wall. Raul didn't have any photographs of himself or his birth parents, or anyone of significance in his life. There'd never really been anyone, and that was fine by Raul, but for their child they were creating a different reality, a myth, and pictures would be a part of that.

In front of the building, they posed for a few more snaps, but when the photographer suggested a kiss Raul responded gruffly, 'That's enough.' He felt Libby stiffen at his side and could have kicked himself. 'It's cold. Time to get inside,' he said, turning to Libby and offering another smile—though it felt stretched on his face.

She nodded, not meeting his eyes.

Back in the limousine, he noticed they sat as far from

one another as possible. Good. Keeping their distance was a wise move.

'You mentioned something about a lunch now?' she asked quietly, fidgeting with her hands in her lap.

Raul closed his eyes as he remembered that particular detail. 'My assistant's idea.'

He missed the hurt on Libby's face, but when she spoke her voice trembled a little. 'We don't have to go. There's not really anything to celebrate here, is there?'

Raul cursed inwardly. 'We just got married,' he said. 'It's the least we can do to mark the occasion.'

'I really can't see that's necessary,' she muttered, the glumness in her voice unmistakable, and she continued to stare at her wedding ring.

Raul reached over, putting a hand on hers without thinking, then wishing he hadn't when he felt the now predictable surge of awareness travel the length of his arm. Touching her was his weakness. The lightest brush of his flesh to hers and he forgot everything he'd promised himself about this marriage, the necessary boundaries and restrictions, and just wanted to exist without constraint.

'We are having a child, and raising them as a family. We both know why that matters to us.'

'Yes,' she whispered, lifting her head but only so she could tilt it away from him, looking out of the window.

'So let's celebrate our commitment to the baby,' he said. 'This is the first day of our new family,' he said, and Libby turned to face him then, eyes wide and so beautiful he couldn't look away.

'Family,' she murmured, as if struck by that idea. Just as he was when he heard her say the word. Struck, and trapped. Terrified. He removed his hand, tried not to look as though the heavens were falling down around him.

'Besides, I'm hungry.'

Libby nodded, then blinked and turned away. Raul resisted the urge to ask her to turn back, to look at him again, but her eyes were quickly becoming an addiction of his. Yet another thing to conquer.

Not only was the restaurant beautiful and exclusive, but Raul's assistant had outdone herself, having a small private alcove reserved for the occasion, decked out in dozens more of the stunning white roses that had formed Libby's bouquet. She brushed the petals of one as she sat down, the softness reminding her of the silk of her dress.

'You look beautiful,' Raul said, as if reading her mind, like he was also thinking of the silk she wore.

Heat suffused Libby's cheeks. 'It's just a thrift shop find,' she said. 'A bit of fun, really. The dress is from the twenties.'

'It suits you.'

'I guess I'm an old-fashioned kind of girl,' she quipped, eyes dropping to her wedding ring, a frown tugging at her lips before she could control it.

A waitress appeared with a bottle of champagne, popped the top. 'It's non-alcoholic,' she said with a bright smile, 'per the request we were emailed.'

They were silent as the drinks were poured, and then, left to their own devices, that silence took on a crackling, electric quality. Libby reached for her drink, wrapped her fingers around the stem but didn't lift it.

'A toast,' Raul said quietly. Libby waited, heart in her throat. 'To our baby's future,' he murmured, and it was so perfectly appropriate because it was a heartfelt sentiment, perhaps the only heartfelt utterance he could have delivered in that moment, and it meant the world to both of them. Libby lifted her glass and clinked it to his.

'To our baby,' she murmured, sipping the drink, finding it every bit as delicious as champagne. She closed her eyes, the moment wrapping around her. 'I can't believe we're married,' she said after a beat.

'I was there. It happened.'

She pulled a face. 'Yeah, I just mean…'

'I know what you mean.'

'In the blink of an eye, I feel like my life has changed so much.' She looked around the room, gesturing distractedly to the grandeur of the restaurant. 'I mean, look at this place. It's the sort of restaurant my clients go to, not me.'

Raul was a study in relaxation. 'What did you see as your future, Libby?'

'I hadn't worked it out yet,' she said honestly. 'I thought I'd study, do something so I could work from home and take care of the baby.'

He nodded. 'I mean if there was no baby. Before meeting me, what was your long-term plan? At one time you wanted to be a chef. But after that, was there anything else?'

It wasn't an unreasonable question and yet, for some reason, Libby felt her defensive hackles rise. 'I didn't think about it. I just had to work and earn enough to get by.'

'I admire that,' he surprised her by saying. 'But surely at some point you wanted something more?'

'No.' She ran a finger over the condensation on her glass. 'Although…'

'What?'

'It's stupid,' she said with a wry smile, but the smile slipped when she saw the look in his eyes—a look of such intense interest that heat bubbled in her veins. 'When I was a kid, I wanted to be a doctor.'

Raul lifted one brow. 'Why is that stupid?'

'Well, I can't stand the sight of blood, for one thing,' she said, sipping her drink. 'But when I was a little girl, maybe seven or eight, my mum passed out. She'd had too much to drink, but I didn't know that then. I just remember seeing her on the floor, not being able to wake her up and panicking. We'd had firefighters come to our school earlier that year, talking to us about what to do in an emergency, so I knew to call emergency services. An ambulance came with flashing lights and kind, confident people who made me feel so good and like everything was going to be okay. My mother was *furious* with me,' she added, grimacing.

'Why?'

'For one thing, she was embarrassed. For another, there was a cost for the callout.' Libby scrunched up her nose. 'But I'll never forget my sense of helplessness, contrasted with the relief I felt when the paramedics arrived and knew exactly what to do. I wanted to be that person who could walk into a room and fix people, make everything okay for everyone.' Libby bit down on her lip. 'Instead, I clean houses. And boats.'

Raul reached across the table, put his hand on Libby's, and her heart jumped into her throat. She felt his sympathy and immediately wanted to push it away.

'It's not like I hate it,' she said. 'In fact, there's a lot to like about it. The pay's okay, and I get to choose my schedule.'

'Not to mention the occasional adventure on the high seas,' he pointed out.

'Right.' She was surprised by how natural it felt to smile. The waitress returned to take their orders. Libby hadn't even looked at the options. Raul suggested a tasting menu and she readily agreed.

'You have some food allergies though, right?' the waitress said, referring to her notepad.

Raul spoke before Libby could respond. 'Shellfish and soft cheeses.'

Libby's eyes widened. He'd read the pregnancy books? Of course he had. Raul was taking no chances with this baby. Her stomach did a funny little loop.

'Got it.' The waitress smiled as she departed.

Libby propped her elbows on the table, resting her chin on one palm. 'What about you?' she asked, fascinated by the strength in Raul's face, the symmetry of his features. 'What did you want to be when you were a kid?'

He grinned. 'A builder.'

'Really?'

'I loved watching high-rises go up. I was fascinated by the way they could be shaped almost as if from the ground. The steel, concrete, the structures. I would skip school and watch the work all day. Sometimes, I'd get to help, earn a few bucks. I loved the feeling of creating something with my bare hands,' he said, looking down at them, almost as if surprised by the admission. 'I haven't thought of that for a long time.'

'But instead you became…well, fabulously wealthy,' she said, crinkling her nose again. 'I don't even know what you do, besides make a lot of money.'

'I started off investing in companies,' he said, as though it were that simple.

'What kinds of companies?'

'Businesses that were failing but which had untapped potential. I exploited their market weakness to get a good deal, then either restructured to turn a profit or pieced them up and sold them off, whichever was going to yield the best return.'

She shook her head. 'I can't even imagine how you got started doing that,' she murmured. 'As someone who comes from nothing, who never had money behind me, just getting by is a struggle some days.'

'Yes,' he agreed with vehemence. 'Precisely. I hit rock-bottom, Libby. I hit it, scraped along it, settled there for long enough to know that I couldn't keep living like that. I had to claw my way off the bottom with my bare hands. It was bloody and hard, and I had to fight tooth and nail to get out, but I swore to myself I would never know that kind of poverty again. I would never be hungry, I would never be cold, I would never be on the streets.'

Admiration for Raul's determination swelled inside of her, and a pride too that she immediately fought. After all, what business did she have feeling proud of him? None of this was down to her. He wasn't even her real husband. It was a sobering thought and her smile momentarily slipped.

'I got a job at a construction company. Just a small one, run by an old couple—they were in their late eighties when I met them. I don't know why they hired me. I was as surprised then as I am now. I was seventeen, skinnier than a nail, but they took a bet on me and I wasn't going to waste the opportunity. I worked my fingers to the bone, and the owner's wife, Maria, would bring lunches to the site. She must have seen how hungry I was. I ate, gained weight, grew stronger, worked harder. I worked for them for three years, got to know them, and then the owner, Pedro, came to me one day and told me he was retiring. That he was leaving the company to me. It was a gift, Libby. A gift. Only, he didn't see it that way. He said I would take their legacy and turn it into something great. He said that he believed in me.'

Raul's eyes widened and Libby's heart felt dangerously soft and aching. 'No one had *ever* believed in me before. It was a gift and a burden. I have spent the last ten years trying to justify his faith.'

Libby's eyes were suspiciously moist. 'Do you still own the company?'

'It's the backbone of all that I do,' Raul admitted. 'It's basically unrecognisable now, but I kept the name, and I think of Maria and Pedro often, I wonder where I would have been if it weren't for them.'

'They didn't have children?'

'No. They couldn't.'

Libby grimaced sympathetically. 'They must have felt that they won the lottery, finding you.'

'I try to make decisions they would be proud of,' he said, again looking surprised by the admission. 'I try to justify the gift they gave me.'

'Raul, even without them, I have no doubt you would be sitting here right now. There's just something about you. Pedro and Maria saw it; I do too.'

His eyes flicked to hers then away again, almost as if he didn't want to believe that.

'Do you ever think about those guys who stole your boat?' she asked, sipping her drink, then easing back in her seat as the waitress appeared with their entrees, a delightful little bowl of velouté.

'Think about them in what way?'

'Wonder about their lives, what they're doing now?'

'I know what they're doing,' he answered simply.

She blinked. She supposed it was possible the police had kept Raul in the loop, given they'd tried to steal his boat.

'Two have been moved into apprenticeship programmes to learn a trade, one is at a boarding school in the city, and another is being helped by a social worker with some childhood trauma he experienced.'

Libby paused, midway through lifting her spoon from the bowl. 'How do you know this?'

Raul briefly looked uncomfortable.

Libby's heart sped up. 'You did that for them, didn't you?'

'Punishment of a judicial nature didn't seem to fit the crime. Besides, I know what kids like that need, and it's not detention.'

Her stomach was in knots and tears sprang to her eyes quickly.

Raul looked terrified.

'I'm sorry.' Libby half laughed. 'It's the pregnancy hormones.' But it wasn't, and she shook her head, dispelling that. 'No, it's more, it's… I think you did a wonderful thing for them,' she said softly. 'Maria and Pedro would be so proud of you.'

Raul looked away before she could see his response, but she knew she'd touched a chord deep within him.

'It was the right thing to do.'

'Yeah,' she agreed in a heartbeat. 'But lots of people wouldn't have done it. I mean, they punched you—'

'He caught me off-guard. He was little more than a child.'

'Still. They stole your boat.'

'I got it back. No harm done. Besides, a boat is just a boat. It's a thing, easy to replace.'

She shook her head. 'Not necessarily, but for you, yes, I can see your point.'

They ate their soup and Libby was surprised to find they slipped easily into small talk. She asked him about the city and he returned those questions, so she found herself sharing stories of her walking adventures, how far she'd gone, how much of the city she'd seen by exploring on foot. He asked about her favourite streets, any cafés she'd found and enjoyed, if there was anything she'd wanted to do but couldn't, and Libby realised she had been develop-

ing a wish-list as she'd walked, of certain sights she'd like
to tour, shops she wanted to explore.

'It's just all so different to what I'm used to,' she said.
'The weather, the streets, the buildings.' She shook her
head. 'I realise how sheltered I've been, in not travelling.
You know, I'd only ever flown once before meeting you,'
she confided. 'To Brisbane, for Mum's funeral.'

Raul's expression was unchanged but something shifted
in the depth of his gaze.

'Now I feel as though my eyes have been opened to this
whole big wide world and I want to see it, Raul. I want to
explore everything.'

'Where else would you like to go?' he asked, as the
waitress came to clear their plates. Libby didn't notice.

'Oh, I don't mean I want to leave New York,' she said
with a wave of her hand. 'Only that I want to inhale this
city while I'm here. I want to see and understand everything. And yes, then I'd like to see more, cities I've read
about and seen in movies and never thought I would have
within my reach. I want to show them to our child, to explore them together,' she said, smiling as she patted her
stomach.

'And you will. You know my plane is at your disposal,
I presume?'

Libby's eyes went round in her face. 'Erm…no, I didn't,
actually, but I…' Her voice trailed off as she realised how
foolish she'd been about to sound. To actually admit that
part of what she'd been envisaging was exploring not just
with their child but with Raul too.

She coloured to the roots of her hair. 'Thank you, I'll
keep that in mind.'

CHAPTER TEN

HE'D SAID SOMETHING WRONG, though he had no idea what it could possibly have been. He was doing everything he could to make this easier for Libby, to offer her what he thought she wanted.

Here she was, sitting across from him, painting him a picture of a life without wings, a life in which she'd been trapped in a rut of hard work and little pleasure, from what he could tell, aside from her God-given ability to derive happiness from the mundane. So he was offering her the keys to the world and he wanted her to use them. He wanted her to realise that their marriage, while necessary for this baby, was not a prison sentence so much as a chance for freedom for her.

Because it was important to assuage his guilt at having pressured her into this?

He could have supported her financially, he could have made her dreams come true without marrying her, but he'd manipulated her emotions, preying on the similarities in their backgrounds to push her into this.

For the sake of their baby, he reminded himself, shifting a little uneasily in his chair, frustrated that the relaxed atmosphere had evaporated and the air was once more crackling with tension and, damn it, awareness.

He didn't want to be aware of his wife.

He didn't want to be aware of the way her silky hair brushed her soft cheeks, of the way her lips parted when she expelled those little sighs, of the way her dress clung to her body like a second skin, of her slender hands as she reached for her champagne flute and took another delicate sip of non-alcoholic wine.

He didn't want to be aware of her in a way that made it dangerously simple to recall the way she'd felt as he'd sunk into her, making her his in a way that had sung to his soul.

'You work very long hours,' she said stiltedly into the silence of the room, and he barely heard her at first because he was absorbed by his own self-critical thoughts.

'Yes,' he agreed eventually.

Libby frowned. 'Is that…have you always?'

'Yes.'

'So it's not just since we…since I got here?'

His brows drew together. 'Do you mean, am I avoiding you?'

'It had crossed my mind,' she said with a lift of one brow.

'My job is demanding.' That wasn't strictly true, though. It didn't have to be. Raul micromanaged out of habit but, for the most part, his team of executives was more than capable of running things with significantly less involvement from Raul. 'It's hard for me to let go,' he explained after a beat. 'I am, I suppose, what you might call a control freak.'

'I'm shocked to hear that,' she said deadpan, and he laughed.

'I probably make my executives' lives hell,' he muttered. 'But it's something about having known that poverty, having been given the gift of a second chance from Maria and Pedro… I can't squander it.'

'So you're afraid that if you take your foot off the ac-. celerator you might lose everything?'

'I'm not afraid of that,' he said thoughtfully. 'And I don't need anywhere near what I have. The money is beside the point. I'm not really that motivated by wealth. Once you can afford to have a roof over your head and three square meals a day, the rest is cream.'

'So what are you motivated by, then?'

'I like to win,' he said simply. 'Succeeding in business is a good metric of victory, don't you think?'

Her smile was enigmatic, as though she were thinking things she wouldn't say. 'I suppose so.'

But that bothered him and he couldn't understand why. 'You don't agree?'

'Success in life is better.'

'How do you measure success in life?'

Libby hesitated, looking self-conscious.

'You can say it,' he murmured, wondering why he was so desperate to hear whatever confession she'd been about to offer.

'I gave this a lot of thought, growing up.' She cleared her throat, then paused as the waitress returned with another course, setting the plates onto the table before disappearing. Libby's eyes fell to the food, but she looked distracted. 'I never wanted much. Just something different to my own experience of home life. For me—' she lifted her gaze then, piercing Raul with the intensity and purity in her eyes '—it was simple. I just wanted a family.' Her voice hitched as she spoke and something rolled uncomfortably in his gut. 'My biggest aspiration was being in a happy marriage, with an army of kids,' she added, a tight smile doing nothing to take away from the sting of her words.

Because how could Raul fail to hear the accusation in

them, even when Libby had said and done nothing to make him feel that way? Their marriage, by its very nature, was a death knell to the hopes and dreams she'd clung to since childhood. They would have just one child, not an army. Raul could barely comprehend becoming a father at all—the idea of parenting more than one child was anathema to him. As for their marriage, while they'd agreed it would be based on respect and a level of friendship, it was never going to be the rosy, heart-warming vision Libby craved.

'Sometimes life doesn't work out how you plan it,' he said gruffly. 'But that doesn't mean it cannot still be a good life.'

'I know,' she answered without missing a beat, expelling a quick sigh and fidgeting her fingers. 'It's okay. I always thought I would find someone who was like my other half. My soulmate. That I'd fall crazy, head over heels in love and live happily ever after,' she added on a small laugh. 'But that's a fairy tale. A silly, juvenile dream.' She rubbed her hand over her stomach. 'I love our baby, Raul. That's enough for me.'

He hoped with all his heart she was being honest, because it was the best he could offer.

Libby stared at the ceiling, ignoring the pang in the centre of her chest.

It wasn't how she'd imagined spending her wedding night. Not that she'd spent much time imagining anything, but deep down, if she were honest, she'd hoped for more than this. She'd hoped against hope for love, real love, and no matter what she said to Raul, she'd never be able to ignore the emptiness inside her chest.

But she had to.

She had to learn.

Libby knew that Raul was right: life didn't always work out how you wanted. In fact, in Libby's experience, most of the time it didn't. Being happy was a question of choice, and she'd *always* chosen happiness. She'd found pleasure in the small things in her life—the golden splash of sunshine against a newly painted fence, the smell of spring in the air and freshly cut grass, the feeling of wet sand underfoot—the things that were hers to marvel at and appreciate without anyone having the power to remove those small delights.

And she knew that the key to her future happiness relied on her ability to keep doing exactly that. To focus on the relief of being liberated from financial stress, the pleasure of growing life inside her belly, of knowing that while Raul might not love her, at least he loved their baby enough to want to be in their life. He would be a great father to their child, and for that she knew she had to be grateful. It had to be enough.

A week after their wedding Raul read his assistant's email for the tenth time, a strange presentiment in his gut.

Will Mrs Ortega be joining you?

Such a simple, and normal, request. After all, Justine would naturally presume that, in the first flush of newly-wed bliss, the couple wouldn't want to be separated. Raul hadn't explained to anyone except his lawyers the real reason for their marriage. It was no one's business.

But what could he say in response?

Just a flat-out no? It wasn't Raul's practice to explain himself to anyone, so why start now?

However, given the necessity of a trip to Rome, the

thought of leaving Libby at home made him feel like a bastard. He grimaced ruefully. It wasn't about explaining himself to Justine, it was the thought of telling Libby that he was going to Europe and not bringing her. He'd wanted her to feel that this marriage was her chance to grow wings, hadn't he?

Was this a way to assuage his conscience at what he knew he'd taken away from her? That being the hope of ever living out her childhood hopes and dreams for a fairy tale happy ending?

Yes, he thought, standing with frustration and pacing across his office. That was precisely the problem. He had a guilty conscience and he didn't want to feel worse than he already did.

She'd cover her response quickly, he was sure, but she'd still feel it. Hurt. Offended. As if he couldn't bear to be with her. Besides, it wasn't like they would need to spend time together if she were to come. Rome was a big city and Raul was travelling for work. So long as he spelled that out when he invited her it would be fine.

With a growl low in his throat that spoke of the regret he knew he'd feel no matter what he chose, he moved back to his keyboard and typed out a reply before he could change his mind.

Yes.

'Libby?'

She glanced at the bedside clock, frowning. It was after ten, and she'd been about to slip into bed.

'Yes?'

'Have you got a moment?'

She glanced at her reflection in the mirror with a sense

of panic. Her pyjamas were hardly the last word in seduction—she wore a pair of comfortable yoga pants and a singlet top but, nonetheless, the idea of Raul seeing her like this did something funny to her insides.

'Libby?' His voice was stern, and it put paid to her indecision.

'Okay.' She wrenched the door inwards and almost lost her footing because he was *right there*, all handsome and businesslike in a button-down shirt with the sleeves pushed up to his elbows, and dark grey trousers that emphasised his slim waist. Her mouth felt dry and her heart fluttered. But it was the way Raul looked at her that sent Libby's pulse into dangerously fast territory. His eyes rested on her face for the briefest moment before travelling all the way down her body, landing on her pale, bare feet, then moving up and clinging to her slightly rounded stomach, so she lifted a hand and rubbed it self-consciously.

'You're—' His eyes widened when they met hers, and she felt a rush of emotions from him. 'May I...?' His hand lifted of its own accord, towards her stomach, and Libby stood very still, her heart in her throat, everything going haywire.

'Of course,' she managed to say, her voice almost a whisper.

He closed his eyes as his hand connected with her stomach, his breath hissing out between his teeth, then his other hand lifted, feeling the other side of her belly, and she swayed a little because it was such a vital, important connection. Mother and father, their baby.

His eyes opened, locking to hers. Libby's heart stammered.

'Did you need something?'

She had meant it innocently. She'd meant it simply because he'd come to her room at ten o'clock, because he'd wanted to talk to her, but she heard the invitation in her words and knew she should say something to retract it. To pull away from him.

Desire was one thing, but Libby had to be stronger than this. She had to learn not to fall into a puddle every time he looked at her as though he wanted to peel her clothes from her body.

Except she didn't. Libby stood right there, blinking up at him, heart pounding, any semblance of resistance melting away in the face of her need for him.

'Libby,' he said darkly, angrily, and something in her chest hurt, but then his hand lifted higher on her side, holding her, and his throat shifted as he swallowed. Libby could only stare at him, as if drawn to him by a force so much greater than any she'd ever known. 'What is it about you?' he said with more anger, more darkness, and both of those emotions were palpable when he dropped his mouth to hers and kissed her as though the world would stop spinning if he didn't.

Libby swayed all the way forward then, pressing her body to his, a complete and willing surrender, not just to this moment but to something bigger, something inevitable and important. Lightning bolts flared inside her mind. She saw stars and felt heaven burst through her. It was nirvana; it was bliss, even when it was also terrifyingly complicated. A simple kiss yet it had the power to detonate something deep in her belly and all through her bones.

'Raul,' she groaned as she leaned closer to him, lifting a hand and curling it into the dark hair at the nape of his warm, strong neck. She felt him grow still. His whole body seemed to tense as though he were fighting something, perhaps the surge of need dominating them. Libby felt it and she refused to allow that fight; she had surrendered and needed him to as well. She kissed him and lifted one foot to the back of his calf, curving it around him, and it was like the unlocking of a door for both of them.

Raul cursed softly against her mouth and then he was moving, taking her with him, deeper into Libby's spacious bedroom, all the way to the king-size bed at its heart. They tumbled to the mattress together, arms, legs entwined, moving frantically now to remove each other's clothes, every touch, each brush of flesh incendiary and divine. Libby had never known anything like it...

Raul wanted to punch himself. No sooner had they exploded in unison, their bodies burning up in a fever of mutual desire, lust and need than he knew it had been a mistake. The whole thing. He lay beside her, a frown on his face, wishing he could take back the last twenty minutes, wishing he could erase their intimacy. For the look on Libby's face had been deeply troubling. Her eyes had softened, her lips had parted, and he'd felt something spark in his chest, something he instantly shied away from, something his brain knew to warn him off.

This was getting messy, and he didn't do mess. Not in his personal life. Not in any sector of his life, in fact. It made him want to run—to run as hard and fast as he could.

He pushed off her bed with an air of casual unconcern, swiped up his boxer shorts and pulled them on, then, when he had chosen a path of retreat, he steeled himself to turn and face Libby.

'I'm flying to Rome tomorrow.' His voice sounded odd to Libby, who was still floating high in the clouds of sensual euphoria after that magnificent coming together, so she didn't immediately understand what he'd said. She pressed a hand to her naked stomach on autopilot, frowning a little.

'I'm sorry?'

'I came here to tell you I'm going to Rome.' He crossed his arms over his chest, looking at her without a hint of emotion on his face.

Whatever glow Libby had been bathing in evaporated and she was suddenly ice-cold. As a child, she'd felt the sands shifting beneath her feet often. She knew nothing was permanent, no one was reliable. Everything could change at a moment's notice. Still, to go from making love as though their lives depended upon it to...this...felt like a kick in the guts.

'You did? You are?'

'I have a meeting.'

'Oh.' She felt like crying. She hated herself for feeling that way, but her responses were innate. This wasn't just Raul, it was every disappointment she'd known in her life, it was a reminder of all the times she'd come home to a 'new daddy', which meant the end of feeling, in some small way, that she mattered to her mother. Change and unpredictability were hardwired to invoke this response in Libby; it was why she'd stayed single rather than dating men who might hurt her, why she'd been waiting for her knight in shining armour to sweep in and love her—love her in a way that would never, ever change.

She glanced down at the sheet, shielding her face from Raul, desperately hoping he wouldn't see a hint of the emotions she was fighting. 'Thanks...for letting me know.' Her voice sounded hollow.

She was aware of him standing just inside the door to her room, his clothes bunched in one hand. She felt his eyes on her but didn't look up. She hardly breathed.

'If you need anything while I'm gone—'

'I won't,' she hastened to say.

'With the baby—' he clarified, and it was the worst thing he could have said to Libby in that moment, because it served to remind her of the truth of their situation. She was simply an incubator to him. This wasn't about her. Not as a person, a woman. Just as a womb. She was stupid to have fallen back into bed with him, to have so willingly given into—no, to have pushed him to surrender to—the undercurrent of desire they both felt.

For all she knew, it was like this for Raul with every woman he slept with. Maybe the only reason they kept ending up in bed together was because she was simply *there*. Available, willing, in his apartment, under his nose. Mortifying thought.

She sucked in a deep breath. 'The baby is fine. I'm fine. Just…go to Rome.'

And then, just like that, he left.

Raul quickened his pace as he passed the Colosseum, barely noticing the beauty of the sun glancing across the ancient structure, the way the stones seemed to glow with gold in the early morning light. He kept his head down, moved faster, weaving around the few people who were on the streets, a Vespa parked across the kerb, a trash collector taking a cigarette break, then onto a busier section of footpath, with cafés set up for early morning patrons. He kept running until his lungs burned, but it didn't matter how fast he went, he couldn't wipe Libby from his mind. More specifically, the look in her eyes when he'd announced he was going to Rome.

It had been worse than he'd anticipated.

Her hurt and surprise were unmistakable.

He was so angry with himself. Not for leaving her to go on a business trip, but for allowing any of the lines between them to become blurred. Raul didn't *do* blurred lines, but there was something about Libby that had made him—temporarily—forget who he was, and how he lived. Except, perhaps it wasn't Libby. Maybe it was the baby instead, the fact that she had his child developing inside of her, that made him uncertain how to treat Libby.

What an idiot he'd been.

In trying to forge a connection with the woman, he'd inadvertently lied to her. He'd led her on. He'd let desire for her cloud his judgement, and now he was in the precarious situation of having to manage the emotions of a person who might very well have come to care for him.

Did she have any idea how stupid that was? What an unsafe person he was to let into her life? Not in a physical sense but emotionally, Raul was the last person in the world who could give Libby what she wanted.

And he had to make sure she understood that.

No more messing around, no more letting things get out of hand. Raul Ortega was married, but he needed his wife to understand that any kind of real relationship was—and always would be—out of the question.

CHAPTER ELEVEN

LIBBY WAS ON the second highest step of the ladder when she heard the door opening and she almost fell sideways, came disastrously close to knocking a half-full pot of paint onto the drop sheet below.

Her insides jolted alarmingly.

Five nights. Raul had been away the whole week and had not contacted her once.

But why would he have? she thought with self-directed anger. He didn't owe Libby anything, and he'd made it abundantly clear he couldn't wait to get away from her after that night.

Anger fired in her veins, a white-hot rage that might have been irrational, that might have been unfair, and yet it fairly exploded through her body. She ground her teeth together, dipped the brush into the tin and returned to the job at hand, carefully painting around the stencils she'd laboriously stuck in place. If he thought she was going to go out and acknowledge his return, he had another think coming.

Her fingers shook a little though as she continued with her work, one ear trained on the apartment, waiting for any indication that Raul was coming towards her. Minutes later, she heard it: the clicking open of the door to this room, a sharp invective in his native language immediately following as he burst towards her like a hurricane.

'What the hell are you doing?'

Libby spun so fast she almost fell—again—but she steadied herself quickly, shooting Raul an angry glare, as though her clumsiness was his fault.

'What does it look like?' she muttered, hating how good he looked, hating how her body immediately responded, and so turning away again quickly, focusing back on the wall of the baby's nursery.

'It *looks*,' he said, with something very near derision in his voice, 'like you have a death wish. Then again, I should have known that from the first time we met and you insisted on storming a boat.'

Libby jabbed the paintbrush angrily at the wall, though it had done nothing to deserve such brutality. 'In case you'd forgotten, we're going to have a baby in a few months. We need somewhere for that baby to sleep.'

'How could I forget, Libby? It's the reason we're married, isn't it?'

Libby's heart popped painfully. She jabbed the wall again.

'Besides which,' he continued, voice deep and gruff and closer than before, and when she happened to glance down she saw he was standing at the base of the ladder, one hand on the metallic rungs, 'we have many places for the baby to sleep. Should you even be breathing that stuff in?' he demanded.

His question *hurt*. As though he couldn't trust her to keep their baby safe.

'It's non-toxic,' she snapped. 'I'm not an idiot. And I don't have a death wish. I'm perfectly safe up here,' she said, ignoring the couple of times she'd almost fallen in the last ten minutes. That had only been because of Raul's unexpected return. 'And your apartment might have many, many bedrooms but none of them is ready for a baby.'

Silence prickled between them, and Libby's anger was dangerously close to morphing into something else, something more like bitter sadness, so she ground her teeth and clung to her annoyance with Raul because it was so much safer than feeling sorry for herself.

'So hire a goddamned decorator,' he snapped.

'Why? I like doing it,' she said, mentally adding that she thought she'd done a good job, but to say as much to Raul might seem as though she was looking for his praise and she definitely wasn't.

'Because you can afford a decorator. Because they can do everything you want, without you risking a broken neck...'

'Far better for them to risk theirs,' she muttered, rolling her eyes. 'It's just a ladder.'

'Then let me do this,' he snapped.

'No.' She was being stubborn and churlish and she didn't care. Emotions were exploding through her, none of them good.

'You really are acting like a child,' he said, but stayed right where he was, one hand firmly gripping the base of the ladder, the other, she suspected, ready to swing into action and catch Libby if she should fall.

She ignored his jibe, continuing instead to paint the sunbeams on the wall, taking her time, refusing to show how unsettling his proximity was. Finally, she was at the end of her reach, and needed to shift the ladder.

'I'm coming down,' she said curtly, expecting him to move. And he did, but only slightly, just enough to make a little more room for Libby. Holding the tin of paint, she gingerly climbed down the treads of the ladder until her feet were on the ground, and then shifted sideways, as far away from Raul as a single step would take her. But here, at ground level, the flecks of anger in his eyes were so much more obvious, and they sparked an answering feeling in her bloodstream. Fire threatened to ravage her internal organs.

She looked away, mutinous.

'Are you finished?'

She pulled a face. 'Does it look finished?'

Raul's nostrils flared as he expelled a loud breath. 'What else?'

'Well, the sun has to go to that corner,' she snapped. 'If you want to help, go out of the room so I have more space to work.' It was a large bedroom and Raul was just a man, but he was a big man, and his presence was at least treble his size.

'Not on your life,' he responded coldly. 'Tell me what you want done, and I will do it.'

She gaped. 'I'm enjoying myself.'

'At great risk to our baby,' he responded pointedly and Libby's insides churned. He didn't care about her; this was all about the baby. And, worse, he thought she *didn't* care enough. He thought she was being reckless. Fear of being like her own mother flooded her; worry that she might be genetically incapable of doing this well gnawed at her. Tears filled Libby's eyes but she desperately didn't want him to see.

'Fine,' she said, bending down to replace the paint tin on the ground rather than handing it to Raul and risking touching him. 'The sunbeams have to hit that corner. I'm going to make a tea,' she said, hands shaking as she ducked her head and left the room, her heart turning into something sharp and blade-like, slashing against the fibres of her chest wall.

* * *

'It's done.' His voice was without emotion ten minutes later when he strode into the lounge room. Libby was calmer now, the space from Raul and a cup of steaming hot tea were exactly what she'd needed to soothe her frazzled nerves. The reprieve was temporary. The moment he entered the spacious lounge, tension prickled along her spine.

She nodded curtly, didn't quite meet his eyes.

'Is there anything else?'

Her lips pulled to one side. 'Obviously.'

'Such as?'

Except Libby wasn't sure she wanted to confide in Raul. She'd chosen the nursery as her project the day after he'd left, when she'd known how important it was to stay busy and focus on something positive. The nursery had become her salvation—something she was tinkering with each day, thinking of their baby, the life inside of her, imagining a future with a little person who simply adored her.

'Nothing you need to worry about.'

He was quiet for so long that Libby felt her eyes pulling towards him, dragged there by the weight of his silence. His expression gave nothing away.

'Do you promise you will not go up the ladder again when I am not home?'

Libby's brows knit together. 'Um, no.'

'No, you will not go back up the ladder?'

'No, I don't promise any such thing,' she snapped. 'I'm not a moron, Raul, and, believe it or not, I care about our baby just as much as you do, or I wouldn't have agreed to go along with all this, would I?' she said, glad to be able to hurl that in his face, though she had no expectation of the sentiment proving as hurtful to Raul as it had been to her, particularly as it had come right after they'd just slept together.

'Then prove it. Don't do anything dangerous when you are alone in the apartment.'

'Going up a ladder is hardly—'

He held a hand up in the air, an instantly recognisable gesture of silence. Libby gawked at him. 'What if you had fallen?'

'I didn't.'

'You could have.'

'Then I would have called for help.'

'Who would you have called? In case you hadn't realised, this penthouse is somewhat isolated.'

She rolled her eyes. 'I have my phone in my back pocket.'

'And if you passed out?'

'You're talking in what-ifs. I could just as easily have slipped when I got out of the shower this morning, or rolled my ankle whilst making the bed...'

His eyes flashed to hers and his jaw tightened. 'You're right.' He crossed his arms over his chest. 'You should not be left alone.'

Libby's lips parted in surprise and her heart began to race. 'That's not what I meant.'

'But it's clear,' Raul contradicted. 'Until the baby is born, I'll work from home.'

Libby's face went whiter than a ghost's. 'N...no,' she stammered, rejecting the idea on some soul-deep level, even when she acknowledged there was a part of her that wanted his company and companionship. 'You're being ridiculous.'

'As ridiculous as a woman who thinks she has to carry

a paperweight to protect someone like me from teenage tearaways?'

At the reminder of how they'd first met, Libby's pulse quickened. 'I'm not here all the time, Raul. I go out—a lot. Are you going to shadow me on the footpath too? Stop me from being hit by a bus or mugged in an alley?'

He ground his teeth. 'If that's necessary.'

Appalled, she glared at him. 'I was being sarcastic.'

'I wasn't.'

'But—'

'You are my *wife*.' He enunciated each word clearly. 'And the mother of my baby. Your safety is important to me.'

Libby spun away from him, hating herself for the way those words pulled at her, weakened her. 'Our baby's safety is important to me too,' she whispered, repeating something she'd already said, needing him to understand that she wasn't being reckless or careless. 'I am not taking stupid risks. I walk in busy areas in broad daylight. I never feel unsafe.'

'Nonetheless,' he said with his trademark authority, 'either I will come with you in the future or I'll arrange an escort.'

She stared at him as if he'd lost his mind. 'Like I'm some kind of heroine in a Jane Austen novel?' she asked, scandalised. 'I'm a twenty-six-year-old woman,' she reminded him, 'and I've been looking after myself for longer than I can remember. Looking after everyone else too. If you think you can crash into my life like some kind of giant, arrogant wrecking ball and start taking over all of my…autonomy…and independence, then bloody think again.'

His features showed irritation. 'I have no interest in curtailing your autonomy, only in ensuring your safety.'

'They sound kind of the same, the way you describe them.'

'Then you're wilfully misunderstanding me.'

'I am not!' she responded with a disbelieving shake of her head. 'You are insufferable.'

'What a shame then that you have a lifetime to suffer me for.'

Libby dug her fingernails into her palms. A lifetime. It wouldn't be a lifetime and they both knew it, but it felt like it in that moment.

'Having regrets?' she asked, bracing her other hand against the kitchen bench.

'Regrets? I'm full of them,' he said, almost to himself, thrusting his hands on his hips with no idea how much his admission cut Libby to the very centre of her soul. 'But nothing changes our position now, does it? We're married, with a baby coming in a matter of months, and I am asking you, for the rest of your pregnancy, to remember you are making decisions for three people, not just one.'

Libby floundered. Her heart hurt. 'You don't need to remind me, Raul, I'm well aware of my pregnancy at every minute of every day. *You're* the one who's carrying on as though nothing has changed, whereas my entire life has been turned on its head from the moment you learned of this pregnancy...'

His eyes narrowed. 'You're right.' His agreement momentarily took the wind out of her sails. 'So I am telling you: my life is about to change too. From now on, I'll be here, with you. If you need a wall painted, I will do it. If you need furniture moved, ask me. You are not to do another job that involves even a hint of risk.'

'Everything involves risk,' she said on a frustrated laugh.

'Don't be argumentative for the sake of it,' he replied. 'You know some things carry greater risk, and scaling to virtually the top step of a ladder is one of them.'

She opened her mouth to say something, to dispute that, but slammed it shut again a moment later. Raul was right. There was an inherent risk in climbing up a ladder whilst alone in the apartment, and she'd known that. She'd been careful precisely for that reason.

She crossed her arms over her chest and glared at a point beyond his shoulder. 'Fine,' she said crisply. 'It's your life. Do whatever you want. But don't for one second think I need you here with me, Raul. I'm perfectly capable of getting through this pregnancy without your help and, news flash, I always was.' And with that she left the room.

A week later Libby felt as though she might burst.

Having Raul constantly around was like some kind of torture. He was *everywhere*. Working in the apartment from early in the morning until late at night, but frequently stepping into the lounge to check on her. If Libby wanted to go for a walk he came too, though he often worked then as well, using the time to make conference calls, so they were like two people on parallel paths, together yet apart. She had taken to walking two steps in front of him and doing her best to forget he was even there, or trying to at least, but Raul's presence was oppressive and overwhelming. Even several paces behind her, she *felt* him, and wished on a thousand stars she didn't.

But on their eighth day in this strange new form of hell, Libby came into the lounge room in the middle of the morning to find another woman standing just inside the apartment, a black leather briefcase clutched at her side, Raul in the process of greeting her.

Libby froze, frowning, wondering at the inclusion of someone else in their odd little arrangement.

'Libby.' Raul forced a smile, but there was a warning in his eyes. 'This is Matilda Roletti—a designer I've called to consult on the nursery. If you tell her what you'd like, she'll arrange it. And the installation.'

Libby's heart tightened and she frowned, because this was the last thing she wanted.

'Oh.' She glanced from Raul to Matilda, then back to Raul.

'I've brought some catalogues for us to look at, but perhaps you'd like to show me the space first?' Matilda spoke with a polished accent. In fact, everything about her was polished and professional and instantly intimidating to Libby, who felt under-dressed and dowdy in comparison. Having not been expecting company, she was dressed in just about the only clothes she owned that still fit—a pair of stretchy yoga pants and a loose T-shirt. She wore no make-up and her hair was long and fluffy around her face—Libby had given up on blow-drying it weeks ago.

'It's just over there.' She gestured to the nursery door— the bedroom beside her own. 'Why don't you go and have a look? I need a quick word with…my husband.'

Matilda nodded once then strode through the apartment with the same sense of belonging as the designer furniture. It was so obvious that Libby sucked in a sharp breath, the sting in the middle of her chest almost felling her. *This* was the kind of woman who belonged in Raul's home. This was the kind of woman who would have been comfortable and content amongst Raul's priceless collection of furniture in his incredibly extravagant penthouse.

Not Libby Langham, a cleaner from Sydney. She swallowed past the constricting feeling in her throat.

'What do you think you're doing?' She rounded on him, hissing the question in a whisper, but her anger reverberated around the room as though she'd shouted. 'I don't need a designer.'

'You said you wanted the nursery to be done.'

'No, I said I wanted to do it,' she responded.

'So you can. Choose what you want with Matilda…'

'That's not what I meant.' Libby groaned. 'God, Raul, you are unbelievable.'

'What have I done wrong?' he disputed with disbelief. 'I'm trying to help.'

'No, you're trying to take over and do things your way, which I'm starting to realise means with an abundance of money and no actual time or feeling.'

The words slammed into the space between them, heavy with accusation and accuracy. She saw him rock back on his heels as though it was the last thing he'd expected her to recognise or say, but Libby didn't apologise nor take the words back. It was true.

'I just hope that when our baby is born you realise they're going to want to spend time with you, not just live in your sky palace and benefit from your fabulous wealth.'

'You think I don't know that?' Raul responded, suddenly pale beneath his tan. 'You think I didn't realise that the moment you told me about the pregnancy? If I wanted to spend money and be done with this, I would have set up a trust fund for the baby and walked away.'

Libby angled her face away from Raul's.

'I am going to be in this baby's life,' he said, the words low and deep but carefully muted of emotion.

It's why I married you.

Raul didn't need to say it again: the refrain was etched in Libby's mind.

'And haven't I been spending time with you?'

It was like waving a red flag in front of a bull.

'You've been shadowing me! That's not spending time together.'

He thrust his hands on his hips. 'I don't know what you want from me, Libby. I really don't.'

She turned away, angry and frustrated. She didn't know either. That was part of the problem. But, deep down, Libby felt like this was all wrong. Everything Raul did seemed to make it worse.

She clung to belligerence, not wanting to back down. Her unreliable pregnancy emotions were zipping all over the place; she felt robbed of her usual optimism and self-control. 'I don't want a decorator.'

There was silence for a moment and when Raul spoke his voice was level, but that didn't matter. Libby heard his frustration, heard his impatience. 'You don't even want to meet with her, to hear her ideas?'

'I have my own ideas,' Libby said quietly. 'I've had plenty of time to think about what I want our baby's room to be like, and it's nothing, *nothing*, like this icescape.' She waved her hand around the lounge room, the impersonal, cold furniture anathema to Libby's sense of warmth and family. '*You* go and hear her thoughts,' Libby snapped. 'I'm sure you'll be a match made in heaven.'

It took him five minutes to dismiss Matilda and he did so without embarrassment, mainly because Raul didn't feel those emotions in the normal course of his life, and for the moment his mind was singularly engaged in decoding and understanding Libby, so he had very little run time to feel something as pedestrian as embarrassment. Besides, he would no doubt get an invoice for the designer's time, even when the visit had been totally unproductive.

Alone once more in the apartment with Libby, he knew the right thing—the wise thing—to do was give her space, and so he returned to his own work, fuming over how unreasonable she'd been, staring at his screen with the sense of a spring being wound tighter and tighter in his belly.

But no matter how frustrated he was with Libby, he still found it impossible to stop thinking about her, and to ignore the feeling that they'd got halfway through an argument they needed to finish properly. Yes, that was it, he thought on a wave of relief. They had unfinished business and for this reason, and this reason alone, he wanted to go to her, to pick up where they'd left off. Until they'd resolved this dispute, he wasn't sure he'd be able to concentrate anyway, so there was no sense in just staring at a blank screen.

He found her in the nursery, one shoulder propped against the wall, eyes trained on the view beyond the window. He stood just inside the door, arms crossed, watching her, suddenly at a loss for words. Her blonde hair again reminded him of an angel's halo, her eyes were sparkling like gems.

'I'm sorry.'

Raul was still searching for what to say, so Libby's softly voiced apology caught him off-guard.

She turned to face him slowly. 'I overreacted.'

He frowned, taking a step deeper into the room and then another, until he was just a short distance from her.

Libby's gaze probed his, as if looking for something important, then she sighed. 'When I was growing up, my room was just a mattress on the floor in a space no bigger than a wardrobe.' Her lips pulled to the side in that way she had; Raul knew it meant she was lost in thought. 'I know neither of us planned for this,' she said, rubbing her stomach distractedly. 'But, at the same time, I've planned for it all my life. As a young girl, I used to imagine what my house would be like, my bedroom, if only I could have it my way. As a teenager, I imagined my future, my family, and from the moment I found out I was pregnant, I've thought about how to make this baby's life everything mine wasn't. It's not about possessions,' she clarified quickly. 'It's about warmth. Security. Love.'

Something tightened in Raul's chest.

He would give their baby the world, but love was the one thing he knew he couldn't offer. Not to the baby, not to Libby, not to anyone. He'd lost that ability a long time ago, and it was something he never wanted to regain.

Fortunately, Raul had no doubt Libby would love their child enough for the both of them, and he would provide everything else that was needed in spades.

'I was trying to help,' he said gruffly, rather than admitting the truth to Libby about the deadened state of his heart.

'I know that, and I appreciate it. But this is what I want to do for our baby. It's important to me, and I enjoy it.'

His gaze moved from Libby to the walls of the room, seeing it with renewed interest. On one side she'd painted a circus theme—a big, bright tent with a waving flag on top, an elephant and a happy clown with a rainbow bursting out of the palm of his hand across another wall, then, on the other, it was a sky theme, with clouds and a gloriously bright sun. Not only was it cheery and warm, it was well executed, so Raul's eyes shone with approval when they met Libby's.

'You're very talented.'

She laughed softly. 'You sound surprised.'

He lifted one hand in the air in apology, and found his lips lifting in an unexpected grin. 'I shouldn't be. You're clearly a woman of many talents.'

She scrutinised the artwork on one wall. 'I drew the outline with pencil first, until I was happy.'

He tried not to think about how many times she'd been up and down the ladder in the week he'd been away.

'I know what I want to do in here, Raul. I was just waiting until you got back in case…'

Her voice trailed off into nothing and his gut tightened in anticipation of what she was going to say. 'I thought you might want to be involved in selecting the furniture,' she said with a shrug. 'But you don't have to. I can do it myself.'

Good. That was the wise choice. She should do it herself.

Raul had to forcibly remind himself of the importance of keeping those lines clear, their boundaries delineated. The less time they spent doing happy family-type activities, the better.

He nodded once. 'I look forward to seeing what you pick out. I presume you can order the necessary items online?'

He ignored the look of hurt in her eyes with difficulty.

She bit into her lip as she nodded. 'I'll get it delivered next week.'

CHAPTER TWELVE

SOME OF THE pieces Libby had selected for the nursery were coming from Europe, and so it took almost a month for everything to arrive. She left each item in its box until the last piece was in the apartment, and by the time that had happened her stomach had become so round it was difficult to get up and down off the floor to do anything, let alone assemble furniture. She and Raul had developed an excellent routine for living in the same space whilst more or less ignoring one another—or at least appearing to.

For Libby, it had become a form of torture. How could she ignore someone who was so intrinsic to the air she breathed? His presence was so overpowering, so overwhelming, he was simply *everywhere*. Not just in the apartment, but in her mind, her thoughts, her dreams. It was truly frustrating because they both treated one another like polite strangers.

Even when he accompanied her to medical appointments, he was more like a chaperone than an expectant father, and misgivings had begun to form in the back of Libby's mind. Doubts. Worries.

What if he was regretting his hasty decision to marry her? What if he was regretting his insistence on being in the baby's life?

It had all happened so fast there hadn't been time for

regrets, but now that the dust had settled and he was faced with the reality of living with Libby—and the impending arrival of their baby—he might very well be wishing things were different.

She'd caught him staring at her several times, frowning, his expression unreadable except for the fact he was obviously thinking *something*—and something that didn't bring him much pleasure. His eyes often fell to her belly—too big to ignore now. Libby had been forced to buy some maternity clothes, and even those were feeling a little tight already.

Twisting the wrench, her hand slipped and the tool fell to the ground, hitting her hard on the ankle.

'Damn it,' she cursed loudly, rubbing the flesh, instinctive tears filling her eyes. She'd been louder than she'd intended, and it brought Raul to the door of the nursery.

When he saw the destruction in there, she realised he hadn't been in the place for weeks. Not since the day of the designer, when she'd apologised to him for overreacting. Almost as if he'd been ignoring the nursery?

'What the hell happened in here?'

She stared at him. 'What does it look like?' She rubbed her ankle. His eyes dropped to the gesture, then he crossed the room, crouching in front of her so his jeans pulled against his haunches, and something powerful ignited in her bloodstream. A desire she'd been trying to ignore, to fight, because he'd made it clear he didn't feel that way about her any more. He hadn't even been close enough to touch her in over a month. So much for being friends. At this stage, she'd have settled for a conversation that didn't feel so stilted it hurt.

'It looks like a bomb went off,' he admitted. 'May I?' His hand hovered close to her ankle but without touching.

Libby was terrified that if his fingers pressed to her skin she might actually explode.

'I'm fine,' she demurred, moving away from him a little, standing with a total lack of elegance and rubbing her belly, then her neck, surveying the room and seeing it as he must have. In one corner, she'd stacked a heap of cardboard packaging. She'd managed to assemble the changing table and was halfway through the crib.

'Libby—' he stood too, moving closer to her; she caught a hint of his cologne and her insides trembled '—why didn't you order these things assembled?'

Heat rushed to her cheeks. 'It cost extra.'

Raul didn't laugh, and she was grateful for that, but she felt his disapproval. She knew how stupid she'd been. He was one of the wealthiest people in the world—as if he would have balked at the additional expense of pre-assembled furniture.

'I needed something to do,' she added defensively. 'I thought it would be easier than this. I've... I've never had anything new before.' She lifted her shoulders. 'I had no idea.'

Raul's voice was gruff. 'Why didn't you ask me for help?'

Libby looked across at him, frowning. 'We've hardly been speaking,' she pointed out. 'I didn't feel like I could.'

His eyes flashed with an emotion she didn't understand. 'I thought space was a good idea for both of us, but you need to know that you can always come to me for help, Libby. You're my wife.'

She pulled a face. 'Yeah, right.'

'What is that supposed to mean?'

'I'm your wife in name only,' she pointed out. 'It's not a real marriage, and we both know that.'

'It's real for us, for our version of marriage.'

That hurt, because he was right. Their marriage wasn't what Libby had wanted, it wasn't what she'd imagined, but it was what she'd agreed to. She nodded awkwardly.

'Pass me the wrench,' he said, holding out his hand.

'You don't have to do this.'

His eyes pinned her to the spot. 'Yes, I do.' Then, after a beat, 'I want to.'

Libby passed the tool over with a massive wave of relief.

It was much easier watching Raul work than doing the work herself, she thought with a grimace ten minutes later as he took over the assembly of the crib with a seeming lack of effort that stole her breath.

He worked for almost an hour and then it was done, but Raul wasn't finished. 'What's next?'

Libby stared at the crib, her heart twisting in her chest. 'It's perfect,' she whispered, putting a hand on the edge of it, tears in her eyes. And it was at that moment, that *exact* moment, that their baby shifted and kicked and Libby gasped, because it was so different to the other movements she'd felt—which had been more like gentle popping sensations. This was a rollercoaster in her belly.

'What is it?' Raul was instantly concerned.

Libby was so overcome by the magic of the moment she didn't stop to question the wisdom of what she was doing; she simply reached out for Raul's hand and pressed it to her stomach, eyes wide as the baby once more flipped and kicked, this time, right against Raul's palm.

It was Raul's turn to react, his expression assuming a mask of shock, his lips parting on an exhalation, his eyes hooded, focused on Libby's stomach.

'That is our baby,' he said, shaking his head as he lifted

his other hand to Libby's stomach and held it there. More somersaults.

They stared at one another and then Libby was laughing, and also sobbing, the emotion of the moment overpowering her, even before Raul lifted one hand to her cheek and held her still, his eyes locked to hers.

'That's our baby,' he repeated, and then he dropped his head, pressing his forehead to hers. Libby closed her eyes, swallowing past a wave of emotion, everything inside of her rolling and twisting so she lost sight of who and where she was.

Instincts overrode everything, just as they had on the boat.

She was an animal, acting solely on biological impulses. She tilted her head, her lips seeking his and finding them, taking them, kissing him lightly at first, curiously, and then hungrily, desperately, needily, and it was a need that only intensified when he kissed her back, his mouth claiming hers with all the heat of possessiveness he'd shown her in the past.

She didn't think. Didn't wonder. Didn't question.

It was too perfect: too right.

Everything inside Libby ignited on a cloud of intense pleasure. Heat built between her legs; her breasts tingled with a need for him to touch them. She was on fire in the best possible way.

'God, Raul,' she groaned into his mouth. 'I want you.' His hand pushed into her hair, fingers tangling in its length as he held her head where it was, against his mouth, his tongue duelling with hers, and Libby said, over and over, 'Yes, yes,' until she was incandescent, her body pressing against his, her hands clasped behind his back, holding him to her. She was exploding with feelings, too many feelings to understand, but they were oh, so powerful and saturating.

In the back of her mind there was a warning bell, but she couldn't hear it, let alone heed it, or perhaps it was just that she didn't want to. After a month of walking on eggshells, being utterly ignored, it felt so good to stand face to face with their desire once more, to know that the heat responsible for initially bringing them together was still a force neither could fully resist.

It was the only thing about their marriage that made any kind of sense.

Until it didn't.

Suddenly Raul was very still, and then he was pulling back, lifting his head and staring at Libby with dazed surprise, dropping his hands from her head, her body, as though she were a scorching-hot potato, staring at his fingers like he didn't recognise them.

'That shouldn't have happened,' he said with self-directed anger.

Libby's stomach rolled and dropped to her toes. She didn't trust herself to speak at first.

'It was feeling the baby move,' he explained stiltedly, then took a step backwards. 'I wasn't prepared.' A frown furrowed his brow. 'I'll finish the furniture tonight, once you are in bed. Don't trouble yourself with it further, Libby.' He moved to the door and then, in a last insult, nodded his head in a businesslike fashion before departing.

Libby stared at the space he'd just occupied, her lips still heavy from the pressure of his, and then she closed her eyes on a wave of desperation.

The emotions inside of her were still hard to understand, but more and more she was starting to fear one of them in particular—an emotion it would be truly awful to feel for her husband. Was it possible that, despite everything, she'd actually been stupid enough to fall in love with him?

Raul couldn't outrun it, not this time. He went faster, harder, the treadmill of his home gym no substitute for the open streets, but at least here he was around should Libby need him.

I need you.

Not *that* kind of need.

But even remembering the soft, desperate way she'd called to him did something strange to his gut, so he had to work hard to stay focused on the rhythm of his steps, one foot after the other. He increased the incline, wanting to sweat, to hurt—to hurt so much he could no longer think, feel, remember.

Flashes sliced through him—other memories, those he tried hardest of all to blank. They were a talisman now, a reminder of why he was the way he was, the self-protective instincts that had served him well since boyhood.

Rejection after rejection. Hurt after hurt—some physical, like being smacked repeatedly by one of his foster parents for coming home with a torn school shirt. Some emotional, like being told he was a waste of skin, that he'd never amount to anything. Being told that no one would ever want him. The last one had been easiest of all to believe.

He ground his teeth, closing his eyes for a moment, hating the memories, hating the experiences most of all, but grateful he'd learned to be truly independent from a young age. By the time he was thirteen, no one had held the power to hurt him. He simply didn't let anyone in.

The closest he'd come was Maria and Pedro and, even then, it had been about making them proud, not letting them love him. Certainly not loving them back.

I need you.

He didn't *want* to be needed, but it was marginally better than his needing anyone else. Raul was determined never to weaken in that regard. He was forged from steel—from rejection, hurt, wounds that had cut him so deeply he'd sworn he'd never allow anyone to cut him again. He was strong now. Physically, mentally, emotionally.

Libby was simply another person in his universe, but she would never have the power to hurt him. He refused to give it to her.

Libby woke early and dressed silently, creeping from her room in what she only acknowledged was an attempt to evade Raul when she reached the front door and slipped her feet into her boots.

He'd been her shadow for a long time, and she'd tolerated it. But yesterday, in the nursery, something inside of her had snapped. Kissing him as though her life depended on it and having Raul back away had been a death knell to her ability to pretend any longer.

He wasn't just the father of her baby. He wasn't simply a man she'd married because of the pregnancy.

He was Raul Ortega and somewhere, somehow, everything had got muddled. Libby wanted more from him. More than a marriage of convenience, more than a businesslike partnership. More than friendship.

Deep down, she was still that little girl who believed in fairy tales and soulmates, and suddenly it seemed possible, if not likely, that everything they'd experienced had been for exactly that simple reason—destiny.

What if they were destined to find one another?

Two people who'd been broken in different ways by their broken childhoods. Who'd known hurt, loss, pain, rejection and fear as kids, who'd fought hard to find their feet as adults, who were now determined to give their own child the best of everything, because they'd never known it.

What if Libby possessed, within herself, everything she needed to heal Raul, and the same was true in reverse? What if they could just be open to that possibility?

Her breath snagged in her throat as she pressed the button for the lift, waiting for it to appear with her fingers crossed, because she didn't want to see Raul yet. She wasn't ready. She needed to think, and for that she required space. She needed to process and understand her feelings, to comprehend the sensations that were expanding inside of her.

The lift doors opened and she stepped through them with gratitude, pressed her back to the wall and then sighed a big breath of relief when they silently zipped shut.

Downstairs and on the corner of the block, she ordered a coffee—her one pregnancy indulgence, which she allowed herself to enjoy only once per day—with caramel syrup, wrapped her hands around the cup then took a sip as she left the café, looking left and right.

It was a beautiful morning, the weather turning incrementally warmer, and she longed to explore the city in all its guises, but especially spring. Trees were beginning to show their first bloom of leaves and blossom. Her mind turned longingly to Central Park, and the beauty she knew she'd find there as things began to grow again. Though winter had also been stunning, with the snow-covered ground and eerie, spindly trees almost seeming to scrape long tendrils of fingers against the leaden sky.

She walked without purpose or destination, simply to move, and with walking came thoughts and clarity, even when she didn't intentionally seek either. It had always been that way for Libby—a walk somehow unlocked things within her.

Each step seemed to cement something, an idea, a concept, that had begun so long ago, and so incrementally, she couldn't even say for sure when the idea had first occurred to her. Not consciously ever but, looking back, she supposed she'd felt a red flag very early on. Perhaps even on the boat, when Raul had suggested dinner. Libby had balked then, because he'd been so *everything*, and she hadn't known quite how to handle that. Or maybe it had been even earlier, when she'd insisted on going with him to confront the boat thieves, as if she'd known that she had to defend him, to protect him, because even when they were total strangers, the idea of anything happening to Raul had been unimaginable.

And then she'd found out about the baby and she'd felt the first rush of love. Unmistakable and all-consuming, it had made her fingertips tingle with possibility and hope. Of course she'd loved her baby, but had it been more than that? Had she loved, even then, the idea of Raul too? Of growing a person who was half him? Of the certainty she would get to know Raul, even if only through their child?

She ran a hand over her stomach, patting the baby distractedly, connecting with that little lifeform, silently promising them the world, as she did all the time.

Libby had always wanted the fairy tale. The dream. But she'd come to accept it might not be possible.

But what if it was?

What if the answer, her hopes, her heart's desire, had been staring her in the face this whole time, and she'd been too shell-shocked to understand? Too stubborn, too *scared* to admit that the pragmatic terms they'd negotiated were just a shield they were both using to protect themselves from any possible fallout?

Libby stopped walking and stared straight ahead. It was early enough in the morning that the street was still quiet, but even if the sidewalk had been brimming with people, she wouldn't have been capable of noticing.

Her breath caught in her throat and she clicked her fingers in the air, the answer seeming so bloody obvious to her now.

They were both scared. They were both using the terms of their arrangement as a shield.

Whenever they got close to breaking through that shield, Raul pulled back, reminding her forcibly of what they were, because he couldn't accept a reality in which he cared for Libby as a person.

She groaned softly and turned on her heel, walking with renewed purpose back to their apartment, a smile tingling the corners of her mouth even when her tummy was tied in a thousand, billion knots with nervousness at the conversation in her near future. It was the only way to move forward, and suddenly she was convinced she could do this.

If fate had brought them together, and she knew in her heart that it had, it was Libby's job to listen—and to make sure Raul did too.

'Come on, baby.' She smiled at the doorman as she returned to Raul's building. 'Let's go tell your daddy how much we love him and just see if he doesn't feel the same way.'

CHAPTER THIRTEEN

RAUL WAS IN the kitchen when Libby returned to the apartment, a cup of coffee in one hand, a large tablet in front of him with one of the daily newspapers on the screen.

He frowned. 'You've been out?'

She stepped out of her boots, then removed her denim jacket, carrying it over one arm. 'I went for a walk.' She held up her coffee as if that explained everything.

'You should have told me,' he said with obvious disapproval. 'I would have come with you.'

She stared at him as if up was somehow down, because it was, in so many ways. An abstract concept whilst walking outside, face to face with Raul now, she had to accept that yes, she absolutely did love him. And that this conversation, while necessary, was the most important of her life.

It was also the most terrifying.

Every time her mother had let a new man move in, Libby had known rejection. She'd lost her mother, not once, not twice, but again and again and again. She'd always been second-best. A consolation prize when her mother was single. Nothing more. She'd never been important, really important, to anyone.

What if she wasn't important to Raul? Could she take that rejection?

Uncertainty pierced the veil of hope that had begun to shroud her; she fidgeted with her fingers.

But Libby had learned to lean into optimism. Perhaps it had been her earliest and best survival skill, a form of delusion even, to hope when hope seemed stupid. She saw beauty, sunlight, brightness, because it had helped her survive the emotionally barren nature of her upbringing, and she saw hope now, even against the odds.

Fate had brought them here; Libby was sure of it.

'I needed to think,' she said honestly, taking a few steps closer, pausing on the other side of the kitchen counter. It was like waking up from a dream, seeing everything for the first time.

This apartment was impersonally furnished, but it was beautiful and she realised she'd been wrong about this too, because it had absolutely come to feel like home. She belonged here. Maybe it wasn't about the picket fence and flowerbeds and cosy furnishings, but about who you were with...

She stared at Raul with a sense of wonder, a sense of dawning comprehension, and she smiled, despite the nerves that were making her stomach loop and twist.

'You look happy.' Raul, in contrast, seemed perplexed.

'Do I?' She bit down on her lower lip. 'I think I am. Or I might be. I don't know. That's kind of up to you, I guess.' She shook her head, because that was the wrong thing to have said. She didn't want to pressure Raul into thinking he had to return her feelings. As if anyone could pressure Raul into anything! But this had to be an act of choice, a decision they both made, if it was ever going to work.

'Is it?'

His cautious tone caused her confidence, and mood, to dip slightly.

'Raul, about yesterday...'

'It was a mistake.' A muscle pulsed low in his jaw. 'I apologise.'

'But what if it wasn't,' she said quickly, the words rushing out of her. 'What if it was the right thing to do?'

His expression was impossible to interpret, but she saw the immediate rejection in the depths of his eyes and it stung, way more than she'd expected. This was going to be hard.

'It wasn't.'

'Why not?'

'Our situation is complicated enough without letting sex enter the equation.'

'Sex *is* a part of our equation,' she reminded him. 'It's disingenuous to pretend otherwise.'

'We can control that.'

'Evidently not,' she said, patting her stomach.

'From now on.'

'Why?'

He looked at her as though she'd started speaking a made-up language.

'Why do we have to control how we feel?' she pushed. 'Why can't we just surrender to what's good in this relationship? And there is so much good, Raul. In fact, I think this could be one of the best things either of us has ever done.'

He looked stricken. 'It was a mistake,' he repeated.

'It was a kiss.'

He shook his head. 'Not yesterday. This.' He gestured to Libby's stomach. 'The boat. Sex. The pregnancy. None of this was supposed to happen.'

She ignored the immediate inflection of pain, held true to her goal in having this conversation, but a part of Libby was falling through the cracks in time, becoming a little girl again, desperate to put her heart on the line because she knew no one loved her.

'But it did. We slept together because neither of us could resist.'

'We had been through something. Adrenalin is a powerful motivator.'

'It wasn't just adrenalin. It was a feeling that if I didn't reach out and grab you, I'd always regret it. How much I wanted you scared the heck out of me. It's why I said no to dinner that night.' She leaned closer, putting her hand on his. 'It's why you asked me for dinner. Isn't it?'

Something shifted in the very depths of his eyes, but he blanked whatever emotion he'd been feeling almost immediately.

'I asked you for dinner because it seemed appropriate, given we'd just had sex. I didn't want you to feel used.'

Her stomach tightened. Was that true? Had it just been a case of going through the motions for Raul?

'I don't believe you,' she said, shaking her head.

'That's your prerogative.'

She flinched. His coldness was worse than anything.

'It didn't mean anything,' he continued in the same tone. 'And if our baby hadn't been conceived, we would never have seen one another again.'

Libby's heart seemed to disconnect from her body. She stared at him in surprise. Surprise that he could say that so calmly, surprised at the version of the world he painted, surprised that the idea of not having Libby in his life didn't bother him at all.

But then surprise faded to understanding. No one had loved her when she was young, and no one loved her now.

Libby's throat felt thick with unshed tears. She'd been

wrong. Not about her feelings, but about the likelihood of Raul returning them.

She had been about to confess something that would make their whole marriage untenable. Worse, it would have made him feel *pity* for her. He was already treating her with kid gloves, acting as though he needed to walk on eggshells around her. Admitting that she'd fallen in love with him would have made that a thousand times worse.

'You're probably right,' she said, shivering, the words trembling a little as she accepted his responses for what they were. Rejection. Even without telling him she loved him, Raul was making his feelings clear.

Libby swallowed past a lump in her throat, tried to force herself to smile but couldn't quite manage it.

'I'm going to be in the nursery.' She spun away from him, almost spilling her coffee in the hasty manner of her departure. 'See you later.'

Everything was perfect, she thought, turning slowly to admire the room, a hand on her stomach connecting her to the baby that all this effort had been for. From the brightly coloured walls to the sleek minimalist furnishings and happy, pale yellow bedlinen, the room was set up for its future occupant in a way that made Libby's spirits lift. At least a little. It was solace. Somewhere to go to remember why she was doing this. To remind herself that things were okay. Everything would be fine.

She could live with this equation. She could live with one part of her life being great—their baby. In fact, it was more than just one part, she reminded herself with a degree of forced optimism. She had things she'd never known existed. She had the kind of financial stability that would allow her to pursue whatever dreams she chose. *Our mar-*

riage can give you wings. She closed her eyes on a shuddery breath, memories of Raul, his promises, making her skin tingle.

Libby had always been determined to see the goodness in life. To give the darkness perspective and make it tolerable. But suddenly she wasn't sure it would be enough.

The idea of living with Raul, of loving him and getting only a limited part of him in return—those parts he was amenable to sharing—made her chest feel as though a whole ton of cement had been dropped onto it. She didn't just want parts of him; she wanted *all* of him.

She wanted him. The real him, flaws, vulnerabilities, everything.

He had to know that, she realised, eyes widening.

For all that Libby's childhood had shaped her, his had too. When was the last time someone had said they loved him and meant it? When was the last time someone had told him he could be broken and imperfect and it wouldn't matter because they accepted him for who he was? She spun quickly, legs carrying her from the nursery before she could question her decision. And even if she were to question it, nothing would change, because she was right. She knew she was right.

No matter how he reacted, no matter what he said he felt, he needed to hear this.

He was still standing at the kitchen bench when she returned, coffee refreshed, newspaper on the tablet lit up. Her heart thumped against her ribs. She loved him. Suddenly the idea of *not* being able to tell him was anathema to Libby. Come what may, she had to do this.

'I wasn't finished,' she said breathily, coming to stand

right beside him, taking comfort and strength from his nearness.

He placed his coffee down on the bench, tilted his face towards hers. There was resignation in his eyes and defensiveness in the tight set of his features. Libby ignored both.

'I know neither of us planned this. I'm not an idiot. Look at who we are, our lives, the way we live—our paths would never normally have crossed. In what world would someone like you even look at someone like me?' she said, missing the way his eyes narrowed and his lips parted, as though he was about to say something. 'Sleeping together wasn't planned, but it wasn't a mistake. And even without this baby, I think we both would have wanted to see one another again.'

His eyes were shuttered, totally inaccessible.

'Did you think of me, after that night?' she pushed, her breath held, her stomach trembling with fear.

Raul's throat shifted. 'Does it matter?'

'Did you think of me?' she persisted.

'I think of lots of things, people, all the time. It doesn't mean anything.'

Libby's smile was sad. 'That's your refrain for everything,' she murmured. 'You think you can cling to the idea that nothing matters and you'll be safe from getting hurt again. But I don't care how many times you say that, it's not true. Not with me.'

He flinched but Libby was on a roll.

'Yes, I see you, Raul. I understand you, maybe better than anyone ever has, because in so many ways we're the same. We've been through the same rejection. The same insecurity as children. The same holes in our lives where loving parents should be.'

'We are not the same.' He spoke quietly, calmly. 'Were

you beaten by foster parents, Libby, for having the temerity to watch television after school? Were you told that the world would be better without you? Not just by one family, but in different ways by each family you were sent to live with, until it became the refrain you heard each night as you fell asleep?'

She closed her eyes on a wave of grief that threatened to envelop her. 'I wish I could take those things away from you,' she said. 'I wish they'd never happened. It's all so wrong.' Tears sparkled on her lashes. 'But Raul, that's why I have to say this, and I know it's not what you want to hear, but you *need* to hear it anyway. I love you.'

He closed his eyes, his nostrils flaring, but Libby carried on. She'd known this would be hard, but it was vitally important. Even when she was terrified, loving someone meant going out on a limb and for Raul she would do that.

'I—' she paused, enunciating each word '—love—' her hand lifted to his chest, fingers splayed wide '—you. All of you, just as you are. I see value in you, strength, kindness, goodness. You are important, and worthy of being loved, of being part of this family. I love you.'

'Stop.' He reached for her hand, put his over it, his eyes boring into hers. 'Just stop.'

She shook her head. She'd expected resistance. She knew he might never be able to accept her love, but that didn't stop her from wanting to say this, to tell him how she felt.

'Why?' She took a step closer. 'Because you're scared to let me love you? Because you're scared to let anyone close?'

'I have been honest with you from the beginning, haven't I?' There was a plea in his voice. 'This wasn't about love. Not ever.'

'It was always about love,' she contradicted. 'I've never really believed in things like fate and destiny. They seem like such dangerous concepts to me. The idea of leaving the happiness of your future in the hands of unseen, intangible forces—how crazy. We make our own futures, our own happiness, our own destiny. But how can either of us deny that fate had a hand in this? I have only slept with one other person, Raul, and that was years before I met you. I'm not someone who has casual sex with strangers, but it never felt like that with you. I didn't understand it at the time, it's only looking back that I can see things with clarity. From the moment we met, I knew you were different. Important somehow. Right from the beginning. Tell me you didn't feel the same about me,' she challenged, then immediately wished she could take the words back, because she desperately didn't want to hear any such thing from his perfect, beautiful mouth.

Yet she stayed the course. Brave in the face of fear, confident in her love being enough to overcome anything.

'I didn't,' he said, but quietly, gently, as though he didn't want to hurt her. 'I don't.'

Her heart cracked but she didn't flinch outwardly. 'You're afraid.'

His eyes flexed. 'Am I?'

'You might not want to admit it, but yes, of course you are. In here—' she drummed her fingers against his chest '—you're still the same little boy who was hurt over and over again and you're scared that if you let me love you, I'll hurt you too.'

'Damn it, Libby.' She'd hit a nerve. He took a step back, dropping her hand, putting space between them, his back ramrod straight. 'Don't act as though you understand me.'

'I do understand you though, Raul, and I love you.'

'Stop saying that,' he demanded, raking his fingers through his hair. 'This is not what we agreed.'

'Yeah, well, I've got news for you, buster. Life doesn't always go to plan. Remember? We've said that before. I didn't know I loved you when we started doing this, but I know now, and I want you to know it too.'

'Why?' he asked, looking at her as if truly, desperately searching for answers. 'Why do I need to know any of this? It changes nothing.'

Her smile was sad, wistful, but she didn't shy away from this conversation.

'Maybe not today,' she said with a lift of one shoulder. 'Maybe not tomorrow, or in a month, but eventually, when you get used to how much our child and I love you, to the fact we're not going anywhere, that there's nothing you can do that will make us love you less, it will change *everything*. One day, you'll wake up and see yourself as I do, you'll see that you're worthy of being loved. That you can accept it, welcome it, maybe even return it.'

'No.' The word was cutting, spoken quickly, an instant rejection. 'It's not possible.'

'How do you know?' she asked, her throat feeling thick, making it hard to swallow.

'Because this is a choice, Libby. I have chosen to live like this.'

'A life without love?'

'A life without vulnerability and weakness,' he corrected. 'The kind of feeling you're talking about is the opposite of everything I want. I refuse to allow it.'

'You can't refuse to allow me to love you,' she said. 'That's preposterous.'

'But I can refuse to be affected by your love, refuse

to be changed by it. I don't want to change. I'm happy as I am.'

'Liar,' she said with a firm shake of her head.

'This is what I want,' he said emphatically. 'I am in control. I depend on no one.'

'What about when our baby is born?' she said, taking a step closer to him, then pausing when he stiffened, obviously not welcoming any contact. He didn't respond, simply looked at Libby with a question in his eyes, so she shook her head gently. 'You don't think you're going to love him or her? That you'll be vulnerable and dependent on how much you adore our child?'

Raul's expression didn't soften. If anything, it grew more determined, more stubborn. 'I will give our baby everything necessary.'

Something shifted inside Libby. 'You'll love our baby.'

'There are other things that matter just as much as love.'

Libby stared at him, her heart slamming through her body. 'Not to a child,' she murmured.

'You will love our baby,' he said, softly though, as if needing to convince himself of this path. 'You will love our baby so much they will never doubt their value and worth. You will fill their heart and soul with belonging.'

'And what will you do?' she asked.

'I'll be here.' The words were dragged out of him, and Libby felt only sadness then for this big alpha guy who'd been so badly shattered by his childhood. 'I will support our child, encourage them, be in their life. That has to be enough—for both of you.'

Libby's eyes swept shut. 'You won't even let yourself love this baby, will you?'

'Does it matter?' The words were bleak.

'Do you really think so little of yourself?' she said with

sad acceptance in her tone. 'You don't think it matters that you will be in our baby's life and not love them?'

He focused on a point beyond Libby's shoulder. 'This is our deal.'

'No, it's not,' she whispered. 'You said you wouldn't love me, but I always presumed you would love our child.'

'Why would you presume that?' he pushed. 'You should know better than anyone that it's not a guarantee in life.'

She flinched.

'I'm sorry,' he said, lifting a hand in the air. 'I did not mean to hurt you. Only you've told me about your mother, how she was with you...'

'And it's exactly what I don't want for my child.'

'I have no intention of treating our child like an irrelevancy,' he said. 'My priority is this family. I will keep you both safe and comfortable, I will do everything in my power to ensure you are both as happy as you can be.'

'But you won't love us,' she whispered, pushing this point because it was the beginning and end of what Libby wanted. Everything else was beside the point.

'No,' he said finally, and even though Libby had been expecting this, it was still, in many ways, the dropping of the guillotine. She took a step back, nodding distractedly, eyes stinging with unshed tears.

'And that's really what you want? You really choose this?'

His eyes met hers and for a moment she felt his anguish and pain and wanted to keep pushing, to try to find the heartbroken little boy inside of him and make everything better for that child. But then he closed himself off, visibly straightening, his features becoming taut and unyielding. 'Yes.'

'Even when I am telling you that I understand? I understand you're scared, I understand why, and I will walk. every step of the way on this journey at your side, understanding that you will make mistakes, that you will need help sometimes, to really let yourself love. You're not even willing to try?'

His eyes slashed through her. 'You're wrong about me, about all of this. I hope you can accept that.'

CHAPTER FOURTEEN

SHE COULDN'T. SHE wanted to. She wanted to because she knew that loving Raul meant accepting this was his way. She couldn't change him, not if he didn't want to change, but she could prove to him that she was different to everyone else in his life, by sticking by him, even when he was doing his level best to push her away.

Wasn't that the point? He'd never had anyone actually stick with him.

He'd been passed around from foster home to foster home; he'd never been accepted and welcomed and loved. He'd learned to develop a thick skin because he'd had to, and now Libby had a chance to show him that she really was different.

But living with Raul after that conversation was a lesson in despair for Libby. She felt it every moment of every day. She was going through the motions of her life, rattling around the enormous penthouse as if in a nightmare from which she couldn't wake. He was there, yet they rarely spoke. He enquired after her health each morning, her pregnancy symptoms, but it was all so cold and business-like, it left a yawning chasm in the centre of Libby's chest.

Raul had worked long hours before, but now he barely seemed to sleep. When he wasn't in his office he was in the home gym, running as though a pride of lions was after him. Libby tried to keep busy with the nursery, with online birth classes, with books and movies and workouts of her own—she chose yoga stretches designed for pregnancy—but she was always aware of him. Always aware of his silence, his rejection.

She wanted to be with him, because Raul deserved that. But what about her?

Didn't she deserve better than this? Could she really live with someone who wouldn't even try to see what they shared?

On the one hand, Libby was tempted to leave. To run away and go home, tail between her legs, and work out how to do this on her own after all. But always the thought of Raul stopped her. She did love him. It was that simple. So she couldn't ignore what he needed, even when it ran contrary to her own needs. She had to stay, to show him she was willing to put her money where her mouth was. She meant what she'd said: she wasn't going anywhere because he was worth loving, even if that hurt her.

In the end, it wasn't really Libby's decision though. Four days after Libby had poured out her heart to Raul, he came into the kitchen while she was fixing a light dinner for herself. She had very little appetite but for the sake of the baby tended to have a small bowl of fruit and yoghurt for dinner.

'This can't go on.' It was hardly a promising start to the sentence.

She stopped slicing the tops off strawberries and gave him the full force of her attention.

'I've bought an apartment downstairs. I'll move out. I've organised for a nurse to come and stay in the guest room; you'll still have around-the-clock care. No climbing ladders,' he added with a tight smile. 'I'll attend medical

appointments with you and, naturally, I'll be at the birth.'
He cleared his throat. 'Once the baby is born, we'll work
out a solution for co-parenting.'

Libby swayed a little and had to reach out and grip the
counter top to stop from falling to the floor.

'Living in the same building will mean we can both
be present in the baby's life. I know that's important to
both of us.'

Libby's body seemed to exist in a strange half-life. She
felt every organ shutting down; her blood seemed to stop
pumping. Every feeling of rejection she'd known in the
course of her life seemed to swirl around her all over again.
She was unlovable. Unwanted.

'Oh,' was all she could say, and it emerged as a strangled, incoherent, breathy sound, garbled by a rush of grief.

Worse than loving Raul and knowing he didn't return
those feelings was being pushed out of his life for good.
Sidelined and having his place taken by paid-for medical staff.

Libby had known she would need to fight for this, to
get through those stubbornly held barriers of his, but suddenly the fight seemed insurmountable. He had to fight
too, just a little bit. Just enough to give her faith she could
get through to him. How could she believe that when he
was literally walking away from her?

'You're not the only one who's been let down,' she said
quietly, staring at him and doing her best to keep emotion
out of her voice and face. 'You're not the only one who's
been hurt, rejected, who's absolutely terrified of what this
might mean.'

A muscle jerked in his jaw; he stayed perfectly still.

'But I'm more afraid of losing you,' she said simply. 'I
love you, and I want this family to be real.'

'That's because it's your fantasy,' he said with obvious frustration. 'You want a family so badly you've deluded yourself into seeing something that's not here.'

She drew in a sharp breath, the charge one that wounded deeply because it could well have been true. Libby knew it wasn't; she understood the accuracy of her heart's desires. But she felt that he'd taken her deepest secrets and weaponised them to win his argument.

'I won't be responsible for hurting you, Libby. That was never my intention. If I had known what marriage and children meant to you, I might not have suggested this arrangement in the first place; that was my mistake. But I can fix it.'

'By moving out?' she asked quietly.

'Yes.'

'You think that will make me stop loving you?'

'It might allow you the necessary perspective to see things as they really are.'

She let out a garbled laugh. 'That's ironic,' she muttered. 'Given you're the one who's blind to the truth, not me.'

His lips clamped together, as if physically biting back whatever he'd been about to say. 'You have my number. Call me if you need anything.'

Libby stared at him, reality sinking in. 'You're seriously leaving?'

'I'll have someone come to collect my clothes later today.'

Libby's eyes swept shut. The pain was immense, but she refused to let him see it. She was too proud, but also, she didn't want to burden him with it.

'Okay,' she said quietly, stoically. 'If that's what you want.'

'It's for the best.'

When she opened her eyes, Raul was gone.

* * *

Raul had intentionally kept his personal possessions sparse. He'd always known in the back of his mind that he would need to be ready to run at any point. If life had taught him one lesson consistently, it was the importance of that. And so he'd run.

Not far.

Just two floors down, to an apartment that was comparatively small but still boasted all of the hallmarks of opulence the building was renowned for. And here, he told himself, he'd find peace and salvation. Here, he'd start to feel like himself again, because Libby was finally away from him.

Except she wasn't.

Libby wasn't just a presence...she was an absence. He felt her even when she wasn't there.

He ached for her. Not just physically, but even the sight of her.

He'd become used to having her in his space. To knowing she was in the kitchen or the nursery, or even her bedroom. He'd found himself staring into space and imagining her reading or watching a movie, curled up on the sofa. Even when he'd stuck to his guns and remained locked away in his office, she'd been a part of his day.

And she still was.

It drove him crazy, and Raul became even more determined to conquer her control over him. To run away not just physically, but mentally too. He'd come dangerously close to forgetting how he lived his life—and why—but he'd escaped in time. He'd run before it got real, hadn't he?

Libby found it was far easier to give paid nursing staff the slip than it had been Raul. For all that Raul had clearly given instructions that Libby was to be shadowed, there was no medical need for her to have a constant companion and she found it simple enough to step out when necessary. The solitude was her godsend.

She had found a small park a few blocks away and she enjoyed sitting on one of the benches with a coffee each morning, watching the parents and nannies playing with the young children, a hand on her belly as she thought of her little one. Libby could easily imagine how nice it would be in summer to come here with her baby, stretch a picnic blanket out beneath a tree and enjoy the sounds of children laughing and playing and all the good things in life.

Except in those fantasies Libby and the baby weren't alone.

Raul was always there, relaxing, smiling, close, doting.

A lump formed easily in Libby's throat these days; tears were never far away. It had been two weeks since she'd seen Raul, though he'd texted each morning to check on her and she knew he spoke to the nurse regularly, to keep tabs on her physical health.

He was making it obvious that he cared for the baby, the pregnancy, that he was willing to look after Libby's medical needs, but that was where he drew the line.

Perhaps she'd been wrong about him?

Or maybe she'd been right, and he did love her, but he just couldn't overcome the damage wrought by his childhood and fight for what they shared. If that were the case, she had to accept it. She could love him with all her heart, but it wasn't enough for Raul. It never would be.

After an hour or so, Libby began to make her way home, pausing at a newsstand on the corner to buy a paper, then heading to the building.

'Good morning, Mrs Ortega,' the doorman, John, greeted her deferentially as she entered.

'Hello.' She smiled back.

'Must be getting close now?' He grinned, nodding towards her stomach.

She patted her round belly. 'Yes.' Even while discussing the baby, she couldn't dredge up a smile. Misery saturated Libby.

'Such lovely news.'

She nodded awkwardly, then moved inside, pressed the button and waited for the lift. When the doors opened, Raul was staring right back at her. Her heart accelerated dangerously, thudding into her throat. She simply stood and stared. The whole world seemed wonky and uneven. Everything inside Libby froze.

Two weeks.

For two weeks she had been striving to make her peace with this, to accept how much she loved and missed him and find a way to coexist with those feelings, to exist in a state of happiness regardless, but just the sight of Raul was like a punch right in her gut.

She stared at him and took a step backwards. The lift doors began to close. Raul's hand came out, keeping them open for her.

'Going up?' he asked, his voice strained even to Libby's ears.

'It's okay. I'll wait.'

'We can ride in the same elevator together, Libby, for God's sake.'

She bit down on her lip, blinking away from him. It was only the possibility of people staring, speculating, that had her taking a step inside the lift and she wished she hadn't as soon as the doors zipped closed and the air seemed to spark with awareness in a way that threatened to pull at all the threads of her sanity.

She tapped her security card to the lift console then pressed her back as hard to the wall as she could. Mercifully, the lift was swift and the doors had opened again before she knew it, onto Raul's floor, but he made no room to leave.

'This is you, isn't it?' she said woodenly.

'I'll see you home.'

She almost scoffed at the stupidity of that. As if he cared. But she wouldn't give him the satisfaction of arguing. She simply shrugged, kept staring straight ahead, and a moment later the doors pinged open once more, this time into the penthouse apartment they'd once shared.

As Libby moved to step past him, Raul put a hand out. Not to Libby, but rather to keep the doors open.

She slowed a little once in the foyer, knowing she had to say something, to at least acknowledge and farewell. She turned, and her heart thumped.

'How are you?' he asked, the question gruff, his eyes raking over her as if the answer lay in her appearance.

'Fine,' she lied. 'And you?'

His smile was bitter. 'Also fine. But then, I am not growing a human inside of me.'

Libby lifted one shoulder. 'Half the time I forget I am. Except at night,' she added, babbling because she was nervous. 'At night, he or she is very active.'

'Are you finding it hard to sleep?'

'Yes,' she said, and she was glad that he would presume it was because of their somersaulting baby, and not the real reason: that she was tormented by thoughts and memories of Raul and what might have been, to the point she found sleep untenable. Their eyes held, yet both were silent. The atmosphere pulsated, and then Libby took a step backwards.

'Well, nice seeing you,' she said quietly. 'Take care.' And she spun away from him quickly, as though her life depended on it.

Raul rode back down to his own apartment with a scowl on his features and a strange feeling in his gut. A feeling that he was going in the opposite direction, like swimming upstream or pushing a magnet against an equal pole. It was really stupid.

He strode into his apartment, changed into his gym gear and left the building, determined to run until he understood himself once more.

Understanding didn't come. The more he ran, the less anything made sense.

Oh, he knew what he *should* want, what was right and smart and safe, but the thought of living two floors below Libby and their baby now seemed preposterous. Two weeks ago, he'd convinced himself it was the right thing for everybody, but how could that be so?

It was clearly not right for Libby—she looked exhausted and shell-shocked. She looked hurt and betrayed.

And for him?

He couldn't analyse his feelings, only he knew everything was wrong. The instincts that had kept him safe for so long, the instincts that had taught him to run at the first sign of connection, to preserve a solid amount of space around himself as though his life depended on it, were pulling him in a different direction now, making him want things that were counter to every goal he'd ever had in life.

He pulled to the edge of the sidewalk and stared across the street, closing his eyes for a moment and letting himself step fully into Libby's rosy dream for them. The family she'd described. The love. The warmth, the promise to *always* love him, no matter what. When he stepped into that vision of his future, he felt a want that was greater than any he'd ever known. For a moment, he let himself imagine it was real, that he could trust her, that Libby would protect him, that he could trust her not to hurt him, that loving her wouldn't mean one day he would have to suffer the most immense loss of his life.

But it was only a fantasy, just like he'd told her. Because at some point the dream would crack. She'd leave him, like everyone else ever had. Or worse, he'd leave her. He'd hurt her, more than he had already, and he'd never be able to forgive himself for that.

Raul began to run once more, but it didn't matter how far he went: he couldn't outrun the tortured nature of his indecision and finally, as he approached the apartment, he stopped running, not just physically, but also mentally.

Libby scared him. She always had.

Right from the beginning, when she'd been willing to put her own life on the line to save his.

But this was different.

She was offering a future that he'd never allowed himself to hope for, because he'd been trained to believe it was beyond his reach.

What if it wasn't?

What if Libby's vision for their family could be a reality? What if he'd been wrong about everything?

'I was informed it's your favourite,' Raul said, holding up a bag of take-out from the Chinese restaurant a few blocks away.

Libby eyed it suspiciously. 'Informed by whom?'

'That would be me.' Her nurse, Veronica, smiled as she pulled her handbag over one shoulder. 'I'll see you tomorrow.'

Libby frowned. 'You're leaving?'

'Call if you need anything,' Veronica said with a nod and wave, disappearing into the lift. Libby watched her go, perplexed.

'Raul, what's going on?'

The smell of the Chinese was wafting towards Libby and her tummy groaned with hunger. She ignored it.

'Can we have dinner? We should talk.'

Libby stared at him, her gut rolling, tightening, confusion making her insides hurt. 'I—' She stared at him, wanting to tell him no. But hadn't she promised that she would love him always? That she would be there for him? While her self-defence mechanism was to push him away now, before he could push her any further, that wasn't right. She needed to *show* him that she loved him, no matter what, not just say it.

'Okay.' She tried to keep her voice neutral. 'Dinner,' she added, as a midway point to looking after herself too.

His eyes showed relief and one corner of his lip lifted in a tight half-smile. 'Thank you.'

His gratitude was unexpected.

Libby busied herself removing plates and water glasses from the kitchen and laying out the table, while Raul removed the lids from the meals and set them up between their two seats. He'd ordered her favourites—she had to credit Veronica for that intel too.

'So,' Libby said, taking a seat opposite Raul, hands folded neatly in her lap, 'what do we need to talk about?'

'The other day…' he said, eyes meeting hers then glancing away.

She frowned. 'What other day?'

'Here, in the kitchen. The conversation we had.'

'That was weeks ago,' she muttered, colouring.

'I'm aware of that.'

'It's just, when you said "the other day" I thought you meant a few days ago, not...' Her voice trailed off.

How could she tell him that a few weeks ago felt like an eternity to her because she'd missed him so damned much? He must know she felt that way, but Libby didn't need to bang him over the head with the truth of that.

'Anyway,' she finished unevenly, 'what do you want to discuss?'

'I think I made a mistake.'

Libby's gut churned; she refused to let hope into the cracks of her heart. Carefully, staying very still, she said, 'Oh?'

Raul's Adam's apple shifted beneath his stubble. His features bore their trademark mask of arrogant control but Libby saw through it. Regardless of her best intentions, hope burst through her.

'Raul,' she murmured. 'What are you trying to say?'

'I don't want to live apart from you.' His brow furrowed, as he concentrated harder. 'I want to live with you.'

For her own sake, Libby had to take this slowly, and also be very specific about what he was saying. This was not a time to rush to conclusions because she *wanted* him to want the same things she did.

'You mean, how we were before? You want it to go back to the way it was before that morning?'

'Yes,' he said with a smile, then shook his head. 'No.' He dragged a hand through his hair. 'I am terrible at this.'

Libby waited patiently.

'I want to live with you, properly. As husband and wife.'

Beneath the table, Libby fidgeted her hands in her lap. It was so close to what she wanted, but still she was careful, cautious, measured.

'Why?' she asked simply, because there could be a dozen reasons for his change of heart. Worry about her health, protectiveness of the baby, a pragmatic preference to be near to one another for the late stages of the pregnancy. None of which equated to the happy-ever-after Libby wanted.

'Why do you think?'

'I don't know, and it's important to understand exactly what you're saying,' she murmured. 'I need to manage my own expectations for this.'

'I think you might be right,' he said slowly, carefully.

Simply for something to do, Libby reached out and took an egg roll, placed it on her plate but then just stared at it.

'I think there might be something fated about our meeting.'

Her heart leaped into her throat.

'Let me show you something,' he said quietly, reaching into his pocket and removing a necklace—a chain with a simple pendant on it. He stared at it a moment, his expression impossible to interpret. 'It's the only thing of my parents' that I possess. It was my mother's. I don't remember her, or him. As I told you, they died when I was very young. This is all I was left.' He moved it from one hand to the other, then handed it over to Libby.

She turned it over to see cursive script on the back, in Spanish. 'What does it say?'

'It's a translation of an old English poem, about the value of living every moment of every day, the importance of not letting opportunities pass one by.'

Libby read the Spanish words but heard Raul's translation, then passed the necklace back to him, still doing her best to be guarded with her heart, even when she was starting to hope against hope that her wildest dreams were coming true.

'You were right about me,' he said. 'About my child-hood, about how it shaped me. I was made to feel worth-less by everyone in my life until I met Maria and Pedro, and éven them I kept at arm's length. Every relationship in my life is transactional. I don't have friendships that are more than skin-deep. I am careful not to get close to any-one. And with you, it felt even more imperative to main-tain those boundaries because, from the very first meeting, I knew on some level that you were a threat to how I live my life. That you could break down my boundaries if you tried to. I have done my best to control this, but I can't.'

Libby's eyes stung.

'I told myself I walked away from this to protect you, but the truth is, I wanted to protect myself. You were of-fering me your love, something I wanted so fiercely that I knew if anything happened, and you stopped loving me, it would be the worst pain I'd ever known. I have never wanted anything like I have this.' He waved a hand around the apartment.

'So you left.'

'But it was too late,' he said. 'The damage is done. You love me, and that means something.'

'It doesn't have to,' she whispered, not wanting him to come back because he pitied her or was grateful to her.

'It means *everything*,' he clarified. 'Even if it is only for now, even if this is temporary, I have to be here, to live this with you. I have to love you back, because I've come to realise there is no alternative. Real love cannot be con-trolled, as it turns out, no matter how determined you are.'

Libby's heart soared now, given freedom by the hope she'd finally allowed to rein in her body.

'Yes,' she whispered, though what question she was answering she couldn't say. But somehow she needed him to know she agreed, she approved, that she understood.

His eyes scanned her face. 'I'm not going to be good at this.'

Libby's laugh was tremulous as she stood, coming around the table and moving to sit in Raul's lap. 'I can live with that.'

'I do love you,' he said. 'I cannot let you—this opportunity I have somehow been given—slip through my fingers. You are my fate, my all.' He stared at her, then shrugged. 'I just… love you.'

'I thought so.' She smiled serenely.

'How on earth could you have that kind of faith in me?'

She pressed her forehead to his. 'I knew you loved me, Raul. I just didn't know if you'd be brave enough to admit it to yourself.'

His hand ran lightly over her spine. 'I hope I can one day be worthy of the faith you had in me.'

She pressed her lips to his. 'You already are.'

EPILOGUE

IF RAUL HAD any lingering doubts about the strength of his love for Libby—and there were none—those doubts would have disappeared entirely in the face of her heroism and courage whilst delivering their baby.

It was not an easy delivery. There were many times when Raul thought he would undo every blissful moment of life with Libby if he could only go back in time and not sleep with her that fateful afternoon, if it meant she could be spared this pain and torment.

For twenty hours she laboured, and he was with her every step of the way until finally, in the small hours of the morning, their baby was delivered and Raul knew, the moment he looked at their daughter, that his heart—what small piece he had kept of it after meeting Libby—was no longer, and never would be, his own. He was beholden to these two women now, utterly and completely. They were his reason for living, his purpose, his life, come what may.

Libby was serene in the hour after birth, her eyes fluttering closed, a beatific smile on her face as she held their daughter cradled to her chest, Raul perching on the edge of the bed. This was his family; it was where he belonged.

Life was never the same after that. Raul and Libby had both been shaped by their experiences, and had developed skills to help them cope with life. Separate, they had existed and they had been okay, but together they really, truly lived. Success took on a different metric for Raul now—if Libby and baby Maria were happy, he was happy.

They lived as the three of them for a single year before Libby was once more pregnant, this time with twin boys, and a year after that another little girl joined their family. Raul had gone from intending to live a solitary life, completely his own person, to finding that his heart simply grew and grew with every new addition to their family—including, to his surprise, the Retriever they adopted when their youngest child was two years old.

They didn't stay in the penthouse apartment for long. One day, while pregnant with the twins, on a drive through the Hamptons, they pulled over to have a picnic on the beach and happened to find a spot right near a big old home that just exuded happiness. From the timber walls to the old tin roof, wraparound balcony and wide steps that led to a porch swing, the house was everything Libby had ever dreamed of. Even the garden seemed to conspire to seduce Libby—huge geranium and lavender bushes lined the gravelled front path, reminding her forcefully of the flowers of home.

'Oh, Raul,' she said, leaning her head against his chest. 'Isn't it the most beautiful thing you've ever seen?'

Raul took one look at Libby's face and knew he would move heaven and earth to gift her this house just as soon as he could. It did not take heaven and earth, just an offer to the owners that was a fair bit above market value, but in Raul's eyes it was worth every penny for the surprise of being able to drive Libby back the following weekend, this time with the keys in his possession.

She wept with happiness, and Raul grinned. He had

wanted to give Libby the world, and this sweet old beach house seemed like as good a place to start as any.

For Libby, the house became a home the moment they crossed the threshold. It was everything she'd always dreamed of. Pretty without being fancy, welcoming and comfortable, the sort of place she could raise her kids away from the opulence and wealth of Raul's world—not that he went in for any of that stuff, anyway. He was finally delegating to his more than qualified executives, accepting that he could zoom out his focus from his business interests and still ensure the ongoing success of his company. Taking a step back from his role had opened the door for new opportunities anyway: he had begun to invest in worthy start-ups, supporting people with big ideas and a lack of resourcing, in the hope that he could do for them what Maria and Pedro's support had done for him.

And then there was Libby, for whom Raul was the biggest champion.

While she was happier than she could express raising their children and being married to Raul, he knew and understood that she had so many skills beyond these, and he never missed an opportunity to remind her she could do whatever she wanted. He would care for the children, he would be whatever she needed, so she could pursue her own ambitions, to really live up to her potential.

It wasn't until their youngest started school that she finally felt ready to turn her focus to something else. Gone was the desire to pursue anything related to bookkeeping, which she'd considered out of desperation what felt like a lifetime ago. That would have been a career of practicality, to enable her to work from home and care for Maria— way back when she thought she would be doing it all alone.

Now, she wasn't alone. She was supported and cherished beyond belief, and in the years since marrying Raul she had come to realise there was one passion she couldn't ignore. Another hand of fate?

Libby enrolled in a course to study jewellery making. 'It's not just the jewellery,' she explained to Raul enthusiastically as she came close to finishing the course. 'It's what it means. It's the idea that each piece becomes a keepsake, something special and meaningful that can evoke emotions all over again. Every time I look at my ring, I think of you,' she said. 'And your mother's necklace keeps her with you,' she said gently, eyes on his face. 'It matters.'

'Yes, Libby, it does,' he agreed, and he kissed her because it was the only way he could think of to express his absolute, all-consuming love for his wife.

Every now and again, Raul found himself imagining 'What if?' What if he hadn't gone to Sydney that weekend? What if Libby hadn't been sent to the boat? What if those teenagers hadn't attempted to steal it? What if he hadn't finally forced himself to understand what he felt for her, what he wanted from her? What if he'd actually been stupid enough to let her go? But then he looked at Libby and she smiled, and he relaxed, because fate had always been driving them to this—Raul was simply along for the ride, and it was a ride he intended to enjoy to its fullest for the rest of his life on earth.

* * * * *

COMING SOON!

We really hope you enjoyed reading this book.
If you're looking for more romance
be sure to head to the shops when
new books are available on

Thursday 24th
October

MILLS & BOON®

Coming next month

HUSBAND FOR THE HOLIDAYS
Dani Collins

In so many ways, this was her dream come true. Could she really complain if it wasn't exactly perfect? "Yes. I will marry you, Konstantin."

"Good." He slid the cool ring onto her finger, then looped his arms behind her.

Eloise's hands were on his lapels, quivering with pleasure at having this right to touch him.

She looked up at him, expecting him to kiss her, but he only caressed the edge of her jaw with his bent finger.

He dipped his head into her throat and nuzzled his lips against her skin.

She gasped and shivered. Her nipples stung and her knees grew weak.

His breath pooled near her ear, fanning the arousal taking hold in her. This was surreal. Too perfect. Like a Christmas miracle. Not that she believed in such things, but maybe it was?

Continue reading
HUSBAND FOR THE HOLIDAYS
Dani Collins

Available next month
millsandboon.co.uk

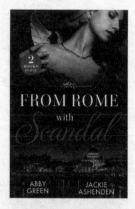
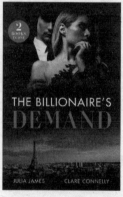
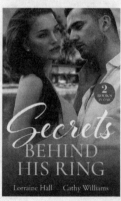

LET'S TALK

Romance

For exclusive extracts, competitions and special offers, find us online:

- **f** MillsandBoon
- **X** @MillsandBoon
- **◉** @MillsandBoonUK
- **♪** @MillsandBoonUK

Get in touch on 01413 063 232

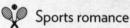
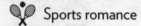
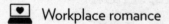

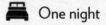

OUT NOW!

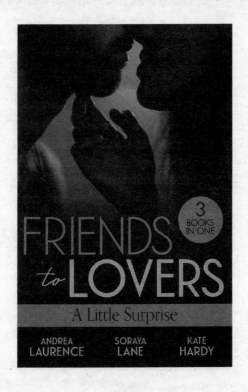

3
BOOKS
IN ONE

FRIENDS
to LOVERS

A Little Surprise

ANDREA
LAURENCE

SORAYA
LANE

KATE
HARDY

Available at
millsandboon.co.uk

MILLS & BOON